camp
CONFIDENTIAL
The Complete First Summer: Books #1-4
W9-BNS-986

by Melissa J. Morgan

Grosset & Dunlap

GROSSET & DUNLAP
Published by the Penguin Group
Penguin Group (USA) Inc., 375 Hudson Street, New York, New York 10014, USA
Penguin Group (Canada), 90 Eglinton Avenue East, Suite 700,
Toronto, Ontario M4P 2Y3, Canada
(a division of Pearson Penguin Canada Inc.)
Penguin Books Ltd., 80 Strand, London WC2R 0RL, England
Penguin Group Ireland, 25 St. Stephen's Green, Dublin 2, Ireland
(a division of Penguin Books Ltd.)
Penguin Group (Australia), 250 Camberwell Road, Camberwell, Victoria 3124, Australia
(a division of Pearson Australia Group Pty. Ltd.)
Penguin Books India Pvt. Ltd., 11 Community Centre, Panchsheel Park,
New Delhi—110 017, India
Penguin Group (NZ), 67 Apollo Drive, Rosedale, North Shore 0632, New Zealand
(a division of Pearson New Zealand Ltd.)
Penguin Books (South Africa) (Pty.) Ltd., 24 Sturdee Avenue,
Rosebank, Johannesburg 2196, South Africa

Penguin Books Ltd., Registered Offices:
80 Strand, London WC2R 0RL, England

Library of Congress Cataloging-in-Publication Data is available.

ISBN 978-0-448-45188-6 10 9 8 7 6 5

Table of Contents

Book #1

Camp Confidential

Natalie's Secret

chapter

ONE

Dear Hannah,

Hey there! I can't remember the last time I picked up a pen and paper to write an honest-to-goodness letter, but desperate times call for desperate measures, I guess. I have no idea whether or not there will be any computer access at—ugh, it's too torturous to even think about—CAMP. Mom insists that it won't be as backwoods as I'm expecting, but at this point I'm not sure I trust her! I mean, really—sending me away to Nowheresville, Pennsylvania, for eight weeks? She is obviously having some sort of mental breakdown, and I'm the one who's going to suffer!

You're so lucky your parents are taking you to Europe. I know you're not that excited about all of the touring around (dusty old paintings and all) but seriously, it has to be better than painting clay pots and identifying different poisonous leaves and whatever else they do at camp all summer long. Promise me you'll take lots of pics of your gorgeous self being all cool and sophisticated in front of the Mona Lisa, Big Ben, the Trevi fountain . . .

Have I mentioned that I'm way jealous?

I think we're about an hour from Camp Lake-puke-joy—so I'm going to put down my pen and start "rethinking my attitude," as Mom suggested. She is totally convinced that the fresh air will do me good. I pointed out that if fresh air was so important, we wouldn't live in Manhattan, but somehow she didn't see things my way.

There is a girl sitting two seats in front of me with awesome clips in her hair. Like little sequins or something. She has the thickest mess of curly red hair I've ever seen. And I bet it's her natural color. Anyway, the barrettes are promising. Maybe I'll go make friends. Or not.

You better miss me! Cross your fingers that this summer is as painless as possible and that we're back in NYC before we even know it (even if it means school again)!

xoxo,

Nat

Natalie signed her letter, folded the crisp lavender sheet of paper into a neat square, and tucked it into the front pocket of her bag with a sigh. Her envelopes and stamps were all packed away in her trunk, which had been shipped separately a week before. Hopefully, her things would be waiting for her when she arrived at camp.

Camp Lakeview. It was all Natalie could do not to shudder at the thought of it. To say that she was not interested in nature was a severe understatement. In fact, Natalie was pretty sure that she was actually allergic to nature. Natalie and her mother lived in the "concrete jungle"—the coolest, most interesting city in the world—New York. The closest Natalie ever came to the great outdoors was when she and her friends went Rollerblading in Central Park on weekends. And that was just fine by her.

Most summers, Natalie would take special classes that were offered by local private schools. She'd study painting or drawing or writing or dancing. The rest of the time, she and her friends would hang out, shop, see movies . . . it was awesome. But not this summer. This summer, Natalie's mother had to travel to Italy. She was an art buyer, and she needed to scout out new pieces for her gallery. Natalie had begged to go with her, but Natalie's mom was firm. "Camp will be good for you," she had said. "A change of pace. A chance to meet different types of people."

"What's wrong with the people I know now?" Natalie had asked.

Her mother had laughed. "Nothing, of course. Your friends are wonderful, sweetie. But everyone you know lives in the same neighborhood as you and goes to the same school. You even go to the same tennis lessons and music programs. It will be good for you to broaden your horizons."

"I like my horizons narrow," Natalie had protested stubbornly. But her mother's word was final.

That conversation had taken place five months ago. Now, Natalie's mind raced as the stuffy charter bus she rode careened down the highway toward Camp Lakeview. Endless grassy pastures dotted the landscape, and she had even seen a few cows and sheep grazing. *Sheep*, for Pete's sake. Was this what her mother meant about broader horizons?

She could go home now, right?

Natalie glanced at the other kids on the bus. She couldn't believe that there wasn't anyone on the bus as miserable as she was, but looking around, most of the other kids were grinning away, laughing, talking to one another . . . Natalie didn't know a soul here. She wasn't especially shy, but she also wasn't thrilled at the prospect of having to make all new friends. Her own friends were cool, and other than Hannah, they were all back in New York City taking a drama intensive offered by a special high school for teenage actors. Everyone was there. Including Kyle Taylor. Kyle Taylor who had, it should be noted, promised to write Natalie over the summer. *That is, if he doesn't forget about me,* she decided. *Which, how could he not, what with me out in the wilderness with the lions and tigers and bears and whatever.*

I should have asked Dad to talk to Mom for me, Natalie thought glumly. *He would have let me go to acting school, definitely.* But as quickly as the thought had popped up, Natalie pushed it out of her mind. Talking to her father was Out of the Question. He and her mother had split up when Natalie was only four years old, and even though Natalie knew her father loved her, they didn't talk very often. It was hard to be in touch with him because . . . no, she wasn't going to think about it. Talking to her father was, at least for right now, a non-option, and therefore, she'd just have to pray that Camp Lake-puke, as she had come to think of the place, wasn't as bad as she feared.

Natalie snapped out of her little daze to see Cool Barrette Girl smiling at her. Well, in her general direction, anyway. Natalie took her chances and smiled back. Success. Barrette Girl stood up from her seat, stretched, and wove her way back to where Natalie sat.

"Hi," she said, still grinning, "I'm Grace Matthews. I'm from New Jersey. Montvale. It's in the north, right by the George Washington Bridge." She stuck out her hand to shake, which seemed a little weird to Natalie. The only people she knew who shook hands were grown-ups—but, hey—she wasn't about to start turning away friendly faces. She reached out her own hand toward Grace.

"I'm Natalie Goode," she said.

"You're new, right?" Grace asked. "I was here last summer."

"Yeah, I'm from Manhattan, so, um, I'm not so used to summer camp," Natalie said. She realized she was babbling. What was wrong with her? She didn't usually get nervous around new people. But this, this whole camp *thing* was totally new and strange to her. "So, yeah, I'm new," she finished, feeling sort of lame.

"You'll love it," Grace assured her. "There are a few other kids from the city here, and they, like, love it even more than the rest of us. I think 'cause they're not used to, you know, trees."

"Oh, hey, no—we've got tons of trees where I come from. I mean, there's a tree right outside my building," Natalie said, hoping Grace would get that she was kidding.

Grace burst out laughing. "Oh, well then, you're ready for the nature shack!" she agreed, shaking out her bright red hair and quickly pinning it right back up. "How old are you?"

"Eleven," Natalie said.

"Oh, cool, me too," Grace replied. "Hey—maybe we'll be in the same bunk! There are eight bunks in every division—four girls' bunks and four boys'. If you're in mine, I can introduce you to everyone. Well, I mean, I'd introduce you, anyway, but you know—it'd be cool if we were in the same bunk!"

"Yeah, cool," Natalie agreed, hoping she didn't

sound as unexcited as she felt. She knew that trees and new people weren't such a bad thing, but somehow, she just couldn't get her enthusiasm together.

"Hey, Grace," shouted a voice from the front of the bus, "we're gonna play hangman!"

Grace rolled her eyes, pretending to be impatient. "Right, hangman. Really important stuff. Do you want to play?" she offered.

Natalie shook her head. "Nah, I'm going to just relax a little bit. Prepare myself for all the trees and stuff."

"Gotcha," Grace said, giggling again. "Well, if you change your mind, I'm just a few seats ahead." She made her way up toward the chattering girls, leaving Natalie alone with her own thoughts again.

Seated in the window seat next to Natalie was a very quiet girl with long, jet-black hair. This girl was hunched over a notebook, scribbling away intently. She hadn't said one word to anyone since they boarded two hours ago, just opened up her notebook and retreated into her own world. She hadn't even looked up when Grace came over to say hi. Natalie couldn't decide how she felt about her seatmate. The fact that this girl was dressed in jeans and a ripped black T-shirt while everyone else was in shorts and tank tops could either be cool or weird. The same went for her refusal to look up and make conversation. Natalie was dying to know what she was writing in her notebook. Lots of her friends from New York were into art and writing and liked to dress differently and wear cool jewelry. So this girl could definitely be sort of cool. Or she could be a total weirdo. It could really go either way.

"All right, guys, listen up!" came a loud voice from the front of the bus. A tall, lanky guy with dark, curly hair pulled into a ponytail stood and addressed them all. He looked a little stressed—a few stray curls had escaped his ponytail and were standing at attention on the top of his head—but also good-natured and friendly. "If I didn't meet you before, I'm meeting you now. I'm Pete, and I'm going to be working in the mess hall this summer!" This announcement brought forth a round of booing and hissing, but Pete waved it off. "None of that," he laughed, "or you don't know what I'll put in the 'tuna surprise.' "

Natalie cringed. "Call me old-fashioned, but I prefer my tuna without any surprises," she mumbled. She was surprised to hear a snort from her right and looked over to see her seatmate stifling a chuckle.

"Agreed," the girl said. She quickly went back to her notebook, as if afraid she had said too much. Natalie was so shocked by the sudden burst of conversation that she forgot to reply. But she didn't have time to, anyway, because Pete was still talking.

"We'll be arriving at camp in about a half hour or so," he explained. "When we get there, you'll come off the bus. There will be a counselor waiting to tell you what bunk you're in and where you're going. So the first thing you want to do is go to your bunk. If fate has been kind to us—and I've got my fingers crossed here—then your trunk or any other luggage you may have shipped will be waiting for you there. You'll meet your counselors and your bunkmates, unpack, and have your bunk meetings." He paused. "Any questions?"

"Yeah," shouted a rowdy boy from the back of the bus. "What's for dinner tonight?"

"Cookout!" Pete said. He sounded highly thrilled at the prospect.

The entire bus erupted into a chorus of cheers. Natalie stared at her fellow campers incredulously. *Cookout?* she wondered. She could not for the life of her understand why something as simple as a barbecue was eliciting such a response. *Sushi, maybe*, she thought. *Hamburgers . . . not so much.*

She glanced to her right again. Her seatmate was still engrossed in her notebook, completely unimpressed by the news of the cookout. Well, that was one thing they had in common, at least. Natalie folded her arms across her chest and leaned back, sighing again.

It was going to be a long eight weeks.

chapter TWO

Natalie rested comfortably in bed, her head cradled by soft down pillows, her body on a mattress that was just the right balance of firm and squishy. The room, a log cabin similar to one Natalie had stayed in on a recent ski trip with her mother, was air-conditioned to the perfect temperature. *Hmmm, I didn't think there would be air-conditioning at camp*, Natalie thought. *I could get used to roughing it.*

Maybe there's going to be sushi for dinner, she thought. *And then afterward we can make frozen-yogurt sundaes.*

"Natalie, wake up," her counselor said, leaning over and nudging her gently. "We're leaving for our field trip in just a few minutes. We'll be going to New York, to the Met."

The Metropolitan Museum? New York? Natalie thought. That was another pleasant surprise. She was pretty sure that Camp Lakeview was at least three hours away from New York. *Some field trip.*

"Natalie, wake up," the voice said again. The

owner of the voice nudged her again, this time not so gently.

"Ow," Natalie said, rubbing her shoulder. "Come on! Quit it."

"Sorry," the voice said, "but we're here. I think you have to get off the bus now."

Here? Natalie peeled her eyes open. *Here.* As in, Camp Lakeview. They had arrived. Natalie groaned.

"Yeah, you were sleeping pretty soundly. You dropped off just after the announcement about the cookout tonight. I take it you're not big into red meat."

"Whatever," Natalie said, rubbing her eyes and feeling grouchy. She looked over to see who was talking to her. It was her seatmate, the maybe-cool notebook girl. "I guess not," she admitted, feeling bad about being so touchy. It wasn't this girl's fault she was so anti-camp.

"Yeah, well, I'm a vegetarian. I get it," the girl said. "My name's Alyssa."

"I'm Natalie," Natalie said with a little smile. A little smile was about the best she could do at the moment.

"I know, I heard you introduce yourself to that girl Grace. You said it was your first summer here. Mine too. And I'm also eleven. So maybe we're in the same bunk."

"There are four bunks of eleven-year-olds," Natalie pointed out. A look of disappointment flickered across Alyssa's face, and Natalie worried that she had unintentionally hurt the girl's feelings. *Nice people skills, Nat,* she scolded herself. "But, you know, I hope we are!"

she said quickly. She was relieved to see a smile return to Alyssa's face.

Natalie and Alyssa gathered their things and stepped off the bus. It took a moment for Natalie's eyes to adjust to the bright sunlight, and when they did, she gasped in surprise. Whatever her expectations had been of camp, she wasn't prepared for *this*.

In a word, it was chaos. All the buses were lined up, parked, in an open field. Just beyond all the buses, though, was a clearing lined with balloons and enormous, hand-lettered signs with greetings like "Welcome, Lakeview Campers!" and "Happy Summer!" And girls and boys anywhere from age eight to sixteen were wandering back and forth, some looking eager, some looking as confused as she felt. In the midst of the crowd were older people—counselors and staff, Natalie assumed—waving clipboards and shouting instructions into megaphones. It was all extremely perky, Natalie thought. She wasn't sure how she felt about that. Come to think of it, she was practically still half-asleep.

"WHAT'S YOUR NAME?" A clipboard was thrust under Natalie's nose. She followed the clipboard up and found herself looking into the face of an older woman wearing a fluorescent orange sun visor and a stripe of zinc down her nose. *No one* in New York City wore sun visors. At least, not anyone Natalie knew.

"Natalie. Natalie Goode," she managed, after taking a moment to recover.

The woman looked at her clipboard briskly. "Natalie Goode. New York City."

"That's me."

"Well, Natalie, I'm Helen Proctor. I'm the camp nurse. Right now, I'm helping all the campers find their bunks. You, my friend, are in the third division. Kathleen is your division head. You'll love her. And you're in bunk 3C," the woman told her. "Your counselor is Julie and Marissa will be your CIT."

"CIT?" Natalie asked. Was that anything like the CIA? Or NPR? Probably not.

"Counselor-in-training," Helen explained. "It's the division between the oldest campers and the counselors. The CITs wait tables in the mess hall, and they're each assigned to one bunk."

Natalie nodded. "Cool," she said. At least, it sounded cool. Time would tell.

Helen leaned forward, crouching next to Natalie. She pointed toward a thin dirt path leading away from the field. "If you follow that path, you'll see that it curves around. That path runs through the main part of the camp—the bunks, the mess hall, and the rec hall. Head down that path and stick to the left. The fourth bunk you pass will be 3C." She patted Natalie on the shoulder reassuringly.

"Great," Natalie said, unconvinced. "Um, thanks." She looked around to see where Alyssa had gone, but she had already disappeared. There could be no more putting it off. She was here at Camp Lakeview, on her way to the bunk.

While on the bus, Natalie had somehow managed to convince herself that camp might not actually be that bad. She had even dreamed of bunks like log cabins, cute little cottages like the ones she and her mother stayed in when they went on vacation. But now, suddenly, her mouth was dry and she felt sweaty and nervous. She willed herself to relax. *Your bunkmates will be cool,* she told herself. *There's going to be a girl there who's into just the same kind of music that you like, and there will be someone who's way funny and wears the same size clothes as you, and you can share jeans and give each other manicures. And you can take a nice, long shower after you've unpacked so you can start to feel human again.* She imagined herself digging her thick terrycloth robe out from her trunk and hanging it just outside a nice shower stall. She'd turn the water on full blast and melt away the travel grime. Then she'd change into her most comfortable track pants and snuggle under her covers until dinnertime. Maybe she'd even blow her hair out—*first day of camp, and all.*

The path curved around, and Natalie hung a left, just like Helen had told her to. Almost immediately, she came upon a cluster of . . .

No. No way.

It just wasn't possible. There was no *way* that these crumbling, paint-chipped shacks were the *bunks*. As in, where she was expected to *live* for eight whole weeks!

The ramshackle structures couldn't have been less

similar to the log cabins of Natalie's fantasies. They barely looked like they would make it through the summer, they were so dilapidated. The bunks were constructed of flimsy-looking planks of wood that had probably been a uniform color once upon a time, but age and weather had rendered them a dull and faded shade of gray. "Windows" were screens without shutters or panes. Natalie wondered what happened when it rained.

Swallowing hard, she counted to the fourth building and stepped up toward it slowly. *Looks can be deceiving*, she reminded herself. *Don't judge a book by its cover.* She racked her brain for any other clichés that could offer any small bit of comfort. Someone had tacked a big pink posterboard to the front door. "WELCOME, BUNK 3C," it said. The sign was decorated with glitter and lots of girls' names. It was hard for Natalie to imagine that in just a few moments all those names would be actual people— people she'd be sharing one big room with for two whole months. She had never shared a room before, ever, other than for a sleepover party. *Just do it*, she decided. It was time to just jump in. *Here goes nothing*, she thought, and pushed the door open, stepping into bunk 3C.

Natalie couldn't believe that her own mother had paid money for her to stay here. Or that there were girls who were looking *forward* to living in a bunk. She didn't know how she was going to make it.

The door clacked shut behind her, bouncing on its hinges. The fact that the door didn't have a knob or any other lock-type mechanism did not escape her. But she couldn't dwell on such matters. Because the bunk itself had many, many other problems.

Six bunk beds were lined up on either side of the small, square room. Two single beds were arranged just beyond the main bunk "area," obviously intended for the counselors. The thin, stained mattresses bore little resemblance to the fabulous bed she'd been dreaming of. And sleeping on a top bunk was clearly out of the question. She'd never fallen out of bed, but she sure wasn't eager to tempt fate from eight feet in the air. The top bunks had some sort of railing, but she wasn't interested in taking chances.

The floor was wooden, scuffed, and looked likely to splinter off. She thought gratefully of having packed her striped, rubber flip-flops. Crooked wooden cubbies were built into the walls, obviously intended for the campers' belongings. She was supposed to unpack her clothes and just leave them in open shelves for everyone to see? Wouldn't they get dusty or dirty or . . . well, she couldn't really think of anything too terrible that would happen to her stuff, but still—it seemed like a bad idea.

Thinking again of her grand plan to shower, Natalie cautiously made her way into the bathroom. *How bad could it be?* she asked herself. She was instantly sorry that she had.

Oh. That *bad*.

It wasn't the sticky, stained floor that bothered her

(she did have those striped flip-flops, after all). Neither was it the no-frills row of stall showers facing the far back wall. Oh, sure, she could see even from the doorway how mildewed and moldy those curtains were. The fact that the toilet-paper rolls were soggy with humidity wasn't a great concern.

No, what freaked Natalie out was the toilet. Specifically, the state of one toilet—one of only *two* that twelve girls were expected to share. On top of this toilet was the hugest, slimiest, squirmiest, and all-out grossest spider Natalie had ever seen. Even if someone had been able to kill this spider—and frankly, she wasn't really sure that that would even be possible—its spidery, icky essence would live on. On the toilet seat.

Well, she just wouldn't use the bathroom. Ever.

Natalie crossed to one of the sinks that stood in a row on the opposite wall of the shower stalls. She glanced at her face in the mirror—no good news there— and splashed some water across her cheeks. She patted her face and walked back into the sleeping area of the bunk.

"So, you're Natalie? Or are you Alyssa or Chelsea or Grace?"

Natalie looked over to see a petite blond girl talking to her. "I'm Julie," the girl continued, smiling widely. "I'm going to be your counselor this summer."

Julie had bright, clear blue eyes and freckles covering every visible square inch of skin. Her hair was short, straight, and shiny. Her skin was scrubbed clean, and her complexion was fresh. Julie looked like a very "perky" person. Natalie had her doubts about "perky" people and couldn't help but be slightly wary of Julie. But of course, she had to at least try, didn't she?

"I'm Natalie," Natalie said, introducing herself. She coaxed what she hoped was a passable smile to her face.

"Right, I knew I had a one-in-four shot because the tri-state buses just arrived. So it was either you or Alyssa or Grace or Chelsea. Chelsea's from Pennsylvania," Julie explained.

Natalie was a little relieved that Julie was just organized, not a mind reader. "A girl named Alyssa was on my bus. So was a Grace. They're both eleven. So it's probably them," she reasoned, feeling a little more relaxed to know that there would be at least two people in her bunk who weren't *total* strangers.

"Well, in that case, I'm sure they'll be here soon," Julie said. "I arranged everyone's luggage—I mean, the stuff that was shipped beforehand, anyway—in front of a bed. Yours is right there," Julie said, indicating the second bunk in the right. "Alex will be in the same bunk bed, so since you're here first, I guess you get to choose top or bottom. Lucky you."

"Well, I personally prefer the bottom. But what if Alex does, too?" Natalie worried.

Julie laughed. "These things usually work themselves out. If Alex is dead-set on a bottom bunk, there will definitely be someone willing to trade with her.

You'd be surprised how many girls actually prefer the top bunk, you know," she said. "Look—Karen does."

For the first time, Natalie noticed that there was another girl in the bunk. She was hunched quietly over in the corner.

"Hey, Karen," Natalie said. "Where are you from?"

Karen spun around. "I'm from Chicago," she said.

Natalie blinked. "That's a long way away," she commented.

"My mother grew up in Pennsylvania, and she used to go to this camp for years and years," Karen said. "So that's why she sent me here. My plane got in really early this morning—I've been here forever."

Natalie nodded, taking Karen in. Natalie wasn't a snob, but she was pretty confident, and she made friends and could read people easily. A quick glance told her all she needed to know about Karen. The girl had thick brown hair pulled back into two braids going down either side of her head. Natalie knew lots of girls who wore their hair that way, but on Karen it really looked babyish, rather than cute. The hair, coupled with Karen's brown-and-green striped capri pants and a T-shirt that said LAKEVIEW ATHLETICS suggested that Karen was weird. Natalie's heart instantly went out to her. "Well, it's good that you had time to settle in before things got really crazy," Natalie told her.

Karen just shrugged and dove back into her trunk, leaving Natalie feeling a little bit foolish. She'd only been trying to be friendly, after all. It wasn't her fault Karen was odd. Also, if she'd been here all day, why was she still unpacking? Bizarre.

Stranger yet was when Karen re-emerged from inside of her trunk with three stuffed animals. *Teddy bears?* Natalie thought incredulously. "Cool bears," she offered, trying again to keep an open mind.

Karen nodded coolly. "The rest are in my duffel."

The rest? Natalie thought. *Yikes.*

Natalie crossed over to the cubby wall and looked around again. Before she could even take a breath, though, Julie's bright, blond face was close to her own. "You can pick any cubby that you like!" Julie asserted, sounding like she thought this was a huge source of comfort to Natalie.

Four weeks, Natalie thought. It would only be four weeks until Visiting Day. Then her mother would come up, see the horror of Natalie's surroundings, and bust her out of Lakeview once and for all. There was no way her mother could be immune to things like moldy shower stalls and spiders on the toilet seats, right?

Was there?

chapter THREE

"Can somebody *please* get the door for me? Ugh, I think I broke a nail!"

Natalie was sitting on the edge of her bed, actually hard at work filing her own nails, when she overheard the cry for help. She had finished unpacking over an hour ago, and had witnessed each new bunkmate walk in. There were only two more left to arrive, and the suspense was killing her. Glad to have something to do, Natalie sprung up and raced to be of help.

She threw the door open to be greeted with the sight of a very pretty older girl. "Hi, I'm Marissa, your CIT," the girl said, green eyes wide. "Thanks for opening the door." She sounded slightly out of breath, and she was balancing a bright pink milk crate overflowing with tons of cool stuff: a metallic blue iPod, a pair of fuzzy purple slippers, a hot pink clip-on lamp . . . Natalie's eyes flickered over the goods, appraising what Marissa had thought to bring. She'd have killed for the purple slippers, now that she saw the floor of the bunk.

"I'm Natalie," Natalie said. "And you probably want to get by." She stepped aside to let Marissa in. Marissa rushed in and immediately dropped her things on the floor next to the unclaimed single, then turned to embrace Julie.

"I'm so glad we get to work together!" Julie squealed, running her fingers through Marissa's wavy, light brown hair. "And I cannot *believe* how long your hair got!"

"You cut yours!" Marissa giggled.

"I did, too," a bold voice interrupted.

Natalie rolled her eyes. After just a few hours in the bunk, she already knew that voice all too well. It was Alex Kim. Alex had arrived just a few minutes after Natalie and had instantly made herself at home. It wasn't that she was so awful, really, just that . . . well, she was a Camp Lakeview regular. This was, like, her fifth summer or something. She knew all the ropes and was definite model-camper material, which made Natalie feel a little weird. Back in New York City, after all, *she* was the one who knew everyone, was friends with everyone, was the center of a million different groups of people. But obviously things would be different at Lakeview. For one, Marissa and Alex were embracing like long-lost relatives on a daytime soap opera.

"It looks great!" Marissa gushed, stepping back to admire Alex's straight black hair. Natalie herself thought the haircut was a little basic, but she supposed it suited Alex.

"Yeah, I needed to cut it to get it out of my face during soccer," Alex said, "but I like it so much that I'm probably not going to grow it back."

"No, short hair's great," Marissa said. "Now we can put all sorts of cool clips and stuff in it. And if you're feeling bold, we can even use some eye makeup, once your hair is pulled off your face."

Alex grimaced. "Gunk around my eyes? No, thanks."

Natalie smiled to herself, thinking of her own makeup kit stashed under her bed. At least that was one thing that she and Marissa could share.

"Are you into makeup?" Alex asked, turning toward Natalie. She was so direct that she somehow made it sound like an accusation.

"Um, yeah, I am," Natalie said, somewhat taken aback. She felt like she was expected to apologize for it or something.

Alex took a long look at Natalie, checking her out. Natalie bristled unintentionally. Who did this girl think she was? Just because she had been here a few summers in a row? That wasn't so special, in Natalie's opinion.

Well, Natalie knew at least one other girl here, and right now, she was especially glad for that. "Hey, Alyssa," she called out in the direction of the ceiling. Alyssa had shown up just after Natalie (the two of them having been on the same bus, and all), and had taken a cool fifteen minutes to put her things away before diving onto the bunk on top of Natalie's (it seemed like Julie had been right about the whole top bunk thing. Alex and Alyssa had swapped almost instantly). Alyssa had been there ever since. Natalie was into her and her whole low-key approach to camp. Alyssa seemed like the type of girl who hardly ever got bothered by anything.

"Yeah?" Alyssa called from her perch on her bed.

"Wanna go outside and play cards until the cookout? I will totally kick your butt at rummy 500."

There was a pause during which Natalie wondered if she'd somehow said the wrong thing. Maybe artsy, sensitive girls didn't like to play cards? Then, finally, "Yeah, right," and the sound of a ballpoint pen being capped. Natalie almost couldn't believe she'd succeeded in tearing Alyssa away from her notebook.

"We're leaving for the cookout in an hour!" Julie called as the girls left the bunk. "Don't go far!"

Natalie wasn't planning on going far, of course. But the stuffy bunk and everyone's unpacking was starting to make her uncomfortable. And for the first time since she'd arrived at Lakeview, Natalie felt like she could use some fresh air.

▲ ▲ ▲

"So, you're new, huh?" Natalie prodded as Alyssa shuffled the deck. They had settled in a grassy patch just outside the bunk and were waiting for the last two campers in 3C to arrive. Natalie had a sinking feeling that once they were all present and accounted for, there'd be icebreakers and more rounds of endless introductions. She was thankful to have a few moments, at least, outside and away from the chaos.

"Uh-huh," Alyssa nodded. "For the past two summers, I've been doing these drawing classes at a college in Middletown—that's right near where I live."

"In Pennsylvania?" Natalie asked.

"Nope, it's Jersey. Way in the south. Anyway, there's nothing special about the school, but, you know, I like to draw, so that was a pretty cool way to spend the summer."

"Why'd you come here?" Natalie wanted to know. Alyssa didn't seem like any more of a camp person than Natalie was.

Alyssa made a face and pushed her long dark hair off her shoulders. "You know. Parents. They decided I need to be more 'social.' " She made air quotes with her fingers and wrinkled her nose.

Natalie laughed. "I know what you mean. My mother told me that camp would help me build character. I told her I already have enough character."

"Totally. And you know"—Alyssa paused conspiratorially—"I bet Alex has enough character for the three of us combined." She winked to take the edge off her words. "Anyway, my mother wouldn't budge. I even tried to sic my dad on her, but he wasn't biting." Alyssa dealt the cards out. "What about yours?"

"What about my what?" Natalie asked, pretending not to get the question. She wasn't prepared to talk about her father just yet.

"Your dad," Alyssa said slowly, as though Natalie were a five-year-old. "Did he think you need more character, too?"

Natalie shrugged. "My dad's not really in the picture," she said simply, hoping that Alyssa would let the subject drop.

Alyssa flipped over the first card of the deck. "Ace of spades." She raised an eyebrow in Natalie's direction.

If she was wondering about Natalie's father, she didn't ask.

"My name is Grace, and I like gummy bears," Grace said, giggling. She gestured to the girl sitting beside her, Indian-style. "This is Chelsea and she likes cheesy music, and that's Alyssa and she likes art class. And Candace likes card games and Jenna likes jewelry." She paused, frowning in concentration. "Alex likes athletics." She exhaled.

Natalie and Alyssa hadn't gotten very far in their game before they had been called back in. The last two girls had arrived and it was time to do the "get-to-know-one-another" thing before dinner. Natalie's suspicion about icebreakers had turned out to be dead-on, and now she and her bunkmates were seated on the floor of the bunk, each offering one piece of information about herself and then forced to recite the names and details provided by the others before her. Based on where in the circle the game had begun, Natalie counted that she would be responsible for remembering every girl but two.

Natalie had a terrible memory.

"I'm Brynn," said the girl seated to Grace's left. Brynn had very short, very dark red hair and very pale skin. Her eyes were a bright, twinkly green. She had been one of the last two girls to show up, and it turned out she was best friends with Alex. They had even requested to bunk together, and they'd been inseparable since Brynn had arrived. Well, nearly inseparable, anyway—at least they weren't sitting next to each other in the circle.

Brynn had a very loud voice for such a small girl. She wanted to be an actress, she explained, and was planning to spend most of her summer in the drama shack. Natalie had to admit that Brynn seemed very dramatic, so maybe that was a good thing. "I'm Brynn and I like Broadway shows. Grace likes gummy bears—so do I, Grace"—she beamed—"and Chelsea likes cheesy music and Alyssa likes art class and Jenna likes jewelry. Candace likes card games. And Alex likes athletics," Brynn said, flashing a blinding grin at her friend.

The bunk erupted in applause. Brynn hadn't faltered on a single name or detail. Even Natalie had to admit that she was slightly impressed. She took a moment to survey the circle of strange faces once more. In addition to the names that Brynn had just rattled off, she had also met Sarah, a friend of Alex and Brynn's and another big-time jock who was very into running (Natalie couldn't understand why anyone would be into running. What was the rush, anyway?), Karen, of course, the strange and youngish girl who'd been there all morning and had arrived with a collection of stuffed animals so large that it almost concerned Natalie, and Valerie, whose dark skin and cornrows reminded Natalie of Hannah from back home. Finally, there was Jessica, who wore her long, light brown hair in a sloppy bun on the top of her head and refused to answer to anything other than "Jessie."

The circle grew quiet, and Natalie realized that everyone was looking at her. *Right, my turn.* She took a deep breath and exhaled loudly. "My name is Natalie and I like . . . new experiences," she said, cringing inwardly at how corny the words sounded coming from her lips. Apparently, it was the right thing to say, though, because Alyssa was giving her a sly grin and Julie was smiling away, full of encouragement.

Anyway, maybe if she tried hard enough, she could make herself believe it was true.

▲ ▲ ▲

"Guys! We have extra hot dogs! I repeat, we have extra hot dogs!"

Natalie couldn't help but laugh to hear Pete

shouting to be heard over the noise. *Good luck,* she thought. The entire camp had turned out for the cookout that evening, and campers were seated in clusters across the lawn, breaking off into countless individual conversations. Seeing everyone seated and enthusiastically eating, Natalie felt overwhelmed all over again. There were more campers at Lakeview than there were students in her entire school! Suddenly, Natalie was wondering if she was as social of a person as she had originally thought.

No, don't think that way, she scolded herself. *You're just freaking out because everything is strange and new. But it won't be this way forever. What would Hannah say if she could talk to you?* She knew what Hannah would say: "Chill out, girl— like it or not, you're at camp for the summer, so you may as well relax and make the best of it." Hannah was totally practical and levelheaded that way. It was so annoying.

And anyway, it wasn't as though Natalie was off in a corner by herself. She and Alyssa had squatted down in a circle with the rest of bunk 3C. Alex and Jenna were big on bunk unity. It was easy to see why they would both be favorites of any counselor.

Natalie felt a finger in her ribs and turned to find Alyssa poking her. "Sure you don't want another hot dog?" The corners of her mouth were turned up in an impish grin.

"Ugh, I don't even want to think about what the first one did to me," Natalie protested. "There must be something wrong with them. You were smart to stick to the side salads." She waved her paper plate in the direction of a group of boys who had jumped up and made a mad dash for the barbecue pit the minute Pete announced second helpings.

"Oh, my brother and his friends'll eat anything," Jenna said. "It's so gross."

"Which one's your brother?" Natalie asked.

"Well, the one who's standing on line like he hasn't eaten in weeks—*so* not true, by the way—is Adam. He's my twin and he's in 3F. So you'll meet him when we have electives and stuff. My sister Stephanie is a CIT. She's good friends with Marissa so you'll meet her soon, I'm sure."

"Oh, we have electives with the boys?" Natalie asked. Suddenly, camp was sounding just a little more interesting.

Jenna shuddered. "Unfortunately. For most of the day, you travel with your bunk to different activities, but twice a day you get to go to your electives, and those are a mix of everyone in our age division. Oh, and they have swim sessions and meals with us, too. We're gonna have to stick together if we want to avoid getting splashed. Although," Jenna leaned in, a mischievous look on her face, "I'm usually pretty good at pulling pranks on them and stuff. They never know what hit 'em."

Natalie nodded. "Good to know." At this point, she was more interested in scoping out the boys than in playing pranks on them. Was that going to be just one more thing that set her apart from her bunkmates? She pushed herself up from the ground and dusted any stray grass off her legs. Nature was turning out to be very . . . well, messy. "I'm gonna toss my trash. Does anyone have anything for me to throw out?" she offered. Jenna and Alyssa shook their heads no.

Natalie fought her way through a swarm of nasty-looking insects and gingerly tossed her plate and utensils into the garbage can. A bit of mayonnaise splashed up onto her arm, making her a prime target of the insects' interest. "Oh, ick," she grumbled, and wandered toward the barbecue table to grab a napkin to clean herself up.

"Look, he *said* there are a ton of hot dogs left."

"But, um, I still have my hamburger, Chelsea."

Natalie turned to see Chelsea and Karen standing next to the barbecue table, apparently in the midst of some serious negotiations. It was plain to see that Karen definitely did have an entire hamburger sitting untouched on her plate. Which Chelsea definitely had designs on. Natalie watched the exchange with curiosity.

"Come on, Karen, I'm starving. And I'm allergic to hot dogs. Don't you want to do me a favor?" Chelsea pressed.

"Well, but . . . I mean . . . how can you be allergic to hot dogs? Or, I mean, if you're allergic to hot dogs, then wouldn't you also be allergic to hamburgers?"

"Well, okay," Chelsea said, quickly backtracking, "I'm not exactly allergic. But it's, like, I really don't like them and they really make me sick. Ever since I was little. Anyway," she continued, "my mother is going to send me up a care package next week, and I can totally hook you up. I mean, wouldn't you want a pack of Twizzlers or something? That's fair, right?"

Karen looked unconvinced, but she was obviously afraid to stand up to Chelsea. "Um, I guess," she said. "Yeah, fine." She pushed her plate at Chelsea and walked away, her head down.

"Wait a minute!" Chelsea called after her, smiling like the cat that had swallowed the canary. "Don't you even want to get a hot dog?"

Karen rushed off, not bothering to answer. Natalie observed the entire exchange silently, thinking. She didn't like what she had just seen. Was Chelsea some kind of bully?

"Where'd you go? We thought you'd, like, fallen into the garbage can or something," Grace teased when Natalie had made her way back to the bunk. "Or were you having a little last-minute hot-dog-eating contest?"

Before Natalie could answer, she was interrupted by the sound of hoots, whistles, and feet stamping on the ground. She glanced over and saw that Alex and Jenna were the cause of the commotion. They were hissing and booing at a group of girls walking by.

"What's the sitch?" Natalie asked, turning to Grace,

who had also joined in on the shrieking and hollering.

"It's bunk 3A," Grace explained between whistles. "They're our rivals."

"Based on what?" Natalie asked.

"Oh, gosh, I don't even remember anymore. They've played all kinds of jokes on us over the last few summers. Somehow, it just developed. I mean, it's all in good fun. You'll see—just don't leave your toothbrush out at night, is all I'm saying," she warned.

Natalie didn't like the sound of that one bit. *All in good fun? Really?* she wondered.

When was the fun going to start, then?

chapter FOUR

Within five minutes of first waking up, Natalie immediately noticed two things. The first was that it was about thirty degrees below zero in the bunk, and her cute little sleep shorts were really not doing the trick of keeping her warm. She remembered that Julie had tried to warn her the night before of how cold it could get in the mountains, but for some reason, she hadn't let herself believe it. *Note to self,* she thought, thrusting her hands underneath the covers and rubbing them vigorously across her bare legs in the hopes of warming them up, *for future reference: Julie knows stuff.*

The second thing Natalie noticed—and this was going to be an even bigger problem, she decided—was the horrible trumpet blaring through the open windows. *We couldn't have just set an alarm clock?* she wondered.

Okay, so she wasn't a morning person.

From across the room, someone groaned. "For Pete's sake, *please* make that noise stop!" It was Grace.

She clearly wasn't a morning person, either.

"What time is it, even?" Natalie demanded. She had worn her cute pink waterproof sports watch to bed (at last, she'd finally have a chance to make use of all of its "outdoor" settings), but she had no intention of taking her hands out from underneath her blanket to check.

"It's quarter of," Julie said brightly, bouncing across the room. She looked as freshly scrubbed and perky as ever. Natalie suspected she even looked that way in her sleep.

"Quarter of *what*?" Natalie pressed. "I don't believe in getting up before the sevens."

"Well, my dear, I'm sorry to have to break it to you, but if that's the case, then you're going to have to stay in bed for another fifteen minutes. But that would only leave you fifteen minutes to get dressed. Your call."

Natalie flew up in bed. "We have *half an hour* to be ready for breakfast?"

She looked around the bunk. To every side she could see girls rummaging through their cubbies in various stages of dress. Karen was sitting on the edge of her bed holding a sock up in front of her face, looking confused.

"But, Julie," Natalie said, careful to keep the edge she was feeling from creeping into her tone, "it takes me at least twenty minutes to shower."

"Well, then you'd better hurry, Natalie. And tomorrow morning, you'll just have to try to get up before the bugle. Does your watch have an alarm?" Julie asked.

She didn't sound unsympathetic, just matter-offact. But that didn't make Natalie feel any better.

"Well, I guess I can rush," Natalie said. "Whatever. I can do makeup when we get back from breakfast."

"I'm sorry, Nat, but after breakfast we really only have a half an hour or so, and that's for our bunk chores," Julie said. "But you don't need makeup to look gorgeous!"

Speak for yourself, Natalie thought glumly, hoisting herself reluctantly out of bed, stepping into her flip-flops, and padding off into the bathroom.

As she shuffled into a shower stall, she was nearly mowed over by Alex, who was running a comb through her wet hair. *Of course,* Natalie thought. It only fit that Alex had woken up on time to shower. She was, like, Supercamper.

Natalie stepped into a stall and turned the hot water on full blast. She ducked under the stream—and let out a startled shriek.

"What is it?" Julie asked, rushing in.

"It's FREEZING!" Natalie shouted. The water was about as cold as the morning air in the bunk had been. Also, a huge clump of wiry hair was poking its way out of the drain. *Gross.*

"Sorry," said a voice from the direction of the sinks. "I might have used up the hot water." It was Chelsea.

"Are you *allergic* to cold water?" Natalie mumbled sarcastically, surprising herself. She hadn't meant to be nasty, it had just slipped out.

"Did you say something?" Chelsea asked.

"No, I didn't say anything," Natalie replied quickly, covering. "I didn't say anything at all."

She ducked back underneath the cold water, resigned to her fate for this morning, at least.

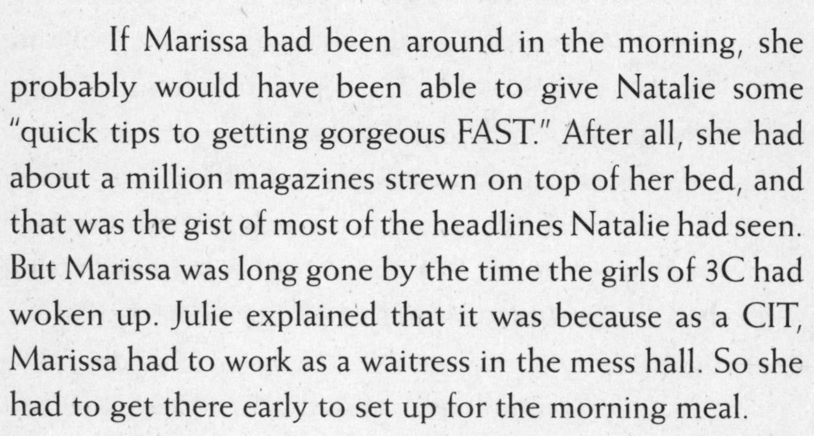

If Marissa had been around in the morning, she probably would have been able to give Natalie some "quick tips to getting gorgeous FAST." After all, she had about a million magazines strewn on top of her bed, and that was the gist of most of the headlines Natalie had seen. But Marissa was long gone by the time the girls of 3C had woken up. Julie explained that it was because as a CIT, Marissa had to work as a waitress in the mess hall. So she had to get there early to set up for the morning meal.

Walking to the mess hall, Natalie was actually kind of excited to see Marissa waiting on them. She wondered if all the CITs had cute matching uniforms that they wore when they served. And maybe Marissa would carry a funny notepad in her apron that she would use for taking orders, like in a real restaurant. Natalie wondered what they normally had for breakfast at Lakeview. If the cookout was any indication, the food wouldn't be any great shakes, but that was no big deal. She could live on scrambled eggs if she had to.

"Oh, and if the bug juice is yellow, don't drink it," Alex was saying to a group of girls.

"Um, why?" Karen asked quietly. By now Natalie had gotten used to the fact that Karen did everything quietly.

"Because you don't know what they put in it," Alex explained. "I mean, I guess you never can be too sure, but with yellow, it's like asking for trouble. I wouldn't put it past them if they peed in it," she said, lowering her voice.

"Ew," Karen said.

"That *can't* be true," Natalie interjected, holding out hope that Alex was just being dramatic.

Jenna nodded solemnly. "It is, though. My oldest brother Matt—he's not here anymore, he's really old, and this summer he's going to a summer college program in science, how boring is *that*?—anyway, his friend used to work in the kitchen. You would not *believe* the stuff that goes on in there. I mean, pee in the bug juice is seriously the least of it. I can tell you stories—"

"—Please don't," Natalie begged.

"Okay, okay," Alex said, breaking into the conversation again like a weary referee. "Let's just put it this way—if we tell you to avoid something, you'll just have to trust us."

"Fair enough," Natalie said.

"This is our table!" Julie shouted, beckoning the girls to a long, cafeteria-style table and bench set just inside the mess hall.

They'd been inside the mess hall for all of three seconds, and already Natalie's head was spinning. For starters, the room was enormous, cavernous, with soaring ceilings held in place with long wooden beams and rafters. Which of course made for the kind of acoustics that sent the racket of at least two hundred separate conversations up into the air only to pour loudly back down. Natalie shook her head. So far, everything about camp seemed to be chaotic. Certainly the paint-splattered banners dangling from the walls, hailing color wars of years gone by. Natalie wasn't sure yet what color war was, and she was almost afraid to ask. It sounded potentially stressful. And there was the clatter of silverware clinking against the surface of the tables. And the laughter coming from her own fellow bunkmates. Was she honestly the only person here who didn't find camp to be one great big party?

She looked up to see Alyssa cradling her chin on her palm, looking thoughtful. Okay, so she wasn't exactly the only one. But that didn't make it much better. Natalie was still hoping that her mother would come up on Visiting Day, take one look at this place, and throw Natalie into the backseat of her SUV and never look back. But Visiting Day was four long weeks away. And Natalie couldn't bear the thought of having to mope her way through each passing day. There had to be some way to make the situation better, more bearable, at least.

Didn't there?

A platter of rubbery-looking blackened pucks

landed on the table in front of her with an unceremonious thud. Natalie gazed intently at the dish. "Nope, nuh-uh," she decided, looking at Alex questioningly. "Not a clue."

Alex leaned forward and put her face closer to the food. The gesture did nothing to encourage Natalie to try the food. She inhaled deeply—*it's always nice when someone breathes directly* on *your food,* Natalie thought fleetingly—and wrinkled her forehead in concentration.

"French toast," she pronounced, pushing the tray toward Natalie. "It's all yours."

Natalie regarded the dried-up slabs of bread again. In no way did they resemble French toast. French toast was what she ordered at her local diner on Sundays, when she and her mother had brunch. French toast was thick and eggy and covered in toasted pecans. It looked nothing like a hockey puck. And it wasn't black. "Oh, I couldn't," Natalie said shortly. "Really."

"Come on, Nat, you have to eat something," Julie prodded. "Here comes Marissa. Maybe she can tell you what else there is for breakfast."

Natalie glanced up. It didn't seem as though Marissa had paid too much attention to any beauty tips this morning. She was wearing a very un-hip plastic apron over cutoff shorts and a tank top, and she had a smudge of something yellow—possibly egg yolk— drying across her cheek. Her eyes looked red and tired, and her hair hung limply at her shoulders. Natalie got the distinct impression that there weren't too many alternatives to the morning menu. Marissa certainly wasn't carrying pen and paper, anyway.

"What's wrong?" Marissa added, sounding harried. "Do you guys need more food?"

"No—no!" Alex said quickly. "I mean, we're fine, we're all good," she corrected.

Natalie could see that working as a waitress was very hard work, and the last thing she wanted to do was add to Marissa's burden. But the French toast was seriously out of the question. "Marissa," she began slowly, "is there, ah, anything else to eat?"

For a moment, Marissa looked as though she wanted to cry. Then she brightened. "I think there's fruit!" she said, darting off in the direction of the kitchen. Natalie's spirits soared. She'd be able to at least make it through the morning on a banana. Lunch *had* to be better than this disaster.

"Here you go," Marissa pronounced, depositing a cracked plastic bowl in the middle of the table. Natalie reached in and grabbed an apple. Her finger immediately sunk through the skin and into a mealy bruise.

"Um, thanks," she said, sighing. "Do you know what's for lunch?"

After the girls had finished eating—or, in Natalie's case, pushing food around on her plate in the hopes that Julie would *think* she was eating—they filed out of the mess hall so that Marissa and the other CITs would be able to clean up. If Marissa was going to be spending so much time in the kitchen, Natalie fretted, she'd never have any energy leftover for the bunk. And then who was going to help her when she flat-ironed her hair? Alyssa was cool, but she didn't seem like the kind of girl who spent a whole lot of time on her hair, after all.

Natalie was so completely lost in her thoughts that she didn't even notice that she had stomped directly into someone. A boy someone, to be specific. The boy someone grunted and stepped forward forcefully. Her foot caught on the back of his shoe and practically pulled it off his foot.

"Hey, what's your problem?" the boy asked, whirling around. He sounded annoyed.

"It wasn't on purpose," Natalie said, feeling defensive. So she was a klutz. Whatever. Just one more reason why she wasn't going to win Camper of the Week.

But one look at her victim, and Natalie felt like maybe there would be some upsides to spending the summer at Lakeview, after all.

The boy, whoever he was, peered at her curiously. He had thick, curly black hair and eyes so deeply blue that it took Natalie a moment to figure out what color they were. Somewhere in the back of her mind, she realized she was staring, but she couldn't help it. It didn't matter, anyway, because whoever he was, he was staring right back at her.

Then one of his bunkmates jostled into him, and the moment was broken. He reached down and coaxed his foot back into his sneaker, stood up, stretched his arms over his head, and walked out of the mess hall without another glance in Natalie's direction.

"His name is Simon," said a voice in Natalie's ear.

"Huh?" Natalie asked, spinning to see Marissa standing just beside her, looking exhausted but eagerly taking in the scene. "Who?" she asked again, trying to sound casual.

Marissa shot her a knowing look. She waved her hand toward Simon's retreating frame. "His name is Simon. He's in bunk 3F."

Natalie shrugged. "Whatever," she said, feeling color rush to her cheeks. She gathered her composure and nodded toward the exit, where Julie and the rest of 3C were making their way out of the building. "I have to, uh, catch up," she said, and took off before Marissa could say anything else.

Simon. Okay. So he had cool eyes. But so what?

What did she care about Simon?

chapter FIVE

The next morning, the girls returned to their bunk after breakfast. By now, Natalie had had a chance to see that Julie hadn't been exaggerating yesterday— there really *wasn't* any time to do any last-minute primping—not that there was any reason to, in this humidity. The morning chill had gradually warmed over, and already little trickles of sweat were forming on the insides of Natalie's elbows and the backs of her knees. She could only imagine what the weather would be like by midday.

For now, though, the girls were responsible for doing chores. Back home, Natalie's mother worked such long hours at her art gallery that she had hired a housekeeper to come in once a week to clean. Natalie often straightened up her room—at least, she made her bed every morning and emptied out the dishwasher when necessary—but that was about the extent of her acquaintance with chores. Julie proudly held up the chore wheel that she had created. On the inner circle of the wheel, she had written up all the tasks, such as scrubbing out the toilets, emptying the wastebaskets, or sweeping the front porch. On the outer circle were all the girls' names. Every day, Julie would shift the outer wheel, so that each day the girls would rotate which chores they were responsible for. "I can't wait until it's my turn to do toilets," Grace quipped as she headed outside with the trash.

"Girls, before you start your chores, listen up. I want to give you your schedules, okay?" Julie called out. "Every day after breakfast, we come back to the bunk and clean for a half an hour. Then after that, we've got a specialty that we travel to as a bunk: nature, arts and crafts, ceramics, woodworking, drama, photography, and the newspaper. It switches every day. After that comes instructional swim. Today you'll be taking your swim tests for placement. After swim comes a free choice, then sports, then lunch, second free choice, then siesta after free swim. While you do your chores, I'll be talking to each of you individually and taking down your selections for your free choices. You should pick three, and I promise I'll do my best to make sure that you get two of the ones that you pick. Okay? Get to it! Karen, come talk to me about free choice."

Dutifully (and, truth be told, somewhat eagerly), Karen put down her scrub brush and scampered over to Julie's bunk. She didn't seem very sorry about having to put off bathroom duty.

As she swept the front porch, Natalie thought about which free choices would be most interesting to her. Photography could be really cool—definitely something she could keep up back in the city if it turned out that she was any good at it. So she would choose that. And secondly, she wouldn't mind writing for the newspaper. Her English teacher in school was always telling her she was a good writer. And for a third choice she would pick drama. Drama was something else that she would probably be good at. After all, it ran in the family. Which was, of course, one of the reasons why she usually steered clear of it. But if it came down to drama or nature, she'd take drama all the way. It was definitely better than any of the other, "campier" choices available. What *was* woodworking, anyway?

Natalie brushed all the excess dust off the porch and directly onto the ground. Julie hadn't given her a dust pan and, besides, the ground was nothing but dirt, anyway. She picked her broom up and walked back inside the bunk.

Inside, though, she was immediately given the shock of her life. Over Alex's bed was a huge poster of Tad Maxwell from his latest movie, *Spy in the Big City*. Instantly, Natalie's blood ran cold. What was that poster doing up? Was Alex a fan of the "spy" movies? Did she know who Tad Maxwell *really* was? No, Natalie decided, she couldn't know. It had to be some sort of coincidence. And if Natalie could keep her cool, Alex would *never* know, either.

She willed herself to maintain her composure. "Hey, Alex, is that your poster?" she asked as casually as she could.

"Huh? Oh, yeah," Alex said, tossing a wet sponge into a bucket of soapy water. She had been working on the sinks in the bathroom."Isn't it cool? My older brother loves Tad Maxwell 'cause he kicks so much butt, and then he got me into the 'spy' movies. I'm a *huge* fan. I think he's really cute, too. What about you?"

"Oh, um, you know. I think Tad Maxwell is cool," Natalie stammered, "but there are, you know, lots of other things I like better. I'm more into chick flicks," she said, pulling herself together.

"Yeah, me too!" Grace said, coming up behind her. "And musicals. Does it get any better than *Grease*?" She broke into a few bars of "Summer Nights," causing all the girls to crack up.

"Nat, you're the only one who hasn't chosen her electives yet," Julie said, interrupting the laughter. "Do you know what you want?"

"Yeah," Natalie said, crossing the room to squat on the floor next to Julie's bed."Anything but nature! Seriously, though," she continued, "I'd be into photography, the newspaper, and . . . drama. Yeah, drama could be cool," she finished, sounding slightly uncertain. She glanced at Alex's poster again.

Natalie thought maybe she already had enough drama in her life.

Julie worked on putting together the girls' free-choice schedules while they were in arts and crafts. Natalie and her bunkmates were hard at work twisting long plastic strands into specially woven patterns. "What are these things for, anyway?" Natalie whispered to Jenna. She was used to being really good at things when she wanted to be, but at camp, everything was different and unfamiliar. She felt really frustrated.

Jenna shrugged. "It's lanyard. It's a camp tradition. You'll have about a million lanyard key chains by the time the summer is over."

Natalie thought about the cool lip-gloss key chain that Hannah had given her at her last birthday. That was way more useful than this . . . *lanyard.* But she had promised herself that she would give camp a try, so she kept her opinion to herself. And, anyway, the pink and turquoise color scheme she'd thought up was looking pretty good, in her opinion. Way tropical.

"Okay, girls, I've got your schedules worked out," Julie announced as the girls worked. "Now, I want you all to know that I did everything I could to make sure that you each got at least one of your three choices, and I'm pretty sure I was successful. But if you're not totally happy with your free choices, just know that we swap every two weeks, okay? So you won't be spending two full months doing something you're not that into. But try to keep an open mind—you might find you're better at something than you would have expected." With that, she called the girls over to a corner of the art room one at a time to let them know their schedules.

Natalie watched in anticipation as one by one, the girls were given their choices. Grace skipped back to the art table after talking to Julie. "Ceramics and drama," she said, beaming. "So awesome. I wanted to be in the school play, and I wanted to learn to use the kiln. Last year, Alex made a really cool coffee mug, and I want to do the same thing."

Brynn was also thrilled with her choices. "Drama," she practically sang. "I heard that the play this year is going to be *Peter Pan*, and I think I'd be the perfect choice for Wendy. And also the newspaper," she said as an afterthought. She began to hum the chorus to one of the songs from *Peter Pan* under her breath. Natalie could see that Brynn already had visions of her name up in lights.

"Natalie?" Julie called.

Natalie pushed her lanyard aside and jumped up. She rushed over to Julie, wishing she didn't feel so nervous. *It's just free choice, Nat*, she reminded herself. "What'd I get?" she asked breathlessly.

"Well, you've got the newspaper for first free," Julie said. "With Alyssa. I thought you two would like to be together."

Natalie exhaled sharply. "Great. That could be fun."

"But," Julie said, looking slightly uncomfortable,

"there were just too many overlaps for most of the rest of the choices, so I had to give you something different than what you asked for."

Natalie bristled. "What'd I get?" she asked, a sense of dread coming over her.

"Keep in mind it's just for two weeks, and you never know what you might learn," Julie said, stalling for time and burying her face in her clipboard.

Now Natalie was really starting to feel anxious. "Julie," she pressed, "come on."

"Well, for second free, you've got nature," Julie said.

"What?" Natalie cried. "Julie, no way!"

"I promise, Nat, it's the only way I could make it work. I swear. And it's only for two weeks."

"Two weeks is a long time!" Natalie insisted. "Julie, I'm pretty sure I'm allergic to nature. I mean, I'm from New York City!"

"Don't be silly," Julie protested. "The truth is, Nat," she said, lowering her voice, "I'm starting to get to know you girls, and I can tell that you're strong. You're a confident chick. And if I stick you in nature, you're gonna do well—even if it's not your first choice. Now, I can't say that about everyone in the bunk. So I need you to be the strong one, and to suck it up and try something new and different. Just think of it as taking one for the team. Can you do that for me?" Julie fixed her bright blue eyes on Natalie, and suddenly Natalie found it hard to say no.

"When you put it that way," Natalie said, rolling her eyes, "how can I argue?"

Julie threw her arms around Natalie. "I knew I could count on you, Natalie! I totally owe you!" she exclaimed.

"Yes," Natalie agreed solemnly. "Yes, you do."

"Oh, you got nature, too?" Chelsea asked, passing by. She didn't sound very sympathetic.

"Uh, yeah. Does that mean you got nature?" Natalie asked.

Chelsea tossed her sun-streaked blond hair over her shoulders. "Yup. But you know, it's different for me. I'm from the country. So I'll be able to identify the poison ivy and stuff—and avoid it," she said snidely. She shot Natalie a self-satisfied grin and stalked off.

Natalie turned back to Julie again, a fresh wave of panic washing over her.

"Nat, she's just kidding. Ha ha," Julie said pleadingly.

Marissa, back from kitchen duty, came up behind Natalie and rubbed her shoulders. "Just think of it as building character," she said.

Great. More character, Natalie thought. *At what point do we decide that I've got enough character?* She sighed. "I'll be a good sport," she said, resigned. "But in that case, have I mentioned how much you owe me?" she asked again.

"Nat, relax. Chelsea was just being . . . Chelsea.

Poison ivy is really easy to identify," Valerie said as the two trudged over to the nature shack. "Besides, I seriously doubt that the nature counselor is going to send us off into a patch of it." She giggled and shook her head, making the beads in her cornrows clink. "I bet you anything we spend today playing with the rabbits or whatever."

"Rabbits?" Natalie asked nervously. "I think I really *am* allergic to rabbits."

Valerie raised an eyebrow at her. "Come on."

"Well, I mean, I've never, like, been tested for it or anything, but who knows? I mean, I *could* be," Natalie said defensively.

"Why don't we wait and see?" Valerie suggested.

"We can wait and see, sure, but I'm telling you, Valerie, even if I'm not allergic to the rabbits or the guinea pigs or the skunks—"

"—Um, I really don't think they keep *skunks* inside the nature shack—" Valerie cut in.

"– *whatever*. The point is, that no matter if I turn out to be the world's biggest animal lover, I would want, you know, some cuddly kittens or something. I mean, there's no way on *Earth* that I'm going to suddenly be all into nature—" Natalie pushed the door open to the nature shack.

And then she stopped her tirade mid-sentence. Because there was one thing, she realized, that could just make nature bearable. One person, to be exact. One boy-person with denim blue eyes. Eyes that happened to be trained directly on her, making her suddenly self-conscious of how incredibly negative she must sound.

Simon.

Natalie stopped short as she walked into the room, causing Valerie to step directly into her and send her forward a few paces. "Ow," she said, barely taking note of the collision.

"God, Nat, stare much?" Chelsea mumbled. She had arrived a few minutes earlier and was already seated.

Natalie ignored Chelsea and went to take a seat at the table—not directly next to Simon, because that would be too obvious, but near enough that she could keep an eye on him during the session.

"Hello, guys, my name's Roseanne," said a woman standing at the front of the table. Roseanne looked like the type of person who would lead a class in nature, if there ever were such a thing: She was wiry, thin, and impossibly tall, with long, dark curly hair shooting off in every direction. She wore faded cargo shorts, a tank top, and broken-in hiking sandals. Natalie guessed Roseanne was probably a vegetarian. "Welcome to nature. In the nature shack—and outside, as well—we're going to learn all about our environment. But if you want to commune with nature, you're going to have to be responsible about it. And that means respecting nature and not disturbing or depleting it."

Scratch vegetarian, Natalie decided. *Vegan. Definite vegan.* Natalie herself had considered becoming a vegetarian, but had to drop it when she realized it meant giving up sushi.

"So first some rules that will help protect *you*," Roseanne continued. She picked up a big hand-lettered chart with some bright pictures of various plants glued onto it. "Does anyone know how to identify poison ivy?"

From her left, Natalie was dimly aware of Valerie stifling a snort and elbowing her in the ribs. But only dimly.

She was much more focused on Simon.

▲ ▲ ▲

Natalie was walking away from the nature shack, eagerly contemplating which magazine from her mother's latest care package she was going to bring to free swim when she heard someone calling after her.

"So, ah, you're not too into nature."

Natalie turned to find Simon slightly out of breath, but walking casually next to her as though he had been there all along. "Well, I like nature, and all," she began, wanting to sound like she had a "positive attitude," "but, you know, it's just . . . okay, I hate nature," she finally conceded.

Simon broke out laughing. "Roseanne can freak you out a little, I know, with her 'avoid this plant,' and 'this thing is poisonous,' but the truth is you're not going to be rubbing up against any poison ivy or anything in the nature shack."

"What about poison oak?" Natalie quipped.

"Negative," Simon replied. "And the thing is that the animals are really cool."

"I guess," Natalie agreed reluctantly. "I'm much more into domesticated animals. Like hamsters. Cats. The occasional lapdog."

"Oh, that's right, you're from New York. I guess they don't really have big dogs in the city, because of all the apartments," Simon reasoned.

Natalie stared at him, puzzled. "How did you know I was from New York City?" she asked, frankly curious.

Simon colored. "I guess, um, someone mentioned it," he offered, shrugging. "I guess."

But Simon was looking *way* too embarrassed to have just found out about her hometown by accident, Natalie decided. Based on his guilty expression, he had definitely done some digging into her background. Not that she minded. *Interesting,* Natalie thought.

Very interesting indeed.

chapter SIX

On Wednesday morning, Natalie woke with enough time to shower. She had somehow figured out how to drag herself out of her bed even amidst the morning chill so that she could get herself together before flag-raising. Maybe it was a survival instinct. After all, this *was* the wilderness, wasn't it?

Flag-raising was a particularly bizarre camp ritual, and even though she'd by now been at Lakeview for six whole days, Natalie still wasn't really getting the point of it. The process was straightforward: All the campers from all the divisions came to the field just in front of the flagpole every morning. This was located in front of the camp director's, Dr. Steve's, office. All the bunks in the divisions met together, along with their counselors and individual division heads. It was important to Dr. Steve that all of Lakeview "greet the day together."

Back in New York, Natalie and her mother liked to greet the day as slowly as possible, and usually with whole-wheat bagels and herbal tea, so this "stand at attention and salute" thing was a pretty big shock to her system.

As Natalie wrapped a towel around herself, she overheard a conversation from the stall next door.

"Are you going to wear your lavender headband?" she heard someone ask in a snotty tone. *Chelsea*, she thought. It had to be. Not that Natalie was a snoop, but suddenly the conversation was that much more interesting. She willed herself inanimate and undetectable.

"Uh, yeah, why?" It was Karen, sounding a little uncertain.

"Well, I was just thinking that it's a shame, because it sort of makes you look like a baby."

Natalie felt a pang of sympathy for Karen.

"Oh, um, do you think so?" Karen asked sadly.

"Totally. You shouldn't even bother—that is, unless you want everyone to think you're a complete *baby*," Chelsea repeated, taunting.

"You're probably right," Karen said. A pause followed, leading Natalie to think that Karen was taking the offending headband out right then and there.

"Much better," Chelsea said, confirming Natalie's thought. "But, you know, you *really* should brush your hair."

"Thanks, Chelsea," Karen said. It upset Natalie to hear the relief in Karen's voice. It certainly wasn't worth getting upset over Chelsea's opinion, annoying as she was!

"So, you know, Karen . . ." Chelsea continued.

Natalie's ears pricked up. Chelsea sounded just a tad *too* casual.

"Yeah?" Karen asked.

"So, now that you're not wearing that headband . . . I guess you wouldn't mind if I borrowed it?"

Natalie had to stop herself from gasping out loud. So Chelsea had manipulated the whole exchange, trying to make Karen feel bad about the headband, just because she wanted to wear it herself? That was just too, too mean.

Then again, she wasn't sure why she was so surprised. After all, it was typical Chelsea.

▲ ▲ ▲

Natalie told Alyssa about the conversation she'd overheard on their way to thc flag-raising. Alyssa agreed that Chelsea could be awful, but she didn't think it was really worth saying anything. "I mean, she didn't do anything to you, right?" Alyssa asked. "So, it's really not any of your business. Karen might even be upset if she found out you overheard. Like, embarrassed."

"You're probably right," Natalie agreed. "But what a pain Chelsea is."

Alyssa put a hand on Natalie's forearm, saying, "Let's not let her ruin our good time."

Natalie had to snicker. Standing in front of a flagpole at daybreak in the freezing cold was definitely not what she considered a "good time"!

"Who's in charge of raising the flag today?" Natalie asked. A different bunk was responsible every morning.

"Three-A," Alex chimed in authoritatively. Just about *everything* Alex said or did was authoritative. She was nice enough, but sometimes her gung-ho attitude grated on Natalie. But she knew what her mother would say about that: *broader horizons, yadda yadda yadda* . . .So she just smiled at Alex and said, "Thanks."

Meredith Bergmont, a petite blonde who weighed, Natalie guessed, less than a hummingbird, stepped forward. She tugged on the rope-pulley mechanism that raised the flag. In fact, Stephanie was so focused on her job that she didn't even notice exactly what she was raising—the American flag, yes.

But that wasn't all.

Meredith finally put the rope down when the first wave of riotous laughter hit the air. She looked up to see all the divisions of Lakeview doubled over, clutching their stomachs with hysteria. Underneath the American flag was a banner that read: "WE SEE LONDON, WE SEE FRANCE. WE SEE 3A'S UNDERPANTS."

And after that?

Strung on the flagpole and waving proudly in the breeze were twelve pairs of girls' underwear. More specifically, the girls' of 3A's underwear.

Natalie's jaw dropped. "Oh my gosh! Who did that?" she demanded, turning to Alyssa. But Alyssa was laughing too hard to answer, pausing only to catch her breath and wipe tears from the corners of her eyes.

Looking around, Natalie could tell that Alyssa wasn't the only one having an extreme reaction. But to her left, three girls looked like they were enjoying the scene just a shade more than everyone else.

Jenna, Grace, and Brynn.

None of the counselors could prove anything, though, and the prank was harmless enough. And so once the panties had been lowered and safely returned to Lizzie, 3A's most embarrassed counselor, flag-raising proceeded as though there had been no interruption at all.

▲ ▲ ▲

"So, today we're going to talk about interviews," Keith, the newspaper specialist said. Keith hadn't ever worked on an actual newspaper—just a small computer magazine published in South Jersey—but Natalie liked him just the same. He seemed very enthusiastic, and nothing about the newspaper office was potentially poisonous, alive, or otherwise natural. Therefore, Natalie had decided that newspaper was just about her favorite place to be at Lakeview. That is, when she wasn't back in the bunk reading magazines while Alyssa sketched. Keith continued, "An interview is a reporter's opportunity to talk to a famous figure or other celebrity, sure, but what people don't always realize is that the interview is also the reporter's opportunity to paint the subject in any light he or she sees fit. Many people assume that interviews they read are a reflection of the subject's true thoughts and words, but often, the interview is strongly influenced by the reporter's vision."

Natalie snorted almost without realizing. "I'll say," she muttered to herself.

Alyssa looked at her friend quizzically. "What do you mean?" she asked.

Natalie looked up to see that not only was Alyssa looking at her, but so were a few other campers. *Whoops,* she thought. She hadn't meant to actually say anything aloud. Now what was she going to do? "Uh, well, I just mean—I read a thing in *Teen People* last week that made Britney Spears look like a total moron. And I don't really think that she is," she stammered, covering.

"Yeah, I'm sure she's, like, a real brainiac," said Claudia, a girl from 3B that Natalie and Alyssa were starting to get to know.

"She's *way* smarter than Christina Aguilera," Natalie protested defensively, hoping to turn the conversation away from her little slip. "Don't you think, Alyssa?"

"Huh? Well, I guess . . . but she's nothing compared to, uh, Mindy Moore," Alyssa said.

Everyone at their table cracked up. Alyssa was so hopeless when it came to mainstream pop culture. That was one of the things Natalie liked best about her—she was into more original music, books, and movies than most of the kids Natalie knew—even her friends back in the city.

"*Mandy* Moore, Lyss," Claudia said, laughing hysterically. "*Mandy.*"

Natalie giggled with her friends, and Alyssa did, too. Natalie was especially relieved for the change in conversation topic. But when Natalie glanced up at her friend, she caught Alyssa gazing at her with a strange expression.

Did her friend suspect that Natalie's comment meant more than she was letting on?

▲ ▲ ▲

"Pass it here! Alex, pass it here!"

Natalie looked up to see a soccer ball nearly glance off Chelsea's face. Naturally, the girl was completely undaunted. Chelsea may have been a total princess in the mornings, spending time blowing out her hair and picking just the right outfit, but when it came to sports, she was a big-time jock. Right now, for example, she dipped backward and deftly sidestepped the soccer ball as it shot toward her. Once it hit the ground, she leaped on top of it and began dribbling swiftly toward the opposite team's goal.

"Go! Go! Go!" Alex shouted, egging Chelsea on. Brynn stood beside Alex, screaming wildly and waving her arms in the air in a wordless show of support.

"Do you think we're supposed to be going after

her?" Natalie whispered to Alyssa, who was also hanging out in the far left field. Natalie was fast learning that in addition to nature, there were several other aspects of camp that weren't exactly her strong suit. Sports being one of them.

Alyssa shrugged. "Not sure. What does 'defense?' mean, anyway?"

Natalie grinned. She and Alyssa really were on the same page.

Suddenly, the players on the field—all the rest of the girls in bunk 3C—erupted into a mixture of triumphant battle cries and booing and hissing. Obviously, Chelsea had scored. No surprise there.

Brian, the head of sports, blew his whistle shrilly, bringing the game to a formal conclusion. "Nice work, girls!" he shouted in his thick Australian accent. "Chelsea, great goal! Alex, awesome assist!"

"I personally think we did some mighty fine standing around," Natalie mumbled to Alyssa under her breath.

Alyssa stifled a giggle. "Somehow, I don't think we're going to get any praise for that."

"Natalie!" Brian called, as if on cue. "Why don't you help me gather up the equipment?"

"Um, sure," Natalie said, slightly taken aback. She headed toward the far end of the field and wrapped her arm around the goal net, dragging it toward the sports shed.

Once she got to the shed, Brian propped the door open for her. "Thanks, Nat, I really appreciate it," he said as she shoved the net through the doorway.

Natalie dusted her hands off on her shorts. "No problem." It was the least she could do, really, given that she had barely moved a muscle all through the sports period.

"So, I noticed that you're not exactly crazy about soccer," Brian observed.

Natalie looked up at him, the very picture of innocence. "Whatever gave you that idea?" she asked, wide-eyed. She could tell he knew she was being sarcastic.

"Wild guess." He ran his fingers through his curly red hair.

Brian looked so frustrated that Natalie actually felt a little guilty. "It's not you, Brian. I'm just, um, not really athletic. But, you know, I think you always find fun things for us to do in sports."

"Thanks, Natalie, but you don't need to reassure me. It's important to me that everyone here has a good time. You don't have to love every single thing we play, but if there's something you'd like to try, let me know. I mean, camp is—"

"—the time for new experiences, I know," Natalie said, cutting him off.

He grinned at her. "It's true."

"It must be, 'cause I keep hearing it," Natalie said, half-kidding. "Look, I'll think about it. I'm sure somehow, somewhere, there's some sort of sport that I like."

"Thanks, Natalie," Brian said.

"I could always be in charge of the whistle," Natalie offered, giggling.

"It's a thought," Brian agreed.

"I'd better go," Natalie said. "Lunch next. Can't miss it."

She ran to catch up to Alyssa, who looked at her quizzically. "Deep conversation?" Alyssa asked.

"He wants me to take a more active interest in sports," Natalie said. "Little does he know the most exercise I get at home is channel surfing." This was an exaggeration, but she was making a point.

"Yeah, it shows."

Natalie whirled around to find Chelsea slithering by. She looked perfect and rosy-cheeked, like an ad for a fitness club or a protein drink or something. *At least I'm not drenched in sweat,* Natalie thought to herself, *on the way to the mess hall.*

She didn't bother to say anything out loud, though. Chelsea just wasn't worth it.

chapter SEVEN

Dear Hannah,

Greetings again from Camp Lake-puke.

I'm just kidding, really. It's not that bad. I mean, I still don't think I'm going to win Camper of the Year or anything, but for the most part I'm enjoying myself. Can you believe it's been almost a week?

Most of the girls here are cool. I really like this one chick, Alyssa, who is from South Jersey. She's very quiet and artsy—always writing or drawing in her journal. Anyway, her parents sent her to camp so she could learn to be more outgoing, but I think she's just fine the way she is. I mean, maybe she doesn't talk that much, but when she does, she always has something smart and funny to say. We're on the newspaper together—she's a really good writer. I guess you could say she's my best friend here. You would really like her.

The rest of the bunk is okay, too. Valerie is cool to hang out with—we're in nature together. Grace is the comedienne, always cracking jokes and making everyone laugh. She's really friendly and never wants anyone to be left out. Then there's Jenna, who has like a million brothers and sisters or at least three that I know of. Her twin, Adam, is very friendly and her older sister Stephanie is good friends with my CIT Marissa. And then I think there's one that's off doing a college prep course. Or something. I can't keep track. They've all been coming to camp for, I think, a hundred years or so, so she knows all the ropes. She's kind of a tomboy and likes to play practical jokes—which sometimes aren't so funny! It doesn't bother me, but one of these days I think she's really going to get into trouble. And Alex is the big uber-camper who knows all the counselors and never complains and kicks total butt in every sport. It's a little intimidating, even for me. She hangs out with Sarah, who also loves sports, and also this girl Brynn, who means well, but ... well, she's a drama queen. Like last week, during chores, she got stuck with the showers. Mind you, the showers are gross, but we all have to do it sooner or later—even me! The way she carried on, you would have thought she was the bunk slave or something. It's kind of annoying.

Still, the only girl I really have an issue with is Chelsea. She's really pretty—blond and skinny, you'd hate her—and also very athletic. But for some reason, she's got a total chip on her shoulder. I don't know what she's got against me—I mean, I'm obviously not vying for the Lakeview MVP award or anything. And it's not just me, either; she's always making little rude comments and not-jokes to people. I guess she's just got a bad attitude. Mostly, I try to ignore her and keep myself positive. Even NATURE'S not so bad these days.

Which brings me to Simon. Yes, the same guy I wrote you about that I met in the mess hall. Well, more like "bumped into," if you want the truth and all. But it turned out he is also in nature, and after the first session, he introduced himself to me (I had to play cool and pretend like I hadn't already gotten the whole 411 from Jenna, since Adam is in his bunk!). It was kind of awkward—I think he's a little shy. Not like all those super-obnoxious boys from school! He could tell I wasn't really "feeling" nature and showed me little tricks, like how to feed the rabbit and which leaves are poisonous out in the wild. Personally, I'm planning to avoid the wild at all costs, but Simon doesn't have to know that! So that's an interesting development, anyway. And it kind of takes my mind off the fact that I still haven't heard from Kyle Taylor yet (in case you were wondering)! Too bad you're not still in the city to spy for me!

Thanks for all your postcards—I save

them and tape them to the wall over my bed, right next to the picture of all of us skating in Central Park last winter. That way, I see your smiling face when the bugle (yes, a bugle—no joke) sounds at the crack of dawn. I think the Mona Lisa is my favorite. What a bummer that it was so crowded when you went! I haven't heard anything from Ellen or Kate, but Maggie wrote to tell me that her summer dance intensive is going well. Lucky girl—she gets to sleep in and spend the day working at the one thing she loves more than anything else! Meanwhile, I toil away at things like kickball and diving practice. Sigh...

I promise I'll write as soon as I've got anything new to report. Maybe I'll help Jenna pull the ultimate prank, and we'll both get kicked out. (KIDDING! Sort of.)

Or maybe I will free all the animals in

the nature shack, and then Simon and I will gallop off into the sunset.

Whatever. I MISS YOU!!! You must be in Italy by now? Eat some pasta for me.

xoxo,

Nat

"Oh, that is so gross," Natalie said, shuddering.

"Come on, Nat—he likes you," Valerie said, sidling up to Natalie teasingly.

Natalie took a gi-normous step backward. "Seriously, stay away from me with that thing," she warned. "I can't believe you're even willing to touch it."

Valerie laughed, and patted the head of the snake that was now wound around her forearm. Valerie had made friends with all the animals in the nature shack, but she liked the snakes the best, and she always made fun of Natalie for being afraid of them.

"Just you wait until one bites you," Natalie warned.

"Afraid of a *garter* snake, Natalie?" Chelsea said

incredulously. She always managed to make everything she said sound like an insult, Natalie noticed.

"I'm not scared," Natalie said hotly. "I just don't see a need to get up close and personal with something cold and slimy."

"For a city girl, you sure can be a baby," Chelsea said, and wandered off to play with the rabbits.

As soon as Chelsea was out of earshot, Natalie rolled her eyes at Valerie. "Funny, I've never seen *her* touch the snake," she commented. "She just likes to annoy me."

"She likes to annoy *everyone*," Valerie pointed out.

"But me especially," Natalie insisted.

Valerie shrugged. "Yeah, maybe. I wouldn't worry about it. She's probably just jealous."

"Of me? Why?" Natalie asked. "What'd I ever do to her?"

"Well, let's see, you're the only other girl in the bunk who's anywhere near as pretty as she is, and you also wear makeup and are into boys, just like her. So you're like some kind of big threat to her."

"That's ridiculous," Natalie scoffed. "She's the one who's totally gorgeous and always put-together. I think her body is naturally programmed to wake up before the bugle! And she's way more into camp than I am. I mean, she's good at all the sports and stuff. I'm no good at anything other than ballet and yoga. I'm, like, the anti-camper."

"It's not ridiculous, Natalie," Valerie protested. "For

starters, you're an amazing swimmer, even if you hate to go in the lake. And let's not forget the one thing you've got that she *really* wants."

Natalie eyed her friend questioningly. Val winked and tilted her head in the direction of the rabbits, where Chelsea was replenishing the animals' water. There was only one other person over by the rabbits. Simon.

"For starters, I do not 'have' Simon, and secondly—do you really think Chelsea likes him?" Natalie asked. But before Val could answer, Roseanne clapped her hands and called for everyone's attention.

"Girls, guys, gather round! I have an announcement to make," she said loudly.

But Natalie couldn't concentrate on what Roseanne was saying. She was still thinking about what Valerie had said. Simon did always go out of his way to talk with her in nature, which was nice, but she didn't know if he *liked* her, liked her. Or if she even wanted him to. Still, when she thought that maybe Chelsea was into Simon—well, the idea didn't make her feel very good. Not good at all.

But there were worse things to worry about at Camp Lakeview, as Natalie was about to learn.

"Next week, on Thursday, we're going on a camp-out," Roseanne said.

Suddenly, Chelsea's feelings for Simon were the least of Natalie's concerns.

"What color today, Nat?" Marissa asked, spreading out a beach towel on the sand next to Natalie.

Natalie was a fantastic swimmer—she'd had all sorts of private lessons in New York. She didn't mind instructional swim, but she wasn't crazy about the lake and all of the actual fish that swam in it. So when free swim rolled around, she preferred to work on her tan.

The head of the waterfront, an extremely tan and fit counselor named Beth, seemed to think this was okay, though she was often trying new and inventive tactics at getting Natalie up and into the water. Just yesterday, she had tried to convince Natalie that lake water was good for the skin. While Natalie appreciated the approach— "A for effort, Beth," she'd said—she wasn't biting.

Natalie's new hobby was lying on the shore by the lake, painting her toes, and watching her bunkmates swim. Fortunately, free swim was the one thing in camp she could get out of if she wanted to, as long as she came down to the waterfront. Lately, Marissa had been joining her, which was especially cool because she always brought her magazines with her.

"Ice Princess," Natalie read off the bottom of the bottle. "Want me to do yours?" Her heart wasn't in it, though, after Roseanne's alarming announcement. Marissa instantly picked up on Natalie's mood.

"No, thanks, Steph did them for me after kitchen duty," Marissa said, wiggling her toes at Natalie by way of demonstration. "Passion Fruit."

"Nice," Natalie said approvingly.

"I brought *People* and *YM*, and if you're nice to me, I'll braid your hair," Marissa promised. "Steph's abandoning us today to flirt with Tyler." She indicated the swim shack, where, in fact, Jenna's older sister was attempting to read the palm of an older and *very* cute swim staffer. "She is shameless," Marissa commented. Then, sensing Natalie's mood, she asked, "What's wrong?"

"Did you know that I have to go on a camping trip with the nature group?" Natalie blurted out.

Marissa nodded her head. "Well, yeah. All the specialties have something big they do sometime during the session. The drama kids do a play, the newspaper prints an issue, ceramics, arts and crafts, woodworking, and photography all have a 'gallery day' where they show their work. Didn't you know that?"

"I do now," Natalie said.

"I thought you were starting to like nature," Marissa pointed out.

"Hey, just because I've managed to avoid walking head-on into a poison-oak patch does not mean that I'm a born-again nature girl," Natalie said. "This trip sounds like bad news. We have to canoe out to some deserted island. When has anything good ever happened on a deserted island?" Natalie demanded.

Marissa laughed. "Slow down, drama queen," she said. "The nature kids go on the same trip every year, and nothing has ever gone wrong. I'm sure this year won't be any different."

Natalie glared at Marissa. "Okay, and then after we dock our boats, we have to hike—which I think is just a fancy term for walk, except maybe it's hilly and rocky and hard. Hike up a mountain, and then set up camp. And then we *cook* on the mountain and sleep there!"

"It's called 'roughing it,' " Marissa said. "Some people enjoy it."

"Not *this* people," Natalie said, frustrated. "I'm here, aren't I? I've tried to be a good sport. I eat the food. I sweep the porch. I come down to the lake during free swim. I haven't had access to my cell phone or e-mail since we got here. Marissa—" Natalie murmured, her voice lowering, "I even clean the toilets. I've *been* roughing it!"

"Well, do you want me to talk to Julie about getting you out of the trip?" Marissa asked with sincerity.

Natalie thought seriously for a moment. Did she? The idea was awfully appealing. It was easy to spot poison ivy in the clearing behind the nature shack, but she had a feeling the wilds on the deserted island would be more . . . well . . . *wild*. Nothing about the trip sounded like fun.

But.

She had promised Julie she would be strong, and for the most part, she had been. She had gotten to know Val, and liked her. She put up with Chelsea's snotty comments. She even learned a little something about nature. Just last week, Roseanne had complimented her on the bird-feeder that she'd built. So being strong wasn't so bad, and even though Natalie really didn't love nature, she wasn't a quitter. And besides, Simon would be on her trip.

Of course, so would Chelsea.

Simon. Think Simon, she reminded herself. That was a reason to go on the trip.

In fact, it might be all the reason she needed.

She turned to Marissa, squaring her shoulders with determination. "No," she said. "Don't worry about it. I'll go."

Marissa squealed and hugged her. "You rock! Scoot over then, sister. I'll braid your hair."

▲ ▲ ▲

Just before dinner that evening, Natalie and the rest of her bunkmates gathered outside the mess hall. Before and after meals was a time when campers could really visit with friends from other bunks, or even other divisions, since everyone ate at the same time. Lots of campers chose to hang out on the steps of the mess hall itself, but Natalie still had the camping trip on her mind, and so she wasn't that interested in socializing. She wandered off a little ways down the path to a nearby wooden pagoda. Once she reached it, however, she realized it wasn't empty.

"Oh, I'm sorry," she said, retreating from the pagoda before she could intrude.

"No, hey, it's totally cool."

Natalie peered more closely into the pagoda and realized with a start that she had actually walked in on Simon! She flushed.

"I guess they haven't let us into the mess hall yet?" he asked.

Natalie shook her head no. "Not that I mind, to be honest."

Simon grinned. "True. I can't decide if it's a good thing or a bad thing that I'm a vegetarian. On the plus side, I get to avoid the random mystery meats. On the other hand, the selection leaves a *lot* to be desired."

"You're a vegetarian?" Natalie asked, nearly swooning. To her, that sounded very cosmopolitan. Almost New York, even.

"Yeah, why? Are you?"

Natalie nodded. "Yeah. I mean no. I mean, I was," she finished, appalled at her awkwardness.

"Why'd you give it up?" Simon asked, sounding genuinely curious.

"Well, I don't eat too much meat, but I guess I just decided that I couldn't go without sushi. It was just too much of a sacrifice. Plus, half the time, it's all that my mom and I even eat," she explained.

Simon raised an eyebrow. "Sushi? Wow. Raw fish—that's pretty brave."

Natalie giggled. "Brave? Hardly. You're talking to the girl who lives in terror of poison oak. I'm like, totally freaked about our camping trip," she confessed.

"It's nothing," Simon assured her. "It can even be fun, I promise."

"I'll believe that when I see it," Natalie said.

"I swear," Simon insisted. "Roseanne does this trip every year, and she hasn't lost a camper yet. I did it last year."

"So you're like a seasoned pro," Natalie teased.

"Totally," Simon said. "I can be your guide."

Yes, yes, you can, Natalie thought to herself. She racked her brain to come up with a reply that wouldn't sound lame or over-eager but came up empty. *Say something, Nat,* she begged herself.

"Nat!"

Natalie looked up to see who was calling her.

"Dinner! Come on! We're all going in!"

It was Jenna. Normally, Jenna's loud voice, bright eyes, and bouncing ponytail were a source of amusement for Natalie, but right now Nat could have killed the girl for her timing.

"Oh, ah," she hemmed, not wanting to walk away from the conversation with Simon.

Simon stood up and dusted himself off. "You go," he said to Natalie. "We'll have plenty of time to talk on the hike, right?" He winked at her and walked off to rejoin his own bunk.

"Ooooh, Natalie, do you have a *boyfriend*?" Jenna singsonged.

Natalie whirled around as if just then realizing that Jenna was still there. She was completely unfazed by Jenna's little joke. "We'll see," she said, with a little smile on her face. "We'll see."

▲ ▲ ▲

At dinner, everyone in 3C was talking about all the activities they had planned in their specialties. "Will you read my newspaper piece before it's published?" Alyssa asked Natalie shyly. The girls had learned that professional writers called their articles "pieces," and they liked to use the grown-up terminology.

Natalie pushed a rubbery piece of chicken back and forth across her plate. Maybe it was time to reconsider vegetarianism again? At least for the summer, anyhow. "Of course. I mean, if you'll read mine," she said. She had conducted an interview with Brian, the sports counselor, on what had prompted him to come over from Australia for the summer, and she was really excited about it, but she knew that Alyssa was the better writer. Alyssa would definitely give her piece a great once-over. "I *may* have gone on a little too long about his accent," Natalie joked.

"How could you not? It's so cool!" Alyssa agreed.

"The best part is that he let me give the interview *instead* of taking sports!" Nat exclaimed, causing Alyssa to nearly choke on her food in laughter.

"Ow," Alyssa grimaced as Jenna slid into the bench

next to her, giggling mischievously. "And you're sitting on my lap because . . ."

"Sorry," Jenna said, slightly breathless. She was peering across the table, over Alex's shoulder, to the table behind them.

"What did you do?" Alex asked, her eyes narrowing suspiciously. Of all the girls in 3C, Alex was most disapproving of Jenna's pranks, mainly because she hated to get into trouble herself.

"Nothing," Jenna said, but she looked ready to burst out of her seat with excitement.

"Something," Sarah, who sat directly to Alex's right, chimed in softly. "Definitely something."

Suddenly, the boys at the table jumped up, all mumbling variations on "ugh," "ew," and "gross." Jenna burst out laughing.

"Isn't that your brother's bunk's table?" Sarah asked Jenna.

But Jenna just looked off to her right, humming a little bit to herself. Whatever she'd done to her brother and his bunkmates, she wasn't telling. And it looked like for now, at least, she wasn't going to be found out.

Natalie knew that whatever joke Jenna had pulled, it was probably really funny. Just like last week, when she had hidden all the silverware from 3A's lunch table. But she was worried about her friend. That was just Natalie's way, when she cared about someone. What if Jenna's little practical schemes were actually a sign of a bigger problem, like something that was on Jenna's mind? Or, if they weren't a sign of a problem, they were going to be the cause of one, soon. How long could she get away with these pranks before she got into serious trouble?

chapter EIGHT

"So, making s'mores is actually really easy—" Jenna explained. She held out a graham cracker and a square of milk chocolate in preparation for a big demonstration.

"—believe it or not, J, I've actually had s'mores before," Natalie said, cutting Jenna off before she could launch into the full-blown lecture. She really liked Jenna, but the girl had at some point decided to "adopt" Natalie and show her the ins and outs of camp. Which was great in theory, but Natalie was independent by nature, and not too crazy about being adopted. Still, she tried to be patient. She knew Jenna was just being nice.

"I thought you'd never been to camp before. When did you make s'mores?" Alex asked, overhearing the girls' conversation.

"Oh, there's a restaurant in New York that will bring them right to your table for you. You cook the marshmallows on these little burners. It's so cool," Natalie said, feeling a little wave of homesickness pass through her. What surprised her, though, was that it was just that—a *little* wave of homesickness. Could it be that she was actually starting to *enjoy* herself at camp? Too weird.

"Maybe you're just too *sophisticated* for sleepaway camp," Chelsea said. She didn't make it sound like a compliment.

"Yes, well, I left my diamonds back in the city. I figured I can do without them for the summer, dahling," Natalie laughed, putting on a fake "proper" accent. She had decided that the best thing to do with Chelsea was to pretend that her comments were intended as lighthearted jokes—even when they obviously weren't. So far, the tactic seemed to be working. Chelsea pursed her lips but she didn't say another word.

From across the campfire, Alyssa nodded to Natalie—a tiny, almost imperceptible gesture. Someone else might not have even noticed it, but Nat knew that her friend was giving her props for not letting Chelsea get to her.

It was Tuesday night, and bunk 3C was having a cookout. After all the camp food, Natalie could understand why so many campers got so excited over barbecued hot dogs and hamburgers. She had eaten one of each, herself, and even though she was stuffed, she still managed to find a tiny bit of room leftover for s'mores. She hated to admit it, but there was something cool about roasting marshmallows over an open campfire—not more special than having them brought to your table in a New York City restaurant, but different. Good different.

The girls in her bunk were good different, too, Natalie had decided. Even though she still wasn't thrilled with things like spiders in the bathrooms and bug juice for lunch, the girls in 3C had a nice chemistry. Even now, they were all huddled in one large circle, stuffing themselves with graham crackers, chocolate, and marshmallows. Julie and Marissa were off to one side of the barbecue talking to Pete, who had manned the grill, and a few of his kitchen buddies, including one named LJ who Natalie really liked. LJ was really funny. He refused to tell her what his initials stood for. He told all the girls in 3C that if they were lucky, he'd let them know at the closing banquet, at the end of the summer.

"Have you girls had your fill?" Kathleen, the head of the third division, walked by, smiling knowingly. Kathleen was energetic and always friendly, and could tell by the girls' expressions that they had eaten more than enough for the evening.

"Oh, gosh, I'll never eat again," Grace moaned, dropping the long stick with her marshmallow to the ground beside her. She bent over and clutched her stomach dramatically.

Kathleen grinned again. "I sort of doubt that," she said, and wandered over to speak with Julie and Marissa.

"Alex, you were smart not to have any," Grace

said, still feigning her stomachache. "I really need to learn some limits."

"Oh, well, uh, you know—I like to take care of myself, for soccer, you know," Alex replied. Natalie looked up. Was it her imagination, or did Alex look slightly uncomfortable? But what would she have to feel uncomfortable about? So she didn't eat junk food. So what?

Natalie offered up her best fake burp. All the girls shrieked with laughter.

"Ugh, that is *so* gross," Brynn said, giggling. "Does *Simon* think that's cute?"

Natalie blushed. "What are you talking about?"

Brynn rolled her eyes. "Oh, come on, it's so obvious. You completely stare at him every time we're in the mess hall. You luuuuuv him," she sang.

"Okay, fine, he's cute, so what?" Natalie protested.

Grace made little gagging noises. "Cute, yak. Boys are icky, not cute."

"Oh, come on," Natalie insisted. "You're telling me there's not a single boy in camp you'd be into?"

All the girls shook their heads emphatically. "It must be something in the Manhattan water, Nat," Sarah said. "You're the only one so far."

"You make it sound like I have some kind of disease," Natalie said, laughing. "Whatever. At least this way I don't have to worry about any of you guys going after him!" She glanced at Chelsea as she said this. But Chelsea was focused intently on fishing out a graham cracker from a newly opened box and didn't—or wouldn't—look up.

"My dad says I can't go on a date until I'm in high school," Karen said. "That's fine by me. Anyway, we play board games on Friday nights. He's a teacher, and sometimes he makes up cool games all on his own."

"Oh, that's so fun!" Candace said. "My dad's a boring lawyer and the only thing he brings home is his laptop."

"Mine's a lawyer, too," Alex put in. "It looks like the dullest job in the world. Whenever we go on vacation, he spends half the time screaming into his cell phone." She shifted her weight and stretched her legs out in front of her, closer to the warmth of the fire. "What about you, Natalie? You never talk about your father," she said.

"Huh?" Natalie said, stalling for time. "He's, uh . . . well, my parents are divorced."

"Oh, that's hard," Sarah said sympathetically. "Do you see him often?"

Natalie shrugged. "Sometimes," she said. "He lives out west. What about yours?" she asked, trying to push the spotlight off herself.

"He's an orthodontist," Sarah replied. "So my older sister got her braces for cheap!"

"Hey, Natalie, when's your campout?" Jenna asked suddenly, a twinkle appearing in her eye.

"Thursday night," Natalie answered, suddenly suspicious. "Why?"

"Well, speaking of boys, I have a fun idea of how we can pass the time between now and then."

"What, you mean instead of evening activity?" Natalie asked. She wouldn't have minded getting out of evening activity. But for some reason, she didn't think that was quite what Jenna was getting at.

"Oh, no—I meant for after," Jenna said quickly. "Later—*much* later—I've got plans for us. *All* of us," she added dramatically.

Natalie glanced around the campfire nervously. She wasn't so sure she liked the sound of that.

▲ ▲ ▲

That evening after the cookout, the girls were all excitable as they prepared for bed. Even Julie could see that something was up.

"Ladies, you're all so hyper tonight. I hope you don't have some sort of mischief planned," she said.

Natalie sort of hoped so, too. But then, a part of her thought that whatever Jenna had in mind could really be fun. So basically, she wasn't sure what to think.

After the girls had all gotten into their bunks, Marissa read to them from the "Trauma-rama" section of *YM*. This was their favorite thing to do before lights-out. Usually, the stories were completely outrageous, and Marissa made the girls vote which ones they thought were true, and which were made-up.

"MADE-UP!" Alex shouted from her bed after an

especially colorful entry. "Please. Who ever really sneezes that much snot?"

"Point taken," Marissa said, closing the magazine.

"Okay, girls, Marissa and I have to go out for a little bit," Julie said. This wasn't a surprise. Julie and Marissa usually went outside for a while after lights-out. No one was totally sure what they did. The counselors rotated their evenings off, and those that had off definitely left camp. Natalie couldn't blame them. There were always two counselors per division—one guy and one girl—who were "OD," or "on-duty," as well, and it was their job to patrol at night and make sure that things were okay with all the campers in their division. But those who weren't off or OD managed to disappear just the same. Jenna's theory was that all the counselors met at the big rock where afternoon snack was held, not too far away from the bunks. "We have a meeting with the rest of the staff. Mark and Kerri are OD tonight. Do you promise you'll all behave?"

"Yes, Julie," the girls chorused in a mocking singsong.

After the door had swung shut behind them, the bunk was quiet for a moment. No one wanted to be the first to speak what was on everyone's mind.

Finally, Jenna sat up in bed. "Do you think they're gone?"

Alex got out of her bed and walked over to the front door. She opened it and peered out. "The coast is clear. No Mark, no Kerri, no problem." She padded back to her bed and sat on the edge of it. "So what were you thinking?"

The lights were still out, but Natalie could practically feel a sly grin creep its way across Jenna's face. "Raid," she whispered.

"Awesome!" Alex said. Even though Alex hated to get in trouble, she was willing to risk it for something like a raid, because raids were just too much fun to resist. She slid back off her bed and poked around in her cubby, pulled out her flashlight, and flicked it on.

"Careful with that thing," Chelsea said, squinting from the bright light. "What is a raid, anyway?"

Natalie was glad Chelsea had asked, since she herself had no idea.

Alex squealed and settled back down on the edge of her bed. "Oooh, it's SO much fun. We sneak out and into someone's bunk—"

"—a *boys'* bunk—" Jenna cut in.

"—yeah, yeah, boys' bunk," Alex continued, looking slightly annoyed at being interrupted. "And, you know, we tp—toilet paper—their bunk and do all sorts of other things while they're sleeping. Like we can put toothpaste on their toilet seats or hide all their toilet paper—"

"So basically we're sabotaging their bathroom?" Natalie asked.

Alex shot her a look. "Well, not necessarily. But that's the kind of thing that's going to get to them."

"*I* always like to tape their bathroom doors shut and pull all their covers down while they're sleeping," Jenna said. There was an edge to her voice that suggested that she didn't really like being upstaged by Alex.

"Do you ever get caught?" Karen asked softly.

"Nah," Jenna bragged. "I mean, it's harmless."

"Counselors practically *expect* you to do it," Alex agreed. "So if you keep it safe and stuff, no one ever says anything."

Natalie found herself warming to the idea. But she still had one question. "Um, which bunk are we going to raid?" she asked.

Jenna snorted. "Every year, I like to raid Adam's bunk," she said. "So, 3F. Is that okay with you, *Nat*?" she finished meaningfully.

Simon's bunk, Natalie thought. *Of course.* "Yeah, sure," she said, trying to act casual.

"I had a feeling it would be," Jenna teased. "Okay, who else is in?"

It turned out that almost everyone was game. Karen was nervous, but she put aside her fears after Alex and Jenna both reassured her that they wouldn't get in any trouble. Candace said she'd rather stay back and read, but she gave in when Sarah guilted her about "acting as a bunk." And that was really it. Chelsea, in particular, seemed very excited. As soon as Jenna had explained her plan, she had hopped out of bed to change into her cutest drawstring capris. Natalie guessed it probably didn't matter what they wore.

But she put on a clean pair of jeans, just in case.

▲ ▲ ▲

"Well, I guess you were wrong about where the counselors go at night," Alex said to Jenna. The bunk was maneuvering slowly, ducking behind bushes when possible, and they were just rounding the big, central rock. They had tiptoed out the front door of the bunk un-detected easily enough—the OD counselors were clearly otherwise occupied. The rock was completely unpopulated. Alex sounded fairly pleased about it. To Natalie, it seemed like Alex and Jenna were locked in a bizarre competition to be the one who knew the most about camp. *Silly*, she thought. *So not worth it.*

Suddenly, someone stomped on her foot. She almost cried out, but the offender clapped a hand over her mouth, muffling the sound. She turned to find Alyssa smiling at her. "Sorry!" she whispered. "I tripped."

"That's what you get for wearing flip-flops," Natalie said. She had tried to convince her friend to wear trail shoes, but Alyssa wasn't having it. "My feet need to breathe," she had protested.

"You win," Alyssa admitted.

"Then why am I the one with the squashed toe, Ms. Breathy-foot?" Natalie kidded.

"Girls!" Alex said in the loudest whisper she could manage. "We're almost there. Keep it down!"

"She is so out of control," Alyssa mumbled.

Natalie almost broke into a giggle, but Alyssa reached out and covered her mouth again.

"Good thing we know how to identify poison oak, right?" Valerie said, catching up to Natalie and Alyssa. "And you thought nature was pointless."

"Not like I could even see it if I were standing right in a poison-oak patch! It's pitch-black out here!" Natalie pointed out.

"Girls!" Jenna said, sounding like Julie. "We're going in. Now, you all have your assignments. Alyssa and Nat, you're going in first. You're going to take the toilet paper out of the bathroom. Then you'll pass it off to Grace and Valerie, who will tp the bunk beds. Meanwhile, Sarah and Brynn will put shaving cream on the toilet seats. Jessie, Alex, and Candace are in charge of rounding up the garbage cans and lining them up outside the front door. That way, they'll topple when the boys try to leave in the morning. Chelsea and Karen are going to hide the shower curtains."

"What will you do?" Natalie asked.

"Oh, I've got special plans of my own for Adam," Jenna said mysteriously.

"Poor Adam," Grace said, sympathetically.

"How about a huddle before we go in?" Alex suggested.

Jenna glared at Alex, but the girls were already grouping together. In the dark, they leaned in to one another and placed all of their hands on top of one another's in the center of the huddle. "Go, 3C!" they whisper-shouted.

Natalie crept up to the front door with Alyssa at her heels. "This may be a dumb idea," Natalie mumbled, suddenly having second thoughts. "But here goes nothing," she said quietly, and pulled the door open.

Instantly, all the girls were engulfed. Natalie was pelted squarely in the stomach with a stream of water, while at the same time covered from head to toe in shaving cream.

"Oh, what the—" Natalie shouted, only to be rewarded by a blast of water into her mouth. She sputtered to herself as the sounds of male war cries filled the room.

Before Natalie could make sense of the scene, her bunkmates had rushed in, screeching with their own war whoops. Jenna whipped a mini water pistol from the waistband of her capri pants and fired from the hip. Karen freaked out, bolted for the bathroom, and locked herself in a stall. Chelsea ran up and down the bunk weaving toilet paper from bed to bed.

Jenna, though, stood stock-still, assessing the scene. Finally, she put her fingers to her lips and whistled.

The bunk was silent.

"Adam," she said, her voice dangerously low.

From the far corner of the bunk, the girls heard chuckling. "Gotcha, sis!" A head full of light brown curls emerged, followed by a male-looking version of Jenna in hospital scrubs and a concert T-shirt.

"How did you know?" Jenna demanded.

"Give me a break, Jenna. I'm on to you. I'm *always* on to you," he said. "I mean, did you think I didn't know what you did with the bug juice the other day?" he continued.

Jenna pursed her lips, planted her hands on her hips, and waited for him to go on.

"And by the way, you plan a raid just about this time *every* summer, J. So this wasn't exactly the hugest shock."

"Well, how did you know it would be tonight?" Jenna asked.

"It makes perfect sense. The counselors are all at that big meeting."

"What big meeting?" Natalie interrupted, suddenly worried. "Julie said they were meeting the other counselors. You know, at the rock. You said they always go to the rock!" she said, turning to face Jenna. But then she remembered. *When we walked past the rock, there was no one around.*

Adam nodded. "Most nights, they do. And you would never have been able to get past them."

"Hey!" Alex protested.

Adam ignored her. "But tonight, they had a meeting with Dr. Steve."

"Dr. Steve? As in, director of the camp Dr. Steve?" Sarah asked, a tinge of dread creeping into her voice.

Natalie understood why she sounded that way. Dr. Steve was very friendly—he made it a point to visit all the activities during the day, and to talk to all the campers—but he was not a pushover. And she didn't think he'd be the kind to look the other way if he found out some campers had gone on a raid while their counselors were out.

"Well, no big deal, right?" came a voice from the corner.

Natalie whirled around to see Simon standing near the front door. He was wearing cut-off sweat pants and a T-shirt with Bart Simpson across the front. *He likes* The Simpsons? I *like* The Simpsons, Natalie thought. *We're perfect for each other!* She realized she was spacing and forced herself to concentrate on what he was saying.

"All they have to do is get back before the meeting's over, and Dr. Steve will never know," he pointed out.

"Right," Natalie said. "That makes sense. But it means we have to get going, like, now. If the counselors come back, that means the meeting's over."

"Duh," Chelsea chimed in. Natalie instantly felt stupid for suggesting something so obvious.

"Well, she's right," Simon countered.

Natalie couldn't believe it. Was Simon *defending* her? "Are you guys okay to clean up by yourselves?" she asked. She felt bad just leaving with everything such a mess.

Adam laughed. "No worries. It's too bad, though—usually raids turn into parties. We would have shared some of our junk-food stash with you."

"Next time," Natalie said, smiling.

"Uh, you guys, there may be a little problem with the plan," Alex said, breaking into the moment.

"Such as?" Jenna asked nervously.

"Such as, where's Alyssa? Nat, wasn't she supposed to come in first with you?"

Natalie glanced around the bunk nervously. Where *was* Alyssa, anyway? "Oh, no," she groaned. "I told her not to wear flip-flops! What if she slipped outside or something?"

In a flash, Natalie and Alex dashed outside, where they immediately found Alyssa kneeled on the porch and clutching her shin.

"I'm the biggest klutz in the world," Alyssa said sheepishly. "Look." She extended her leg. "I *really* shouldn't have worn flip-flops, Nat."

Natalie gasped. "I won't even say 'I told you so,' " she promised. Alyssa had mangled her leg really badly. It was raw and oozing, and the ankle was looking a little bit puffy, as well. Alex and Natalie quickly helped her back into the bunk so that the group could assess the situation together.

"Oh, jeez. We need to take you to the infirmary and get that cleaned out," Natalie said. "What if you sprained your ankle?"

"The infirmary's closed," Grace said. "Plan B?"

Natalie's stomach turned over. "Uh, I think the only real plan B is to go find the counselors." The thought was not appealing.

Jenna's face went white. "We can't! Julie will *kill* me!"

"Jenna, look at her leg!" Natalie pressed. "What would you rather we do?"

"I have some Band-Aids in the bunk," Jenna offered.

"Jen, I'm sorry, but look at that. It's, like, dripping, and not even ankle-shaped. I don't think your Band-Aids are going to do the trick. Can you even walk on that, Alyssa?"

Alyssa leaned into her leg tentatively. "It's sore," she admitted.

Simon stepped forward. "Why don't you let Nat and me walk you to find the counselors?" he suggested. "I mean, it was her idea, but you know, if you can't walk or whatever, I could carry you better than she could."

Natalie didn't know if Alyssa really needed two personal escorts, but she wasn't about to argue. Besides, how sweet was it of Simon to offer? "Sounds like a plan," she said, crossing over to where Alyssa stood.

"That's ridiculous," Chelsea cut in. "Simon, I can go with you."

Natalie seethed. How low could Chelsea stoop?

"It's okay, Chelsea. It looks like Nat's got this covered," Simon insisted.

It was all Natalie could do not to stick out her tongue and do a little victory dance in Chelsea's face. *Be the bigger person,* she reminded herself.

"Whatever," Chelsea snapped.

Natalie decided to take charge. After all, Simon

seemed to think that she knew what she was talking about. "Okay, um, Alyssa, why don't you put one arm across my shoulder and one arm across Simon's?"

Alyssa maneuvered forward and awkwardly draped one arm over each of them. The three of them hopped toward the front door like losers in a strange three-legged relay, when suddenly the door opened, and the overhead lights flew on. The room was blindingly bright.

"It's the mother ship!" Grace shrieked.

"Shh!" Natalie said. "*So* not the time for jokes."

"*What* is going on here?!"

It was Nate, the counselor for 3F. He didn't look very pleased.

And standing beside him was Julie.

chapter NINE

"I can't believe Julie let you off with just a warning!" Grace said, reaching over Natalie to grab the pitcher of milk that stood in the middle of the breakfast table.

"I know, she was really cool about it," Jenna agreed. "But she was *not* pleased. She made it clear that this was my last get-out-of-jail-free." She shook her head, causing her sandy ponytail to bob up and down. "I'm just relieved that Dr. Steve didn't find out. If he had, I don't think Julie would have been so understanding."

"What did you even tell Nurse Helen, anyway, Alyssa?" Grace asked.

In the end, Julie had gone with Natalie and Alyssa to the nurse. They had explained that Alyssa had been "outside" and had tripped, and Nurse Helen had been good enough to leave it at that. She took a look at Alyssa's ankle and declared it not sprained, cleaned it out, wrapped it in an Ace bandage, and sent the girls on their way. Today, Alyssa was still limping slightly, but was basically okay.

Just then, Simon walked to their table with a group of his friends.

"Hey!" Natalie called out, getting Simon's attention. "Thanks for offering to help me take her. That was cool of you."

"Oh, no problem. But you were awesome," Simon said.

"Huh? What do you mean?" Natalie asked, surprised.

"Well, just the way that you took charge," Simon explained. "You knew that the only answer was to go to the infirmary, even if it meant getting in trouble, and you were willing to go and accept the consequences. Not everyone would have done that."

"Well, I mean, when your friend is practically an amputee," Natalie joked, shrugging off the compliment.

"Come on, Nat. You would have done that no matter who was hurt," Simon insisted. Natalie couldn't decide which was more exciting—hearing Simon say such nice things about her—or the fact that he was calling her "Nat." She liked hearing him use her nickname, like they were old friends.

"Excuse me, Simon," Chelsea cut in. "But I believe the boys' table is over there." She pointed to the other side of the mess hall.

Natalie rolled her eyes as Simon walked off.

"I'm sure he'll talk to you at the campout," Alyssa whispered.

"The campout? That's hardly going to be my finest hour!" Natalie groaned. She flung her head down onto the table in mock despair.

"You do realize you're getting cornflakes in your hair," Grace said dryly.

▲ ▲ ▲

When breakfast was over, the girls slowly filed out of the mess hall. It was gray and overcast as the girls stepped outside.

"What do you think's going on over *there*?" Brynn asked suddenly, stopping short.

Natalie glanced over to where Brynn was pointing, just a few paces in front of the mess hall. Sure enough, an enormous stretch limo idled on the dirt path, and in front of it stood a small entourage of rock-star types—a super-skinny blonde; a tall, beefy man in black; and a small, nervous, wiry type. From where she stood, Natalie couldn't quite make out who the would-be celebrities were, especially since they were completely mobbed by campers. But she had some idea.

"Oh my God!" she heard one girl from an older division yell. "I LOVE you!"

"Dude, your last movie *rocked*!"

"Can I have your autograph?"

"What are you *doing* here?"

"Is that your limo, man? Sweet!"

Natalie's stomach lurched, and a feeling of dread washed over her.

"Oh my *God*!" Brynn shouted, recognition dawning. "I can't believe it!"

"That's Tad Maxwell!" Alex shrieked excitedly. "*What* is he doing here?" Her faced turned bright red. "I think I'm going to hyperventilate. I mean, I'm his biggest fan! I can't *believe* it! I just can't *believe* it!"

"Alex, relax. You're gonna blow a gasket," Natalie said, uncomfortable.

Alex whirled around to Natalie, eyes flashing with excitement. "Of *course* I am, Nat! Do you even *realize* who that is? That's Tad Maxwell! *Spy in the Big City* Tad Maxwell. *Spy in the Far East* Tad Maxwell! *Spy in the Jungle* Tad Maxwell! And he's here! Right before our eyes! I mean, it's not a poster, it's really him! That's Tad Maxwell! That's—"

"—that's my father," Natalie finished.

Then she turned and ran away.

"I'm sorry."

Natalie tilted her head up to regard her father. He did look genuinely sorry to have surprised her.

"I thought it'd be fun for you," he insisted.

After her terrible experience at the mess hall, Natalie had run back to the bunk as fast as she possibly could. But once she was there, she didn't know what to do with herself. After all, her secret was out now. And it wasn't like anyone wouldn't find her back at the bunk. Not to mention, her father was here on one of his unexpected visits, and she had to face him sooner or later.

She really, really wished it could be later. But no such luck.

The thing was, Natalie really liked her father. He was fun and sweet, and she totally knew how much he loved her. Unfortunately, his work was very demanding, and he was often away on location for months at a time. When he wasn't on location, he was touring to promote his latest movie or shooting magazine covers or training for his next role . . . one way or another, he was always occupied. And so Natalie had learned to appreciate him when he was around, but not to expect more of him than he was able to give. It was sad, but it was life. The most important thing was that she had a mother and a father who both cared about her.

Back in New York, Natalie went to a pretty fancy private school. Most of her friends were either the children of celebrities, or else their parents were just so rich that they couldn't even be bothered with the whole starstruck thing. Hannah's mother, for example, was an African ambassador, and their friend Maggie's mother was actual royalty, though Natalie couldn't even pronounce the name of the country that she came from.

Natalie's friends thought the fact that her father was a big-time action hero was pretty cool. But it really wasn't a big deal to them. Natalie never knew how other people would react to the information. Some kids were really weirded out and just assumed she was a snob or spoiled or something. Others got really nicey-nice, wanting to get in and meet a real-life movie star. Natalie was tired of people seeing her for who her father was first, before they got to know her on her own terms.

So when her mother first told her about "Operation Lake-puke," Natalie had decided that she wasn't going to tell anyone about her father. For once, she wanted to be anonymous. It would be nice, she decided, to be just "Natalie"—no strings attached.

Fat chance of that now. For Pete's sake—he'd brought his girlfriend, his bodyguard, and his personal assistant! To *Lakeview*! Not exactly low-profile . . .

Natalie's father had eventually tracked her down to her bunk. Julie had suggested that they go out on the porch to talk privately, which was where they now sat. Her father explained that he was between shoots and wanted to stop by and see how her summer was going. He seemed really sorry that he had just popped in like that.

Natalie sighed. "It's not your fault," she said. "I know you were trying to do something special."

"You used to like it when I surprised you," he pointed out.

"I did! I mean, I do. But I was really liking the way that no one knew who you were," she said. Her father looked hurt. "I mean—well, it was cool to be meeting people on my own terms, you know? I mean, I didn't want anyone to act weird or different once they knew who you were. I wanted them to like me for me. Or not like me for me, whatever. You get the point."

Her father smiled and pushed her hair back from her face. "Believe it or not, Nat, I know exactly what you mean. I have to deal with that every day. Agents, actors, directors—everyone telling me what I want to hear."

Natalie smirked at him. "That must be awful."

He laughed. "Well, okay, not always. Point taken."

"You look good," she said. "The 'spy' training is always a good thing." And he did look good. He was tanned and fit and actually even looked relaxed, which was rare for him.

Her father fake-flexed a bicep. "Not bad for an old-timer, right?" he laughed.

"One of the girls in my bunk has your poster up on the wall," Natalie said. "Shc thinks you're cute. It's pretty gross."

Her father arched an eyebrow. "Gross? Should I be offended?"

Natalie giggled. "Sorry." She stood up and walked toward him. "I'm glad to see you."

Her father reached out and pulled her close for a hug. "I'm glad to see you, too, sweetie."

She pushed away and looked at him again. "What have you got on tap for today? I'd give you the grand tour but even with all your personal training I don't think you could handle the *real* great outdoors," she teased. "Also, you wouldn't be able to walk a foot in any direction without being attacked by legions of fans."

"Well, hang on, that could be fun," her father protested, pretending to consider his options. "Legions, you say? . . . Nah, I get enough of that in L.A.," he decided. "How about I bust you out of this joint for the afternoon? I already cleared it with Dr. Steve. Who, by the way, does not strike me as a medical professional. Has your mother checked his credentials? Anyway, we could do lunch, go shopping—"

"Shopping? Please don't be kidding," Natalie said, eyes lighting up at the prospect.

"Of course I'm not kidding! Josie couldn't go a day without spending some of my money."

Natalie knew that her father's girlfriend, Josie, *loved* to shop.

"I don't know what sort of shops we'll find up here," Natalie warned her father.

"Oh, I'm not worried. Somehow, between you and Josie, I bet we can sniff out the bargains," her father said, patting her on the head. "I have one call to make—"

"How very Hollywood of you—" Natalie quipped.

"—and then I'll get Skylar to bring the car up," her father finished, ignoring her.

"Don't be ridiculous, Dad. Go make your call, and I'll meet you at the front entrance to the camp. No more drama, okay?" Natalie said.

"Fine." He kissed her on her forehead. "See you in fifteen."

Her father trotted off in the direction of the camp entrance, and Natalie squared her shoulders and prepared herself to go back into the bunk. She had no idea what she was going to say to any of her friends, but it was now or never.

As she walked into the bunk, she was aware of the room going utterly silent. She suddenly had the distinct impression that just moments before, she'd been the subject of conversation. *Don't be paranoid, Nat,* she told herself, but she couldn't shake the sensation that all eyes were on her. She kept her head down as she crossed to her cubby to fish out her bag.

"How's your father, Nat?" Julie chirped, breaking the silence.

"Um, he's okay," Natalie managed. "Tired, I guess, because he just finished filming."

Julie didn't seem to know what else to say. In the end, she decided on a nondescript, "mmm," before turning back to her book.

"God, he is really great-looking in person."

Natalie turned to find Chelsea gazing at her with stars in her eyes. It was like she'd had some sort of personality transplant or something.

Just what I didn't want to happen, Natalie thought, dejected. She glanced up to Alyssa's bunk—but all she could see were feet. Alyssa was either sleeping or playing dead. Natalie hoped she was sleeping.

"Why didn't you say anything?" Alex said. She looked a little bit sad. "We wouldn't have cared. But I feel so stupid for all of those times I went on about him, and he—he was your father . . ." Her voice trailed off.

"I know," Natalie whispered. "I just . . ."

Just what? she asked herself. But she just couldn't come up with a good enough answer. "I'm sorry," she finished finally. "I have to go. I'll be back later."

"Sure!" Julie agreed. Her enthusiasm was out of sync with the mood of the room.

Natalie trudged out the front door, wondering how she was going to make things right with her friends. Why had she lied to them? Why had she hidden the truth about her family? How could she expect them to trust her again?

"Hey, uh, can I talk to you?"

Natalie looked up and gasped. "Simon," she said. "I, uh . . . what's up?" *Duh. What's up is that your father is a movie star and you never said anything and now everyone thinks you're weird and secretive and probably all stuck-up and spoiled. That's what's up.*

"So, uh . . . your father. Tad Maxwell," Simon said, stating the obvious.

"Yup," Natalie said, swinging her arms back and forth nervously. "That he is. And I, um, didn't want to say anything . . . I don't know why I didn't want to say anything," she said at last. "I guess I suck. I wouldn't blame you if you were mad at me." *Oh, please don't be mad at me,* Natalie thought.

"Well, it's just—"

Natalie's heart dropped to her stomach. "Well, it's just" was not the same thing as "of course I'm not mad." Not at all. And suddenly, she wasn't sure she wanted to hear the end of that sentence. Her friends were upset with her, her secret was out, and now Simon—well, whatever was on his mind, it was too much. She couldn't deal with it just then. And her father was still waiting for her down at the entrance to the camp.

"Look, I'm really sorry, okay?" she said pleadingly. "I know I wasn't completely honest with you. And I know you probably hate me. But I can't talk right now. My father . . . my father's waiting. And I have to meet him. Now." She turned and began to walk off down the path, doing her best to ignore the hurt look in Simon's eyes.

Quickly, almost against her own will, she turned back again. He was still staring at her, looking very confused and disappointed. "I'm sorry," she repeated.

Then she took off to find her father.

chapter TEN

"Well, Natalie, I do have to give you credit. I don't know if I would be able to survive in the wilderness all summer long," Josie said, delicately picking at a salad.

After several hours of attempting to shop, Natalie and Josie had finally given in and accepted that rural Pennsylvania didn't have that much to offer them. There were lots of cute crafts shops and antiquey places, but the truth was that Tad's house in L.A. was totally done out in an ultra-mod design, and none of the things they would find in Pennsylvania would really mesh with his decor. And the outlet shops, it turned out, were hours away. Once the trio had gotten past the disappointment (well, Natalie and Josie had been disappointed, and Tad had just done his best to seem sympathetic), they opted to drown their sorrows in milkshakes and burgers at the nearest roadside stop. Her father thought it would be great fun to eat at an authentic diner. Josie, however, was accustomed to healthy California food and was busily picking out the cheese and croutons from her salad.

Natalie laughed. "It's not quite the 'wilderness,' you know. I think you just got the wrong impression when they told you they didn't have low-fat dressing here. I mean, we do have running water and indoor toilets." She flashed back to the spider she'd encountered on her first day of camp and shuddered. "Most of the time," she amended. "Anyway, I'm told it builds character."

Her father laughed heartily. "Kid, I think you've got more than enough character already."

"Tell that to Mom," Natalie groaned, giggling.

"Seriously, Natalie—how are you liking camp? Because I've spoken with your mother, and we both agree that if you're really miserable, you can come home. She says your letters—the few that she's gotten—are written with your typical sarcasm, and she can't make out how bad it really is. So you have to fess up."

"You spoke to Mom?" Natalie asked softly. Accepting as she was of her parents' love lives, a part of her still couldn't quite believe that their marriage was over. They had divorced when she was four, so she'd had some time to get used to it, and she and her mother were happy and doing well. But the fact that the separation had been so . . . *amicable* almost made it harder to accept. If they were screaming and yelling about things like child support all the time, she might be more willing to let go of the fantasy that they'd someday get back together.

"She called last week," Josie chirped, breaking into Natalie's little imaginary tour of the alternate reality where her nuclear family was still intact. "Because she knew we were coming to surprise you."

"Yes, we're all in on it, sweetie. If you're unhappy, we'll take you right home. Well, technically, you'd have to come out to L.A., because your mother won't be back from Europe for a few more weeks. But I have about a month before I head off on location again, so the timing would be perfect."

Natalie frowned. She wasn't sure how she felt about it. A week ago, being offered the chance to go home would have been a dream come true. Could it be that so much had changed in such a short period of time? There were things about camp that she could *definitely* do without—spiders in the bathroom, for example. Or that horrible food three times a day. Or having to put up with Chelsea's snipes. But then she thought of smart, sensitive Alyssa, and outgoing Grace. Boisterous Jenna, and energetic Alex. Assuming those girls still planned on talking to her, she couldn't just bail on them. What would Val do in nature without her? Or Simon? *That is, if he doesn't hate me,* Natalie thought.

But if her friends *did* hate her, she knew she had to stay and smooth things over. Going home wasn't the answer. Hannah wasn't in New York City, and Maggie and Ellen were away, too, so what was the fun in that?

And as for visiting her father in Los Angeles . . . well, she loved being out in California (she especially loved his huge house and heated swimming pool), but she had already planned a trip to see him at the end of the summer, just before school started. Now was camp time. And to Natalie's surprise, she found that she was determined to stick it out.

"You know what, Dad?" Natalie found herself saying. "It's okay. I've kind of gotten used to camp. I can't walk away now."

Her father grinned, his bright blue eyes twinkling. "What did I tell you? More than enough character! That's what I like to hear, honey. I'm proud of you."

"Me too," Josie echoed, pushing her plate aside and flagging down the waitress. "Do you think they have fat-free frozen yogurt in this place?"

▲ ▲ ▲

"I'm just disappointed that you didn't find anything today that you wanted," Tad said to Natalie. They had finished their lunch and driven back to camp, stopping only at a farm stand on the side of the road. Now his limo was parked just outside the front entrance to camp. Natalie didn't want to risk generating attention by bringing her father back onto the campgrounds. She'd had enough time in the spotlight already that day—and somehow, she had a feeling that she hadn't seen the last of it.

"Not true," Natalie pointed out. "Everyone in

my bunk is going to be *really* into the peanut butter and chocolate fudge we got at the farm stand." She grinned devilishly in Josie's direction. "Want to take some home with you? I think it's fat-free."

Josie swatted Natalie playfully. "You're terrible. But he's right, we wanted to bring you stuff."

"Are you kidding? You've got a whole wild retail wonderland stuffed in the trunk!" Natalie's eyes had almost popped out of her head when her father and Josie had shown her their idea of a "care package"—they'd loaded up the car with industrial-sized boxes of cereal, cookies, chips, and soda ("Have you heard of this place called Costco?" Josie had asked, wrinkling her nose with distaste.), as well as CDs, DVDs, books, hair accessories, and more than a few cute T-shirts and skirts. "Trust me," Natalie said, "I've got plenty of stuff."

"Are you *sure* you want us to drop this all off in New York, then?" her father asked doubtfully.

Natalie shrugged uneasily. "The thing is, Dad, some of the kids might think it was weird, me bringing all that stuff in. I mean, that's enough food to carry us through to next summer! I just . . . I really don't want to seem different, you know?"

Her father sighed. "I understand. But if you won't let me spoil you, what have I got left?"

Josie patted his shoulder reassuringly. "You could spoil *me*."

Tad laughed and hugged both of his girls close to

him. "All right, then, I guess, if we can't convince you to take this stuff, and we can't convince you to run away with us, then the time has come for us to be on our way. We have a suite booked at the Soho House for tonight, and Josie has a trainer coming early tomorrow morning."

Natalie thought fleetingly of the luxurious Soho House hotel and its rooftop swimming pool. Her father was just one of the many celebrity guests who stayed there, and the pool club was considered a real scene. All she had to do was say the word, and she'd be sipping ice-cold soft drinks on a lounge chair all afternoon. She groaned. "You're killing me, Dad," she said. "But I'll just say good-bye now." She threw her arms around him and gave him a huge hug. "Thanks for stopping by. It was a fantastic surprise."

"You know I'd still love a tour of the camp, kiddo. Especially the famous nature shack."

Natalie groaned. "Haven't you already caused enough of a stir?"

Her father laughed. "You're right. At least I got to talk to the camp director before I met up with you. And that woman—Kathleen, is that her name? Very energetic woman. And I got that great twenty minutes of quality time on the porch of your bunk. I hope I didn't get you in too much trouble with your friends?" he asked.

"Either that, or I'm going to be *really* popular for the rest of the summer. It could go either way. But whichever it's going to be, I'm going to have to face things sooner rather than later." She squared her shoulders dramatically.

"You're a trooper," her father laughed. He gestured toward the trunk again. "Your things will be waiting for you when you get home in August. Sort of a reward for sticking it out."

Natalie nodded. "Cool. And thanks." She paused and thought for a moment. "Well, maybe I'll just take one box of cookies. And some chips. And soda. You know, for the girls."

Josie nodded knowingly. "The girls deserve it."

"And, um, maybe that really cute tank top with the ribbons on the shoulders."

Josie and Tad smiled. "Do you want to have another look in the trunk before we go?" Tad asked.

Natalie grinned sheepishly. "Well," she said, "if you've brought it all this way . . ."

By the time Natalie had finished saying her good-byes to her father and Josie, dinner was long over and the entire camp, it felt like, was off at evening activity. Natalie realized she didn't even know what evening activity was supposed to be that night. She figured maybe it was for the best. She'd return to her bunk, and put away her things. Then maybe she'd have some time to relax before having to face her bunkmates again.

She pushed open the door of her bunk to find Marissa and Pete sitting on Marissa's bed, talking quietly.

Natalie had the feeling she was interrupting something. *What's going on between Marissa and Pete?* she wondered. After all, she knew they were friendly.

But if either of them were feeling awkward, they didn't show it. Marissa sat up straight on her bed and beamed at Natalie. "Hey, girl, how was your day with your dad?" she asked.

Natalie blushed. "Oh, you know . . . fun. Unexpected," she said.

Pete smiled. "I'll say!"

"I guess I should have said something," Natalie admitted. She dropped her clothes and books on her bed, and brought a bag of chips over to where Marissa and Pete sat. She popped the bag open and offered them a snack.

"Parents are the best," Pete said, crunching down on a handful of chips.

"My dad's got his issues, but he means well," Natalie agreed.

"He's got great taste in snack food," Marissa said.

Natalie couldn't believe it. Were they really not going to give her a hard time for not coming clean with them about her father? "Okay, so what's the deal?" she demanded abruptly. "Why are you being so normal about this?"

Marissa and Pete glanced at each other briefly, and then back at Natalie. "What would you rather we do?" Marissa asked softly. "It's your family, and it's your business. I think you're a great girl, Natalie, and I respect you. If you didn't want to talk about what your father does, then that's your call. I don't blame you. I bet you have to deal with a lot of weirdness, growing up as Tad Maxwell's daughter."

Natalie felt relief course through her in waves. Leave it to Marissa to be totally understanding. "Exactly," she said. "I didn't mean to lie, I just . . . wanted to spend the summer without having to deal with that. I mean, you never know how people are going to react, and I just wanted to be here on my own terms this summer."

"I totally dig that," Pete said. He reached forward for more chips.

Marissa rolled her eyes. "He's just easily bribed. A little salt and vinegar goes a long way." She suddenly lowered her voice, slightly more serious. "But I think you have to be prepared for the fact that some other people might react a little differently."

"Is everyone mad at me?" Natalie asked nervously. "Not that I blame them. I mean, I sort of lied."

"I don't know that people are 'mad,' Nat, but definitely, some of your friends are going to wonder why you didn't trust them enough to come clean," Marissa replied.

"And then there are others who might just be really weird now that they know who your father is," Pete said. "People react really strangely to fame, you know?"

Natalie sighed heavily. "Actually, I do." She looked

up at the two of them. "So where is everybody now?"

"Capture the flag tonight," Marissa explained. "Up in Far Meadow. But it's half over, anyway. You can stay here with us if you want."

"I really appreciate it, Marissa," Natalie said. "But I guess I have to deal sooner or later.

"It might as well be sooner."

▲ ▲ ▲

Natalie could hear the sounds of cheering and laughing long before the sprawl of Far Meadow actually came into view. She wasn't really sure what "capture the flag" was and she didn't much mind having missed half the game. Now, she was almost deliberately dragging her feet. She did and she didn't want to deal with her fellow campers just yet.

Rounding the corner, she could see Alex in a huddle with Sarah, Brynn, Valerie, and Alyssa. She broke into a jog and ran over to where they stood.

"Can someone fill me in on what this game is about?" she asked, trying to sound more confident than she felt.

Everybody jumped. "Nat!" Alex said. She looked startled, and it was obvious that she was making a deliberate effort to compose herself. "Hey," she said coolly. "Did you have fun with your dad?"

Natalie nodded. "Well, you know, it was a big surprise. It's always a surprise to see him." She tried desperately to catch Alyssa's eye, but her friend just looked away.

The rest of the girls all nodded in unison, as though they understood. To Natalie, the moment seemed to occur in slow-motion, and it felt very awkward. But if no one was going to say anything, then she wouldn't, either.

"Natalie!"

Natalie turned to see Chelsea sprinting toward her as though they were long lost friends. "Are you on our team?" she asked breathlessly. Her tank top was streaked with grass stains and a few blond wisps had escaped her ponytail, but if anything, the flush in her cheeks made her look even prettier than usual. "We've got a no-lose strategy. Did Alex fill you in?"

Alex shrugged. "I didn't have a chance yet."

Natalie's head was spinning. The scene felt almost completely surreal. Her friends were being polite but awkward, and Chelsea was suddenly her bestest best friend in the world? This was so not what she wanted! *This* was why she hadn't wanted to let people know who her father was!

Chelsea leaned in again. "Look, Betsey is our offense." She gestured to midfield where a lanky brunette from 3A hunkered, hands on her knees. "Jenna's gonna create a distraction—see? Bennett's playing defense, so Jenna's on top of him. Then Betsey will go long and grab the flag. We'll go wait just outside of the goal zone, and once she's got the flag, she'll pass. Then we can run it back to our side."

Natalie stared at Chelsea in disbelief. "I'm, uh, not such a fast runner." To say the least.

Chelsea burst out laughing and gave Natalie a playful shove. "Come on. It's fine." She grabbed Natalie's arm and began to drag her upfield. "All you have to do is act like you know what you're doing."

"You guys—" Natalie protested, and glanced fleetingly at Alex.

"It's a solid strategy," Alex said, wrapping her glossy black hair back into a sloppy ponytail. "Go for it."

The girls ran up the meadow, Chelsea pausing to high-five Betsey behind her back. Once they were within spitting distance of the other team's goal, Chelsea shoved Natalie hard. "Go distract the goalies."

"Huh?" Natalie asked as she stumbled forward. Three boys stood in front of the goal, which she assumed was where the flag would be. One was Jenna's brother Adam, and one was a boy named Caleb who was on the newspaper with Natalie.

One was Simon.

Before Natalie could even begin to think of what to say to him, Caleb was in her face, growling and pretending to be tough. "Don't even think about it, girlie," he said, puffing his chest out and standing really close to her. "We're all over this flag."

"Dude, do you know who her father is?" Adam

asked. "Tad Maxwell. You know, huge action spy. She might be able to kick your butt!"

"It's just a movie," Natalie said desperately. She looked over at Simon, but he wasn't looking back. "I mean, he's really not that tough."

"Oh, yeah?" Caleb asked thoughtfully. "I've got an idea. How about you hook me up? I get to meet your dad, you get to capture the flag?" He winked and then burst out laughing as though this were the most hysterical joke ever told.

"You know who I want to meet? Josie McLaughlan!" Adam said. "Her father's girlfriend. She's so hot, I could cry. Do you think she'll come up for Visiting Day, Natalie?"

"I doubt it," Natalie said. "I think my father's going to be shooting." *Do we* have *to talk about this?* she thought anxiously.

"But you could get us, like, an autograph or something, right?" Caleb pressed.

"Ah, sure, maybe," Natalie said. Out of the corner of her eye, she could see Chelsea creeping behind the flag, waiting for Morgan from 3B to break in and away. She was racking her brain for the right thing to say to Simon but drawing a blank. It didn't matter—he didn't look like he wanted to talk, anyway.

Suddenly, Betsey burst forward, cutting between Natalie and Caleb in a blur of long brown braid and legs. She snatched the flag from its pole and circled around Simon, passing it off to Chelsea and backing away again.

"YEAH!" Chelsea screamed, tearing forward and making a break for the far end of the field.

"Dude, are you asleep?" Caleb shouted to Simon, taking off after Chelsea. After a moment, Adam followed him. Now Natalie stood alone, facing Simon. The tension in the air was thick. A thousand ways to open a conversation raced through Natalie's mind, but she rejected them all.

Finally, Simon spoke. "You should go after them," he said quietly.

Then he ran off to follow his teammates.

chapter ELEVEN

"Nat, do you want to borrow my extra flashlight for the camping trip?"

Natalie looked up to find Chelsea beaming down at her, waving a bright yellow flashlight. "Oh, ah, I've got my own," she managed. "But, thanks." She pressed her toiletries case into her daypack and zipped it shut. Everyone who was going on the camping trip had packed a larger duffel that was being driven to the campsite separately. That baggage had been delivered to the rec hall the night before. But all the campers were responsible for bringing their own daypacks and carrying them on the hike.

"Do you have enough bug repellant? I have two bottles," Chelsea offered. "And also sunscreen."

"It's okay, Chelsea," Natalie insisted, trying her hardest not to sound testy. "I'm all set." She knew Chelsea was just trying to be nice—well, she assumed so, anyway—but the girl was starting to drive her crazy. Most of Natalie's friends had been remote and aloof since yesterday. And for her part, Natalie didn't know how to behave around them, either. But not Chelsea. Chelsea had been all buddy-buddy on the way back from evening activity the night before, and now she was practically trying to pack Natalie's bag for her. Meanwhile, everyone else in the bunk was tiptoeing around her, and all the other campers were acting like she was some kind of rock goddess. Natalie felt like she was losing her mind. She couldn't believe it, but she was almost looking forward to the camping trip! At least it would help her get away from everything and clear her mind. When she was back home and feeling stressed-out, she always went for long walks in Central Park. This camping trip was the closest she was going to get to that for at least six more weeks.

"All right," she said to no one in particular. "I've got to go. I'm in charge of picking up the lunches for the group and bringing them to the rec hall. That's where the van is meeting us." She shouldered her backpack. "Chelsea, Valerie, I'll meet you there. Good-bye, everyone! Wish me luck avoiding snakebites!"

Her bunkmates laughed and offered vague reassurances. None of it was especially comforting.

Natalie started out toward the mess hall for the lunches. She hadn't gotten farther than the front porch, though, when she heard the door creak open and bang shut again behind her. "Nat, wait," she heard. She stopped walking.

It was Alyssa. "Look, I'm sorry I've been avoiding you," she said, biting her lip. "I feel terrible." Alyssa hadn't exactly been rude to Natalie, but she definitely hadn't been overly friendly the evening before. Natalie had tried to convince herself that it was because of Alyssa's deep-seated aversion to capture the flag, but inside she knew better. Which was probably why she herself had been reluctant to approach her friend. She just wasn't sure what to say.

"*You* feel terrible?" Natalie cried in disbelief. "Are you kidding me? I'm the one who lied to you guys! I feel awful! I wouldn't blame you if you never wanted to speak to me again!"

"Of course I want to speak to you again," Alyssa said. "Listen, you have the right to want to keep certain things secret. God knows, I haven't told you everything about my crazy family. Just wait until we're back home in the fall, and you meet my older sister. What a freak *she* is!"

Natalie giggled. "I guess everyone's family is a little bit nuts."

"Excuse me, but have you *seen* Jenna when she and Adam bicker? It's like they're possessed or something. Anyway, I don't blame you. Especially now that half the people in camp are your biggest fans. I can totally get why you wanted to keep this quiet. It must be so annoying to feel like no one knows the real you."

"Exactly!" Natalie said, relieved that her friend understood.

"But I never knew anyone who was famous before,

and when I saw who your father was, I guess I flipped," Alyssa continued softly. "I mean, you're so pretty and funny and sophisticated—you're from New York, after all. So I knew you were definitely a character."

"Why does everyone keep telling me how much character I have?" Natalie asked wryly. "It could really give a girl a complex."

"Will you shut up and let me finish?" Alyssa asked. "Character, I like. But when it started to seem like maybe you had this whole alternate-Hollywood lifestyle or something, I got nervous. Like maybe I wasn't cool enough for you anymore." She looked down at the ground as though maybe she thought she'd said too much.

Natalie's eyes flew open. "Okay, first of all, I am *so* not more sophisticated than you! You've read, like, every book *ever*, and you have the coolest taste in music! And you draw so well, and you're the best writer on the paper! And second of all, most of my friends in New York are really, really normal. Maybe some of them have money, but they don't go riding around in limos everywhere. That's just my father. And if you want the truth, well . . . I don't see him that often. I mean, he means well. I know he loves me. But he's pretty involved in his own thing. So if you think my life is one big Hollywood party after another, well . . . you have no idea. Honestly? I spend most of the time watching TV at home with my friends." She crossed her arms in front of her chest and regarded her friend. "Okay?"

Alyssa nodded, clearly glad to have everything out in the open. "Okay. Can we stop being idiots now? Because yesterday when we weren't talking was really bad."

Natalie smiled. "You're telling me? *Chelsea* is, like, my new best friend!"

"Ha ha," Alyssa said. "Have fun on the camping trip!"

"Very funny," Natalie said, making a face. She glanced at her watch. "Now I *really* have to go," she said. "Can't keep the poison ivy waiting."

▲ ▲ ▲

"What are in these lunches, anyway?" Pete asked, pretending to struggle under the weight of the garbage bag he was carrying. He and Marissa had been in the mess hall when Natalie came by, and they had packed up the lunches for her, offering to help her carry them to the rec hall.

"So, Nat," Marissa said, "how was everyone last night?"

"Pretty much what I expected," Natalie said. "Half the girls in our bunk have no idea how to act around me. Like Alex and Brynn and Sarah. They're behaving like robots. Very polite, stiff robots."

"What about the other half?" Marissa asked.

"Oh, they're really into me now that they know who my father is. All fake-nice and stuff."

As if on cue, Chelsea stepped out in front of them.

"Hey, guys!" she said. "Need help?"

Pete stifled a chuckle. "I think we're good, Chelsea. Are you all ready for the camping trip?"

"Totally!" she said. She looked the part, too. She had done her hair up into two cute braids down either side of her head, and she was wearing a crisp white tank top and lightweight cargo capris. Her trail shoes looked appropriately broken-in, and a disposable camera peeked out from one pocket.

"Chelsea, why don't you show Pete where to bring the food," Marissa suggested.

"Totally!" Chelsea repeated. Her enthusiasm was slightly scary.

Marissa poked Natalie in the ribs as they watched the two make their way into the mess hall. "Okay, I can see what you mean," she said.

"Right?" Natalie asked. "I get that all the time. I just didn't want to have to deal with it here. This place was supposed to be a whole new experience."

"Well, I think it's safe to say it *was* a whole new experience, right?" Marissa said. "I mean, look at you. When you first got here, you wouldn't shower without wearing your bathing suit."

"Let's not exaggerate," Natalie protested.

"Almost," Marissa insisted. "And now you're going on a camping trip! In the actual wilderness! Nat, you should really be proud of yourself."

"I guess I sort of am," Natalie admitted. She never

liked to say those kinds of things out loud for fear of people thinking she was stuck-up, but in this case, it was definitely true.

"And I think you should know," Marissa continued, "that your true friends are going to stick by you no matter what. Whatever you did or didn't tell them, or whoever your father is, they'll still be on your side. That's how you know they're your friends."

"You're right," Natalie said, thinking of Alyssa. Then she remembered the look on Simon's face just before he ran off after the flag. "At least, I hope you are."

"Okay, I want you all to line up, boy-girl-boy-girl," Roseanne shouted. She seemed to have forgotten how to speak at a normal decibel today. Of course, Natalie had to give her credit for dragging a group of fifteen immature eleven-year-olds into the woods overnight with only LJ from the kitchen as support. The line snapped into place and Natalie found herself at the end of it, behind Chelsea, due to an uneven number of boys and girls. "Now I want you to break off into pairs," Roseanne continued. "The person you pair off with is your buddy. No matter where we are or what you're doing, you are always responsible for your buddy. Do you understand? That means *always* knowing where your buddy is and what he or she is doing. The woods aren't dangerous, but we all have to be alert at all times. Devon, Eric, you're buddies," she said, pointing to the first boy-girl combo at the front of the line. Dutifully, the rest of the campers began to partner up.

Natalie glanced down the line. *Paige and Eric,* she ticked off mentally, *Shari and Ross, Michael and Valerie, Topher and Melanie, Brian and Lizzie, Seth and Adrianne . . .* with a sinking feeling, she realized who the threesome would be. After all, there were only three of them left.

Simon and Chelsea . . . and me.

Natalie didn't know which was worse, the chafe of her backpack against her shoulders, or the deafening silence between Simon and herself. Both were extremely irritating and slightly painful. And both showed little signs of letting up anytime soon.

Fortunately, Chelsea was doing enough chattering for the both of them. She had, thankfully, taken it upon herself to play the role of group leader. Each pair (or, in their case, trio) was responsible for identifying and gathering several types of flora and fauna along the way. The idea was that they would all share their findings around the campfire that night. Natalie was more open-minded about this trip than she would ever have dreamed, true, but try though she might, she just couldn't get jazzed over rocks, leaves, and twigs for show-and-tell. So it was a good thing that Chelsea was eager to pick up the slack. "Pine needles are so totally obvious," she was saying, waving her map in front of her buddies. She was either completely oblivious to the awkward tension coursing through the air, or deliberately ignoring it. "We totally lucked out."

Natalie frowned at the path beneath her feet, and kicked at a rock. "Totally," she echoed.

"Have you seen any?" Chelsea asked. "'Cause I just haven't yet. But I know we will." She stopped short, tossing her head so her braids flew back over her shoulders dramatically. "Let's take a picture."

"Oh, uh, now?" Natalie asked with alarm. They'd been hiking along at the tail end of the group for about an hour now, Natalie imagining entire conversations with Simon in her head. It didn't seem quite the right time for a Kodak moment. "Why don't you wait until we hit the campsite? Roseanne says there are amazing views."

"Well, duh, I'll take pictures then, too!" Chelsea said, speaking as though Natalie were five years old. "Oh, look—" she squealed. "A rabbit!"

Sure enough, a tiny spotted rabbit leaped out from the trees and landed just before Chelsea's feet. It froze, blinking furiously. Then it hopped away.

"Oh, I *so* need a picture of that!" Chelsea exclaimed, darting off after it. The rabbit bounced off to the left of the path and down a sloping hill.

Natalie glanced up ahead to where Roseanne and the group were continuing along. Everyone in the group was busy collecting samples from the trail and didn't seem to have noticed that Natalie, Simon, and Chelsea were lagging behind. Suddenly, Natalie felt nervous. They really weren't supposed to go off on their own. But then again, she and Simon were Chelsea's buddies. They couldn't let her out of their sight. That was the rules.

"Shoot," she muttered. "What should we do?"

Simon looked equally panicked, in his own low-key way. "I guess we have to go after her, pull her back," he said.

They took one last, fleeting glance at the group and started down the slope after Chelsea. "Chelsea, come on!" Natalie shouted. "We're not supposed to go off the path!"

"Don't be such a freak, Nat!" Chelsea called back over her shoulder. "We've barely been gone five minutes! Come on! The rabbit's trying to hide! It would make a really cute picture."

"If the rabbit is hiding, Chelsea, it's probably scared of you," Simon pointed out. He slid a few paces and skidded to a stop in front of her.

"*Uf*," Natalie grunted, tripping over her feet and landing inches behind Simon. She grabbed at him for traction then pulled back as if she'd been electrocuted. "Sorry."

She blew a thick clump of hair off her face gracelessly. "Where's Thumper?"

"You scared him off," Chelsea snapped, suddenly cranky. "Thanks a lot."

"Um, sorry?" Natalie said. "I practically skidded down the hill on my butt. It was hardly on purpose." She was hot and tired and not in the mood for attitude. "Anyway, you know we're not supposed to run off." She rubbed at her shoulders and thought absently that it was probably time to reapply the sunscreen.

"Guys," Simon said, breaking into the heated moment. "Forget the rabbit. I think we have other problems."

Natalie put her hands on her hips. "What?" she asked. It was humid, buggy, and they still had at least another hour to go before they reached the campsite. What other problems could there possibly be?

He jerked his head back in the direction of the group. "Well, for starters, I don't see them anymore," he said.

Natalie glanced over to where he was pointing. He was right. She couldn't make out even the faintest forms on the path. She had no idea where the rest of the group had gone.

They were on their own.

▲ ▲ ▲

"I *knew* I shouldn't have paired up with Miss New York," Chelsea grumbled, trudging along. Since they had gotten separated from the group, she had completely reverted back to her old self. She was sour and angry, taking constant jabs at Natalie. It was as though her whole about-face thing had never happened at all.

For her part, Natalie was mostly exhausted and exasperated, and more than ready to meet up with the group again to set up camp. "Yeah, yeah, I know," Natalie muttered. "You're my best friend, too, Chelsea. Look, for now, let's just concentrate on finding Roseanne. I never thought I'd say this, but I'm dying to set up the cooker and roll out our sleeping bags. I'd even be willing to bathe in the river." She stopped for a moment, having a thought. "The river!" she said excitedly.

Chelsea glared at her. "Yeah? What about it?"

"Roseanne said we were camping a quarter mile upstream from where the river forked." Flustered, she pulled the map out of her back pocket. It was damp and sticky, like everything else, but she ignored that and unfolded it. "Here's where we last saw the group," she said, pointing to a spot on the dirt path. "That's where we went when we saw the rabbit—I think." She slid her finger down and off to one side. "But I think we thought we were going parallel, but really, we veered off west. And the river is north."

Simon peered at the map over her shoulder. "I think you're right."

"So what does that mean?" Chelsea demanded.

"It means if we head north again, we'll find the river," Simon explained.

"—and if we find the river, we'll find the group," Natalie finished.

"Why should I listen to you two, anyway?" Chelsea whined. "Natalie, you're just a stuck-up city girl, anyway. *Not* exactly the ideal trail guide!" She smirked to herself at her own nasty joke.

"Why should you listen to me?" Natalie asked. "Because if it weren't for *you*, we wouldn't be in this mess, anyway! Now come on—we don't have time for this. What other choice do we have?"

"Ugh, *fine*," Chelsea agreed. "But I don't trust you at all."

"I can live with that," Natalie said. She fished a compass out of her backpack. "Simon, can you read this thing?"

He took it from her and held it flat in his palm. "Yup," he said. "Follow me."

"Natalie!"

Natalie thought she had never in her life been so glad to hear thc sound of Roseanne's voice. For her part, Roseanne sounded thrilled beyond belief to see Natalie, Simon, and Chelsea.

"*Where* did you guys get off to? We've got LJ driving the van off in every direction trying to find you."

"Well, obviously not *every* direction," Natalie quipped wearily. "Have you got any water?" She tossed her pack off her back and collapsed down next to it, taking her hair out of its ponytail and shaking it out.

"Of course, of course," Roseanne said, offering her canteen to Natalie. "The others are pitching the tents over in that clearing—" she pointed to a spot in the distance. "And then when LJ gets back, he's going to start cooking dinner."

"Thank God," Natalie said. "I dropped my granola bar in the river a mile or so back, and I'm starving."

"Whatever," Chelsea interrupted. "It's totally Natalie's fault that we got lost."

"What? But—" Natalie began, then stopped. She was too tired, anyway.

"Chelsea, dear, why don't you go help the others pitch the tents, okay?" Roseanne suggested. Chelsea marched off in the direction indicated without offering even a second glance at Natalie or Simon.

Once she was out of earshot, Natalie turned to Roseanne imploringly. "It is so *not* my fault that we got lost—" she started.

Roseanne laughed. "Why do I not doubt that? Sweetie, don't get yourself all worked up. You've had a long afternoon. Just relax and take a load off. Simon can fill me in on the rest."

Natalie had to admit, the idea of resting for a bit sounded awfully appealing. From across the clearing, she could hear the laughter of the group. The thought of making conversation and explaining what happened felt overwhelming. A moment to regroup seemed like the right thing. And regardless of where their friendship was, she trusted Simon to relay the truth to Roseanne. So she smiled at the both of them, stood, brushed herself off, and walked away—though not *too* far away. She'd learned her lesson, after all.

Natalie found a quiet spot in the shade. She crouched on a flat rock and looked out over the hilltops. She could see the river down below—and if she turned around, she could see the other campers chilling out at the site. She exhaled deeply and took in the scenery.

Central Park had nothing to compare to this. True, she could ride horseback or canoe in the lake, eat ice cream or watch Shakespeare performed outdoors. New York was a special place, no doubt about it. But then, so was Lakeview. Natalie realized that she didn't care that Chelsea was being bratty again—in a way, it was even a relief. At least it felt natural. And she would somehow apologize to Simon. Even if he didn't want to be friends, she owed him that much, and she would gather up the courage to tell him so. But not now. Right now, she was just going to breathe in the clean mountain air.

I'm like a commercial for Grape-Nuts or something, she realized with wonder. *What's going on with me? Am I, like, a real camper now?* She glanced down at her legs. The scratches and bruises she'd gotten while trying to link up with the rest of the group were proof-positive that she was definitely gaining a new perspective on the great outdoors. The thought made her smile to herself.

"I've got something that'll *really* make you smile," she heard.

She looked up to see Simon holding out a granola bar. "Since I knew you lost yours."

She took it eagerly. "Have I mentioned I'm *dying* of hunger?" she asked.

He gave her a look. "I think once or twice."

She swatted at him jokingly. "Sit. Share," she commanded.

Simon lowered himself onto the ground next to her and took half of the granola bar willingly. "So," he started, suddenly sounding nervous.

"No, me first," Natalie cut in. "I need to tell you that I'm sorry. I'm sorry I didn't say anything about my father. I shouldn't have been so secretive. And I'm sorry I ran away the other day. I could tell you were upset, and I just wasn't ready to deal."

Simon nodded thoughtfully. "I know. I get it. I mean, I'm not gonna lie—I was really upset yesterday, Nat. It really hurt me to think that you didn't feel you could tell me."

"It's not that—" Natalie started.

"—listen," Simon pressed. "The point is, I get it now. I saw how everyone reacted to your father, and I can see why you wanted to keep it a secret for a while."

"I wanted people to like me for who I am," Natalie explained.

"People?" Simon asked.

Natalie blushed. "Some people more than others."

Simon put his arm around Natalie's shoulders. Rockets went off in her stomach. "I just hope that from now on, you know you can always be straight with me."

Natalie tilted her head to look him straight in the eyes. "I know. I will. I promise."

"I think you were awesome today, the way you knew how to find the way back to camp," he said.

"Come on—you knew, too."

"You had the compass. We would have been lost without you," Simon said.

"Fair enough," Natalie agreed. "Let's just compromise and say that we're a great team."

Simon slipped his hand around Natalie's own. "Absolutely," he said.

chapter TWELVE

"Okay, so is it true that Chelsea was, like, trapped by a bear and almost eaten?" Brynn asked. She sounded sort of excited at the prospect.

"Not even!" Natalie exclaimed. "Where did you hear such a thing?"

"Well, Simon's telling everyone how you rescued Chelsea after she got lost," Alex said.

The three girls were on their way out of the mess hall following dinner. Natalie and the rest of the campers from the overnight had returned back to Lakeview early that afternoon, but they were given a few hours to kick back and do whatever they wanted. For Natalie, that meant sitting out on the front porch of 3C reading *Entertainment Weekly*. She only counted two wild rumors connected to her father. To her that was progress. One said he was having hair transplants done before his next movie. To the best of her knowledge, Natalie's father had never had any plastic surgery done. She'd have to make sure and give him a hard time about that gossip the next time they spoke.

Since Natalie had spent the afternoon by herself, she was totally unaware of the rumors that were flying around camp about *her*. Simon had let it slip—intentionally, she guessed—that the three of them had been separated from the group and had been forced to find their way to the campsite with little more than a compass and some bug spray. But somehow, the story had morphed into a tale of daring rescue. One that made her sound like a cross between Lara Croft and the Crocodile Hunter. It was too funny. She had to admit, she didn't mind the attention that much. It seemed to have superceded people's obsession with her movie-star father, so for now, at least, she was okay with it.

"It was so not a big deal," Natalie said, shaking her head. "Chelsea ran off, and we ran after her." It was the truth, after all.

Chelsea had been quiet since they'd all returned. Those who were talking about her didn't seem to have the guts to go right up *to* her and ask her about the trip. She and the rest of bunk 3C were still milling outside of the mess hall while Brynn, Alex, and Natalie killed time in the nearby pagoda. Natalie was finding that her opinion toward Alex had mellowed slightly. The girl was definitely a type-A model camper, but she was friendly and sincere, and she was one of the few of Natalie's bunkmates who had really gone out of her way to be as normal as possible after she found out the truth about Natalie's father.

"Well, I heard that when she realized that you guys had lost the rest of the group, she totally freaked, and you had to, like, talk her down," Brynn said.

She seemed pretty unwilling to entertain any other version of the story, and Natalie decided she wasn't too interested in correcting her, after all. It *had* been a pretty harrowing experience, and she deserved at least some of the glory, didn't she? "Someone had to step up," she said airily.

"Tell us, Nat, how does it feel to have barely escaped from the wilderness with your life?" Alex asked jokingly. She held out an imaginary microphone, pretending to be a newscaster.

"No comment," Natalie said, cracking up. She saw Marissa talking to Pete, Brian, and Beth, and she ran over to them.

"Hey!" Marissa said, smiling. "You made it out alive."

Natalie groaned. "Just barely."

"Yeah, so we heard," Pete teased. "Aren't you glad all those hours in the nature shack finally paid off?"

"Ahem," Brian interjected. "I believe it was her excellent training during sports that prepared her for the physical challenges of her outdoor adventure."

"Definitely," Natalie agreed, laughing.

"Too bad she *still* won't go into the water for free swim!" Beth protested.

"Excuse me, but after my harrowing experience,

shouldn't I get a get-out-of-jail-free card?" Natalie asked.

"Fair enough," Beth conceded.

"We heard that Chelsea, ah, isn't recovering quite as well," Pete said delicately.

"Well, she wasn't exactly thinking positively when we got lost," Natalie said, thinking back to how incredibly negative she herself had been when she got to camp. She actually felt a little bit sorry for Chelsea. Now that they were back, no one had a good word to say about her. "But, I mean, it was a hard day. It was hot, and we were tired—and we had *no* idea where we were going. I was just crossing my fingers that the compass was going to work. I can't really blame her for being suspicious."

"Oh, gosh, Nat, that's so *generous* of you," hissed a voice in her ear.

Natalie turned to find Chelsea shooting her a look of death. The girl had obviously overheard the entire exchange. "No, Chelsea, we were just—" Natalie began.

"—Like I care," Chelsea spat, and stormed off.

"Yikes," Pete said, raising an eyebrow.

"But, well . . . I guess at least things are back to normal?" Marissa asked, shrugging tentatively.

"Exactly," Natalie agreed. "And you know what? You were right."

"What about?" Marissa asked, puzzled.

At that moment, Alyssa emerged from the mess hall, notebook tucked under one arm and black hair piled up on the top of her head. She squinted into the sunlight, then spotted Natalie and smiled, making her way over to her friend.

"Hey there, superstar," she said, tossing an arm around Natalie's shoulder. "Let's get going."

"You were the one that told me, Marissa—that my true friends would always stick by me," Natalie said, sticking out her tongue at Alyssa. "And you were right."

"Trauma-rama or horoscopes?" Julie asked, waving two magazines in the air by way of comparison.

"Oooh, horoscopes," Jenna said. "I need to know whether or not—" she stopped abruptly.

"What?" Julie asked, narrowing her gaze. "What have you got planned, my little terror?"

"Nothing," Jenna sang innocently. "Nothing at all."

"Trauma-rama," Natalie put in. "Do they have one where, like, this city girl goes off to this weird place in the country where kids voluntarily sleep on threadbare mattresses and pee in beaten-up, bug-infested stalls, and then after almost two weeks of pretending she isn't the hugest fish out of water, her big movie-star father shows up and outs her as a Hollywood brat?"

"Um, no, that one's not in here, Nat," Julie said sarcastically. "But have you got something on your mind?"

"First things first," Natalie said, reaching under

her bed and sliding out the economy-sized box of cookies. "Snacks."

"Natalie, you know you're supposed to tell us what you've got and clear it before giving it out," Julie said, pretending to be more annoyed than she was.

"Do you want one?" Natalie asked knowingly.

"Actually, I kind of want two," Julie admitted, scooting over to the box. "Okay, ladies, we'll have a little extended evening activity before lights-out. Courtesy of Natalie."

"Courtesy of Tad Maxwell," Natalie said. "You are eating cookies purchased by Tad Maxwell."

"That's a very tough offer to turn down," Alex said, pretending to swoon. But Nat noticed she passed the box without taking any cookies.

"Or, at least purchased by his assistant," Natalie amended. "My dad can get a little busy."

"I'll bet!" Grace said.

"I owe you all an apology," Natalie said, growing serious for a moment. "I didn't mean to lie. Or omit. Or whatever. I just really wanted to have a chance to get to know you all without having the thing with my father be a part of it. I mean, I wanted you to like me on my own terms."

"Well, come on, that would never be an issue," Grace said. " 'Cause of how we don't really like you, anyway." She grinned to show that she was teasing and reached for another cookie. "Hey, does anyone have anything to drink?"

"My dad also brought me some sodas," Natalie said,

feeling slightly embarrassed. "I guess sometimes he goes overboard."

"Hey, when it comes to Diet Pepsi, he can go as overboard as he wants!" Valerie said. "Maybe now I'll even go see his next movie!"

"I have an idea for lights-out," Karen suggested quietly. Everyone turned to stare at her. She almost never spoke out in large groups. "How about Natalie tells us some good Hollywood dirt? That's better than anything you read in a magazine, because we know it's real."

"Oh, I don't know," Natalie hedged . . . But then she stopped herself. *Why not?* she thought. *It's not like they don't read all about him in* People *magazine every day. And since I've been keeping my dad a secret, I haven't been able to dish about him since I got here.* "Cool, I'm in!" she decided. The girls whooped and cheered.

"Hey, the first two weeks are almost up and we have to pick our next electives," Alex reminded everyone. "Does anyone have any idea what they want?"

"Ceramics," Chelsea said sullenly. "I guess I'll take ceramics and drama."

"Photography!" Jenna said. "And maybe woodworking."

"I really want to stay on the newspaper," Alyssa said. "I'll have to think about what else I want to do."

"I wish they offered an elective for napping," Grace quipped. "That or eating." She stuffed another cookie into her mouth for good measure.

"What about you, Nat?" Sarah asked. "Are you and Simon gonna, like, pick your free periods together?" she teased.

Natalie laughed, feeling a little flustered. "Um, not quite," she stammered.

"So is he your *boyfriend* now, or what?" Grace sang, kissing the back of her hand furiously in a bizarre imitation of, Natalie assumed, her and Simon.

Natalie shrugged. "I don't know. He's my friend. And he's a boy. And maybe he's also a little bit more than a friend. But I've never really had a boyfriend before, and I don't know what that means."

"Translated, that means she *likes* him, likes him," Alyssa translated, smiling at her friend.

"Ugh, *gross,*" Karen said, echoing the sentiment of all the bunkmates. Everyone erupted into a chorus of, "eew," and, "barf," and Brynn leaned over and made hearty retching noises.

"Enough, people," Marissa broke in. "Trust me—soon enough, you won't be thinking that boys are all that gross."

"Boys like Pete?" Natalie asked. "Or other boys?"

"*Any* boys," Marissa confirmed, dodging the question skillfully. "And anyway, Nat, you never answered the question. What electives are you gonna go for next?"

Natalie scrunched up her face as if in deep concentration. "You know? I think I'll stick with nature," she joked.

Her bunkmates cracked up and pelted her with their pillows. Natalie found herself laughing, too. She couldn't believe that just two weeks into the summer, she'd already made some amazing friends and a maybe-boyfriend—and survived overnight in the woods. She had no intention of taking nature again—and she knew Julie would say she'd already paid her dues. So now she could try anything else she wanted. Even something she'd never done before. Something that could be hard or scary or different. Something that she might not even be good at.

No matter what, Natalie knew she was ready. After two weeks at Camp Lakeview, she could handle anything that came at her. And more than that?

She'd probably even enjoy herself, too.

Book #2

camp CONFIDENTIAL

chapter ONE

Dear Matt,

Hey, Big Bro! How's everything at science school? Are you bored to death yet? Just kidding. I'm sure you're having the bestest best time of your life, being that you're such a monster science geek. Ha-ha.

Anyway, thanks for the letter and the "Honk If You Love Cheese" bumper sticker. It's perfect for my collection. I have over thirty now, and they're all taped up to the wall above my bunk. All I need is a car to stick them on and I'm all set. But seriously, I know you're worried about me getting into trouble at camp this year, but I swear, so far I've been really good. Well, sort of good. Almost totally good. I've only pulled a couple of pranks, and they were way small. So don't worry. Mom and Dad won't be getting any freak-out phone calls from Dr. Steve. Like you said, I know they don't need that right now.

But you know, if those two didn't want to get any freak-out phone calls in their lives, maybe they should have thought of that before they had four kids, right? Ha-ha.

Okay, gotta go to lunch. Alex is blowing her top because I'm holding up the bunk. Can you say "control freak"? (I mean, she's one of my best friends, but come on. One of these days she's gonna give herself a way-early heart attack.) Anyway, I don't have much to send in return for the bumper sticker, so I'm enclosing this leaf from one of the Camp Lakeview trees to remind you of the actual fun summers you used to have here before you became Science Boy. (Kidding!)

Love,
Jenna

P.S. I love you, too! But don't let it go to your head.

"Cupcakes for everyone!" Jenna Bloom called out, placing the big, foil-lined box in the center of the creaky bunk floor. She had returned from lunch to find yet another care package from her mom, this one filled with chocolate-on-chocolate cakes, each covered in sprinkles. Her mother had even put in these cardboard divider things she had invented a couple of years ago so each cupcake had its own little compartment, and there was hardly any mess at all. (Except for some icing on the top of the box. Jenna's mom was all about minimal mess.) As soon as Jenna set the box down, all her friends in bunk 3C dropped what they were doing and hit the floor in a circle.

"You know, I've been trying to get you guys to huddle up for ten minutes, and no one listens to me," Julie, the bunk counselor, said. Jenna could tell by her half-smile that she was only pretending to be annoyed as she stood over them. "Are you telling me all I had to do was bribe you with sweets?"

"All you ever have to do is bribe us with sweets," Grace joked. She dropped the book she was reading and quickly wrapped her curly red hair back in a ponytail. "We *never* get good desserts around here unless Jenna's parents send them to us."

It was true. Jenna's mom and dad *had* been responsible for most of the sugar highs in 3C this summer. Jenna was proud and happy that her parents were so popular with her friends.

"I call the one with the most icing!" Chelsea said, leaning over the box until her long blond hair fell forward and almost got stuck in one of the cakes.

"Which one is that?" Valerie asked.

"I don't know yet, but it's mine," Chelsea replied in her ever-bossy way.

"Well, I'm taking this one," Brynn announced, her voice booming. She grabbed a cupcake from the center and licked half the icing off the top. As soon as one was gone, everyone in the circle attacked, laughing and fake-whining over how small or big their choice was.

"Sheesh. It's like they've never seen a cupcake before," Jenna joked to Alex Kim, who was the only girl in the bunch not grabbing for the snacks. "Don't you want one?"

"Nah," Alex said, shrugging one shoulder. "I'm still stuffed from lunch."

Jenna felt her face flush, and she looked away. Alex was the only person who never took her up on her offers of candy bars and cookies whenever her mom and dad sent packages. It was like she thought she was too good for the Blooms' gifts. Jenna didn't get it. She and Alex had both been coming to camp at Lakeview for four years—the longest legacies in the bunk—and they had always been good friends. They both knew more about Lakeview than anyone else, and together they felt kind of like the leaders of the bunk. But as close as they were, there were certain things about Alex that Jenna didn't understand. Like how she was sometimes so blunt—even when what she said might hurt someone's feelings—and she acted like that was the only way to be. And Jenna *really* didn't understand this whole turning-down-chocolate thing.

"You sure?" Jenna asked.

"Yeah. Thanks, anyway," Alex said, smoothing her hand through her short, dark hair.

"More for us, then," Jenna said, diving in. She grabbed a cupcake and sunk her teeth in, savoring the gooey sweetness. Her mom was the best baker in the world.

"Your parents are so cool," Sarah said, taking a napkin from the box to wipe her mouth. She pushed her Boston Red Sox baseball cap up on her forehead a bit so Jenna could actually see her eyes. "They send you, like, two packages a week!"

"Yeah! Like two packages! It's crazy!" Candace put in as she licked some icing off her finger. Short and pale with cropped brown hair, Candace was one of those people who agreed with everything anyone else said. Her parents didn't believe in sweets and only sent her letters, so Candace spent most of her summer at camp eating as much sugar as possible and feeling ill half the time.

"You're so lucky, Jen," Natalie added with a grin. Her cupcake was neatly displayed on the floor in front of her, standing in the center of its wrapper. Clearly, Nat was trying to figure out the best way to dive in without ruining her new tank top. Natalie's clothes were very important to her.

Yeah, really lucky, Jenna thought, her heart squeezing in her chest as she tried to smile. *Double the care packages. Yee-ha*. She didn't even want to think about the real reason she was getting so much mail this year, so she forced herself to ignore it.

"You know, it's really nice how you always share your goodies with the bunk," Julie said, reaching out and tousling Jenna's curly brown hair.

Jenna brushed aside her unhappy thoughts and beamed over the praise. She glanced at Alex, who looked away quickly as if she hadn't noticed. Jenna knew Alex couldn't stand it when anyone else was singled out.

"Well, when you have two brothers and a sister, you kind of have to learn to share," Jenna said, earning a laugh from her friends.

"Everyone! Let's thank Jenna!" Julie announced.

"Thank you, Jenna!" shouted ten half-full mouths. Then everyone fell into a group giggle fit, crumbs flying everywhere. Even Natalie gave up on trying to stay neat and took a huge bite of her cupcake, letting the sprinkles fall all over the place.

"All right! So now that I've got you all in one place, I have the list of electives!" Julie announced, tucking her short blond hair behind her ears. She pulled out her ever-present clipboard and sat down on Natalie's bunk.

Jenna's heart thumped with excitement. Every two

weeks at Camp Lakeview, the campers got to concentrate on two elective programs. Last week, they had given Julie their top three choices, and now they would find out which two classes they had been placed in. Jenna was hoping for photography and sports. She had always wanted to learn how to take good pictures of her friends (and maybe how to take some secret, spy cam–style shots of her brothers and sister as well—very useful for bribery). Plus, sports was always a top choice. Jenna had a lot of extra energy to expend, and she loved all kinds of athletics. She, Alex, and Sarah were the biggest jocks in the cabin, and they always signed up for sports.

"So, Nat, going for nature again?" Jenna teased, nudging her friend as Jessie—the camper who always had her nose in a book—went up to Julie to get her electives.

"I don't *think* so," Natalie replied, flipping her long, dark hair behind her shoulder. "The whole campout thing is a great story, but I *so* don't need to go there again. I'm hoping for the newspaper and ceramics."

"Ceramics?" Alyssa asked, looking surprised. Alyssa was an artist, writer, and all-around creative type. Half her clothes were spattered with paint, and she was always doing cool and creative things with her dark hair, like twisting it into tiny braids or crazy buns. Jenna knew Alyssa had requested arts and crafts and the newspaper as her top electives.

"What? I could be artistic and not even know it," Natalie replied. "This time next year I could have a line of high-end vases and bowls in all the best boutiques in New York."

Jenna, Alyssa, and Valerie, another of Jenna's longtime camp friends, all cracked up laughing.

"Fine! See if I invite you to my red-carpet gallery opening," Natalie grumbled, hiding a smile.

"Maybe she wants to make a ceramic statue of *Simon*!" Jenna teased, watching Natalie's face go red. Everyone laughed even harder, and Jenna giggled happily. She loved making people laugh, and this joke was too easy to make. Simon was a boy in Jenna's twin brother Adam's bunk whom Natalie had been crushing on since the first week of camp. Most of the girls in the bunk thought boys were gross and annoying, so they loved to tease Natalie about Simon.

"Okay, okay. Are you guys ever going to stop picking on me about this?" Natalie asked, still smiling.

"Sometime, maybe," Jenna said. "Check back with me next summer."

"Nat! You're up!" Julie called.

"Ha-ha," Natalie said, nudging Jenna's leg with her toe as she got up and walked over to Julie.

Jenna kicked back and munched on her cupcake while the rest of the bunk went up one by one to get their electives. Suddenly, the door banged open and in walked Marissa, her CIT, along with Jenna's older sister, Stephanie, who was also a CIT. Stephanie had been stuck with bunk 3A, who happened to be the rivals of bunk 3C.

Normally, CITs would at least be semi-cold to the CITs of their rival bunks, but not Marissa. She and Stephanie were best friends and couldn't care less about the rivalry.

"Hey, Boo," Stephanie said. "You got cupcakes, too, huh?"

"Steph, I told you not to call me that here," Jenna said, scrambling to her feet. At home, her family nickname didn't bother her, but the last thing she wanted was for her bunkmates to start using the cutesy name for her. Then the guys would find out, and suddenly everyone at Lakeview would be calling her "Boo," which was only her nickname because she had apparently loved peekaboo so much when she was, like, two.

"Oh, right. Sorry," Stephanie said, reaching out to smooth Jenna's hair behind her ears. "God, did you even wash up today?" The girl actually licked her finger and went to wipe something off Jenna's cheek.

"Ew! Do not touch me with that!" Jenna pulled away, her face turning beet red as a couple of her bunkmates giggled. "Okay, *why* did you bring her here?" Jenna asked Marissa.

"I'm not getting in the middle of this," Marissa replied, backing away.

It wasn't like Jenna hated her big sister. She actually loved her—most of the time. But when they were away at camp, Stephanie always acted like she was suddenly supposed to be Jenna's mom or something. And she was only sixteen—just five years older than Jenna. It drove

Jenna up the wall. It also didn't help that Stephanie was totally gorgeous and cool, which meant all the girls looked up to her, and all the boys followed her around like puppy dogs. Totally sickening, if you asked Jenna.

"Sorry!" Stephanie said, her blue eyes sparkling as she raised her hands in surrender. "I just came by to borrow some nail polish from Marissa. Pretend I'm not even here."

Marissa and Stephanie walked over to Marissa's bed and started to go through the CIT's big pink box of cosmetics. Jenna let out a sigh. Sometimes it was cool having her sister and Adam at camp with her at the same time. It was nice having family around and knowing there were people she could go to if she needed someone or got homesick. But those things hardly ever happened to Jenna, and in the meantime it was like everywhere she went, there was a sibling watching her or picking on her or trying to tell her what to do. Plus, because her oldest brother Matt had also gone to Lakeview, half the grown-ups here couldn't keep all the Bloom kids straight, so they just called her "Bloom." It was totally annoying. Sometimes she just wished she could get away from them all.

"Jenna, you're next," Julie said.

Jenna quickly wiped her cheek, wondering what Stephanie had seen on there, and sat down next to Julie.

"Okay, you got photography, which was your first choice," Julie told her. "But for your other elective, I could only get you your third choice, the newspaper."

"No sports?" Jenna asked, disappointed.

"No, not this time," Julie said. "But don't worry. You still have a million active activities to keep you busy. And, hey, Natalie and Alyssa are on the paper, so that'll be cool."

"Yeah. Welcome to our world," Alyssa said with a smile, overhearing.

"Cool," Jenna said, brightening.

Since camp had started two weeks ago, she had really gotten to know and like the two new girls. It might be fun working on the paper with them. Besides, she liked hanging out with newbies. Jenna had been coming to Lakeview for years, and the new kids always needed her help finding their way around. It made her feel important. Instantly, her disappointment was forgotten. Jenna had never been one to dwell very long on the bad. She was all about the good. And, besides, Julie was right: They had swimming every day—either lessons or free swim, which was the best part of camp. Plus, the bunk competed in various sports with other bunks in their age group almost every day. She would have plenty of exercise.

"So, Bo . . . I mean, Jenna," Stephanie said, stepping up with a bottle of silver nail polish. "What did you get?"

"The newspaper and photography," Jenna replied.

"Oh, that's so cool!" Stephanie exclaimed. "I just saw Adam before I came over here, and he got photography, too! I guess you guys will be spending a lot of time together!"

Jenna tipped her head back and groaned. Perfect. So much for getting away from her family. Two whole weeks stuck in the darkroom with her twin brother. Wasn't it enough that they'd had to share a womb for nine months? When was the torture going to end?

chapter TWO

That night in the mess hall, everyone was even rowdier than usual. There was a rumor going through camp that there was going to be some big announcement, and all the campers were buzzing, wondering what it might be. Voices and laughter bounced off the wooden rafters high above, filling the room with a crazy mix of happy noise. It was so loud, Jenna swore she could even see the cobweb-covered lights swinging on their wires overhead.

"What do you think the big news is gonna be?" Karen asked Jenna excitedly, digging into the orange sherbet that the kitchen staff passed off as dessert. Usually, Karen was the shyest girl in the bunk. She kept to herself during free period and barely spoke at meals—or ever—but even she couldn't help but be affected by the excitement in the air.

"It's going to be a dance," Alex said, cutting in before Jenna could answer. "It's *always* some kind of dance."

"Really?" Natalie asked, leaning forward in her seat. "That could be cool!"

"Yeah, they actually are," Jenna said, eager to share her Lakeview info. "They usually have all these great decorations and crazy amounts of snacks, and everyone gets all dressed up."

"Well, as dressed up as you *can* get around here," Grace put in. "I've been saving my favorite rhinestone barrette just in case," she added with a grin. "Last year, I had *nothing* cool to wear."

"Well, my mom called ahead to see what I would need, and when she found out about the yearly dance she bought me a new sundress," Chelsea said, tossing her blond hair back. "I haven't even cut the tags off yet."

Jenna caught Alex's eye, and they both stifled a groan. Chelsea was new this year, and they had found out early on that she was smart and funny. But she could also be a bully and was totally into her looks. Plus, she *loved* to show off.

"This is so beyond cool," Natalie said. "I brought all kinds of stuff that I never thought I'd get to wear once I got here. Like my new denim miniskirt and that purple tank top with the appliqué flowers . . . I'm going to have to do some serious outfit planning."

"Well, I have no dance-worthy clothes," Alyssa said. "Who knew they had dances at camp?"

"You can borrow something of mine, if you want," Natalie offered. "So, do people have, like, dates for this dance?"

Please! Dates? Jenna thought. *I'd rather eat all the leftover sloppy joe surprise!*

"Some of the older kids ask each other," Alex said. "But I don't think anyone in our year will."

"Oh," Natalie said, her face falling.

"Why? Did you want *Simon* to ask you?" Jenna asked. "Natalie and Simon sitting in a tree! K-I-S-S-I-N-G!"

She glanced over at Simon and Adam's table and found them and a bunch of their friends trying to get their spoons to stick to the ends of their noses. Adam's spoon clattered to the table, and they all cracked up laughing. "What do you see in them, anyway? They're such losers," Jenna said.

"But cute losers," Chelsea put in, raising one eyebrow.

Jenna stuck her finger in her mouth to fake gag. Two weeks ago, Chelsea had claimed to be just as grossed out by the boys as the rest of them, but clearly that was a big fake out. Lately it had become obvious that she was almost as boy-crazy as Natalie.

"I just hope none of you think my brother is cute," Jenna said, pushing away from the table. "Because that would just give me nightmares."

"You're going over there, aren't you?" Natalie asked as Jenna stood up.

"Yep. I have to talk to my evil twin," Jenna replied.

"Tell me if Simon says anything about me?" Natalie begged.

Jenna tried not to roll her eyes. "No problem," she replied.

"Uh, Jenna? Where are you going?" Julie asked, sounding worried.

"To talk to my brother," Jenna replied.

"To talk to him? Not to pull some prank on him?" Julie asked.

Jenna smiled. "No, Julie, I swear." She crossed her heart with her pinkie for good measure.

"Okay, then!" Julie said with a smile, though she still looked doubtful.

Wow. Pull a few lousy pranks and one raid and nobody trusts you anymore, Jenna thought. *Well, one raid each summer. Maybe two.* She walked over to Adam's table and dropped down into a chair next to him.

"Jenna? What are you doing over here?" Adam's bunk counselor Nate asked, with an expression that looked a lot like Julie's just had.

"I'm not pulling a prank!" Jenna half-shouted.

"Like you could really pull one over on us," Adam said.

"Hello? I've only done it, like, a million times before!" Jenna reminded him.

"But not tonight," Nate said.

Jenna rolled her eyes. "Not tonight. I promise," she told Nate. She turned to her brother while the rest of the guys continued their stunning spoon tricks. "So, Adam, we need to talk."

"I know," he said. "Did you get the cupcakes from Mom today?"

Jenna's heart turned over in her chest. "Yeah, but that's—"

"Unbelievable, right? I mean, it's like they're trying to bribe us or something. I didn't even finish the candy Dad sent over the weekend yet," Adam said, looking down.

Jenna did not like the way this conversation was going. "Yeah, well, that's because you don't share," she said. "So listen, do you really *have* to take photography?"

"Photography?" Adam asked, blinking. "That's why you came over here? I thought you wanted to talk about—"

"Yeah. I want you to drop it," Jenna said, cutting him off. "Drop photography and take something else."

Adam sat up straight in his chair, and she knew she finally had his full attention. "Why?"

"Because I'm taking photography. And, you and me? We can't be in the same elective at the same time," Jenna said.

"Why not?" Adam asked.

"Because! You . . . you . . ." And that was when Jenna realized she didn't have a real reason. What was she supposed to say? *"I don't want you around me?"* Adam had thick skin, but even he would probably be upset by that. It didn't even really make sense to her, but it was how she felt.

"Because I what?" Adam asked.

"Because you smell!" Jenna said, blurting out the first thing that came to her mind.

All of Adam's friends cracked up, and her brother's face fell. For a split second Jenna felt beyond awful. She couldn't believe she had just made fun of her brother like that in front of everyone. But then his face broke into his silly, wide grin. He lifted his arm and took a huge, long whiff of his T-shirt at the armpit.

"Ugh!" Jenna groaned, along with some of the guys.

"Fresh as a flower patch," Adam said, picking up his spoon and digging into his dessert. "Sorry, sis, but if you want to avoid me, *you're* gonna have to drop photography. You'd better get back to your friends. I'm sure you're missing some very important lip-gloss tips or something."

All the boys cracked up laughing, and Jenna felt her skin turn blotchy and red. She stood up and stalked back to her table, humiliated. She knew it was a little jerky to ask Adam to quit photography, but she just wanted one thing to herself. Why couldn't she have been an only child? Or, at the very least, the only one born on her birthday?

"All right, everyone! Settle down, settle down."

Dr. Steve stood in front of the microphone at the

front of the room next to the long table where the camp directors and coordinators ate. An excited twitter raced through the mess hall.

"This is it! The big announcement!" Grace said with a grin. She pulled her legs up and tucked them under her to give her added height so she could see better. Ever positive and always up for fun, Grace had a way of getting excited about everything—even Dr. Steve's unsurprising announcements.

The camp director was a tall man with thinning blond hair and a high forehead. His face was constantly pink because, no matter how much sunblock he wore, he always seemed to burn. During the day, he was always seen in a fisherman's hat, shorts, and a white Camp Lakeview polo. But at dinner, he wore khaki pants and a dark blue Camp Lakeview polo. He had worn this uniform every single night since the beginning of time. Even Jenna's older brother Matt had confirmed this. In fact, Matt had asked Jenna to let him know the first time Dr. Steve changed his outfit, because Matt would have to throw a party to celebrate the event.

Dr. Steve tapped at the mike. He tried to shush the campers with a few dozen "shhhs" and "ahems," but it wasn't until a huge peel of feedback split the room that everyone finally shut up.

"Thank you," Dr. Steve said, blinking rapidly as he leaned toward the mike. Jenna glanced at Alex, and they shared a smile. They had noticed Dr. Steve's crazy blinking habit their first summer at Lakeview, and Alex had come up with the nickname "Dr. Flutter Bug." Ever since then, neither of them could see him without thinking of it.

"First off, I'd like to remind everyone that Visiting Day is in just two weeks," Dr. Steve announced.

The entire room exploded in a roar of cheers and applause, and Grace even threw her fists in the air as she whooped. Everyone loved when their parents came to visit, no matter how embarrassing they were. Visiting Day meant three things: tons of food, clean clothes, and lots of presents.

As Dr. Steve tried to get the room to "settle down" once more, Jenna picked up her spoon and dipped it into the orange soup her dessert had become. She lifted it and stared as the goo dripped off the end and back into the bowl. Lift, turn, drip. Lift, turn, drip. It was mesmerizing.

"Jenna? You okay?" Julie asked as the room began to quiet again.

Jenna dropped her spoon with a clatter. "Yeah. Fine. Why?"

"You don't seem too psyched about Visiting Day," Julie pointed out.

"Yeah. Even I can't wait, and my mom's a total freak and my dad's a total flake," Alyssa put in. "At least you know both your parents will show up."

Yeah. Sure. Right, Jenna thought, a pit of sour sadness forming in her stomach. *The perfect Blooms will definitely be here to see all their perfect kids.*

"Everything okay?" Julie asked again.

Jenna opened her mouth to reply, but Dr. Steve tapped the microphone again before she got a word out.

"But before Visiting Day, there is one other event that I think you will all be very excited about," Dr. Steve put in. "The night before Visiting Day, we are going to have . . ."

Jenna saw Natalie cross her fingers. Valerie and Chelsea sat up a little higher in their seats. Grace was beaming so brightly, she could have lit up the entire camp. Even Sarah, the bunk's major jock, who would never even *think* about getting dressed up, looked excited.

"A camp-wide social!" Dr. Steve announced, just as Alex mouthed the words, *"A camp-wide dance."*

Half the room gasped in excitement, and Jenna glanced at Alex.

"Dance, social. What's the difference?" Alex asked.

"What *is* the difference?" Natalie asked.

"Nothing, really," Marissa replied, sitting down at the end of the table with Julie. As a CIT, Marissa also had the job of waitressing at meals, and she always joined the table when her duties were done. "There will still be dancing. They just decided not to call it a dance because the younger kids get all weird about it."

Jenna knew this was true. Every year while all the older girls danced with the older boys, the younger girls stood around and looked awkwardly at the boys across the room. Some kids didn't want to dance at all because they felt silly. Other kids were terrified of asking someone to dance and even more terrified of being asked to dance. A lot of kids got stressed out about it in the days leading up to the event. Of course, Jenna had never been one of them. She just saw the camp dance as a chance to eat snacks and hang with her friends. And she didn't think that using the word "social" was going to fool anyone. They all knew it was still the camp dance.

"We'll be having all kinds of sweets and snacks, and Pete, the assistant cook you all know and love, has graciously offered to deejay the event," Dr. Steve continued.

Pete took a step away from the wall where he had been lounging and threw his fists in the air to loud cheers and hoots from all the guys. Gangly and sweet, Pete was a camp mainstay. Up until this year, he had been a counselor and definitely one of the cooler ones. This summer, he had taken a job in the mess hall, although Jenna had no idea why. Even looking after the boys had to be better than working with the so-called food they served around here.

"A DJ? That's so cool!" Valerie said, her eyes wide.

"I hope he's got some good music," Alyssa put in.

"Last year at the camp-wide dance, they actually played Kenny G.," Grace said, scrunching her face up. "I mean, my *grandmother* listens to Kenny G."

"Who's Kenny G.?" Jessie asked. For the first time, she lifted her nose from the book it had been buried in the whole time she had been eating.

"Exactly!" Grace said, raising a hand. "No one knows! He's, like, this weird old guy with freaky long hair who plays elevator music. I swear he hypnotizes old people into liking him. Oooh! But wouldn't it be so cool if you could hypnotize people into liking you?" she added, her eyes bright.

Jenna and her bunkmates laughed at this latest babble of Grace's. "Don't worry. Everybody already likes you," Jenna assured her, causing her friend to blush under her freckles.

"We would like the campers to be as involved as possible in planning this event," Dr. Steve continued. "After all, this is your party. To that end, we'll be creating a planning committee made up entirely of campers."

Jenna's eyes widened, and she looked from Alex to Brynn to Grace. Now *this* was new. Campers had never been involved in the planning of the annual event before. If Jenna could get on the committee, she could make sure that it was the best social/dance/whatever in the history of Lakeview. And she could help them avoid the classic mistakes. Like Kenny G.!

"This is so cool!" Grace said, clasping her hands together.

"Counselors, we will be taking two volunteers from each cabin. Please bring the names of your volunteers to my office tomorrow morning," Dr. Steve said, shouting now to be heard over the excited chatter. "Thank you for your attention," he said. Then he gave up and sat down at his table again.

"I totally want to be on the planning committee!" Chelsea said instantly.

"Me too!" Jenna put in.

"So do I!" Natalie added. "Don't you, Alyssa?"

"Yeah," Alyssa said. "It could be fun."

The whole table erupted as everyone tried to volunteer for the committee.

"You guys, you can't *all* be on the committee," Julie said, holding her hands up. "Then none of you would get to be surprised on the night of the social."

"And besides, Dr. Steve said there could be only two from each bunk," Brynn added.

"You're right," Alex said, sitting back. "I'm out. I wanna see what the rest of you come up with."

Jenna couldn't have been more surprised if Alex had just unzipped her face and revealed that she was actually an alien. Alex didn't want to be in charge of something? Not possible.

"Yeah, it's okay," Candace put in. "I'm not really into it, anyway."

"Me neither," Karen added.

"I don't have to do it, either, Julie," Jessie offered.

Julie looked at the rest of them expectantly, waiting for more of them to back down, but no one did. "The rest of you want in?" she asked.

The table erupted again as everyone tried to make her case.

"All right! All right!" Julie said, attempting to quiet them. "Like Brynn said, I'm only supposed to submit two names." She picked up her ever-present clipboard from under her chair and tore off a page of blank paper. "I'll write everyone's name down on strips of paper, and then we'll pick—sound fair?"

Natalie and Grace and a few others nodded their approval, but Jenna's heart sank. Her name was *never* pulled out of hats or barrels or bowls. She was just not lucky with those things.

"Sarah? Can I borrow your hat?" Julie asked when she was done tearing paper and writing names.

Sarah pulled off her Red Sox cap, her ponytail flopping through the hole in the back, and handed it to Julie. All the names were dumped in the hat, and then Julie shook it up.

"Alex, since you were the first to gracefully bow out, how about you do the honors?" Julie asked, holding the hat out to Alex, who was sitting to her right.

Alex sat up straight and made a very serious face as she dipped her hand into the hat. Jenna held her breath. Alex unfolded the first strip of paper and held it up for everyone to see. "Chelsea," she said.

"Yes!" Chelsea cheered.

So unfair, Jenna thought. *Why should a newbie get to be on the committee and not me? At least I've been to these things before.*

Julie shook the cap again, and Alex put her hand inside.

Please just say Jenna, please just say Jenna, please just say—

"Jenna!" Alex announced.

"No way!" Jenna blurted, causing everyone to laugh. Alex leaned over to high-five her, and Jenna slapped her friend's hand. She couldn't believe it. Her name had actually been chosen! She was going to be on the planning committee!

"So Chelsea and Jenna will represent us," Julie said, dumping out the rest of the names and handing the hat back to Sarah. The rest of the bunk sat back, disappointed.

"Don't worry, you guys. We'll all come up with ideas, and then Chelsea and I can give them to the committee," Jenna suggested.

Everyone brightened a bit at this plan, and Julie grinned. "Now that sounds fair, doesn't it?"

"Yeah," Grace replied, chorused by the others. "Thanks, Jenna."

"No problem," Jenna said, her mind already brimming with possibilities. She couldn't wait to put her own personal touch on the camp-wide social. Now all she had to do was figure out what her personal touch would be.

▲ ▲ ▲

"I can't believe Chelsea got picked," Brynn complained

as she, Jenna, Alex, and Grace walked back to the bunk together after dinner. "She's a newbie. Julie should have done it by seniority."

"You only think that because I said no, and then you and Jenna would have been after me in line," Alex said.

Jenna, Brynn, and Alex would have been at the same point in line, actually, but Jenna didn't bother to point that out. They all knew it, anyway.

"So?" Brynn said, kicking at a stone on the walkway.

"Don't worry, Brynn. Like I said, if you have any ideas, I'll bring them up at the meetings," Jenna told her.

"Good, because I have about a million," Grace put in, fiddling with her colorful plastic rings. "We could have a fifties theme! You know, like *Grease*? Or like a *Gone with the Wind* theme? Like a Southern ball? Ooh! Or maybe it could be a Mardi Gras theme! I went to Mardi Gras with my aunt and uncle one year, and it was so cool! Well, I didn't get to see a lot of it because I had to go to bed early, but in the morning there were beads *everywhere*."

"Good ideas," Jenna said. "Maybe you should write them down or something so I remember them."

"Totally!" Grace said, putting a little skip in her walk that made her crazy red curls bounce all around. "I'll do it when we get back."

"Just make sure you give it to Jenna and not Chelsea," Brynn suggested. "I don't trust that girl yet."

"That reminds me," Alex said, walking backward to look at Jenna. She glanced around at the other random campers walking and talking nearby and lowered her voice. "Whatever happened to the initiation prank?"

Jenna blinked. She couldn't believe it. She had entirely forgotten about the initiation prank this year! *Wow. I've been* really *distracted*, she thought.

"Yeah! What about that? You did it to me, Jessie, and Candace last year," Grace said.

"And Val and Sarah and the others two years ago," Brynn added.

"Yeah. Everyone in the bunk who came after us has been a victim at some point," Alex pointed out. "Don't Chelsea, Nat, and Alyssa need to be initiated, too?" she added, raising her eyebrows.

Jenna glanced over her shoulder at Natalie and Alyssa, who were walking with Valerie, Jessie, and Sarah, gabbing about the social. Now that she knew them so well, she wasn't sure she wanted to prank Natalie and Alyssa. They didn't feel as new to her anymore. They were already her friends.

"Maybe I waited too long," Jenna said.

"Hey! Don't wuss out on us," Brynn said. "It's a tradition."

Jenna caught a glimpse of Chelsea now, who was walking with Simon, Eric, and Adam, tossing her hair and flirting. Ew! Flirting with *Adam*? And even worse, Adam was smiling and laughing. He seemed to be *enjoying* it.

Maybe some newbies *did* need to be pranked.

"All right," Jenna said, her eyes sparkling with mischief as she turned back to her friends. "Let's do it."

"When?" Alex asked, her dark eyes bright with excitement.

"Why wait?" Jenna said, a skitter of excitement racing over her skin. "Tomorrow we make a plan. And tomorrow night, the newbies get initiated."

chapter THREE

The next morning, Jenna stood on the edge of the wooden planks that made up the beginner's diving pier at the Lakeview lake. The sky was a gorgeous blue with just a few whispy-white clouds. The sun was hot on her shoulders and all around the lake, campers laughed, splashed, and squealed, having the time of their lives. Across the water, in the deep end, the senior boys and girls were doing relay races while their friends shouted encouragement from the sand. Jenna watched them, wishing she were over there having fun instead of standing over the rippling water, terrified.

In the water below Jenna, Chelsea and Alex dog-paddled, having already made their dives. Behind her were a bunch of other boys and girls in her swim skill level, all gossiping and messing around while they waited their turns. Everyone was happy and relaxed and looking forward to that night's movie-night viewing. Everyone except Jenna.

The water looked so far away. Even though she could probably reach down with her toe and touch the cool surface of the lake, it still looked so far. Was she really supposed to launch herself from the safety of the platform and crash headfirst into the water? What if there was something down there? Like a rock? She could crack her head open and die and her body would sink to the bottom of the lake and no one would ever find her and—

Sometimes having a good imagination really stinks, Jenna thought.

The whole camp was divided up into colors according to their swimming ability. Those who were just learning to swim were reds and had to stay in the shallow end. Those who could swim but weren't experts yet and couldn't dive were yellows, like Jenna. Those who could dive and were practicing for their deep-end swim test were greens. The experts, who had passed the final test and could do it all, were blues.

At the end of last summer, Adam had accelerated right through green and straight to blue, and Jenna had been totally jealous. Not many eleven-year-olds were blues, and it killed her that Adam was so far ahead of her. But staring at the water just then, she felt she wouldn't have minded staying a yellow forever.

"Okay, Jenna, just put your hands together over your head like a V," Tyler Bernal, the swim instructor, told her. He was in the lake, one hand holding onto the ladder to the pier, the other treading water.

Tyler was new to camp this year, and with his curly dark hair, tanned skin, and killer smile, every girl at Lakeview was in love with him—especially Jenna's sister Stephanie. Half the camp was whispering about the possibility that Tyler and Stephanie would be a couple before summer's end. Even Jenna thought Tyler was pretty cool. But if he really made her dive headfirst into this lake, that opinion was going to change.

Jenna did as she was told, but her knees were shaking so violently, they were actually knocking together. This was something Jenna had thought only happened in cartoons.

"Good, now bend forward toward the water," Tyler instructed.

Jenna bent at the waist. She felt like she was going to throw up. This whole feeling was new to Jenna. Normally she wasn't scared of anything.

"Come on, Jenna! You can do it!" Alex called out from the water, clearly sensing her terror.

"Good, now bend your knees a little, tuck your head, and dive," Tyler said.

You make it sound so easy, Jenna thought. *Like I'm not about to die.*

"Okay, Jenna, on the count of three," Tyler prodded gently.

Jenna squeezed her eyes shut. She could hear the first-year campers giggling and splashing at the shallow end of the lake. She could hear the water lapping against the platform. She could hear Tyler counting up.

"One . . ."

I can do this, I can, Jenna told herself. Though her pounding heart didn't seem to agree.

"Two . . ."

I can. I can. I can . . .

"Three!"

Jenna opened her eyes, saw the water, and panicked. She stumbled back from the edge of the platform, and her bare heel caught in one of the grooves between the boards.

Luckily, Grace caught her before she could fall on her butt.

"Are you okay?" Grace asked, pulling off the little nose clip she always wore for swimming.

"I can't," Jenna heard herself say, shaking her head. "I can't do it. I just can't."

Tyler was out of the water in an instant, walking over to her with his red swim trunks dripping all over the planks. "It's okay, Jenna. You don't have to do it today," he said. "We can work on it some more."

"Yeah, don't worry, Jenna. You don't have to do it today," Candace said, repeating Tyler's words like she always repeated everyone's. "It's no big deal."

"Remember last year? It took me, like, forever before I could even put my head under the water," Grace reminded her. "I felt like such a total freakazoid! But you were the one who told me to just take my time, and by the end of the summer, I was swimming."

Jenna's heartbeat started to return to normal, and she managed to smile at her friends. They were right. She didn't have to get everything on the first try, did she? Besides, she was the best softball player in the bunk and the best kickball player. She didn't have to be great at *everything*.

Just when she was starting to feel better, Chelsea and Alex stepped up from the ladder.

"Omigosh! You looked hil-*ar*-ious standing up there all shaking," Chelsea said, holding her stomach as she laughed. "I can't believe Jenna Bloom is afraid of diving!"

"Chelsea!" Alex said reprovingly.

Jenna's cheeks reddened in embarrassment.

"You know you're not going to move up to green if you can't dive—right, Jenna?" Chelsea said. "You'll be stuck in the kiddie end next summer while we're all hanging out over here."

"Like I really want to hang out with you," Jenna shot back. Why did Chelsea have to be so mean? And only some of the time. If she were mean *all* of the time, at least Jenna and the others would always be prepared, but it was like one second she was a completely normal friend and the next second she was being a total jerk.

"All right, girls. That's enough," Tyler said, putting his hands on Chelsea's shoulders and steering her to the back of the line. He rejoined Jenna and crouched next to her. "Check it out," he said, lifting his chin toward the next platform where the diving boards were.

Jenna watched as her brother Adam climbed the five steps to the mid-level board, walked confidently to the edge, and dove off. He barely made a splash when he hit the water. All his buddies and some of the other blues cheered for him when his head popped up again. Even Sarah, who had been in blue forever, and Natalie, who had been put in blue right away after taking her swim test, applauded for him. Adam's grin was practically blinding.

"If your brother can do it, you can do it—right?" Tyler said.

Jenna swallowed hard. There it was again, the Bloom Curse. Now she felt like an even bigger loser because Adam was so far ahead of her. Back when Grace couldn't duck under the water, everyone was patient and cool about it. But now, if Jenna didn't catch up with Adam, everyone would tease her for being so far behind her brother. It was so unfair.

"Want to try it again?" Tyler asked.

Jenna shook her head. "No."

"You sure?" Tyler asked.

"Can't we just do it at the next lesson?" Jenna asked. She crossed her fingers behind her back and added, "I'm sure I'll be ready by then."

"Yeah. I'm sure she'll be ready by then," Candace echoed.

"Okay," Tyler said, standing up again. Jenna felt

relieved that he was no longer staring her straight in the eye. "Why don't you sit with your feet in the water while the rest of the campers take their turns? When we're done we'll all go for a swim."

Jenna nodded silently and sat on the edge of the pier. She stared down at the surface of the lake as she swirled her legs around, keeping her back to the diving platform. The last thing she wanted was to have to keep watching her brother show off his skills. For the first time in her life, Jenna couldn't wait for swim period to be over.

▲ ▲ ▲

Jenna sighed as she used her fork to make crisscross designs in her puddle of ketchup. Lunch was almost over, and most of the girls in her bunk were gathered around a new magazine Marissa had gotten in the mail, taking a quiz titled "What's Your Style Personality?" Jenna was so not interested.

"Want my Tater Tots?" Alex asked from the seat across from Jenna.

Jenna eyed the pile of potatoes that were left on her friend's plate. Did this girl never eat? "Sure," she said, pushing her plate toward Alex's. Alex used her fork to shovel the Tots over to Jenna, who promptly drowned them in ketchup.

Alex glanced down the table. Once she seemed convinced that everyone else was occupied, she leaned in toward Jenna. "So, you were really scared this morning, huh?" Alex asked.

Jenna's eyes flashed, but then she looked at her friend and realized she wasn't teasing her. Alex's dark eyes were open and concerned. Jenna looked down at her plate.

"I just don't get how you do it," Jenna said. "I mean, you're *not* scared?"

Alex shrugged one shoulder. "Maybe I was the first time. A little. But once you do it once, it's no big deal."

"Really?" Jenna asked, doubtful.

"Yeah. It's actually fun," Alex said.

Jenna couldn't believe that one. How could something so terrifying turn out to be fun? But then, she supposed most of the older kids did laugh and mess around as they did their crazy dives. And when they came out of the water again, they were usually smiling like Adam had been that morning.

"I can help you during free swim if you want," Alex suggested. "Tyler said my dive was the straightest in the group."

The Tater Tot Jenna was munching on turned to dust in her mouth. Alex wasn't trying to make her feel better, she was just trying to show off. It was one more way for Alex to prove she was the better camper. She was about to tell Alex that she could handle her own diving when Marissa got up from the other end of the table, leaving the magazine with the other campers. She walked over and dropped down into the chair next to Jenna's.

"You guys were in such an intense conversation, I just *had* to see what was up," Marissa said, looking from Jenna to Alex. "So what's up?"

"I was just offering to help Jenna with her diving," Alex said.

"Oh, yeah. I heard about what happened this morning," Marissa said, looking at Jenna like she felt *so* bad for her.

It was all Jenna could do to keep from crawling under the table. "How did you hear about it?"

"Pete told me," Marissa said.

Jenna's jaw dropped. It wasn't surprising that Marissa had heard gossip from Pete. The two of them had been hanging out a lot this summer, and everyone suspected they might be dating. But she couldn't believe *Pete* had found out about it.

"How did Pete know?" Alex asked defensively, getting Jenna's back.

"I think Tyler told him," Marissa replied.

"Omigosh!" Jenna said, holding her head in her hand. "Everyone's talking about what a huge loser I am!"

"No! Jenna! It's not like that," Marissa said, putting her hand on Jenna's back. "I think Tyler was just asking for Pete's advice on how to help you."

"Great. So that just means that I'm so bad, even the swim instructor doesn't know what to do with me," Jenna said, slumping.

"Wow. Since when did you become so negative?" Marissa asked.

Since now, Jenna thought. *Or maybe it started before I left home to come here*. It had been pretty tough to stay positive for those last few weeks of the school year. Normally Jenna looked forward to camp even more than she looked forward to Christmas, but this year everything had been different. Even leaving for camp wasn't as fun as it normally was.

"Want to hear a secret?" Marissa whispered.

Both Jenna and Alex perked up. There was nothing better than a secret. They all leaned closer to the table.

"I was afraid to dive until I was thirteen," Marissa told them.

Jenna and Alex glanced at each other, disbelieving.

"No way," Alex said.

"Way," Marissa said. "I was so pathetic. I was light-years behind my friends."

"So what finally made you do it?" Jenna asked, eyes wide.

"Well, I was standing with the younger campers on the beginners' pier, still petrified to dive, when I saw Marcy Brachfeld flirting with Tommy Catherwood by the diving boards," Marissa said. "I had a huge crush on Tommy, and there was no way I was letting Marcy have him, so I closed my eyes and dove off. Two days later

Tommy was flirting with *me* by the diving boards," she added with a casual shrug.

Jenna and Alex giggled uncontrollably. "Okay, but I don't have a crush on anyone, so that's not going to make me dive," Jenna said finally.

"All I'm saying is, you never know what's going to get you over that hurdle," Marissa told her. "But I think that having Alex help you during free swim is a great idea. It'll be much less pressure than trying to do it with all the yellows watching. And I'll be there, too, if you want. As a former non-diver, I should support you."

"Yeah?" Jenna said, glancing from Alex to Marissa. Everyone in the bunk loved Marissa, and the idea of getting the CIT all to herself made Jenna smile. Well, not *all* to herself, since Alex would be there. But Marissa wanted to take time out to hang with Jenna. And that was pretty cool.

"Yeah," Marissa said. "But Jenna, you've got to want to learn, or you'll never be able to do it."

"I know," Jenna said halfheartedly.

"That doesn't sound like someone who wants it," Marissa said.

That's because I'm still scared out of my mind, Jenna thought. "I do," she managed to say. "I want to learn how to dive." *But only so Chelsea can't pick on me, and I won't be compared to Adam or get left behind next year.*

"Good," Marissa said, patting her on the back.

"Good," Alex repeated with a confident nod.

"Good," Jenna said, trying to smile. But she shuddered when she thought of the lake looming below her. Jenna would never admit it in a million years, but suddenly she wished her mom and dad were there.

chapter FOUR

"Jenna, you are a genius! Have I ever told you that you are a genius?" Grace whisper-giggled that evening.

"I know. I know. It's a gift, really," Jenna said with a shrug.

Jenna, Grace, and Alex were alone in the cabin with Marissa, who had turned on her Walkman and told them to pretend she wasn't there. Marissa knew what they were doing and, as a long camp legacy herself, had no problem with initiation pranks, as long as they were harmless. And of course, Jenna's initiation prank was always harmless.

Plus, it was fun. Messing around with Alex and Grace was even helping her forget about her awful afternoon. She, Alex, and Marissa had spent an hour on the pier, and Jenna hadn't done one dive. They were going to help her again tomorrow, but just thinking about it made Jenna ill. So she wasn't going to think about it.

"Here, put this in Chelsea's cubby," Alex said, handing Alyssa's art supplies to Grace. "Jenna, give me Chelsea's diary and I'll put it in Alyssa's cubby."

"Here. Hide it good and deep," Jenna said, handing over the glitter-covered book. She was still irritated with Chelsea for picking on her that morning at the lake. After that, Jenna was happier than ever that Alex had reminded her to pull the initiation prank. Chelsea *so* deserved it. "And let's put Natalie's makeup in Alyssa's, too," she added. "Oh, and give me that mix CD Alyssa's always listening to. We'll put it in Nat's."

"I mean, the way you got them out of the cabin!" Grace said, still giggling. "Telling them about the guys' nightly Wiffle ball game? That was perfect!"

"Yeah, especially for the guy crazies like Nat and Chelsea," Alex added, rolling her eyes. "I bet they're over there right now cheering on their favorite guys."

"Blech!" all three of them said in unison, sticking out their tongues.

"Yeah, but I thought Alyssa was never going to leave," Alex said, tossing Chelsea's favorite sandals into Natalie's cubby. "Brynn saved the day there."

"Totally," Jenna agreed.

At the last minute, when Alyssa had insisted for the tenth time that she did not have any interest in watching the guys play Wiffle ball, Brynn had stepped in and told her it would be a great story for the paper. The rivalry between Adam's bunk, 3F, and bunk 3E was almost as big as the one between Jenna's bunk and 3A. Tonight, 3F and 3E were playing each other during their free period, and Brynn had told Alyssa that she *had* to cover the game. Alyssa had finally, grudgingly, agreed and taken off with her pad and pencil. Jenna would really have to thank Brynn later.

Satisfied that they had switched up enough of the newbies' stuff to be confusing, Jenna slapped her hands together and turned around. Now for the best part: the beds.

"You guys do Natalie and Chelsea," Jenna said. "I'll get Alyssa's. The top bunks are always harder."

"This is going to be so great!" Grace said as she tore the sheets off Natalie's bed. "I can't wait to see their faces."

Jenna grinned. For the first time all day she was in a perfectly giddy mood, and there wasn't a thought of diving or siblings or anything else in her mind. There was nothing like a good prank to cheer her up.

That night, Jenna's heart pounded as she crawled into bed early and stayed near the edge, all the better to see the action. No one had noticed anything before dinner, and right after eating they had all gone to Classic Game Night in the main cabin. Sitting through several rounds of Coke and Pepsi, playing Red Rover with the guys, and watching the first-years go nuts during the Duck, Duck,

Goose tournament had seemed to take forever. All Jenna wanted to do was see how Alyssa, Natalie, and Chelsea reacted to their initiation. Now, it was showtime.

Jenna caught Alex's eye as Chelsea went over to her cubby. She had to slap her hand over her mouth to hide her smile as Chelsea dug through the stuff that clearly wasn't hers. "Hey! Has anyone seen my diary?" Chelsea asked.

"No," Natalie said, pulling a few things out of her own cubby. "Have you seen my monogram pajamas?"

"Why would I have seen those?" Chelsea asked as Alyssa stepped up behind her.

"Oh, I don't know. Maybe because you have my paint set in your cubby," Alyssa said, whipping the tin out and holding it up. "What are you doing with this?"

Jenna buried her face in her pillow to keep from laughing. She could hear Grace and Brynn in the bathroom, wheezing for breath as they listened in.

"I didn't take your paints," Chelsea replied. "You must have put them in the wrong cubby."

"Wait a minute. Whose is this?" Natalie asked, pulling a black T-shirt out of her own cubby and holding it up between two fingers.

"That's mine, too!" Alyssa exclaimed, grabbing it away. "What's going on around here?"

Chelsea stalked over to Alyssa's cubby, pushed some things aside, and pulled out her diary. "Oh! And you accused *me*!" she shouted at Alyssa. "Who said you could read my private thoughts?"

"Trust me, I didn't even know you had thoughts," Alyssa said flatly.

Natalie cracked up laughing, but Chelsea just blinked as the joke went over her head. Jenna pounded her fist into her bed, practically crying, she was laughing so hard.

Then Chelsea finally got the insult and started shouting at Alyssa, who shouted right back. Natalie jumped between them, trying to calm them down, but it soon grew into a three-way fight.

"All right! All right! What's going on in here!?" Julie said, storming in from the porch, where she had been talking to another counselor.

Natalie, Alyssa, and Chelsea tried to explain all at once, and Julie's face gradually broke into a smile. She glanced from Jenna to Alex to Brynn and Grace, who were now standing in the bathroom doorway. All of them shrugged innocently.

"I don't know what's so funny!" Chelsea said to Julie. "Alyssa's a thief!"

"Girls! Girls! Calm down!" Julie finally said, holding up her hands. "I think you've officially been initiated."

"Welcome to bunk 3C!" Jenna and the other girls shouted, gathering around the newbies, cheering and clapping.

Natalie and the others looked stunned. "What?"

"Sorry, Nat," Jenna said, looping her arm around

her friend's shoulder. "It had to be done."

"She's done it to all of us," Val explained.

"Except for the ones who started with us the first year," Alex explained.

"You're one of us now!" Grace shouted, hugging all three of the newbies in turn. "Congrats!"

Finally, Natalie, Alyssa, and Chelsea all seemed to get what was going on and started to smile.

"Omigod! I was ready to kill Alyssa for taking my diary," Chelsea said, covering her mouth.

"Not before I killed you for taking my paints," Alyssa replied, laughing as well.

"I *still* don't know where my pajamas are!" Natalie mock-whined.

"Here!" Jenna shouted, pulling them from the back of Alyssa's cubby and tossing them to Natalie.

"All right! Now let's everyone get to bed!" Julie announced. "The fun's over, and it's time for lights-out. You can sort your stuff out in the morning."

Everyone groaned, and Natalie, Chelsea, and Alyssa quickly changed into their pajamas. Jenna and the other veteran campers climbed into bed and waited. Julie only *thought* the fun was over.

Natalie pulled back her blanket. Alyssa climbed to her top bunk. Chelsea fluffed her pillow. And then they all shoved their feet in under their sheets.

"Hey!" Chelsea exclaimed.

"What the . . . ?" Alyssa said.

"You *guys*!" Natalie wailed.

"Short-sheeting!" Jenna, Alex, Brynn, and Grace shouted, tossing their pillows toward the new girls.

And then, no matter how much Julie protested, the pillow fight of the century was launched.

▲ ▲ ▲

"Okay, Jenna, what scares you the most about diving?" Marissa asked as she, Jenna, and Alex stood on the edge of the beginner's pier again the following afternoon.

"Everything," Jenna replied.

"It can't be *everything*," Alex said, crossing her arms over her chest.

"Okay, fine. I just don't get how you're supposed to go headfirst," Jenna said, gesturing toward the water. "The water is so far down. And doesn't it hurt?"

"It doesn't, I promise," Alex said. "You just need to do it."

Jenna was starting to get tense with Alex breathing down her neck. It seemed like her idea of helping Jenna was standing there telling her to just do it. She was like a walking, talking Nike ad. It was a good thing Marissa had offered to help. If the CIT hadn't been there, Jenna probably would have given up by now.

"Okay, how about this?" Marissa said. "Why don't you try jumping into the water feetfirst? You can do that, right?"

"Everyone can do that," Jenna said with a scoff, stepping to the edge.

Marissa reached out and touched her arm before she could jump. "But this time, I want you to pay attention to your feet. Really think about how your feet feel when they hit the water, okay?"

Jenna blinked. Think about her feet? Was Marissa losing it? "Um . . . okay," she said.

She jumped off the platform, closed her eyes, and concentrated on her feet. They hit the water, Jenna felt the splash, and then went under. The water rushed up around her, refreshing and cool. Jenna smiled as she swam back up to the surface. She really did love to swim. If only she could just avoid the diving.

"Well?" Marissa asked.

"Well what?" Jenna replied, paddling over to the ladder.

"Did it hurt? Did your feet hurt when they hit the water?" Marissa asked.

Jenna paused as she climbed, thinking about it. "No."

"So if it doesn't hurt your feet when they go in first, it's not going to hurt your head, especially when your hands are breaking the water first," Marissa said happily.

"Wow. She's good," Alex said.

Jenna couldn't have agreed more. Marissa definitely had a point. Why would diving hurt any more than jumping?

"Okay, but what if I hit a rock?" Jenna asked, pulling her wet bathing suit away from her stomach to make the sucking sound she loved and then letting it go.

"Did you even hit the bottom of the lake when you jumped in just now?" Marissa asked.

Jenna felt her face flush slightly. "Um . . . no."

"Well then you're not going to hit it when you dive," Marissa told her. "Besides, there are no rocks down there. It's all sand."

"Swear?" Jenna asked.

"Cross my heart and hope to never wear eyeliner again," Marissa said. She crossed her heart with her finger and held up a flat hand like a Girl Scout.

"And for her, that's serious," Alex said.

Marissa and Jenna laughed, and Jenna walked to the edge of the platform once more, looking down. Suddenly, the water didn't seem as far away. Her stomach was still full of nervous butterflies, but for the first time, she felt like she might actually be able to do this. Marissa had done it when she was scared. Even Alex had told her that she had been a little frightened on her first dive. If they could both do it, why couldn't she?

Jenna turned to Marissa and Alex with a smile. "Okay! I think I'm gonna—"

"Hey, Marissa!"

Jenna's face fell when she saw her sister Stephanie walking the planks toward them. She was wearing her new pink tankini and her hair was back in a perfect French braid.

"Hold that thought, J," Marissa said.

"What are you guys doing out here?" Stephanie asked, slipping on her Hollywood-style tinted sunglasses.

"We're helping Jenna with her diving," Alex announced.

Stephanie looked at Jenna sympathetically. "Oh, yeah, I heard about that, Boo." She stepped over and gathered Jenna's hair behind her head, running her fingers through it like Jenna's mother always did when Jenna was sad. Who did Stephanie think she was, Jenna's personal babysitter? This whole mothering thing was worse than ever this summer. "Anything I can do?" Stephanie asked. She stuck out her bottom lip slightly like she was talking to a pouting baby.

"Yeah. Stop calling me Boo," Jenna replied, stepping out of her sister's grasp.

"Oh, right! Sorry!" Stephanie said with a quick smile. She didn't actually seem sorry at all. "Listen, can I borrow Marissa for a sec? It's kind of important."

"Sure," Jenna said, mostly because Stephanie was already dragging Marissa aside.

"So, we *need* to talk about the social," Stephanie said.

"I know!" Marissa said. "We have to decide on wardrobe, makeup, and, most importantly—"

"Guys!" Marissa and Stephanie said at the same time, then giggled like a couple of crazy people.

Jenna and Alex looked at each other and rolled their eyes. It seemed like all the older girls talked about was which boys they liked and which boys liked them. Didn't they know there were about a million more important things in life? Like the fact that five seconds ago, Jenna had been ready to announce that she was going to take her first dive. Marissa was helping her with the most embarrassing problem of her life, and Stephanie had stolen her away. To talk about what? Stupid boys!

I'm never going to be able to dive now, Jenna thought, staring down at the water sadly. The moment of confidence had passed. She was back to being petrified. What had she been thinking?

"Hey! Here come the newbies," Alex said.

Natalie and Chelsea jogged toward the pier, both practically bursting, they were so excited.

"Omigod, you guys! You are never going to believe what just happened!" Natalie said, grabbing Jenna's arm. "Simon asked me to the social!"

"And Eric asked *me*!" Chelsea exclaimed.

Jenna's and Alex's jaw dropped. "What?" they both said in unison.

"I can't believe it! We have dates for the social!" Natalie trilled, grinning.

"Why?" Jenna asked. It was the only word in her head. "I mean . . . why?"

"What do you mean, why?" Chelsea asked with that superior look on her face. "It's a dance. You *have* to have a date for a dance or it's no fun."

"Uh, none of us has ever gone with dates before, and we always have fun," Alex said.

"Well, maybe things are going to be different this year," Chelsea replied.

Jenna could not believe it. Dates for the social? What was wrong with these girls? Why would they ever want to spend time with boys voluntarily? Jenna was forced to spend time with her brother and his friends all the time and it was just plain annoying. Plus, they were newbies and they were acting like the social was *their* thing. Like *they* knew how to make it fun. They had never even been to one before!

"Here they come!" Natalie whispered. "Act cool."

"Great. And your uglier half is with them," Alex joked.

Ugh! Could things get any worse? Adam, Simon, and Eric were all walking toward them, and Adam had that look on his face. That self-satisfied look he always got when he was feeling proud of himself about something. What had he done now, dove off the high dive?

Nat and Chelsea walked up to meet the boys and stopped a few feet up the pier. Alex shrugged and joined them while Adam stepped up to Jenna at the edge of the planks.

"Hey, Jen," Adam said. "Why so bummed? No date for the dance?"

"Like I want one," Jenna said. "Wait. Don't tell me *you* have one."

"Uh . . . no. No ball and chain for me," Adam joked. "So if it's not a guy, then what's with the face? You're all scrunchy."

"I don't know, it's like all anyone can talk about is the social. Like it's *so* important. Look at Stephanie," Jenna grumbled, glaring at her sister and Marissa over her shoulder. "Marissa was helping me out, and Stephanie came over to discuss wardrobe and guys or whatever and now it's like I'm invisible."

"You could never be invisible!" Adam said. "Especially not in that bathing suit," he added with a laugh, eyeing her yellow and pink Hawaiian-print tank.

"Shut up!" Jenna shot back.

"Okay! Okay!" Adam said. "God! Freak out a little more, why don't you? What's the big deal?"

Jenna glanced at Stephanie and Marissa, laughing and whispering. The big deal was Marissa was supposed to be hanging out with *her*. But once again one of her siblings had to come along and ruin her afternoon for her. And now Adam was here to rub salt in the wound. "Just forget it," Jenna told Adam.

"Well, if you want help with your diving, I can help you," Adam offered.

Like I really want my twin brother coaching me. How

humiliating, Jenna thought. "Thanks, anyway," she said.

"Come on, Jen, I'm already at *blue* level," Adam said. "I can help."

"Oh, you're so cool," Jenna said, annoyed. "You're already at blue level." *I would* kill *to be at blue level*, she added silently.

"I'm sorry I'm ahead of you, all right? But if you don't learn how to dive, you're going to be stuck back here in yellow while the rest of your friends move on to green and blue," Adam said.

Like I don't know this, Jenna thought, heat prickling at the back of her neck. Why couldn't everyone just leave her alone? Why did they have to keep reminding her of what a failure she was?

I want to call Mom, Jenna thought, then felt like a big baby. Her mother had plenty of other things to worry about this summer. She didn't need her daughter calling her up to whine about diving like she was some kindergartner.

"Come on. I'll practice with you," Adam said.

Why did everyone feel the need to push her? All it did was make her feel worse. Jenna had to get out of there before she did something embarrassing. Like burst into tears. Thinking about her mother had already made the hot prickling move into her eyes. The last thing she wanted to do was cry in front of everyone.

"Thanks, anyway, but I . . . uh . . . I kind of need to go to the bathroom right now," Jenna said, backing up. It was the first excuse that came to mind.

"Jenna—"

"Really, Adam," Jenna said, turning. She was so frustrated, and somehow, even with all these people around, she felt really alone. "I gotta go."

She turned and jogged to the beach, grabbing up her board shorts and flip-flops from the end of the pier. Jenna would have loved to have run back to the bunk and cry her eyes out, but she wasn't allowed to leave the lake area during free swim. Some of the girls from 3C were lounging over by the first-aid shack. Jessie and Grace both had their noses buried in books while Candace, Valerie, and Alyssa flipped through magazines. Everyone else was swimming in the shallow end, but she couldn't face her friends when she was all red-eyed and upset. Instead, she headed for a huge oak tree behind the water sports cabin, which also housed the bathrooms. She dropped to the ground in front of it, pulled her knees up under her chin and hugged them to her.

I am so sick of my brothers and sister, Jenna thought, burying her face behind her legs. *Next year I'm going to a different camp. Or better. I'll make Mom and Dad send all of them to a different camp.*

"Jenna? Are you okay?"

Sniffling quickly, Jenna was surprised to find Chelsea hovering over her. Had she actually left the precious boys to see if Jenna was all right?

"I'm fine," Jenna said grouchily.

Chelsea tucked her blond hair behind her ear and

sat down next to Jenna. After two weeks at camp, Chelsea already had a deep tan, and the freckles across the bridge of her nose were more defined. She was wearing a baby blue bathing suit that brought out the stunning color of her eyes. In fact, Jenna now realized that all of Chelsea's bathing suits were blue, and for the first time she wondered if Chelsea had matched her eyes on purpose. Jenna looked down at her own bright suit. Matching her clothes to her eyes was something she never would have thought of doing. But that was Chelsea.

"Hey, I'm sorry I picked on you the other day," Chelsea said, putting her arm around Jenna. "I didn't know it was such a big deal."

"It's not," Jenna replied automatically.

"Okay," Chelsea said quickly.

They both stared at the ground for a moment. Jenna watched a trail of ants returning to their anthill in a perfect line.

"I am *so* glad I don't have a brother," Chelsea said finally.

"Adam is such a jerk," Jenna replied. " 'I'm in blue, you know.' Like we don't *all* know he's ahead of the rest of us."

"He's so obnoxious," Chelsea agreed. "We need to get back at him."

Jenna lifted her head fully for the first time. Chelsea's eyes gleamed with mischief. "Get back at him? How?"

"Nothing big," Chelsea said with a shrug. "Just a small, innocent prank—like the one you pulled on us last night. To remind him who he's dealing with."

Jenna smiled slightly. A prank. Yes. That would make her feel better. Pulling a prank always made her feel better. It would take her mind off diving, off Adam and Stephanie, off her parents. She grinned at Chelsea. Just yesterday Jenna had been beyond mad at the girl for picking on her fear of diving, but suddenly that didn't matter anymore. If there was one thing Chelsea would be good for, it was pranking. She was fearless and smart. And she didn't care what anyone else thought of her, which could be a pain sometimes, but it made her the perfect partner in crime. And that was exactly what Jenna needed at the moment.

"We need a plan," Jenna said. "A really, *really* good one."

chapter FIVE

Chelsea and Jenna stood in the bunk bathroom that evening, huddled in the corner by the second toilet. It had started to drizzle outside toward the end of free swim, and the light rain tapped against the windowpane above their heads. As always, the rain brought out the slight moldy smell of the bathroom and made the air thick. Out in the bunk, the rest of Jenna's friends killed the free time before dinner by writing letters to their parents and friends. Jenna, however, was doing what she did best: plotting.

"Are you sure you can do this?" she asked Chelsea under her breath. "I can, if you want me to. I can fake it better than anybody."

"Come on, Jenna. Julie's never going to believe you have a stomachache," Chelsea said. "You're you."

"Yeah. I guess I have used it too many times," Jenna said, checking her plastic watch. "Okay, we gotta do it now or we won't have time."

"Let's go," Chelsea said with a nod.

Jenna lifted a twenty-ounce bottle of Sunkist her dad had sent in a care package. She nodded at Chelsea, who coughed so that no one would hear the hiss as she popped the bottle open. Then Jenna nodded again, and Chelsea started making some of the most convincing barfing noises Jenna had ever heard.

Stifling a laugh, Jenna quickly dumped the Sunkist into the toilet so it would sound like Chelsea was actually throwing up. When they heard an "Ew" and some movement in the bunk, Jenna tossed the bottle into the trash and Chelsea hit her knees, quickly flushing the toilet. Seconds later Julie appeared in the doorway with half the bunk gathered behind her.

"Who's sick?" Julie asked, her eyes darting to Chelsea.

Chelsea took a deep, heaving breath. Her hair stuck to her forehead as she looked up at Julie with heavy eyes.

"I don't feel so good," Chelsea said.

"She threw up. A lot," Jenna confirmed, doing her best grossed-out face.

Julie crouched next to Chelsea and pushed her hair back from her face. Jenna was impressed to see Chelsea swallowing hard and hanging her head. The girl knew what she was doing. If Jenna didn't know better, even *she* would have believed Chelsea was ill. Suddenly Jenna had a whole new respect for this particular new girl.

"Can you make it to the nurse's cabin?" Julie asked.

"I don't know," Chelsea said weakly.

"I'll take her," Jenna volunteered. As if the idea had just come to her.

Julie helped Chelsea to her feet, where she stood, leaning sideways slightly like she was about to fall over.

"Chelsea? Do you need me to go with you, or is Jenna okay?" Julie asked.

"No. Jenna's fine," Chelsea said, adding a burp. "You have to take everyone to dinner." She put her hand over her stomach and grimaced. "Ugh. Dinner."

"I'd better get her out of here before she ralphs again," Jenna said, wrapping her arm around Chelsea. Together they staggered to the bathroom door, where everyone parted to let them through.

"Here, you guys," Grace said, helpfully grabbing their windbreakers from the pegs by the door. "It's raining out, and you don't want Chelsea to get even sicker."

"Yeah, you don't want her to get even sicker," Candace repeated.

"Thanks," Jenna said, feeling a little guilty over Grace's concern and thoughtfulness. She and Chelsea struggled into their jackets and headed out into the drizzle.

"Feel better!" Val called after them.

Then the screen door slammed shut, and Jenna and Chelsea made their way around the bunk. As soon as they were safely out of sight, Jenna stopped pretending to hold Chelsea up and they took off at a run, heading for the mess hall. The plan was simple, but it had to be done within the next five minutes, or they were sure to get caught.

Jenna's heart pounded as her feet slammed along the muddy path through the woods. She loved this energized feeling she got whenever she was about to pull a prank. She was half-psyched, half-nervous, but couldn't stop grinning. When Jenna was pulling a prank it was like the rest of the world and all its problems melted away. All that was left was fun.

Chelsea emerged into the clearing behind the mess hall first. Jenna looked both ways. The coast was clear. They sprinted to the back of the building and leaned against the wooden planked wall.

"Whew. Made it," Chelsea said, wiping some rain off her cheek.

"I'll peek inside," Jenna offered.

As always, the back door to the kitchen was open to let the air in while the cooks slaved over the hot stoves. Ever so slowly Jenna checked around the side of the door. The three cooks and Pete were all standing at the huge silver stoves, talking and laughing as they stirred huge vats of torture food.

Ugh. Smells like beef Stroganoff, Jenna thought, scrunching up her nose. This would be one of those bread-only nights for her, but it was good news for the prank. Her brother *loved* that gooey brown mess.

"Jenna! Come on!" Chelsea whispered.

Pulse pounding in her ears, Jenna reached up to the shelf next to the door and grabbed down a five-pound bag of sugar. She was pressed back into the outside wall again before anyone was the wiser.

"It's so great how they keep all this stuff right by the door," Jenna said, hugging the bag to her. "It's like they're *asking* us to steal it."

"Okay, let's go," Chelsea said.

Crouching low below the windows, Jenna and Chelsea made their way around the side of the mess hall to the front. Mud splattered Jenna's sneakers, and rain dripped from her hood onto her nose. When they reached the door, Chelsea peeked inside and quickly jumped back. "The CITs are still setting the tables," she informed Jenna.

"Count to ten and check again," Jenna said.

Together, they counted up to ten Mississippis, then Chelsea checked.

"Okay! They're all back in the kitchen. It's now or never," Chelsea said.

They locked eyes, filled with excitement, then Jenna nodded. "Go!"

Jenna and Chelsea ran into the mess hall, right over to Adam's table. There were three sets of plastic salt and pepper shakers, and Jenna grabbed them all up while Chelsea slid under the table. Jenna joined her and opened the salt bottles while Chelsea ripped open the bag of sugar. They sat, cross-legged and facing each other. That was when Jenna noticed a snag in the plan.

"What do I do with the salt?" Jenna whispered, her heart pounding wildly.

"Oh, God! Why didn't we think of that?" Chelsea asked.

Jenna looked around and was hit with an idea. "My pockets!"

"Nice!" Chelsea replied.

Jenna quickly emptied all three salt shakers into her jacket pockets. Chelsea grabbed the bottles one by one and dipped them into the sugar bag to fill them.

"This is gonna be so great," Chelsea said with a snicker.

"I know!" Jenna whispered back.

Just as Jenna was replacing all the shaker tops, they heard the door from the kitchen bang open.

Jenna froze, a chill of fear sliding over her from head to toe. Chelsea grabbed her hand. Their palms were both covered in sweat—or maybe it was just rain.

Either way, Jenna could practically hear her friend's heart beating.

"You were supposed to make sure all the glasses from lunch got cleaned!" someone scolded. "What are we supposed to do with ten dozen dirty glasses?"

"Whatever. It's too late to do anything now. Don't say anything and no one will notice," another voice answered.

Jenna and Chelsea both stuck out their tongues. So much for drinking any bug juice tonight. The two sets of feet clomped right by their table and out the front door.

"That was close," Chelsea said.

Jenna nodded her agreement. "Let's get out of here."

They checked first to make sure the coast was clear, then quickly replaced all the salt and pepper shakers on Adam's table. It was all Jenna could do to keep from laughing out loud as they raced out the front door and turned their steps toward the nurse's cabin.

"Omigosh! This is going to be so funny!" Chelsea cried, dumping the rest of the sugar in the nearest garbage can.

Jenna shook the salt out of her pockets and it rained down, disappearing into the grass. "I know! Beef Stroganoff is bad enough, but beef Stroganoff with sugar? Gag me!"

"Come on! We have to get to the nurse's station and tell her I was sick but that the fresh air cured me," Chelsea said. "There's no way I'm missing this!"

They grabbed hands and ran for the nurse's station to cover their tracks in case Julie followed up with Nurse Helen later. Jenna could barely wait to get to dinner. So much for Adam thinking she couldn't pull a prank on him. He had no idea what was about to hit him!

▲ ▲ ▲

The key to getting away with a prank was to keep from laughing before everyone else did. Only the prankster herself would know to laugh *before* anything happened. Jenna had learned this when she had planted her first whoopee cushion on her teacher's chair, then cracked up before his butt hit the seat. He had stopped, found the cushion, and sent her directly to the principal's office. But even though she knew this very important rule, Jenna was having a very hard time keeping a straight face while Adam and his friends covered their dinner in sugar.

"I can't take it," Chelsea whispered in her ear. There was a laugh right on the edge of her voice. "I really can't take it."

"When are they going to eat it already?" Jenna replied.

"Are you okay down there, Chelsea?" Julie asked from the head of the table. "Only eat the bland stuff."

"Oh, I am," Chelsea replied, tearing off a piece of her white bread for good measure. Neither she nor Jenna had touched their drinks *or* their dinners. Later, after lights-out, they planned on raiding Jenna's candy stash to keep away the hungries until morning.

"Here we go," Jenna said into her napkin.

She and Chelsea stared as Adam, his friend Eric, and his counselor Nate all took their first bites of food. Adam's eyes bulged. Then he gagged. Then Eric knocked over Adam's bug juice while grabbing for his own, splashing the yellow liquid all over Adam.

"Hey!" Adam shouted, jumping up.

At that point, Jenna and Chelsea couldn't take it anymore. They cracked up laughing. Luckily, half the kids at Adam's table and the rest of the kids at neighboring tables were laughing, too. Spilled bug juice always got a big reaction.

Adam, meanwhile, seemed to forget his wet lap and remembered the taste in his mouth. He stuck his tongue out a few times like a frog and grabbed Eric's glass right out of his hands, chugging down half the bug juice.

Jenna nearly doubled over, she was laughing so hard. Chelsea had tears coming out of her eyes.

Before they realized what was going on, a couple of the other guys took huge mouthfuls of food. One of them grabbed his napkin and spit the beef into it. Another just spit it right back onto his plate.

"Ew!" Grace squealed.

"Ew!" Candace echoed.

"Pete! What's with the Stroge?" Nate called out. Nate had a habit of shortening any word with more than two syllables.

"Oh, that is so gross," Brynn put in as another of the boys tasted his dinner, then spit it out half-chewed.

Pete walked over to the table. "Problem, man?" he

asked Nate. "Did you salt it? You know you always gotta salt the Stroge."

Jenna and Chelsea laughed even harder. This was too perfect for words.

"Of course we salted it," Nate said.

Pete shrugged and bravely grabbed a fork to take a bite of Nate's food. His lips pursed, but he somehow managed to swallow. "Dude. That beef is covered in sugar," he said.

"Sugar?" Nate replied. He grabbed a shaker and shook some sugar into his palm, then tasted it. "I don't believe it."

Adam and Simon tested the other shakers. "They're all full of sugar," Simon announced.

"Oh, gross! Sugar on beef?" Alex said, sticking out her tongue. "Who would do *that*?"

Instantly everyone at the surrounding tables looked over at Jenna. Jenna and Chelsea stared back, their eyes wide with innocence.

"Jenna? Chelsea? Did you really go to the nurse's before dinner?" Julie asked, sounding weary.

"What? Julie! I was barfing. Of course we did," Chelsea said.

Julie narrowed her blue eyes. "You *have* made a stunning recovery."

"Nurse Helen said her lunch just didn't agree with her," Jenna told Julie. "You can ask her yourself."

"I think I will," Julie said as Pete and Nate started

clearing away all the plates of food from Adam's table. "And, Chelsea, don't take this the wrong way, but I hope, for your sake, that you actually were sick."

chapter SIX

"So, you guys did it, right? I mean, you have to have done it," Grace said, her eyes shining with excitement as she questioned Jenna a few days later. They were at their photography elective and since it was raining again, they were inside, working on printing the nature photos they had taken earlier in the week.

"Grace! Adam is *right there*!" Jenna said through her teeth. She was trying to feed the film through the negative carrier doohickey, and she kept getting it jammed. This photography thing wasn't as easy at it looked.

"So you did! I knew it!" Grace said with a grin. The rain had made Grace's curly hair frizz out, so she had tied it into two short braids. The hairdo and her excited face both made her seem about four years younger than she was.

Jenna glanced at her brother over her shoulder. Everyone she knew had been asking her the same question ever since beef Stroganoff night, but Jenna always denied it. The last thing she needed was for Julie to find out and punish her somehow, or for Adam to find out and fight back. But she was dying to tell someone that she had pulled it off. What good was pulling a prank if you couldn't take credit for your creativity? Luckily Adam was busy studying his film strips. He seemed to be taking this whole photography thing very seriously.

"Come on, Jenna. Tell me," Grace said. "I'm dying over here."

"Okay, yeah, we did," Jenna said with a sly grin.

Grace squealed in delight and slapped her hand over her mouth.

"But don't tell anyone!" Jenna added. "Nurse Helen backed up our story, but if Julie finds out, she's going to murder us."

"I'll never tell. Even if they torture me," Grace said with a grin. She kept giggling as she sorted through her film negatives, and Jenna knew that Grace was happy to be the only one let in on the prank. "Chelsea totally tricked me. I thought she was really sick."

"Yeah. Sorry about that," Jenna said, her guilt from the other day returning. "I felt bad for making everyone worry."

"Eh. It was Chelsea. We weren't *that* worried," Grace joked. Then her face fell. "Oh! That was mean! I was just kidding!"

"I know! I know!"

Jenna laughed and finally managed to get the film strip straight in the negative carrier, which was a flat plate with a slot in the middle.

"Grace? Can you read me the next step?" Jenna said over her shoulder.

Faith had given them all a list of the steps for printing photographs, and Grace had one on the table in front of her.

Grace looked down at the paper and shrugged. "Here," she said, handing the list to Jenna. "I . . . I don't know how much you've already done."

"Oookay," Jenna said, taking the page from Grace. She read the directions quickly and found the next step: *Insert negative carrier into enlarger.*

The enlarger looked kind of like a projector. She put the carrier into the machine. Then she turned on the light, and her picture appeared on the empty tray below.

"Wow! It actually works!" Jenna said.

Her picture was of a squirrel holding an acorn. She could see the image projected onto the tray in front of her. Jenna was sure that Faith, the photography instructor, had explained the science behind the whole process, but Jenna had zoned out during that part, replaying in her mind the scene of Adam choking on his beef Stroganoff.

She had been replaying the scene a lot over the last few days, actually. It was just so perfect!

Jenna focused her image so it would print as sharply as possible. Then she switched off the light so she could insert the photographic paper into the tray without exposing it. Once it was ready, she flipped on the light that was going to magically affix her picture to the paper. She sat back to wait. In her mind she saw Adam, hands grabbing for his throat in slow motion as he tasted his beef-with-sugar. She saw him gagging, saw Eric knocking over the bug juice, saw the splash and Adam's surprised face. Jenna only wished she could have videotaped the whole thing to show over and over and over . . .

"Jenna! What're you doing!?"

Startled out of her daydream, Jenna stood up to find Adam glaring at her. Oh, no! Had she zoned out so far, she had actually confessed to the crime or something?

"Your paper's not straight! Your picture's gonna be all crooked," Adam said, gesturing at her enlarger.

"Geez! Sorry, Mr. Perfect."

She undid the little flaps that held the paper in place and adjusted it.

"No! You can't move it once the light's already on!" Adam said, his eyes wide.

"Oh, right," Jenna said, remembering the instructions. Her face flushed, and she resecured the paper, but it was too late now. She had already moved it. What was going to happen to her photo?

"And how long has the light been on, anyway? Did you even set the timer?" Adam asked.

"The timer!" Jenna exclaimed. She had been so

focused on daydreaming about her prank, she had missed the most basic step. She reached over and turned the light off, and Adam shook his head like he just couldn't believe how stupid she was.

"What?" Jenna said, pulling her photo paper out of the tray. "I'm sure it's going to come out fine."

Trying to look more confident than she felt, Jenna walked over to the tubs of chemicals near the wall and slid her photo into the developing liquid. Much to her disappointment, Adam followed as if he was determined to see if she had messed up. Jenna snapped on a pair of plastic gloves and waited.

See? I remembered the gloves. I know what I'm doing, Jenna thought. *I paid attention!*

Grace joined Adam and Jenna at the developer and they all leaned in to watch as the image appeared. This was the best part, as far as Jenna was concerned. Watching Faith's photos magically appear during her demonstration had been totally cool.

"Which picture did you choose, Jenna?" Faith asked, joining them. Her small glasses were perched at the end of her nose, and her long brown hair was pulled back in a low ponytail. She wasn't much older than Julie and the other counselors, but she tried to make herself look like she was.

"It's a picture of a squirrel holding an acorn," Jenna said proudly. "I think it's really good."

That moment something started to appear on the

page, but it didn't look anything like a squirrel. At first, there was a big black blob right in the middle, surrounded by other fuzzy blobs that could only be the leaves and rocks the squirrel had been sitting on. Behind the center blob, there were a bunch of gray speckles. Then the image started to turn darker and darker.

Pressing her lips together, Jenna grabbed the photo out of the developer and put it into the stop bath, which was what they called the liquid in the next bin. At least she remembered that part.

"Oh, Jenna," Faith said. "It's okay. The great thing about having a negative is that you can try to print from it again and again until it comes out the way you want it."

"And you definitely didn't want it *that* way," Adam said.

"Don't listen to him," Grace said. "Your next one will be fabulous. I know it," she added, looping her arm around Jenna and sticking her tongue out at Adam.

Jenna couldn't have been more grateful for Grace's save, because she never could have said anything herself. She knew that if she opened her mouth, she was going to burst into tears. She stared down at her blackened photo, her face burning with embarrassment. For a veteran Lakeview camper who thought she knew how to do everything, Jenna was certainly getting a lot wrong lately. And she didn't like the way it felt.

▲ ▲ ▲

By that afternoon the rain had stopped, though the sky remained overcast. It was a little windy and chilly, but as long as there was no water falling from the sky, free swim was still on. As the rest of the campers streamed from their bunks, laughing and screeching, their towels billowing behind them as they ran for the lake, Jenna trudged behind her friends. It used to be that free swim was Jenna's favorite part of the day. Now she was just wishing the rain would come back so they could all hang out in the cabin and play cat's cradle and checkers and Clue. Jenna was starting to hate the lake.

"Cheer up, Jenna," Julie said, falling into step with her. "If the weather keeps up like this, at least we'll still get to have the scavenger hunt tonight."

Jenna brightened a bit as Julie quickened her steps to catch up with Marissa at the head of the crowd. Scavenger hunts were the best evening activity there was. And since Jenna knew the camp like the back of her hand, her group always completed their lists and brought home the blue ribbon.

"What's a scavenger hunt?" Natalie asked as she and Valerie caught up with Jenna.

"What's a scavenger hunt?" Jenna repeated, her jaw dropping. "You've never done one?"

"Um . . . no," Natalie said. "Doesn't sound like a New York kind of event."

"Omigosh, scavenger hunts are the best," Jenna said, warming to the topic. She loved being able to teach the newbies like Natalie about camp traditions. "You get this whole long list of things that you have to find, and whoever finds the most stuff on their list, wins."

"What kind of things?" Natalie asked, interested.

"Everything from a single acorn to a four-leaf clover to a napkin from the mess hall, or one of Pete's baseball caps," Jenna said. "It's different every year."

"Yeah, but last year we were the only ones to get one of Pete's caps," Grace added, joining the group. "Thanks to Jenna."

"You stole one of his caps?" Natalie asked.

"I would have, but he found out that they were on the list, so he hid them all," Jenna replied. "Not even his own bunk could find them."

"So how did you get one?" Natalie asked.

"She talked him into giving her one," Valerie replied, hooking her arm around Jenna. "The girl is good."

Jenna grinned as everyone agreed. It was the baseball cap that had helped them beat out bunk 4A last year and take first place.

"So? How did you talk him into it?" Natalie asked.

"Well, last year my big brother Matt was still a counselor here and he had these two tickets to that AlternaFest concert at the end of the summer," Jenna said. "Everyone knew he had them and that he hadn't decided who to bring yet, so I just told Pete that if he gave me the cap, I'd tell Matt how he had helped me out. Then Matt would think he was really cool and take him to the concert. After that, he finally gave in."

"Jenna? That's not talking him into it, that's bribery," Natalie said with a laugh.

"Whatever it was, it worked," Valerie said.

"So did Pete get to go to the concert?" Natalie asked.

"Nah," Jenna said. "Matt took his new girlfriend, Keira, but Pete said he understood because she was 'so totally hot,' " she added, doing her best Pete impression.

Everyone laughed as they reached the lake. As Grace and Valerie dropped their stuff, a couple of guys from 3F walked over to them.

"Hey, Val. You swimming?" one of them asked.

Valerie flushed and smiled. "Yeah. I'll be right in."

"Cool," he said. Then he and his friends turned and ran for the water.

"Who was that?" Jenna asked.

"His name's Christopher. He's a newbie," Val said. "He asked me to the social this morning."

Jenna's heart dropped. "*You* have a date, too?"

Val shrugged, and Grace groaned. "Everyone is going to have a date except me!" Grace said.

"No way," Jenna said. "*I* am not going to have a date, and neither is Alex or Sarah or any of us who haven't gone totally boingo bonkers."

"Yeah, Grace," Natalie said. "Don't feel like you

have to have a date or something. It's not a big deal."

"All right, but you have to swear that you will not have a date," Grace said to Jenna, her face more serious than Jenna had ever seen it. Apparently this whole date thing was really getting to her.

"I swear on my life I will not have a date," Jenna said.

Grace broke into a grin. "Thanks, Jenna. Come on, Val. Let's swim!"

Valerie and Grace raced to the water, but Jenna hung back. Natalie placed her bag on the ground and glanced at Jenna.

"You going in?" Natalie asked.

"I don't really feel like swimming," Jenna said. She wrapped her arms around herself, trying to look cold.

Natalie looked from her friends splashing in the water back to Jenna. "Do you want to practice diving? 'Cuz I could come with you."

Jenna instantly tensed. "That's okay."

"I learned how to dive when I was really young. My mom made me take lessons from the time I could, like, stand up," Natalie said. "It took me a while, too, but it's totally fun once you get into it. Maybe I could help."

"Why does everyone think I need help?" Jenna snapped, her good mood gone. Her arms dropped to her sides, and her fingers curled up into angry fists.

Natalie's face fell. "Well, I just—"

"I don't, okay? I don't need help from you or Adam

or anyone," Jenna said. "I just don't feel like swimming."

With that, she placed her towel down on the grass and sat, her knees pulled up under her chin. Natalie hovered for a second, but Jenna just stared out at the gray sky and the even grayer water. She couldn't believe that Natalie, a first-year camper, was offering to help her out with something. Jenna was a total veteran compared to her. *She* was supposed to be helping *Natalie* with stuff. Not the other way around.

"All right," Natalie said with a shrug. "I'll be hanging out with Simon if you change your mind."

Jenna stayed angry for only a few seconds as she watched Natalie join the boys and saw the rest of her friends doing gymnastic moves in the water. Then she started to feel awful. Jenna had practically bitten Natalie's head off, and Natalie had still left the door open for Jenna to ask for help. Natalie was so friendly, and Jenna had just treated her like a jerk. What was wrong with her?

Normally, Jenna was pretty easygoing, but she just couldn't seem to take it anymore. She couldn't take everyone reminding her of what a loser she was. She had thought that coming to camp would help her get her mind off the things that were going on back home, but it was like the longer she stayed here, the worse she felt. And the worse she felt, the harder it was to keep from showing it. The first two weeks of camp had been okay, getting to know new people and getting back into the swing of things, but the more she settled into her routine, the harder it was to act like everything was okay. All she wanted to do was go back to last summer, when camp was still fun—back when she knew what she was doing.

chapter SEVEN

After half an hour of sitting by herself in the sand, Jenna got bored and asked Tyler for a special pass to go back to her bunk. She told him she didn't feel well, and all he had to do was take one look at her sad face and he believed her. Normally campers weren't allowed to wander off by themselves, but Tyler took pity on Jenna. He told her that since she knew the camp so well, being a fourth-year and all, he would let her go, but she had to keep to the path and go straight back. For once, Jenna had no problem following a rule. At that moment, all she wanted to do was lie down on her bunk and sulk.

But as she cut through the woods, Jenna started to feel a little better. Here she was, walking back to her bunk all by herself. Natalie never would have been allowed to do that. She wasn't experienced enough and didn't know her way around. There were still perks to being Jenna.

High above, the sun started to break through

the clouds, causing the droplets of rain on the leaves to dance and sparkle. The birds in the trees woke up and started chirping as if it were morning and not late afternoon. Jenna passed by the rock where she, Alex, and Brynn used to hang out and trade gum when they were second-years. She saw the tree where Matt had carved his initials with the rest of his bunk. When she came to the edge of the clearing by the cabins, she saw the old, crumbling tool shed where she and her friends had hid last year after raiding the boys' cabin. This was Camp Lakeview, her home-away-from-home. It was impossible to stay depressed here for long.

Hey, maybe Marissa's hanging out in the cabin, Jenna realized suddenly, quickening her steps as she passed by the other bunks. Marissa and the other CITs usually got a break during free swim since they had to work meals and all other hours of the day. Hanging out with Marissa would cheer her up. Maybe Jenna could even get her to tell the story of her first dive again and try to get back some of that confidence.

Jenna bounded up the steps and yanked open the screen door, hoping to find Marissa on her cot, flipping through the latest copy of *Allure*. Instead, she found Marissa and Stephanie sitting cross-legged in the middle of the bunk floor, doing their nails. The whole bunk was filled with the sour scent of nail polish remover. Jenna stopped in her tracks.

"Hey! What are you doing here?" Marissa asked.

Her tone was totally normal, but the question made Jenna feel like an outsider in her own bunk.

"I didn't feel well, so Tyler said I could come back," Jenna replied.

"What's wrong?" Stephanie asked, her face all-concern. "Is it your stomach? Your head?"

"Don't worry about it, *Mom*," Jenna said, instantly grouchy again. "I just want to lie down." She so didn't want to be babied right now. Why did her sister have to be there? Couldn't Jenna ever get Marissa all to herself? Marissa was supposed to be Jenna's CIT. She was supposed to be here for *Jenna*, not Stephanie.

"Okay, but if you need anything, you just let me know," Stephanie said. "We Blooms have to take care of each other," she added with a wink.

Gag me, Jenna thought.

"You're lucky you have your sister at camp with you," Marissa told Jenna with a smile. "Especially since I never know what to do when campers are sick. I become Panic Girl. The not-so-super-hero," she joked.

"Yeah. So lucky," Jenna said flatly. "Nice polish, Marissa," she added, standing awkwardly off to the side. She wasn't sure whether she should join them or stick with her story and crawl into her bunk. Could she really just lie there while Marissa and Stephanie had fun without her?

"Thanks," Marissa said, snapping her gum as she held up her fingers to check them. "It's called Very Berry. Wanna try some?"

Jenna was about to say yes when Stephanie cut her off. "Oh, please. Polish is pointless on Jenna. She bites her nails to bits."

Flushing, Jenna hid her hands behind her back. Her nails *were* a little destroyed, but Stephanie didn't have to announce it like Jenna was some kind of joke.

"So, you're going to wear your red sundress?" Stephanie asked Marissa.

"I think so," Marissa replied. "And you have to wear that new mini. The boys will go speechless."

"You guys are talking about the social, aren't you?" Jenna asked, dropping onto Natalie's bottom bunk. "*Again.*"

"Like there's anything else to talk about around here," Stephanie said with a laugh.

How about we talk about you getting out of my cabin? Jenna thought, though she knew she'd never say it.

"So, Jenna, what are you going to wear?" Stephanie asked. "I hope you brought something cool this year."

Jenna's expression darkened. Was Stephanie trying to say she had looked like a dork at every other camp dance? Jenna thought of the lavender dress with the lace on the sleeves that she had brought for this year's event. When she had packed it she'd thought it was perfect, but with Stephanie and Marissa talking about red dresses and denim minis, now it just seemed way too babyish.

"Who cares what I wear?" Jenna said. "It's just the stupid camp dance."

"Social," Marissa and Stephanie reminded her, then laughed as if there was some kind of personal joke between them.

"Whatever," Jenna said, finally giving up. She climbed up into her bunk and lay down on her side, on top of the covers. Staring at her colorful collection of bumper stickers that were taped to the wall, Jenna fumed over her sister. Who did she think she was, criticizing her clothes and trying to take care of her like a mother? And why did she have to hang around Jenna's bunk so much? Couldn't she just leave her alone?

Jenna sighed. She reached out and flattened the bent corner on her Six Flags Great Adventure sticker.

I should prank her next, she thought as she listened to her sister and Marissa discussing all the CITs and counselors at camp, predicting who would kiss by the end of the summer and which couples would break up. Totally boring. *Oh, yeah, Stephanie is in total need of a pranking*, she thought. *If only because it'll give her something else to talk about!*

▲ ▲ ▲

"Where are they?" Jenna asked, bouncing up and down on the balls of her feet.

"I don't know, but I'm getting worried," Alex said. "3A just ran by, and they looked psyched."

"We cannot let 3A win," Brynn said. "We just can't."

It was the middle of the scavenger hunt, and Jenna

and the rest of her bunk were waiting for Val, Sarah, and Grace to return from the sports shed. At Jenna's feet was a pillowcase full of items from the list. All they needed to complete it were a horseshoe, which Val and the others were getting, and the last bonus item, which even Jenna hadn't figured out how to get. Not yet, anyway.

"There they are!" Natalie cried, pointing toward the edge of the woods.

Sure enough, Valerie, Grace, and Sarah were all running toward them, red-faced and gasping for air.

"We got it! We got the last horseshoe!" Valerie whispered.

"Did 3A get one?" Chelsea demanded.

"Yeah," Sarah said, bending at the waist. "They got there right before us."

"Now we *have* to get this last item to win," Jenna said, holding up the list. "But how are we supposed to get a picture of the top of a counselor's head?"

"What kind of scavenger hunt *is* this?" Alyssa asked.

"Yeah! What kind of scavenger hunt *is* this?" Candace echoed.

"An unfair one," Sarah said, gesturing at a couple of counselors as they walked by. "They all saw the list beforehand, so they're all wearing hats. We can't get a picture of the top of their heads if they won't take their hats off."

"We can't even get a picture," Jenna pointed out.

"We don't have a camera! I have to return mine to the lab after each class."

"Jessie has a camera," Karen piped up. "A Polaroid."

Everyone turned to look at Jessie, who was leaning against the flagpole, staring off into space.

"You have a Polaroid camera?" Chelsea asked, nudging her.

Jessie blinked a few times as if she'd just woken up. "Oh . . . yeah. I forgot about that."

Jenna and Alex exchanged a glance. What a space case! She was holding onto the one item that might help them win, and she just forgot about it?

"Let's go!" Alex said.

Together the whole bunk ran back to their cabin. On the way they saw a bunch of boys from 2E trying to jump up and grab Nate's hat off his head. As far as Jenna could see, they didn't even have a camera, but it didn't matter, anyway. Nate was dodging and weaving and ducking and running. He wasn't letting them anywhere near his head. Back at 3C, Jessie dug through her cubby until she found the unused camera. Luckily there was a whole cartridge of film in it.

"Great. Now all we have to do is come up with a plan," Brynn said.

"What if we just tackle one of them?" Grace suggested breathlessly. "We could tackle Julie and hold her down and take her hat and—"

"I don't think we should gang-tackle Julie," Alex said. "We have to live with her for the rest of the summer. But we do have to get one of them down low so we can grab their hat."

"And then *we* need to get up high so we can take the picture," Valerie pointed out.

"We just need to get creative here, people," Alyssa said, biting her lip.

Get them down low and get us up high, Jenna thought.

Suddenly she was hit with a brilliant idea. "I've got it, you guys! I know what to do!"

▲ ▲ ▲

"Um . . . Jenna? Nat? Don't you think this is kind of dangerous?" Jessie whispered as they tiptoed their way through the storage room on the second floor of the main cabin.

"Come on, Jess! Don't you want to win?" Jenna asked, sidestepping a very dusty stack of ancient board games. What in the world was Uncle Wiggly, anyway?

"Yeah, but um . . . I'm kind of afraid of heights."

Outside, a bunch of girls squealed and a few other people applauded. Time was running out. They had to get this last item before someone else won the scavenger hunt.

"Don't worry. Natalie and I will do it," Jenna said. "Right, Nat?"

"I grew up in a skyscraper," Natalie said, determined. "No problem."

They got to the window above the cabin's front porch, and Jenna undid the latch. Her pulse pounded in her ears, and she pulled up on the old window. It wouldn't budge.

"I don't think this thing has ever been opened," Jenna said.

"Here. Let's all try," Natalie suggested.

Together, the three girls gripped at the bottom of the old window and suddenly, without warning, it flew open, slamming into the top of the frame. Jenna and her friends froze, but luckily someone outside shouted at the exact same moment. It didn't seem like anyone down below had heard.

"No screen. Thank goodness," Jessie said.

"Okay, Nat. Let's go," Jenna said.

"Good luck, you guys!" Jessie whispered.

Jenna was the first to crawl out. She placed her foot on the roof of the porch's overhang and carefully put all her weight on it. The roof was sturdy as could be, and she realized she had been silly to worry. Matt had once told her that he and the other counselors sometimes snuck out here to look at the stars. Of course it would hold her.

"We're good. Come on," Jenna said to Natalie.

Natalie swung her leg over the windowsill and followed Jenna out. They crept to the edge of the roof and lay down on their stomachs to stay out of sight. Jenna picked her head up carefully and saw Alex signal her from the trees across the way. Jenna lifted her hand in response, and Alex nodded.

"Here we go," she said to Natalie.

Giggling, they pulled themselves forward so they could see over the edge of the roof. Down below, Pete, Tyler, Marissa, and Stephanie were all hanging out, each wearing a baseball cap. A bunch of boys from 5F ran by, and the counselors cheered them on. They were followed by four very familiar faces.

"Here they come!" Natalie whispered.

Jenna held her breath. Valerie, Karen, Grace, and Chelsea all came running into view, right in front of the counselors. Val was holding the horseshoe again. A little touch to make it look real. It had been Alex's idea.

"Get ready," Natalie whispered.

Jenna propped the camera up and focused in on Tyler's head. One of these counselors was going down.

"We got it!" Valerie shouted again. "We got the last horseshoe!"

Just then, Karen tripped and fell right in the dirt in front of the counselors. Everyone stopped.

"Omigosh! Are you okay?" Chelsea asked.

And then, Karen started to wail. "My ankle! My ankle!" She even produced actual tears. Jenna and Natalie looked at each other. Little, quiet, mousy Karen was not a bad actress.

"She's like a secret weapon," Natalie said, her eyes bright.

"No joke," Jenna replied.

Instantly, all the counselors rushed to Karen's side. Tyler crouched down next to her and pulled her shoe off.

"Karen? Can you move it at all?" Marissa asked.

At that second, Alex and Sarah sprinted out of the trees across the way. Before anyone could even look up, Alex snatched the baseball cap off Tyler's head and Sarah got Pete's. Jenna snapped the picture, ripped the print from the side of the camera, then snapped another for good measure.

"Hey!" Pete shouted at Sarah.

"Where did you come from?" Tyler cried.

But Alex and Sarah were already sprinting away, followed by the rest of the bunk, who poured out of the trees, laughing and whooping all the way.

"Oh my God! We did it! I can't believe we did it!" Natalie cheered.

All the counselors looked up, and their jaws dropped when they saw Natalie and Jenna holding the camera triumphantly above their heads. Down below, Karen stood up, took a little bow, and raced off with Val, Grace, and Chelsea. Her ankle was totally fine.

"Hey! She didn't even hurt herself!" Pete shouted, picking up his hat from the ground where Sarah had tossed it. "Foul! Foul!"

But he was laughing. They all were. The counselors knew when they had been outsmarted, and they appreciated a game well-played.

Jenna held the pictures in front of her as they came into focus.

"Did they come out?" Jessie asked from the window.

"They're perfect!" Natalie announced. "We got both of them!"

"We are so awesome!" Jenna cheered, and she and Natalie stood up and hugged. "Ha-ha! Bunk 3C rules!"

"Jenna Bloom!" Stephanie shouted up. "Get down from there! You'll kill yourself!"

"Oh, I'm coming down!" Jenna shouted back. "We have a scavenger hunt to win!"

chapter EIGHT

By the time the bugle sounded to wake the camp the following morning, Jenna was still glowing from her bunk's scavenger hunt victory *and* she had a perfect prank in mind for Stephanie. The only problem was, she had no idea how she was going to pull it off. The planning was going to require some inside knowledge—some info even Jenna didn't have. And the even bigger problem was, the only people who could help her were the girls in Stephanie's bunk. The dreaded bunk 3A.

At breakfast, Jenna glanced over at the table where Stephanie was sitting with her campers, trying to figure out which one of the girls might help her. Danielle? No, everyone knew she was a total jerk. Christa? Not likely. That girl talked even less than Karen did. Ashley? No way. She had hated Jenna ever since Jenna planted that frog under her pillow two summers ago. Of course Jenna had only done it because 3A had short-sheeted all the beds in 3C. It was all just part of the rivalry.

"Jenna, why do you keep staring at 3A like that?" Alex asked toward the end of breakfast.

"She's probably trying to send them psychic 'I hate you' messages," Grace joked, munching on her toast.

Brynn, Valerie, and Alex all giggled, throwing dirty looks at the other table. Jenna wasn't even sure when the war between the bunks had started. It was as if it had always been there.

"Oh! Leave the poor girls alone!" Brynn said, pretending to be sympathetic. "They're probably still all boo-hooing about how we beat them in the hunt last night."

"Yeah, we did!" Jenna cheered, high-fiving with her friends and letting out a little cheer. Bunk 3C had been the one and only bunk to get the bonus photo and had brought back the blue ribbon for the third year in a row. 3A had been on top until Jenna's bunk had raced in with the pictures just before the time had run out. Victory was sweet, but it was even sweeter when your lifelong enemies ended up moping all night.

"They're such losers," Alex said, rolling her eyes.

"I don't know. Some of them aren't that bad," Alyssa put in. "Like that girl Regina? She works on the paper with us, and she's really funny."

"Oh. My. Gosh. You did not just say that," Val said, dropping her hand to the table.

"Only a newbie would *ever* say that," Alex put in.

"You cannot like a 3A girl, Alyssa. It's, like, totally

against the code," Chelsea said. Even though she was a newbie herself, she seemed to live for the rivalry as much as the veterans did.

"The code?" Natalie said with a laugh. "You sound like you're in the army or something."

"Well, pretend we are and they're the enemy," Brynn said. "Right, Jenna?"

Jenna looked guiltily at her friends. Normally, of course, she would be the first one talking about how annoying and jerky the 3A-ers were. But now, she needed them. Pretty soon one of her friends might even see her talking to them. What was she supposed to say?

"Well, *most* of them are awful," Jenna replied. "But not *all* of them."

"I can't believe I just heard Jenna Bloom say that," Alex said. "Do you have a fever or something?"

"Yeah, J, way to go against everything you've ever said. *Ever*," Sarah put in.

Jenna reddened and was relieved when breakfast was dismissed. Alex and Brynn rushed out, whispering, and Jenna knew they were talking about her and how she had turned on them. At the moment, she didn't care much, though. Jenna would do pretty much anything for a good prank, and that included letting her friends think she liked the girls in 3A. While the rest of her bunk trailed out the door, Jenna slowed her steps until bunk 3A caught up to her.

"Oh, look! It's a Bloom!" one of the veteran 3A girls, Sharon, said with a sneer.

"Oh, look! It's a slug!" Jenna shot back.

Two girls, including Regina from the paper, laughed at her joke, and Jenna realized that Alyssa was right. Regina was pretty cool. And her friend Marta had also been around forever, and had been in on some good raids. (Not as good as 3C's raids, but still good.) These two were definitely Jenna's best bets.

"Hey, Regina! Marta!" Jenna said, falling into step with them as they walked outside. "Can I talk to you?"

Regina glanced at Marta, who shrugged, and all three of them stepped aside to let the other campers pass by.

"Listen, I want to pull a prank, and I need your help," Jenna whispered, glancing around.

"Our help?" Regina asked, tucking her short blond hair behind her ears. "Don't you have enough people in your own bunk?"

Even with the nicer, more normal girls, the bunk rivalry was strong.

"Yeah, but this prank only you guys can help me with," Jenna said. "I want to prank my sister."

"Stephanie? No way! We love Stephanie!" Marta said, pushing her big glasses up on her nose.

"I know! I do, too!" Jenna said, growing impatient already. She couldn't let too many people see her talking to girls from 3A. It was way too suspicious. "She's my sister. And I swear I wouldn't do anything to her if she didn't love pranks as much as I do," she added, crossing her fingers behind her back. "She'll think it's funny."

"I don't know . . ." Regina said, looking at Marta. Marta twisted a strand of her long black hair over her finger until her fingertip turned purple.

"Come on, you guys, it'll be fun," Jenna said. "And your bunkmates will think it's totally cool, right? Everyone loves a good prank."

Marta released her hair and started to smile slightly. Jenna knew she had her. The girl had some mischief in there somewhere. All Jenna had to do was wake it up.

"Well . . . what were you thinking of doing?" Marta asked.

Yes! Jenna thought. *Let the games begin!*

"You're absolutely sure she's in there? She always does her beauty routine on Sunday nights when we're at home," Jenna whispered on Friday afternoon. She, Regina, and Marta were all crouched below the back window of bunk 3A. Jenna had Jessie's Polaroid camera clutched in her sweaty hands, filled with film and ready to go. She had "borrowed" it out of Jessie's cubby, but was sure the girl would never notice. Aside from the scavenger hunt, she hadn't used it once all summer.

"Well, she's been doing it on Fridays ever since we got here. I promise. Every Friday during free swim,"

Regina said. She pressed her fingers into the ground to keep her wet bathing suit from hitting the dirt. They had all snuck out of free swim to do the deed, and Jenna could tell that the others were as nervous about getting caught as she was.

"Let's just do this and get back to the lake," Marta said, blinking rapidly.

"Okay, do one of you guys want to take the picture?" Jenna offered. "You got me the info, after all."

"No way. I don't know how to work that thing," Regina said.

"I can't even see without my glasses," Marta put in, swinging her long dark hair over her shoulder. "You're just a big yellow blur right now."

"Okay. Then I guess it's me," Jenna said, her heart slamming into her ribs. "Here goes nothing."

Jenna stood up and lifted the camera to her eye. The second she saw her sister, she almost cracked up laughing. Stephanie was lying on her cot a few feet from the window, her hair wrapped up in a towel, her face covered in a blue facial mask, with cucumber slices over her eyes. Where she got cucumbers out here, Jenna had no idea, but she was glad her sister was so resourceful. It made the picture all the more funny.

"Just take it!" Regina whispered.

Jenna quickly snapped the photo and hit the dirt. "Let's go!"

The girls got up and ran, giggling, all the way back

to the edge of the path that led to the lake. By the time they got there, the photo had already developed. There, in full color, was Jenna's perfect sister, looking like some kind of creature from the black lagoon.

"Omigosh! It's so great!" Marta said.

"I thought you couldn't see," Jenna reminded her.

"Yeah, but I can imagine how great it is," Marta said.

Jenna rolled her eyes. "Do you have the note?"

"Here. I wrote it in my mother's handwriting so no one would know it was from me," Regina said, handing over a piece of Stephanie's own pink stationery.

"You can do your mother's handwriting?" Jenna asked, impressed.

"She never lets me go on class trips. I had to learn to do her signature," Regina said with a shrug.

Wow, Jenna thought. *Wish this girl was in* my *bunk*.

She quickly scanned the note:

Dear Tyler,
Roses are red,
Violets are blue,
I love cucumbers, Hope you do, too!

Love,
Stephanie

"I love it!" Jenna squealed. Regina was *good*! "Now

all we have to do is slip it into Tyler's bag. This is going to be so great."

"I hope Stephanie isn't too mad," Regina said, biting her bottom lip.

"Don't worry. She'll think it's funny. I swear," Jenna said, crossing her fingers again.

"I can't wait to see what happens next," Marta said with a grin.

Neither can I, Jenna thought, grinning. *I cannot wait.*

That night all the campers in Jenna's year, along with their counselors and CITs, gathered by the lake to tell ghost stories. A campfire blazed on the sand, the lake shone in the moonlight, and the stars twinkled high overhead. All around them the woods were black as pitch. There wasn't a sound except for the crackling of the fire, the chirping crickets, and Pete's deep voice. Everyone was riveted by his story of the little old woman in the deserted house. Even people who heard it every year were still on the edge of their seats.

"The little old lady felt an icy chill creep down her back," Pete said in his most spooky voice. "All the tiny white hairs on her neck stood on end . . ."

Jenna, herself, felt like she was on red alert. Every nerve in her body was sizzling. But it was not because of Pete's story. On the edge of the crowd were the CITs. Tyler was lounging back against the lifeguard's chair with some of the other guys while Stephanie and her friends sat on the old, overturned boat in the sand where the campers painted their bunk numbers at the end of each summer. Every once in a while Tyler would shoot a look at Stephanie, and every once in a while Stephanie would notice and smile back.

Tyler had to have seen the picture and the note. There was no way he could have missed it sitting right on top of his sunblock in his bag. Something was going to happen tonight. Jenna could feel it.

"Slowly . . . slowly . . . the little old lady crept toward the door," Pete said, the light from the fire dancing in his eyes and throwing eerie shadows across his face. "Step after step, she knew she might be walking to her doom . . ."

Suddenly Tyler pushed himself away from the lifeguard's chair. Jenna's heart hit her throat. Across the fire her eyes met Regina's, then Marta's. They were watching, too. They were all dying to know what was going to happen.

Stephanie saw Tyler coming. She stood up a little straighter, tossed her hair behind one shoulder, and smiled slyly at Marissa.

"Her gnarled old fingers shook with fear as she reached for the doorknob . . ."

Tyler's hand went to his pocket. He pulled something out. The envelope! The pink envelope!

"Her hand grasped the cool brass handle. She closed her eyes and said a prayer . . ."

Stephanie blinked in confusion. She took the envelope and opened it. Her face went white as she saw the picture. The envelope fluttered to the sand. Jenna looked at Regina and slapped her hand over her mouth to keep from laughing. Marta already had her face buried in Regina's back, her shoulders shaking.

"The little old lady opened the door and—"

"*What is this!?*" Stephanie shrieked at the top of her lungs.

All the campers around the fire jumped. Jenna saw Natalie grab Simon out of fear, then flush and look away. Even Adam looked like he had just seen a ghost.

"Who did this!?" Stephanie shouted, kicking up sand as she stalked toward the fire.

"Stephanie, come on," Tyler pleaded, following her. "It's no big deal. I mean, I knew it was a joke."

It seemed like Stephanie hadn't even heard him. She stepped into the center of the circle and glared at the girls in her cabin, holding the photo up.

"I know it had to be one of you!" she shouted. "You're the only ones who know when I use my mask. So who did it, huh? Who took this picture?"

Still barely containing her laughter, Jenna glanced at Regina and Marta again. But now, neither one of them was laughing. They both looked upset and guilty. Regina turned accusing eyes toward Jenna, and Jenna knew what she was thinking. She had promised Regina that Stephanie would think the prank was funny. And from the way Stephanie was reacting, it was clear that that was not the case.

"No one has the guts to confess?" Stephanie asked.

There was total silence aside from the crackling of the fire.

"Fine," Stephanie said, clenching her jaw. "I'm outta here."

Then she turned and stalked through the circle and headed back for the bunks. Marissa got up and ran after her, and Tyler shrugged. "Well, I thought it was funny," he said, causing a quick round of laugher and breaking the tension.

Jenna leaned back on her elbows and sighed happily. Forget Regina and Marta. It wasn't her fault they didn't have the stomach for a good joke. As far as she was concerned, it was another successful prank. At least Jenna Bloom was still good at something.

chapter NINE

Jenna could not believe her luck. She was sitting at the social planning committee meeting after dinner on Monday and there were more than a dozen kids sitting around her, boys and girls from every age group. But not one of them was a brother or sister. Stephanie and Adam were both absent. She was actually the only Bloom on the committee.

"What's with the freaky big smile?" Chelsea asked her.

"Just happy to be here," Jenna said with a shrug as Shira, the camp's events coordinator, welcomed them.

Shira was an ever-peppy college student who always wore shirts with Greek letters on them. She had curly black hair, a huge smile, and could talk faster than anyone Jenna had ever met. Just then she was babbling on about how they should all be honored to be part of such an important event.

"Okay, the first thing we need to decide on is a theme for the event," Shira said, once she was done with her welcome speech. Her crazy black curls framed her face as she looked up at the table. Her pink-ink pen was poised above a bright green clipboard, ready to take suggestions. "Any ideas? I know you kids are just bursting with creativity!"

"How about *The Lord of the Rings?*" a boy from 3E suggested. He had a cowlick the size of New Jersey and wore a faded Frodo T-shirt.

"Nice!" Pete cheered. He, Nate, and a couple of other counselors were hanging out by the wall, listening in on the meeting.

"Um . . . interesting, but not exactly appropriate for a social," Shira said, shooting Pete a look. "Good start, though. Anyone else?"

"Hey, I liked it, buddy," Pete said, leaning over to slap the Frodo kid on the back. The Frodo kid turned fire-engine red and slumped a little bit, crossing his arms on the table.

"We could do Hollywood," Chelsea put in, sitting up straight. "We could have a red carpet, and stars hanging from the ceiling and stuff like that."

"Ooh! That could be so glam and romantic," an older girl said with a grin.

"I like it!" Shira said. "Anyone else?"

Romantic? Yuck! Jenna thought, looking around as some of the younger kids squirmed. *Who wants romance? Well, besides all my crazy friends who are going with dates.*

"What about a square dance?" a fifth-year girl

named Gwendolyn suggested. "We could learn all the different dances and maybe we could have a competition for the best dancers."

Jenna sat up a little straighter at this idea. A square dance competition sounded like a lot more fun, and a lot less "romantic" than Chelsea's Hollywood idea.

"A square dance! How fun!" Shira trilled, scribbling on her clipboard. "We could get bales of hay and horseshoes and cowboy hats. Great idea, Gwen!"

"A square dance? That's so third grade," Chelsea said, brushing the idea off.

The third-graders at the table sank lower in their chairs, and Jenna elbowed Chelsea in the ribs. Jenna still remembered how annoying it was when older kids had brushed *her* ideas off just because she was younger.

"Ow!" Chelsea said.

"I think it's a great idea," Jenna put in, covering up Chelsea's complaints. "It would be a lot of fun. Like, all bright and happy and stuff."

"Yeah, and learning the dances would be cool," another girl put in.

"Would we *have* to dance?" the Frodo boy asked.

"Not if you don't want to," Jenna said. "But if you wanted to, you would be matched up with someone as your partner. You know, for the contest. Right?"

Frodo Boy actually brightened. "So I could actually dance without having to go up to a girl and ask her? I like *that* idea."

"Jenna's got a good point," Nate said. "A square dance is actually perfect."

Jenna felt a little flutter in her heart as she beamed. Nate was agreeing with her! One of the coolest counselors at camp!

"Come on!" one of the older girls said. "A square dance is silly."

"Hey!" Gwen replied.

"Everyone calm down and listen to what Nate has to say," Shira suggested. "Nate?"

"Well, whenever we have one of these things, all the girls stand on one side of the room, and all the boys stand on the other side, and it takes half the night for anyone to get up the guts to ask anyone else to dance," Nate said. "If we do the square dance, everyone will be dancing all night. I think it would be much more relaxed."

Exactly what I was thinking, Jenna thought with a smile. "Plus, lately everyone has felt all this pressure to come with a date," Jenna said, thinking of how serious Grace had been when she had made Jenna promise to go solo. "If everyone knows they're going to get to dance with someone even if they *don't* already have a date, then everyone could, you know, chill about it."

"Well put," Shira said. "Well, we have two theme ideas. Let's put it to a vote. All for the Hollywood theme?"

Chelsea and a bunch of the older girls and guys raised their hands. Shira counted quickly and made a note on her board.

"And all for the square-dance theme?" she asked.

Jenna, Gwen, Frodo Boy, and all the younger kids, plus Nate and the rest of the counselors raised their hands. Shira counted again, but it was already clear which idea had won.

"Square dance it is!"

Yes! Jenna thought as a few kids cheered and clapped. Nate grinned at her, and she felt as if she were on top of the world. This was going to be the coolest camp dance-social-thingie ever.

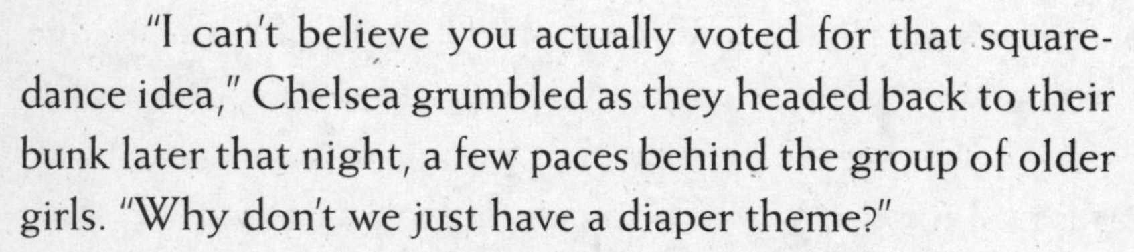

"I can't believe you actually voted for that square-dance idea," Chelsea grumbled as they headed back to their bunk later that night, a few paces behind the group of older girls. "Why don't we just have a diaper theme?"

"Come on, Chelsea! It'll be fun!" Jenna said.

Jenna knew Chelsea was just upset that her idea had been outvoted, but the square dance was such a better idea. It was more important that the entire camp have a fun social than it was to keep Chelsea happy.

"Yeah, bales of hay, cornbread and beans, and a bunch of uncoordinated boys bouncing up and down," Chelsea said, pausing in front of the nature shack. "Yee-ha."

"Chelsea . . ."

"It's my first date ever, and now I'm always going to remember that Eric took me to a hoedown," she said.

"What's the big deal? You still get to dance with him,"

Jenna said. "Even thought I still can't figure out *why* you want to."

"Whatever, Jenna. You just don't get it yet," Chelsea said. "But one day you're gonna want to go out with a boy. I swear."

"Not unless somebody sucks my brain out and replaces it with yours," Jenna said.

Chelsea scoffed. She glanced behind her at the nature shack, then looked at Jenna with a sly smile.

"You know what? It's too bad there aren't any animals for our Old McDonald's farm dance," she said. "That would just make the whole thing *perfect.*"

With that, Chelsea walked off, huffily stomping along the pathway toward the bunks. Jenna, however, couldn't make herself move. Was Chelsea suggesting what Jenna thought she was suggesting? Whether or not Chelsea had realized it, she had started a brilliant idea forming in Jenna's mind. She stared at the nature shack, her wicked brain already putting together the details.

Animals for Old McDonald's Farm . . .

She couldn't. She shouldn't. Especially not after the way Stephanie had reacted to the last prank. She should be hanging up her thinking cap for the rest of the summer and leaving the pranks to the other kids. Besides, if she kept it up, sooner or later she was going to get caught. And if she got caught, her parents would wig out—not to mention her brother Matt, who had made her promise to be good.

But it would just be so totally amazing! It would be the biggest, most creative, most legendary prank ever pulled in the history of Camp Lakeview. Jenna would be talked about for years. Everyone would know her name. If she could pull it off, she would be Jenna the Champion Prankster, not just another Bloom.

It really is a good idea, Jenna thought, smiling. *A really good*, bad *idea . . .*

▲ ▲ ▲

"Okay, I'm totally bored," Jenna said, slumping back in her chair at the newspaper.

She looked at Natalie and Alyssa, who were busy going through a stack of photographs for the next issue. All around the room, campers huddled over desks, tapped away at the two ancient computers or flipped through old issues of the camp paper—*The Acorn*—for ideas. Various bulletin boards hung on the walls displayed unused pictures of campers from every age group, eating lunch, playing volleyball, smiling for the camera. But even with all the activity inside the cabin, it still felt stifling just to be there. Jenna could hear the squeals and shouts of the kids playing soccer on the field outside and was practically green with jealousy.

"Do we really need to print a list of all the competitions and who's won them?" Jenna asked, tossing her pen down and stretching out her aching fingers. The fan in the corner swung slowly in their direction, and she lifted her ponytail to feel the cool air on the back of her neck. It actually seemed hotter in here than it was outside. Why wasn't she out in the sun kicking a soccer ball around right now instead of being cooped up inside doing busy work?

Natalie stopped tapping her red pencil against the edge of the long wooden table and smirked at Jenna. "I thought you would love doing that list. Your name is on it, like, at least five times."

"Yeah. You're like Queen of Camp Lakeview," Alyssa put in.

Jenna couldn't help smiling at the compliment and almost wished Alex were there to hear it. She did have to admit, her name and her bunk appeared very often on the rundown she was working on. Bunk 3C had not only won the scavenger hunt, but they were in the semifinals of the summerlong capture-the-flag-tournament and had won the girls' kickball competition. Jenna herself had taken home the blue ribbon in the obstacle course in her age division and second place in the cross-country race (just behind Sarah). It *was* kind of cool getting so much recognition. Maybe putting this list together wasn't as boring as she had thought.

"Okay, but when I'm done with this, I get to do something fun," Jenna said, sitting up again. She sifted through the stack of slips on which the counselors had written their campers' many triumphs. Even though Julie's slip had Jenna's name all over it, the list couldn't record

Jenna's biggest news of the summer. She had pulled two huge pranks, and no one had figured out it was her! That should have been front-page news.

"Hey! Maybe I'll write a story about all the pranks that have been going on!" Jenna suggested.

Natalie and Alyssa exchanged a look as the newspaper supervisor, Keith, walked by. Keith was Nate's older brother and had been a counselor at Lakeview until a couple of years ago. He worked on a computer magazine in South Jersey and was going to be some big reporter one day. He looked just like Nate, only taller, skinnier, and nerdier.

"I don't think that's such a good idea, Jenna," Keith said, pausing by their table. His thick glasses hung on the edge of his nose, making him look like an owl.

"Why not?" Jenna asked. "It's an interesting story. And funny. I mean, you guys think those pranks were funny . . . right?" she asked her friends.

"Yeah . . . sure," Alyssa responded slowly, looking away.

"I understand why you think it would be a fun story, Jenna, but this issue is for parents' day," Keith said. "I don't think the parents really want to hear about pranks being pulled on their kids, do you?"

Jenna flushed slightly. The only parents who would be reading about pranks pulled on their kids would be her own. After all, the only pranks so far this year had been pulled on Adam and Stephanie. And Keith was right. Her parents would not want to hear about those jokes. Not this summer, especially.

"All right," Jenna grumbled, never too willing to give up, even when she knew she should. "But I think you should check the Constitution. I know there's something about the press being able to write whatever they want."

Keith smiled. "Well, not *whatever* they want, but that's a lesson for another day."

Jenna sighed and returned to her repetitive task, wincing when she heard a huge cheer from outside. Someone had clearly scored a goal. Jenna was missing all the fun.

"Oooh! I *love* this one," Alyssa said, holding up a picture across the way. "It's so artistic."

"Totally," Natalie agreed. "Who took it?"

Alyssa flipped the photo over. "Adam Bloom," she read, sounding surprised. "Hey, Jenna, your brother's a great photographer."

Jenna looked up from her work. "Let me see," she said, sure it was going to be some random picture of Adam's friends making faces or something.

Alyssa turned the photo around and held it up for Jenna to see. It was a shot of the lake at sunset with the light reflecting all the trees in the water. Even Jenna had to admit it was totally gorgeous. It was like something a person could frame and hang on the wall.

"Wow," she said, burning with jealousy. "That *is* good. But you can't use that for the paper, right? I mean, there are no campers in it and it doesn't show an activity, so what's the point?"

"Oh, well, Keith said we could print some of the more artsy shots in the parents' day edition," Natalie said, placing Adam's photo aside. "You know, to show off to the parents what we're doing at camp."

"Yeah. We're picking out the best ones," Alyssa said.

Jenna shifted in her seat, staring at Adam's photo. "Oh. So you're picking that one?"

"Definitely," Alyssa said. "That's the best one yet."

"Hey! You're in photography now, right?" Natalie said, her eyes bright. "Why don't you hand in some of your pictures?"

Jenna pressed her pen into the page in front of her, scowling. "I don't think so," she said. Natalie and Alyssa had no idea that Jenna had basically underexposed, blurred, or blackened out almost all of her pictures when she'd tried to print them. She just couldn't seem to get that machine to work right.

"Why not?" Alyssa asked. "If Adam's are this good, yours are probably awesome. I mean, he *is* your brother."

"Yeah! Maybe it's in your blood!" Natalie added with a grin.

"My pictures stink, all right?" Jenna said flatly. "Can we please talk about something else?"

Natalie and Alyssa fell silent for a moment. A long moment that seemed to drag out forever. Jenna couldn't believe she had snapped at her friends again. What was she doing—turning into an even jerkier version of Chelsea or something?

"Hey! I know what we can talk about!" Alyssa said finally, glancing around the room as if to check if anyone was watching. Jenna leaned forward, curious, as Alyssa bent down and rummaged through her black messenger bag. "Check it out," she said, lifting a small box just into view at the end of the table. Jenna's eyes nearly popped out of her head. It was a box of hair dye. Red hair dye.

"Who is that for?" Jenna asked as Alyssa slipped the box out of sight again.

"For me," Alyssa said, grinning wildly.

Jenna stared at Alyssa's long black locks. She couldn't believe she was actually thinking about dyeing her hair! Alyssa had always been a little . . . *different*, what with her wardrobe of ripped jeans, paint-spattered cargo shorts, and black T-shirts. But this? This was totally off the deep end!

"Where did you get it?" Jenna asked.

"That senior girl Daphne gave it to us," Natalie said, lifting her chin toward the other end of the room. "Plus, the bleach we have to use first."

"Bleach?" Jenna said, her mouth dropping open. "Are you crazy?"

"Daphne says she does it all the time," Alyssa replied. "It's no big deal."

Jenna turned around to check out Daphne, a

thirteen-year-old girl with white-blond hair. She was sitting at a table in the back of the room, chopping up newspapers with a pair of huge scissors. Jenna wasn't sure what good her task was doing anyone, but as always, no one was bothering her. Daphne had been wearing black eyeliner ever since Jenna could remember, and whenever anyone asked her a question, she just grunted. She also cracked her knuckles constantly. Jenna had always been totally afraid of Daphne. Most of the *counselors* were even afraid of her. How had Natalie and Alyssa even gotten her to *talk* to them?

"She changes her hair color every five minutes," Natalie said.

"Yeah, wasn't she a brunette last week?" Jenna asked.

"Yep," Alyssa said. "She was saving the red for the end of the summer, but I traded her my pastel set for it. I wanted to do something cool and different for the social."

"Wow. Well, it'll definitely be different," Jenna said. "So, when are we going to do it?"

"Tonight," Natalie whispered. "It's Julie's night off, and you know Marissa sleeps like she's practically dead or something," she added with a giggle.

"Aren't you afraid of getting in trouble?" Jenna asked Alyssa.

"It's never stopped you, has it?" Alyssa said with a grin.

Jenna grinned back. How cool! She was inspiring Alyssa to take a chance! "No, I guess not."

"Besides, what are they going to do to me?" Alyssa asked with a shrug. "By the time they see what I've done, it'll be too late. And it is *my* hair."

They could do a lot of things to you, Jenna thought. *Like give you extra chores or make you help out in the mess hall.* Jenna had gotten enough punishments in her life to know that Alyssa could get in big trouble. But still, it was cool to see how calm Alyssa was about it all.

"Wow," Jenna said, leaning back in her chair again. "I'm impressed."

"And she's going to look so *fabb*-u-lous with red highlights," Natalie said, fluttering her lashes and tilting her head back.

"Thank you, *dah*-ling," Alyssa replied, flipping her hair.

Jenna giggled, her boredom and irritation over Adam and his pictures entirely forgotten. Tonight was going to be so much fun. And for once, she wasn't going to be the one getting yelled at or having suspicious looks thrown at her. For once, something big was going to happen, and no one would be able to blame it on her.

chapter TEN

Dear Matt,

I can't believe you think it was me who pulled the pranks on Stephanie and Adam. First of all, they're total whiners for telling you about them, anyway, because they were no big deal. But just because I am the "common link" (your words) between them, that doesn't mean I did it. Besides, the sugar prank was pulled on Adam's entire table, not just Adam. How do you know someone wasn't trying to prank

Eric? Or Simon? Or Nate?

Besides, you know that if it WAS me, I wouldn't be able to tell you, anyway. The less people that know you did a prank, the better—right? And when did you get so parental? Wasn't it you who replaced the morning bugle sound track with "You Gotta Fight for Your Right to Party" that summer? People still talk about that. And you KNOW you love it.

Just in case you're interested in the good things I'm doing this summer, we won the scavenger hunt AGAIN, and I'm on the planning committee for the camp social. It's going to be the best one ever. And Mom and Dad still haven't gotten any freak-out phone calls. So there.

I hope you're having fun with your beakers and test tubes!

Love,

Jenna

P.S. Thanks for the "I Eat Glue" bumper sticker. Very funny, you know, since I actually used to eat glue. Yum! Ha-ha. I swear I don't eat glue anymore.

That night, after lights-out, Julie left to meet up with the other counselors and do whatever it was they did on their nights off. *Probably a lot of kissing and holding hands,* Jenna thought. *Gross.*

Jenna lay in her top bunk, staring at the ceiling, holding her breath and listening to the sound of her heartbeat. In the other bunks the rest of her friends were doing the same. Jenna turned her face and stole a glance at Valerie who grinned back. Everyone was psyched for what they were about to do.

The minutes dragged on for what seemed like days, but soon enough Jenna heard the soft whistle of Marissa's snoring. Somewhere in the bunk someone snorted a laugh and clapped her hand over her mouth. Jessie and Karen giggled and twittered until Alex shushed them. Finally the tiny beeping alarm on Sarah's sports watch went off, and everyone sat up. Fifteen minutes had passed. Nothing but the trumpet reveille could wake Marissa now.

Ever so quietly Jenna slipped from her bed and down the ladder, bumping butts with Alex as she came down from her own.

"Are you ready?" Grace asked Alyssa as they all gathered in the center of the bunk in socked-feet.

"Yeah. Let's do this," Alyssa said.

"Yeah," Candace added. "Let's do this."

A few of the girls giggled and started to whisper.

"Shhh! No more talking till we're in the bathroom!" Jenna hissed, causing everyone to immediately shut up. Jenna smiled, happy she had come up with the order before Alex, and they all tiptoed past Marissa's cot and into the bathroom.

Brynn went for the light, but Alex grabbed her hand to stop her.

"Pull the curtain first!" Alex said in a whisper.

Jessie yanked the burgundy curtain across the door opening to shield some of the light from spilling into the bunk area, and then Brynn flicked the light on.

Alyssa, Natalie, Valerie, and Grace were already gathered at the back sink.

"This is going to be so cool!" Natalie said, tearing the box open. It made a hugely loud noise, and Jenna's heart jumped into her throat. Everyone looked at the door. When they heard Marissa snore again, they let out a big sigh of relief.

"She's in dreamland," Chelsea said. "Don't worry about her."

"Okay, we've already read the directions about ten times," Natalie said. "Let's just go for it."

"Are you sure you want to do this, Alyssa?" Alex asked, ever the cautious camper. She looked at Alyssa's reflection in the mirror, and Alyssa gazed steadily back.

"I'm sure," she said with a nod. "Let's go."

"I can't believe we're doing this. I can't believe we're doing this!" Grace babbled excitedly.

Jenna grabbed one of Alyssa's towels and draped it over her shoulders. Natalie wiggled her fingers into the plastic gloves while Grace removed the safety cap from the bottle of dye. Valerie used a comb to help Natalie work parts into Alyssa's hair. Then Natalie held up the dye bottle.

"This is it!" Natalie said with a grin. Alyssa nodded quickly, and Natalie applied the dye. After a few seconds of watching them work, a sharp, sour smell hit Jenna's nostrils, and she scrunched her nose.

"Ugh! That stuff smells gross!" she whispered.

"Sometimes you have to suffer for beauty," Natalie replied, still working. "Or at least that's what my dad's girlfriend always says."

Everyone nodded at this piece of wisdom. Natalie's dad was Ted Maxwell, the huge Hollywood star. His current girlfriend, Josie McLaughlan, was a starlet on the rise who had appeared on the cover of nearly every women's magazine last spring. If anyone knew about beauty, she did.

"Everything okay out there, Karen?" Valerie asked, glancing toward the door.

Karen moved the curtain slightly and peeked out. "Yep," she whispered with a nod. "She's still asleep."

"Okay," Natalie said when the bottle of dye was empty. "Now we just wait fifteen minutes and rinse it out."

Sarah pressed a few buttons on her watch and nodded. "Okay. Timer's set."

Jenna looked around the bathroom. What were they going to do for fifteen minutes? With no other options in sight, she finally shrugged and sat down on the rough wooden floor. The other girls soon joined her and they all sat in a circle, breathing in the fumes from Alyssa's head.

"How does it feel?" Jenna asked.

"It burns a little, but the box said it would," Alyssa replied calmly. Jenna couldn't believe how brave she was, sitting there like there was nothing going on. If Jenna was changing the color of her own hair, she would be losing it right then.

"I can't wait to see how it looks," Grace said.

"Me neither," Jessie put in. "I just read the part in *Anne of Green Gables* where she tries to dye her red hair black and it comes out all green and horrible . . ."

Everyone stared at Jessie until she realized what she was saying and all the color drained from her face.

"Not that your hair's going to be green and horrible," she added quickly. "I'm sure it's gonna look great."

Jenna rolled her eyes and leaned back on her hands. Sometimes Jessie could say the most spacey things. There was a moment of awkward silence, which Grace finally broke.

"I love the movie version of *Anne of Green Gables*," she said. "Actually I think it was a miniseries. My mom bought it for me on tape."

"Have you read the book?" Jessie asked.

Grace flushed slightly. "No . . . just seen the movie."

"Oh, well, the book is *so* much better," Jessie said. "I can lend it to you if you want."

"That's okay," Grace said.

"Actually, you kind of look like Anne, Grace," Karen said. "Your hair is the exact same color as hers."

"Really? Well, soon Alyssa's gonna look like her, too!" Grace announced, bringing the attention back to the hair dye at hand.

"I was actually hoping for more punk rock than prairie-girl chic," Alyssa said.

Everyone laughed, and after that they pretty much stayed quiet until the beeper on Sarah's watch went off again.

"Time to rinse!" Natalie said, jumping up.

Alyssa scrambled to her feet and followed Natalie to the sink. She dipped her head forward under the spout.

"How does it look?" Alyssa asked. Her eyes were scrunched shut to keep the dye out.

Jenna's mouth was totally dry. The water pouring from Alyssa's hair and down the drain was bright red, like the color of blood. It was totally gross. Jenna was really worried. If Alyssa's hair was the same color as that water, she wasn't going to look as *fabb*-u-lous as Natalie had predicted at the newspaper. She was going to look *scary*.

"It's . . . hard to tell," Grace said. "Because, you know, your hair is still wet and the color always looks different when it's wet."

"So let's dry it," Chelsea said, pulling her hairdryer out. The girls all kept their toiletries in plastic crates near the wall and Chelsea's was on the top shelf, always overflowing with headbands, barrettes, and various ribbons.

"No!" Alex whispered. "You can't turn that on!"

"She's right," Alyssa said, lifting her head and wrapping the towel from her shoulders around her hair.

"I know Marissa's a deep sleeper, but that could definitely wake her up."

Jenna felt as disappointed as the rest of her friends looked. "So what do we do?" she asked.

"We just wait until the morning," Alyssa said. "It'll dry overnight."

"Wow. Can you really wait that long?" Jenna asked. There was no way she would be as calm as Alyssa was right then. Dyeing her hair was a huge thing! How could she not be freaking out?

"I kind of have to," Alyssa said, leading the way to the door. "Come on, girls, let's get some sleep. Tomorrow you'll get to see the whole new me!"

▲ ▲ ▲

The next morning Jenna woke up super early, just like she always did on Christmas morning. For a moment she couldn't figure out why she was so excited, and then she remembered. Alyssa's top bunk was across the room from Jenna's, so she rolled over to take a look. Maybe she could be the first person to get a look at the hair! Unfortunately, Alyssa must have been sleeping all the way back against the wall. All Jenna could see was her blanket and the edge of her pillow.

As patiently as she could, Jenna waited until reveille. She must have dozed off again, because when the trumpet went off, she sat up so fast, she smacked her head into the ceiling.

Alex, Chelsea, and Natalie, always up before the trumpet, all ran in from the bathroom. The rest of the girls shot one another glances from their bunks, grinning with anticipation. Finally Alyssa, the second heaviest sleeper next to Marissa, sat up and swung her feet over the side of the bunk.

Jenna let out a gasp that was echoed by the rest of the girls. Suddenly she felt sick to her stomach. Alyssa's hair, all knotted and stringy from being slept on wet, was Ronald McDonald red!

"What?" Alyssa said, her eyes still closed as she stretched her arms out at her sides.

"Alyssa! Your . . . your hair!" Natalie wailed.

Suddenly Alyssa's eyes popped open, and her hands flew to her head. She grabbed her long hair and slowly brought the ends in front of her face. Her eyes widened to the size of softballs.

"Omigod!" she gasped, sliding down off her bunk and dropping to the floor. She ran to the bathroom, followed by the rest of the bunk, and stared into the mirror. "Oh . . . my . . . God!"

It looked even worse in the bright lights of the bathroom. Alyssa's hair wasn't just red. It was flaming, fire-engine, hot-sauce, ketchup red. She looked like a Raggedy Ann doll. All around her reflection were the faces of her eleven stunned bunkmates. It was clear to Jenna that no one knew what to say. It was Natalie who finally broke the silence.

"Alyssa, I am so, so, so, so sorry," she said, holding her hands over her mouth. "I swear I followed the directions. I don't know what happened."

Alyssa was just opening her mouth to say something when Julie walked into the room, all smiles in her gray sweats and white T-shirt. All the campers froze in place.

We are so dead, Jenna thought. *So very, very dead*.

"Good morning, girls!" Julie said, grabbing her toothbrush and taking it over to the sink. "Are you guys ready for another beautiful—ACK!!!"

Julie dropped her toothbrush in the sink with a clatter and whirled to face the little group of campers. Everyone tightened in around Alyssa as if to protect her.

"What happened?" Julie asked. "What did you do to yourself?"

"I . . . I . . . dyed it," Alyssa said, looking at the floor.

"With what? Paint from the arts-and-crafts cabin?" Julie cried. She reached out and took a few strands in her hand. "Oh, Alyssa, what were you thinking?"

"I thought it was just going to be highlights!" Alyssa said, lifting her big brown eyes to look at Julie. "I didn't know!"

Julie sighed and put her hands on her hips. "Did you girls help her do this?" she asked, looking around.

"No!" Alyssa piped up immediately. "They didn't even know until this morning."

"Lyss," Natalie said.

"I swear, Julie. If anyone should get in trouble, it should just be me," Alyssa said, turning to look in the mirror again. "Ugh! I look like a horror movie!"

Julie sighed again and shook her head. "All right, everyone but Alyssa, back outside," she said, pointing a thumb at the door.

Everyone shot sympathetic looks at Alyssa. On top of looking like an oversized rag doll, she was about to get in major trouble. It didn't seem fair. Back outside the bathroom, Jenna and Alex both hovered near the door to hear.

"Alyssa, why did you do this?" Julie asked, her voice low.

"I thought it would be cool for the social tonight," Alyssa replied.

"And who gave you the dye?" Julie asked.

There was a pause. "No one. I brought it with me to camp."

Wow. Alyssa's a good person to have on your side, Jenna thought, sharing a look with Alex. *She's not even giving Daphne up.*

"Well, technically, I should revoke your privileges and at least make you stay home from the social," Julie said, causing Jenna and Alex to gasp. "But I won't," she added.

"Really?" Alyssa said.

"I think looking at your reflection for the rest of the summer will be punishment enough," Julie said. "Now go tell your friends you're not in trouble. Except for the two nosy nosersons standing by the door, because they already know."

Caught, Jenna and Alex jumped back and joined the rest of their friends to wait for Alyssa to come out.

"I'm not in trouble!" Alyssa shouted, throwing her hands in the air.

Everyone cheered and started to go about getting ready for breakfast. Natalie, Grace, and Alyssa huddled in the corner, brushing out Alyssa's hair and trying to figure out a way to make it look better. In the end, they borrowed a baseball cap from Sarah and decided to deal with it later.

As Jenna headed for the sink to wash her face and brush her teeth, her mind was working overtime. She couldn't believe Alyssa hadn't gotten in trouble. If Jenna had dyed her own hair, she was sure Julie would have sent her right to Dr. Steve. Jenna *always* got in trouble when she was caught.

Or maybe not, she thought, looking at her reflection in the mirror. Maybe Julie was softening a little. And there hadn't been any big drama over either one of her last pranks. As far as Jenna knew, the camp director and the counselors still didn't know for sure who had pulled them. Maybe the whole camp was getting a little easier on pranksters and jokesters. If Alyssa could turn herself into a clown and not get in trouble, there was no telling what Jenna might be able to get away with.

Tonight was the social, and she could still pull the all-time greatest prank . . . if she dared. Sizzling with excitement, Jenna brushed her teeth quickly and headed outside for some alone time while everyone else got ready. She had a lot of thinking to do. Tonight, Jenna Bloom could become a legend.

chapter ELEVEN

That night, the social was in full swing in the mess hall and all the campers seemed to be having a great time. Jenna hung back against the wall behind the huge punch bowl and took in the scene. Nate had been right. Instead of everyone being divided, boys against one wall and girls against the other, most of the kids were in the center of the floor, laughing while the counselors tried to teach them some square-dance moves. A lot of the girls had done their hair in double braids, and many of them had tracked down plaid and denim clothing to go along with the theme. Some of the boys were wearing brown plastic cowboy hats that Pete had found at a local party store, and Julie stood in the corner, handing out colorful bandannas for the campers to tie around their necks.

Bales of hay were stacked against the walls and around the snack tables. Silver and gold stars were hanging from the ceiling—the only idea left over from Chelsea's Hollywood plan. But now they were stars of the desert night instead of stars of L.A. There were even a few inflatable cacti leaning against the DJ table where Pete played old square dance records someone had dug up from the AV room. Everything had come together just as the planning committee had dreamed it.

"Hey, Jenna! Aren't you going to dance!?" Natalie called out as Simon grabbed her arm and swung her around. Natalie tipped her head back and laughed, and Jenna couldn't help but smile. Nat looked like she was having an amazing time.

"Maybe later," Jenna said. "I'm in charge of punch right now!"

Natalie waved and twirled away. Jenna looked down at her lavender dress and sighed. She wasn't actually in charge of punch. The punch could take care of itself. The problem for Jenna was, she just couldn't get into party mode. It turned out that dancing with boys, even silly square dancing, was not her thing. The very thought of letting one of Adam's grubby friends spin her around and grab her hand made her cringe.

But everyone else seemed to be enjoying it, so what was wrong with Jenna? She always had fun at the camp dance, even when she just spent the night talking to her friends. What was wrong with her this year?

Jenna saw Adam approaching the punch table and pushed herself away from the wall. She went about filling cups from the punch bowl, trying to look important and busy.

"Hey, Jen," he said, pausing in front of her. He looked kind of pale and tired, but that was what he got for spending half his summer in the darkroom. Adam may have been good with photos, but he was going to go back to school in September looking like a vampire.

"What's up?" Jenna said, lifting the ladle from the bowl.

"You having fun?" he asked. He fiddled with the cord that held the plastic cowboy hat that hung down his back.

"Sure," she said. "You?"

"I guess," Adam said, scanning the room. "So . . . listen, who's that new girl in your bunk? The one with the red hair?"

For a moment, Jenna thought of Grace, who had red curly hair. But she had been new *last* year and Adam knew her. She followed his gaze across the room and her jaw dropped. Adam was staring at Alyssa, who was standing by the far wall chatting with Daphne. Alyssa had her tomato-red mop pulled back in a ponytail and had made a belt by tying five of the multicolored bandannas together. Alyssa probably thought she looked cool, but Jenna thought the outfit just made her look even more like a clown.

Jenna glanced back at Adam. He looked as if he had stars in his eyes. He could have been that old cartoon skunk whose heart always thumped out his chest whenever he saw that black-and-white girl cat. Oh, God! Did Adam have a *crush*? On one of her *friends*? Could this summer get any worse?

"Jenna? Are you in there?" Adam asked.

"That's Alyssa," Jenna said finally. "She's from south Jersey and she just did that to her hair last night. Kind of bright, right?" she said, attempting a laugh. She felt bad for picking on Alyssa to her brother, but she didn't want Adam to like Alyssa. She *really* didn't want that. She already shared *everything* with her brothers and sister. Was she going to have to share her friends, too?

"Actually, I think it's kind of cool," Adam said. "Is she into art?"

Jenna swallowed hard. "Why do you say that?"

"She has paint all over her sneakers," Adam pointed out.

"So what? You like artsy girls all of a sudden?" Jenna asked. "Why? Because you're such an *amazing photographer* now?"

Adam looked at her like he felt sorry for her. "You could be, too, you know, if you just paid attention to what you were doing."

"Well, maybe I'm not into lame-o photography," Jenna shot back. "I'd rather be playing kickball than sitting in that cave all darn day."

"Okay! Okay! Forget I said anything," Adam replied, raising his hands in surrender. "So, what's Alyssa into? What are her electives?"

"Uh . . . she's on the paper with me and she's in arts and crafts," Jenna said, filling another cup. "You don't, like, really *like* her, do you?"

"I don't know," Adam said, reaching back and placing his cowboy hat firmly on his head. "Let's find out!" he said with a smile.

Oh, ick! Jenna thought, watching as Adam walked across the room and struck up a conversation with Alyssa. She couldn't have looked away if she'd tried. This couldn't be happening. Adam couldn't be crushing on one of her bunkmates. If Adam and Alyssa got together it would be such a nightmare! Her brother would be in her face even more than he already was.

And why this summer of all summers? Why was this the year Adam had chosen to suddenly become interested in girls? How could he, with everything else that was going on?

At the sound of a familiar laugh, Jenna turned her head and saw her sister and Marissa dancing with a bunch of the guys in the corner. They were busting out their best club moves, even though the Texas Reel was playing over the speakers. The guys clapped and hooted, and Marissa and Stephanie looked like they were having the time of their lives.

Adam was getting to know Alyssa, and Stephanie was dancing up a storm. They were both having so much fun. Why was Jenna the only Bloom kid who seemed to be miserable? Didn't they care about their family at all?

Soon, Adam and Alyssa were dancing and laughing it up with Simon and Natalie. Tyler came over and grabbed some punch for Stephanie so she could cool off. The two of them bent their heads close together and whispered and laughed as they sipped their drinks. Finally Jenna couldn't take it anymore. Everyone was having fun but her. And there was only one thing she could do to change it.

Decision made, Jenna waved to Chelsea, who grinned wickedly, nodded, and headed out through the kitchen. Jenna dropped the ladle and tromped outside. It was time to pull the prank of the year—maybe even of the decade. It was time for Jenna Bloom to truly make her mark on the Camp Lakeview social.

▲ ▲ ▲

"Omigod! Aaahhhhh! Snake!!!!"

"What is nibbling on my foot? Hey! Is that Snowball!?"

"Get it away from me! Get it away from me!!!"

Jenna and Chelsea doubled over laughing in the corner as the animals from the nature shack took center stage at the camp social. Now *this* was fun. Rabbits, squirrels, snakes, iguanas, turtles—everything but the fish and the birds had been released amidst the dancing, stomping feet.

"This was the best idea you ever had," Chelsea told Jenna.

"Couldn't have done it without you!" Jenna replied.

Ten minutes ago Chelsea and Jenna had snuck into the nature shack, using the extra hide-a-key that Roseanne kept in a fake rock by the door for those mornings when she was spacey from lack of coffee. Chelsea had seen her use it once during her time in the nature elective and had remembered the exact placement of the fake rock. Once inside, Jenna and Chelsea had each grabbed as many cages as they could handle and raced through the darkness back to the rear door of the mess hall kitchen. After three trips they had stacked up almost every cage in the shack and the animals were running around inside their pens, twittering and clawing and raring to go.

"Okay. Let's turn this in to a real hoedown," Chelsea had said, crouching in front of one of the bunny cages.

"Ready?" Jenna had added, her heart pounding. "One . . . two . . . three!"

They both opened the doors to their nearest cages and . . . nothing happened. Brownie the mouse just looked at Jenna with his beady black eyes. Snowball the rabbit ran to the back of his cage and crouched there.

"No, silly! You're supposed to go out! Out!" Chelsea ordered.

"Come on," Jenna said coaxingly. She reached in and picked up Brownie in her hands, then placed him by the door of the kitchen. "Run! You're free! You're free!"

The mouse started looking for crumbs.

"Maybe they just need some friends," Chelsea said.

So Jenna and Chelsea ran around, opening every cage in sight and dumping the animals out on the floor. Then, working together, they wrangled them toward the door, grabbing Leaky the lizard as he tried to make a break for it and giving Todd the turtle the nudge he needed. Finally . . . *finally* . . . the animals got the picture and, following Sandy the squirrel's lead, they fanned out into the mess hall.

Now, campers had scattered everywhere. Girls clambered up onto the snack tables, knocking over bowls of Cheetos and plates of brownies. A first-year girl screamed and launched herself toward the punch bowl, splashing the contents all over Stephanie, who was running to help. Stephanie screamed at the top of her lungs.

"Omigosh! Look at my sister!" Jenna cried, grasping Chelsea's hand as Stephanie's flattened hair dripped red punch onto her dress. Her mascara was already running, and she looked like the ax murderer from some bad scary movie.

"Check it out!" Chelsea shouted, pointing.

The Frodo Boy from the meeting was running away from, of all things, a chipmunk. He looked terrified as he ran out the front door and ran off screaming into the night.

"This is the best!" Jenna cried, beyond proud of herself.

"Everybody, calm down!" Dr. Steve said into the microphone. "Counselors and staff, please try to wrangle the animals!"

Pete dipped to the floor and swooped up a snake

that was slithering toward a huddled group of senior girls. Daphne grabbed two of the iguanas and held them against her, cooing to them with a gentleness Jenna had never thought the girl could produce. Nate came running out of the kitchen, loaded down with buckets and boxes to try to contain the creatures. In every corner of the room there was screaming and chaos.

"Omigod! Somebody get the rabbit! The rabbit is getting away!" a second-year girl screamed from her perch on the DJ table.

Jenna watched as Adam tore across the room and grabbed Snowball, the white rabbit, by its haunches just before it slipped out the door.

At the sight of Snowball's panicked eyes, something inside Jenna's chest dropped, hard and fast. She hadn't thought of the fact that the animals could get away. Suddenly it seemed like all the creatures were scampering for the door, terrified by the screaming and running and crying.

Crying? Who's crying? Jenna glanced around the room and saw Marta, the girl from bunk 3A, standing with a drenched Stephanie bawling her eyes out. Julie was on the floor next to her with a Band-Aid and a wet cloth.

"What happened?" Nurse Helen asked, appearing on the scene.

"It was Rocco, the guinea pig," Marissa said, lifting the little pink-nosed animal in her arms. His eyes were darting around wildly. "He got scared and bit her ankle."

Nurse Helen pressed a piece of gauze into Marta's wound and when it came back all bloodstained, Jenna almost fainted.

"This is great!" Chelsea said as the chaos continued around them.

But it wasn't. It wasn't great at all. The animals were petrified and in danger. Marta's crying had sparked off a wave of tears among the younger girls. Everyone was miserable. And it was all her fault.

For the first time in her prank-filled life, Jenna knew immediately that she had gone too far.

chapter TWELVE

"I'm very disappointed in you, Jenna," Dr. Steve said, leaning back against the front of his desk. Jenna had to tip her head back to see up into his face. He blinked rapidly, as always, but now it wasn't funny. His expression was so harsh—so serious. Before Jenna knew it, she was looking at the floor again. "I know you've always been a prankster. Your whole family is famous for it. But you've never done anything that caused injury or true harm. What were you thinking?"

I was thinking I was miserable, Jenna thought, sinking lower in her seat. *I was mad at my sister and my brother for having fun. I needed to do something.*

She wasn't about to say any of this to the camp director. It hardly made sense to her—how was it supposed to make sense to him?

"Is Marta okay?" she asked finally, her voice small.

"She'll be fine," Dr. Steve said. "Of course

each of our animals have had their vaccinations, so there's no chance of rabies or infection."

Jenna let out a sigh of relief. If Marta had been mad at Jenna after Stephanie's reaction to the love-note prank, she must have hated Jenna now. But that didn't really matter. As long as Marta was okay, Jenna could deal with getting dirty looks from 3A for the rest of the summer. It was nothing new.

"But that's not the point, Jenna. The point is, it took over an hour to round up all the animals. Roseanne was beside herself with worry," Dr. Steve said, getting up and pacing to the other side of his desk. "On top of which, the camp social was ruined. There are over a hundred campers here who are none too happy with you."

"I know," Jenna said, her heart heavy.

She looked out the window at the bright blue sky. Even from here she could see the colorful helium balloons that were tied up all around the mess hall, welcoming the parents to camp for Visiting Day. Car doors slammed and kids shouted as they greeted thc families they hadn't seen in four full weeks. Shira raced around, playing the happy hostess. Jenna knew that back in her bunk, all her friends were putting on their best clothes, brushing their hair, getting ready for one of the biggest days of the summer. And where was she? Stuck in the director's office, waiting for her mom to come in for a meeting.

The prank had not been worth it. Not by a long shot.

Jenna wondered how many of the kids had already told their parents about the social. By the end of the day she *was* going to be famous—but in a bad way. Not exactly what Jenna had imagined.

There was a quick rap on the door, and Jenna's stomach turned.

"Come in," Dr. Steve said.

Jenna looked up to find her mother, brow wrinkled in concern, stepping into the room. Her curly hair was pulled back in a low ponytail, and she was wearing her favorite blue sundress and white sneakers. But her eyes looked tired and worried, and Jenna was instantly sorry for giving her anything negative to think about today.

Out of habit, Jenna looked for her father to step through the door after her, but of course, he didn't. It was like there was a big empty hole where he should have been.

"Jenna," her mother said. And Jenna was out of her chair like a shot, hugging her mother as tightly as she could. Jenna had no idea how much she'd missed her mom until that very second. "Honey, are you okay?" her mom asked. "Shira told me to come right to the office. Is there anything wrong?"

"I'm afraid we have to have a serious talk, Ms. Bloom," Dr. Steve said.

Jenna looked up at her mom, who looked back at her with that disappointed expression that Jenna knew so well from other after-prank meetings. She felt like she was about to cry. "I'm really sorry, Mom."

"It's okay, baby. Just wait outside while I talk to Dr. Steve," her mom said, running her hand over Jenna's hair. "I'll be right out."

"Hello, Mrs. Bloom," Dr. Steve said as Jenna slipped through the door. "And will Mr. Bloom be joining us?"

Jenna closed the door before she could hear her mother's response. She dropped down into a chair in the deserted waiting room, closed her eyes against her tears, and waited.

▲ ▲ ▲

"Let's go for a walk," Jenna's mother said when she stepped out of Dr. Steve's office. She was clutching her purse, and her mouth was set in a thin line. This was not a happy mom.

Jenna stood up quickly, her knees shaking almost as badly as they had on the diving pier. "I'm not kicked out of camp, am I?" she asked.

"No. You're not kicked out of camp," her mother said, opening the door for her with a loud creak. "Though I have to say, I find that decision surprising after what you pulled."

Thank you, thank you, thank you! Jenna thought, practically skipping out into the sunshine. Even though her mother was clearly upset with her, Jenna couldn't help being relieved that she wasn't going to have to go home. There was no way she could have handled living for four summer weeks at that house without her brothers and sister. They may have been annoying to have around camp, but she would need them at home. Especially with everything that was going on.

Jenna and her mother stepped onto the main drive where Pete and a bunch of the counselors were directing parents to parking spaces. There wasn't a paved lot at Camp Lakeview, so they made do with a wide expanse of dirt and did the best they could to fit in all the cars. The tires kicked up a lot of dust, and Pete and the guys were using the bandannas from last night's social to cover their mouths while they coughed.

"So, do you want to go find Stephanie?" Jenna asked brightly, hoping to change the subject.

"Eh! You're not getting off that easily, kid," her mother said. "You are going to be punished for what you did last night."

Jenna's heart fell. She had known this had to be coming, but she still didn't want to hear it. "What's my punishment?" she asked as they turned their steps toward the picnic tables at the edge of the woods.

"You'll be getting up early every morning for the next two weeks and helping Roseanne feed the animals and clean their cages," her mother said.

"Every morning?" Jenna blurted.

"Yes. Every morning," her mother replied. "And if you ask me, Dr. Steve is going lightly on you. This is the least you can do to make up for that ridiculous prank."

Jenna tucked her chin and tromped along, her hands hanging heavy at her sides. She knew what she had done was wrong, but that didn't make taking the punishment any easier.

"Jenna, is there anything you want to talk to me about?" her mother asked, dropping down on a bench at one of the tables. She hefted her large purse onto the grainy wood and turned her intent gaze on Jenna.

Suddenly Jenna's insides squirmed. "Like what?" she asked, sitting next to her mom.

"Like why you did this?" her mother asked. "I know you like to play jokes and mess around. I know you have a free spirit. But you're a smart girl. This wasn't a whoopee cushion or a trick pack of gum. You couldn't have thought this prank was harmless."

"I know," Jenna said quietly.

"So what made you do it?" her mother asked, reaching out and running her fingers through Jenna's hair, untangling it down her back. Usually Jenna loved her mother's gentle, comforting touch, but after everything she had done, it just made her feel worse—like she didn't deserve the attention.

"I don't know," Jenna said, knowing it was a lame answer.

"Well, let's think about it," her mother said, still combing. "What were you thinking about just before you let the animals into the dance? What were you feeling just then?"

Jenna flushed at the memory, her heart twisting in her chest.

"You can tell me, Jen," her mom said. "You know you can tell me anything."

"I was . . . I was mad," Jenna said finally. She stared at her sandaled feet, kicking out one, then the other, from under the bench.

"Mad at whom?" her mother asked gently.

"At Adam. And Stephanie," Jenna said.

"Your brother and sister?" her mother said, sounding surprised. "Why?"

"Because they were having so much fun!" Jenna blurted, finally looking at her mom. "And I don't get it! I don't get why they get to have so much fun while I'm so . . . so . . ."

"So what, Jenna?" her mom asked her.

"So sad!" Jenna half-shouted, a tear spilling over onto her cheek.

Her mother's eyes softened slightly, and she wrapped an arm around Jenna, pulling her to her side. Suddenly Jenna was crying loudly, pressing her face into her mother's shoulder to hide in case anyone happened to walk by.

"You're sad about me and your dad splitting up?" her mother said quietly.

Jenna nodded into her mom's arm and sniffled. "And no one else cares! They all act like there's nothing going on! They act like dad is still going to be living there when we get home. Like . . . like everything hasn't changed!"

"Oh, Jenna, I'm sure that's not true," her mother said. She wiped Jenna's tears with her thumbs and smiled down at her. "Everyone reacts to this kind of thing in his or her own way. Are you really telling me that neither of them—not Adam, or Stephanie—has acted any differently this summer?"

Jenna sniffled again and thought hard. She thought about Adam and how he had tried to talk to her a couple of times about the upcoming divorce—how she had avoided talking about it. And come to think of it, Adam *had* been spending a lot of time taking pictures and sitting alone in the darkroom, when in the past he had been as active and athletic as Jenna was. Plus, Stephanie was even more mothering than usual this year. Maybe each one of them *was* just dealing with their family's troubles in a different way.

"I guess," Jenna said finally. "I guess they have been acting a little weird."

Her mother sighed and looked out across the camp, watching as parents hugged their kids and walked off with them to tour the grounds. Jenna wished she were one of them. She wished she was happy and excited and rushing her mom and dad to meet her friends, like she had on every other Visiting Day. Jenna was sick of being upset.

"I'm sorry this is so hard for you guys," her mother said. "I wish there was something I could do to make it easier."

"I know," Jenna said sadly. "I'm just sorry I made it harder for you," she added, thinking about Matt's letters and how he had warned her to not get into trouble this year. He had been trying to protect her parents because they had enough to deal with: the divorce, her father moving. But instead of helping him protect their parents, Jenna had made things worse.

"Oh, sweetie!" her mother said, kissing her quickly on the forehead. "Please! I'm not your responsibility. I'm supposed to worry about *you*, not the other way around."

Jenna smiled slightly. "Well, okay, but I promise I'm not pulling any more pranks this summer," she said. "You're not going to get one more freak-out phone call."

"Freak-out phone call?" her mother asked.

Jenna laughed. "Long story."

"You're a good kid—you know that?" her mother said, reaching out to hug her again. "A little nutty, but generally good," she joked. Jenna grasped her mother tightly and closed her eyes. Everything was changing. She wished she could just stay here, hanging on to her mother forever, and that the rest of the world would just go back to the way it was.

"Hey! Look who's here!" her mother said, releasing her.

Jenna turned around to follow her mother's gaze, and her jaw dropped. There, walking toward her with her brothers and sister behind him, was her dad. He had a huge grin on his tanned face and was carrying a picnic basket bursting with food.

"Daddy!" Jenna shouted, running to him. Her brother laughed as she nearly tackled her father to the ground, but she couldn't help it. She was so surprised to see him—to see them all together—that she could hardly control herself.

"Hey, Boo!" he said, planting a kiss atop her head. He handed the basket to Stephanie and put his hands on his hips. "I have a bone to pick with you."

Jenna's heart skipped a beat. Was her dad mad about the prank as well?

Her father pulled a folded copy of *The Acorn* out of his back pocket and opened to the list of awards.

"Now, I really think you should stop winning so many events," he said. "It's just not fair to the other kids."

Jenna laughed as her dad ruffled her hair and draped his arm over her shoulder. Stephanie and Adam greeted their mother, and they all gathered around the table.

"Hello, Christine," Jenna's dad said, nodding as he sat at the other end of the bench.

"Hi, David," her mother replied with a small smile. "How was your drive?"

"Fine, thanks. Yours?" he asked.

"Great. Such a beautiful day," her mother replied.

Jenna exchanged a look with her siblings as their parents made small talk and unwrapped various sandwiches from the basket. It was weird, having them sit so far apart—having them talk to each other like strangers. But at least they were here, together. Things were definitely going to be different when Jenna got home after this summer, but maybe they wouldn't be as horrible as she had thought. She had imagined that her parents would never want to see each other again, that they would never be sitting all at the same table together like they were just then.

So her family wasn't perfect, but they never *had* been (especially not with Adam as part of it). Now they were just going to be a different kind of imperfect. Maybe, just maybe, Jenna could get used to it.

"I know what Jenna wants," her father said, opening the waxed paper around a white-bread sandwich. "A little peanut butter and banana?"

"Ugh!" her sister groaned as Jenna happily took the sandwich. "You're such a freak!"

Jenna took a huge bite and smiled a peanut-buttery smile. "I know," she said, her mouth full. "I like me that way."

And she meant it. However imperfect her family was, however imperfect *she* was, Jenna liked her life. From this moment on, she was going to start remembering that.

chapter THIRTEEN

Jenna sat in the darkroom that afternoon, determined to get at least one picture right before her two-week elective was over. Her parents had left half an hour earlier, after showering their kids with food and new clothes. Jenna had watched them talking as they'd walked to their cars, and even saw them hug good-bye. She knew enough to not hope that her parents were getting back together, but at least it seemed like their divorce wasn't going to be nasty and full of fights, like some of the divorces her friends had lived through.

"How's it going over there, Jenna?" Faith asked. She was working on her own pictures in the corner and now she looked up and checked her digital watch. "There's only about a half hour more of free time before dinner."

"I think it's going okay," Jenna replied, though she was at a total loss.

"Well, if you need any help . . ."

"I'll ask," Jenna assured her. But she didn't want to ask for help. She wanted to prove she could do it on her own.

Just then the door opened and in stepped Adam from the curtained area outside the darkroom. He glanced in Jenna's direction and closed the door quietly. Great. Had he come to mock her photography skills again?

"Hi, Faith," he said.

"Hey there, Adam," she said, not even looking up from her work. Apparently she was getting used to having him around all the time.

Adam weaved his way around the tables and took the stool next to Jenna's. "Hey," he said, looking at her supplies. "How's it going?"

"Fine," she lied. In the twenty minutes she had been in the darkroom she hadn't printed one good picture.

"So, was Mom pretty mad about the prank last night?" Adam asked.

Jenna glanced at Faith, but then realized it didn't matter if they talked about it here. Everyone in camp knew she was responsible for the Great Animal Escape, which was what Pete had called it that afternoon.

"Not really," Jenna said. "She was cool about it."

"That's good," Adam said. He started lining up her film strips on the table, organizing them for her. "I mean, she probably would have been *really* mad if she knew what else you had done this summer."

Jenna froze. "What do you mean, what else I've done?"

"Oh, you know, the sugar in the salt shakers . . . that picture you took of Stephanie," Adam said. "You know, that was a nice shot. Maybe you should just stick to Polaroid. It's more your speed."

Jenna was too stunned to even whack him on the shoulder for the insult. When had Adam figured out that she was behind the other pranks? "What do you . . ."

Jenna stopped when Adam gave her an "oh, please" look. He was her twin, after all. He knew her better than anyone. There was no point in trying to act all innocent around him.

"All right. How did you know?" Jenna asked, her shoulders slumping.

"Well, first of all, the salt shaker thing was just like the trick you played on Uncle Earl last Thanksgiving," Adam pointed out, shifting on his stool. "You remember? When you put apple cider in the gravy boat?"

Jenna laughed. "Right! And he didn't even notice."

"Said it was the best gravy he'd ever had," Adam said with a smile.

"Aunt Jo did not like that," Jenna said. "Okay, so maybe the sugar prank wasn't the most original idea I've ever had. But what about the Stephanie thing?"

"Well, you and I are the only ones who know about that gross mask thing of hers except for the girls in her bunk," Adam said with a shrug. "I knew it wasn't me, and all the girls in her bunk worship her . . . so I figured somebody had to talk them into it. Who else would do it but you?"

Jenna let out a little whistle. "Wow. You're good. Maybe you should become a detective or something."

Adam grinned wickedly. "Why do you think I'm so interested in photography?" he said. "P.I.'s make tons of money, you know."

Jenna was struck for the millionth time by how much her brother's thoughts were like her own. Back when she had decided to take photography one of the reasons was so that she could learn to take spy pictures of her family. Clearly Adam was thinking along the same lines.

"So if you knew all along . . . why didn't you tell on me?" Jenna asked.

"I don't know," Adam said, toying with a lever on the exposure machine. "I guess I just figured . . . you know . . . we already had enough stuff going on. I didn't want you to get in trouble on top of everything else."

Jenna's heart squeezed, and for the first time since she was about five years old, she felt like hugging her brother. She resisted the urge, though. It was just too weird. He probably would think that she was taping a "Kick Me" sign to his back.

"Is . . . is that why you've been hanging out in here so much?" Jenna asked him, looking down. "Because you're upset about Mom and Dad?"

Adam shrugged again. "I dunno. Maybe. It's just weird hanging out with the guys and trying to have fun when all these bad things are going through my mind.

It's like one second I'm laughing and then all of a sudden I remember that Dad moved out and I don't really think anything's funny after that. Would you believe that Eric and those guys actually started calling me Adam-Moody? Like it's all one name. Adamoody."

Jenna laughed at the joke, then covered her mouth. "I totally know how you feel," she said. "It's like one second I'm happy and the next second I'm yelling at people. No one's given me a nickname yet, though."

"Huh," Adam said, his eyes wide. "You really do know how I feel."

"Yeah. I do," Jenna said. She felt about a million percent better to know that her brother was going through the same emotions she was.

"Wow," Adam said, looking as surprised and relieved as Jenna felt. "We should have talked about this ages ago."

"Tell me about it," Jenna replied.

They sat there smiling at each other for a long moment. *Huh. Maybe Adam's not so bad after all,* Jenna thought. And somehow she knew he was thinking the same thing about her.

"So, you want me to show you how to do this or what?" Adam asked, sliding closer to her.

Normally Jenna would have gotten all defensive if Adam, or anyone else, had forced his help on her, but for the first time all summer, she felt calm. She felt like she could deal with the fact that she wasn't good at photography. She felt like she could, and should, ask for help.

"Yes, I do," Jenna said. "I really, really do."

▲ ▲ ▲

The next day, Jenna trailed behind the rest of her bunk on the way to free swim. Ever since the Great Animal Escape all her friends had been sort of cold to her. They weren't ignoring her completely, but they weren't being all that friendly, either. The very idea of sitting by the lake on the outskirts of their crowd made her cringe. All she could do was hope that they wouldn't be mad at her forever.

"Hey, Jenna! Wait up!" Marissa called out, jogging to catch up with her. As always, the CIT was perfectly coordinated with a red bathing suit, red flip-flops, and a red-and-white striped plastic bag full of magazines and suntan lotion.

"Hi," Jenna said, surprised that Marissa wanted to walk with her. The CITs, especially Marissa and Stephanie, had been looking forward to the social more than anyone else in camp. Jenna had figured they would be madder at her than the rest of the campers.

"So, how's it going?" Marissa asked, her ponytail swinging back and forth as they walked.

"Okay," Jenna said, pulling her towel more tightly around her body. "Except everyone hates me."

"Everyone does not hate you," Marissa said, slinging

her arm over Jenna's shoulders. "It was just the camp social. Half the people there didn't want to be there, anyway."

"Really?" Jenna said.

"Please! You remember what it was like when you first started here," Marissa said. "All the younger kids don't know what to do at dances, whether they're square or otherwise. And, you didn't hear this from me, but all the CITs want to do is sneak off and smooch somewhere," she added, lowering her voice.

"Oh, ick!" Jenna said, sticking out her tongue with a laugh.

"All I'm saying is, people will get over it," Marissa said. "You'll see."

Just then, Marissa tripped forward a few steps and Jenna caught her arm.

"Stupid flip-flops," Marissa muttered. One of her red sandals was lying on the path a foot back, having slipped off. "Hang on a sec, will you? I want to put on my tennis shoes."

"Sure," Jenna said, following Marissa over to a rock so she could sit. Jenna didn't see what the big deal was. The lake was about fifty yards away, and Marissa could definitely make it without changing her shoes. But Jenna wasn't in any hurry to get to free swim, anyway, so she waited, watching the other campers laughing and chatting as they streamed by.

Marissa pulled out a pair of white tennis shoes and shoved her feet into them, then placed the flip-flops back into her bag. She retied the knots in her laces and finally stood up.

"Okay, all ready," Marissa said, dusting herself off. They started toward the lake again, side by side. "So . . . you think you want to try diving again today?"

"I don't know," Jenna said, feeling that familiar pit of fear start to form in her stomach. "Maybe I could give it a try . . ."

Her words trailed off as she and Marissa came to the end of the pathway and stepped onto the sand. There, directly in front of her on the beginners' diving pier, was her entire bunk, along with Tyler, Stephanie, and Adam. They were all lined up on either side of the platform like they were forming a runway.

"Let's go, Jenna!" Stephanie cheered. Everyone clapped and shouted and called out her name.

"Omigosh," Jenna said, stepping to the edge of the pier. "What are you guys doing?"

"We're helping you dive," Tyler said, stepping forward and walking her to the edge of the platform. "This whole scaredey-cat thing? It's definitely not you."

"You think?" Jenna said.

"Come on, Jen," Stephanie said. "You're the bravest chick we know. I mean, what you pulled the other night might have been totally beyond stupid— ow!" Adam had nudged Stephanie in the side to get her to stop talking. She rubbed her ribs and continued. "But it takes guts to do stuff like that."

"Yeah, if you can coordinate the Great Animal Escape, you can totally dive," Natalie put in.

"Not that we're saying you should ever do anything like that again," Julie put in. *"Ever."*

"Don't worry. I am all pranked out," Jenna assured her.

"Come on, Jen," Marissa said. "Do you really want to be standing on the planks all summer, or do you want to dive in and join the rest of us?"

Jenna stepped up to the edge of the platform. Maybe it was because her heart was so full, thanks to her friends and family for supporting her. Or maybe she just didn't care anymore. But either way, the fear was barely there anymore. Marissa was right. It was time for Jenna to take the plunge. It was time for her to do something really daring.

Jenna stood with her toes hanging over the edge of the pier and raised her arms over her head the way Tyler had taught her. With all her friends, her counselors, her brother and sister cheering behind her, Jenna grinned, took a deep breath, and went for it.

Book #3

camp CONFIDENTIAL

chapter ONE

Dear Emily,

Hey there, chiquita! What's up back in Boringtown, U.S.A.? I bet you've been spending the whole summer just lying by the pool, right? I'm having a blast here at Camp Lakeview, as if that's any surprise! My bunkmates rule—they're almost as cool as you. (Calm down, I said almost!) I'm in the same bunk as Brynn, Jenna, and Alex again, which is so much fun. It's hard to believe I haven't seen them since last summer—we just slipped right back into our old friendship. I'm lucky to have so many friends here. Not that they'll ever replace you, my bestest friend in the world! I wish you could come to Lakeview, too. It's weird not seeing you for the entire summer. And I know you're probably mad at me. I'm sorry I haven't written yet, Em, but you know how it is. I keep meaning to, but then—

Whatever. I haven't told you the most amazing thing. One of the new girls in my bunk, Natalie, is the daughter of Tad Maxwell!! Can you believe it?? He came to Lakeview with his girlfriend once in the early days of camp, but he couldn't make it for Visiting Day last week. If only my parents were famous movie stars so they would be too busy to get here for a visit. But no, they showed up. With another boring book for me to read. Ugh. Can you believe it? Jenna's parents brought a truckload of food *in their care package, and my parents bring The Jungle Book. Why would anyone want to read that when they can just watch the cartoon? Anyway, Mom and Dad spent the whole time lecturing me, as I'm sure you can imagine—*

Grace Matthews sighed and put down her pen. Her best friend, Emily, deserved a letter. She'd already sent three letters to Grace at Camp Lakeview, and Grace hadn't answered even one. But it took so long to write a letter . . . and there was always so much fun stuff to do at camp. Her copy of *The Call of the Wild* lay upside down at the foot of her bed, open to the last page she'd read. Grace grabbed it and pulled it halfheartedly onto her lap. Reading was almost as boring as writing. She glanced around bunk 3C at all her friends. Sure, some of them were reading or writing letters, but lots of them were busy doing more interesting stuff. Well, except for Chelsea, who seemed to be doing nothing but staring at herself in her hand mirror. Chelsea was beautiful, but it still had to be pretty boring to spend all your time looking at your own face. Grace shrugged and turned her attention to one of the other old-time campers like herself.

"Hey, Brynn," Grace called down from her top

bunk. "What on earth are you doing?"

Brynn stood in the center of the small room, her feet planted about ten inches apart on the scuffed wooden floor. She was bent over at the waist, her arms hanging down and her short dark red hair falling over her face. She'd been standing like that for at least two minutes. "It's yoga," Brynn said, her voice muffled. She was speaking into her knees, after all. "My mom gave me an article on Visiting Day about how lots of actors do yoga to keep themselves focused."

Grace grinned. She loved acting, and she knew Brynn did, too. In fact, it was the only real interest Brynn had. "Mind if I join you?"

Brynn shook her upside-down head. Grace jumped down from her bunk, took her place next to Brynn, and copied the strange position. Just before she bent over, she noticed Julie, their counselor, shoot a look up at the unfinished letter and book on Grace's bed. Grace felt her cheeks grow warm, and she quickly leaned over so she wouldn't have to meet Julie's gaze.

Hanging head-down wasn't much better, though. All the blood rushed to her head, making her cheeks and neck feel hot. Her curly red hair was longer than Brynn's, and it kept getting in her eyes and covering her face. She moved to pull away a strand that had gotten caught in her mouth, but Brynn protested. "You're supposed to keep still," she said. "Don't move; just pay attention to your breathing and to the stretch in your back muscles."

"That's right, Grace, don't forget to breathe," Jenna Bloom said from across the room. Jenna put on a slow, deep voice as if she were trying to hypnotize someone. "Breathe in . . . breathe out. Breathe in . . . breathe in some more," Jenna said in her "soothing" voice.

Grace couldn't help it—she got the giggles. "How can I pay attention to my breathing when I can't breathe?" she asked. Leaning over like this made it hard to take a deep breath, and she felt herself getting a little dizzy. She stood up quickly and got a head rush. "Whoa," she cried, stumbling backward. Luckily Marissa, bunk 3C's CIT, or counselor-in-training, was there to catch her.

"I'm not sure you're mellow enough to do yoga, Grace," Marissa joked.

Brynn stood up very slowly. "It's too bad," she commented. "You could be such a good actress if you tried. Yoga could really help you be more centered."

Grace decided to ignore her. Brynn's whole goal in life was to be a famous actor, and she could never understand why Grace wasn't as focused on that as she was. But to Grace, acting was just something fun to do. She loved it—she *totally* loved it—but mostly because it was easy, and she was good at it, and it gave her a chance to be someone else for a few minutes. She didn't need to be famous or anything. She just loved acting. Whenever things got tough in school, acting was her favorite way to escape from the pressure. But none of her bunkmates knew that. None of them had any idea how it was back at school. Summer camp was for fun, not stress, and that was exactly how Grace liked it.

"There's no more time for yoga now, anyway," Marissa said. "Dinner's ready. I just came back to grab my hair band—I forgot it." Marissa snatched a pink elastic band from her cot and took off, letting the screen door bang shut behind her as she scooped her long hair up into a ponytail. She and the other CITs were responsible for serving the meals in the mess hall. If you could call them meals.

"Okay, everyone, let's go chow down," Julie called.

"You don't have to tell me twice," Jenna joked, heading for the door. She was so athletic that she spent lots of time eating—she needed plenty of fuel to burn out on the soccer field. She, Alex, and Sarah were the big jocks in the bunk. Grace liked sports well enough, but she wasn't as obsessed with them as some of her friends.

"I think it's spaghetti night," Alex said. She rolled her eyes at Brynn, her best friend. "In other words . . ."

". . . cardboard strips in tomato soup," Brynn finished for her. They both laughed.

Grace had to admit, the food at Camp Lakeview wasn't gourmet. In fact, it was even worse than the cafeteria food back at school. But eating every night in the noisy mess hall surrounded by all the other Lakeview campers was enough fun that the food didn't matter.

She climbed down the two rickety steps from the cabin and followed her bunkmates along the path toward the mess hall. Natalie and Alyssa, another 3C camper, walked right behind her.

"I didn't even get to dance with him," Alyssa was saying. "It's no big deal."

"But he obviously likes you," Natalie replied.

Grace grinned and turned around to walk backward so she could talk to them. "Still talking about the camp social?" she asked. "It was almost a week ago!"

Alyssa shrugged, making her orange hair swing. She'd dyed it that color the night before the social—by accident. It was supposed to be red, but something had gone horribly wrong. Grace was secretly a little relieved not to be the most Ronald McDonald-like girl in the bunk for a change. But on Alyssa, the strange color actually looked good—sort of punk. Alyssa was so artsy that she could make anything weird seem stylish.

"Adam was totally flirting with Alyssa at the social," Natalie said. "And I know she likes him, too. She's just being shy."

Alyssa stuck out her tongue at Natalie. "And *you're* just trying to make us forget about you and Simon," she teased.

Grace laughed. It was true, Natalie's relationship with Simon had been the big topic of discussion in bunk 3C for the past few weeks. Well, first it had been Natalie's famous father, and then Natalie's sort-of boyfriend, Simon. But for the past few days, talk had been a little more serious in the bunk.

Grace glanced over her shoulder to see where Jenna was. She was tromping through the trees at the head of the group, as usual. "Hey, do you guys think Jenna's doing okay?" she asked, lowering her voice.

Natalie squinted at Jenna's back. "She's been kinda sticking to herself, I guess," she said. "But I think that's normal."

Alyssa nodded. "She's probably still embarrassed about the Great Animal Escape."

Grace shuddered just thinking about it. Jenna had always been a prankster—some of the best memories Grace had from the previous summer were of helping Jenna prank their rival bunk, 3A. But the night before this year's Visiting Day, Jenna had gone too far. She'd let all the animals from the nature shack out of their cages . . . and into the camp social. It had been mayhem, and Jenna had gotten in a lot of trouble.

"Adam says she'll be fine," Alyssa said. "And he should know, he's her twin!"

"Oh, is that what *Adam* says?" Grace joked.

Natalie laughed, but Alyssa didn't even blush. She could be pretty impressive sometimes. When Grace had first met her, she'd thought Alyssa was shy because she was so quiet. But in the past month, she'd discovered that Alyssa wasn't shy—she just didn't see the need to talk unless she had something to say.

"It must be nice to have a twin," Natalie commented. "It's like having your own built-in best friend for life."

"Yeah, must be nice," Grace agreed. She turned back around to walk forward. Suddenly Grace realized that her whole bunk was lined up in pairs. Jenna walked along chatting with Julie, whom she'd known for years because her whole family had been coming to Lakeview since forever. Then Brynn and Alex, Sarah and Valerie, Candace and Jessie, Alyssa and Nat . . . even Chelsea had a buddy. She was walking with Karen, one of the most timid girls in the bunk. That was sort of a weird combination, but the rest of the pairs were totally normal. They were all best friends. Everyone had a partner...except for Grace.

Grace felt a pang of homesickness. Well, maybe not *home*sickness, exactly. More like *friend*sickness. She missed Emily. They'd been best friends since kindergarten, and Emily knew everything about Grace's life and her family and all her issues . . .

Why don't I have a best friend at camp? Grace suddenly wondered. *Everyone else does.*

The thought had never occurred to her before, and it was so shocking that she stopped in her tracks. How had she managed to spend a whole summer here last year without making a best friend? And she'd been here for half the summer this year without one, too.

"Whoa, Grace, did you fall asleep standing up?" Natalie laughed, pushing her gently in the back. "I almost walked right into you!"

"Oh. Sorry," Grace mumbled. Nat and Alyssa stepped in front of her, and Grace trailed after them.

"It was nice to meet your mom on Visiting Day," Alyssa told Natalie. "She's more my speed than your father. No offense."

"Don't worry. Even I can't keep up with my dad's crazy life," Natalie replied. "But I always have fun with my mother. And she really liked your parents—she told me so."

"Yeah, maybe over the winter we can all hang out," Alyssa said. "Our parents can keep one another busy, and then we can get away with doing whatever we want!"

Natalie grinned and gave her a high five.

Grace sighed. If only her parents were the kind of people she could have fun with. But they never even seemed to understand the idea of fun. Lately the only thing they did was give her lectures or "talks" or "suggestions." Even at Visiting Day, they hadn't wanted to talk about camp. They'd wanted to give her another lecture.

Snap out of it, Grace ordered herself. *Mom and Dad aren't here now. So I don't have to think about it.* She was here at Lakeview, her favorite place in the world, and she was going to enjoy every minute of it. Or at least she was going to try. It would be easier, though, if she could talk to someone about what was going on . . .

Grace quickened her pace, catching up to Natalie and Alyssa. They were still talking about Visiting Day, but Grace's mind wasn't on their conversation. She just watched the two of them, walking along close together, teasing and laughing with each other . . . they'd only known each other for a month, and yet they acted like old friends. Best friends.

I can't believe I didn't finish that letter to Emily, Grace thought, horrified. What if her best friend really was mad at her for not writing all summer? Grace had promised and promised that this year would be different. That this summer she'd actually keep in touch. The whole time, she'd known that Emily didn't believe her. Emily assumed that she wouldn't get a single letter from Grace, and so far, she was right.

Grace took a deep breath. Of course Emily wouldn't be mad. Emily understood how hard it was for Grace to write . . . that it took too long and kept her from relaxing and having fun at camp. Emily would just shake her head and laugh, because that's what best friends did.

A burst of laughter erupted from Natalie and Alyssa in front of her, and Grace felt a little flicker of jealousy. If she had a best friend at camp, she wouldn't have to keep this all to herself. She'd be able to talk about her parents' annoying behavior at Visiting Day. She'd be able to talk about . . .

Oh, never mind, Grace thought. *I have lots of friends here. And that's better than just one. Isn't it?*

chapter TWO

"Whoo-hoo!" Grace yelled the next day on the path from bunk 3C. "Time for drama!" She pumped her arm in the air like a demented football fan.

Alex giggled, but Brynn rolled her eyes. "It's time for drama, Grace, not time to be *over*dramatic."

Grace stopped pumping her arm and instead draped it over Brynn's shoulders. "Okay, I'm just playing around," she admitted. "But I *am* psyched for drama. It's my favorite free choice."

Alex pushed back a branch that stuck out into the path, then held it so it wouldn't hit Grace and Brynn. "Then why didn't you take drama last session?" she asked Grace.

Grace shrugged. "Everybody likes drama. I figured I'd give some of the other kids a chance. And besides, I did put it as my number three choice last session. Julie just didn't give it to me."

"She always gives me drama for my free choice," Brynn said. "She knows there's no way I'd be cooped up with the smelly animals in the nature shack when I could be honing my craft."

"Phoning your what?" Grace teased.

Brynn laughed. "That's what my mother calls it. 'Honing my craft.' I think it means rehearsing."

"Wow. All that practicing *and* big, new words. I'm impressed," Grace said.

"What's your other free choice, Grace?" Alex asked.

"Arts and crafts."

Alex wrinkled her nose. "Yuck, I hate arts and crafts. The clay smells so bad."

"Maybe I'll do an improv scene about that in drama," Grace joked. "I'll pretend to be throwing a pot on the wheel, and then I'll act as if I'm overcome by fumes." She staggered backward, pretending to gasp for air.

"Very convincing." Alex giggled. "You'll definitely get a role in the camp play."

A little thrill of excitement ran down Grace's body. It was true, she wasn't as consumed by drama as Brynn. But that didn't keep her from being psyched by the idea of the play. "Now *that* would be fun," she said. "I wonder what play they're doing this year."

"*Peter Pan*," Brynn said. "I'm so excited!" She nudged Grace in the side. "And remember, we have unfinished business from last summer."

"Oh. That's right. I forgot." Grace tried to sound casual, but inside she felt a rush of humiliation. She'd been hoping Brynn wouldn't remember their deal.

"What unfinished business?" Alex asked.

"Grace and I made a pact at the end of last summer," Brynn explained. "She was so mad at herself for not auditioning for the camp play last year that we promised we'd audition together this year—and that we'd both get parts!"

Grace kept a smile plastered on her face. Now was not the time to tell Brynn that she might not be able to keep up her end of the bargain. *Maybe I can audition,* Grace thought. *Maybe.*

"I can't believe you made a pact and you didn't tell me," Alex teased Brynn.

"I don't have to tell you everything," Brynn said.

"Yes you do. That's what best friends do." Alex playfully rolled her eyes. "Tell her, Grace."

"It's true. Best friends tell each other everything," Grace confirmed. She thought about Emily. Emily was the only one who knew what was going on in Grace's life right now. If only she were here . . .

"Okay, I broke the best-friend rule," Brynn said. "Can you ever forgive me?"

"Sure. That's also what best friends do. But don't let it happen again!" Alex joked. "Here we are."

They stopped in front of the dilapidated cabin that housed the drama department. Grace knew from last summer that the place was bigger inside than it looked from outside. The whole cabin was one big, open room, painted black, and the only furniture were black wooden boxes that acted as chairs, tables, couches, and whatever else was needed. All it took was a little imagination to make the place feel like a palace or a diner or a store in the Wild West. That's what made drama class so much fun.

"Uh-oh," Alex murmured, stepping closer to Brynn and Grace. "Looks like you're in for trouble." She pointed with her chin toward a tall, skinny girl just entering the drama shack.

"Oh, no," Brynn said. "A spy from bunk 3A!"

They all laughed. Their bunk had an old rivalry with bunk 3A. Grace wasn't sure how it had started—when she arrived at camp last summer, one of the first things she learned was that 3A was the enemy. It didn't really matter why. The play rivalry was just for fun, anyway. Last week the girls from 3A had jokingly sprinkled food coloring on 3C's fried chicken at lunch. They hadn't noticed it on the food, but by the time they finished eating, Grace and her entire bunk had bright orange coloring on their fingers and lips. Not even swimming in the lake had gotten the color off their hands. So the 3A girls probably figured that 3C was planning some kind of prank as payback.

Alex and Brynn sneered at the 3A girl as she walked inside, then cracked up.

"We'll just have to *act* like we don't mind her," Grace joked.

"Have fun!" Alex gave her friends a little wave and headed off toward the newspaper shack for her own free choice.

Grace followed Brynn into the cool darkness of the drama shack, her heart beating fast with anticipation. "I can't wait to hear about the play," she told Brynn as they sat on the floor with the kids who were already there. "I mean, being on the stage crew was a lot of fun last summer, but I'd rather at least be one of the background actors."

"Yeah, that was pretty cool," Brynn replied. In last year's play, she had been one of the youngest kids onstage, even though she didn't get to say any lines. "If you don't goof around this year, you can get a part, too," she added.

Grace didn't answer. Brynn was right—she'd been so busy clowning around during drama last summer that she hadn't even managed to memorize the lines for her audition scene. But she'd learned her lesson. That was the reason she'd made the pact with Brynn—so that she'd be serious about auditioning this year.

Suddenly she felt a head next to her own. "Geez, she sounds like a teacher or something, lecturing you like that," a voice whispered in her ear.

Grace turned in surprise to see who was talking to her. It was the tall girl from bunk 3A. Up close, Grace could see that every inch of the girl's face, neck, and arms was covered in freckles. *Wow, she's even more freckly than me!* Grace thought.

"If you don't goof around, you'll get a part," the girl said in a fake high-pitched voice, making fun of Brynn.

Brynn shot her a nasty look and scooched farther

away, but Grace couldn't help smiling. Brynn *did* sound like a nag sometimes. She always wanted Grace to be more serious about acting. Grace knew it was because Brynn thought she was talented. But still, sometimes her friend got a little too intense.

"You're in 3C, right?" the tall girl asked.

Grace nodded. "I'm Grace."

"I'm Gaby." She pulled her long brown hair back and tied it in a careless knot. "I'll forgive you for being in a lame bunk."

"Oh." Grace wasn't sure what to say. It was hard to tell if Gaby was kidding or not. "Thanks."

"Okay, everyone, let's get started!" Bethany, the drama instructor, strode into the room and stood in front of the group. She was tiny, with the wiry body of a dancer and wispy dark hair. But Grace knew from last summer that Bethany was a powerhouse when it came to acting. As soon as she got into a character, her whole appearance seemed to change. "I know what you're all wondering, so I'm just going to get it out of the way right now," Bethany went on. "The play this year will be *Peter Pan*."

Brynn turned to Grace excitedly. "I'm totally trying out for Wendy," she whispered.

"But that's a big part," Grace whispered back. "Are you sure?"

"Absolutely. How else am I going to get experience?" Brynn replied.

Gaby let out a loud snort. "You don't stand a chance,"

she said loudly. "Our CIT said that nobody from the third division ever gets a lead role. You're too young."

"Well then, *you're* too young to get a good part, too," Brynn shot back. "You're in the third division just like us."

"Girls!" Bethany interrupted. "I need everyone to pay attention. Now, for the record, any camper from any division is eligible for any role in the play. Since the beginning of the summer, all the kids who have taken drama have been given audition pieces to work on, so auditions aren't limited to just this class. You don't have to try out, but you can if you want to." She looked right at Brynn and Gaby. "No one is kept out because they're too young."

"Right. It's just because you're too dumb," cracked one of the boys from the fifth division.

"Speak for yourself," Brynn murmured.

Grace bit back a laugh. Brynn was usually really nice. But if you got on her bad side, she had no problem defending herself.

"I don't care what anyone says. I'm going to play Wendy," Brynn announced loudly.

Several of the other kids snickered or rolled their eyes. Grace sighed. She liked Brynn—she always had—but she had to admit that sometimes Brynn could get a little overbearing. During auditions last year, Brynn had spent one whole weekend being in character as Annie Oakley, just to get herself ready for her audition piece from *Annie Get Your Gun*. She wouldn't even speak to her bunkmates unless they called her "Annie." She called it "method acting." Apparently lots of famous celebrities use the technique to prepare for a role. Was 3C in for the same thing this year?

"Auditions are next Wednesday," Bethany went on. "There are two audition scenes to choose from for the girls and two for the boys. Everyone will have a partner, and your job is to help each other prepare. The first half hour of every class will be devoted to practicing for your auditions."

Grace leaned toward Brynn, but before she could say anything, she felt Gaby poke her in the side. She glanced over at the tall girl.

"Wanna be partners?" Gaby asked. "You're the only fun one here."

"Thanks, but . . ." Grace wasn't sure what to say. She'd assumed she would partner up with Brynn since they were bunkmates. But Brynn didn't even seem to have heard the whole "partner" speech. She was staring straight ahead, her lips moving as she recited a scene to herself. Grace knew all too well how being Brynn's partner would turn out—they'd spend all their free time working on their audition scenes, and Brynn would constantly tell Grace that she should practice more. It wouldn't be any fun at all. And besides, Brynn had Alex to help her practice. Grace got the feeling that being partners with Brynn would really mean being partners with Brynn *and* her best friend. Except for free choice, Brynn and Alex were always together. Grace would just be the third wheel, the way she always seemed to end up with her bunkmates.

"Well?" Gaby was grinning at her, and Grace had to admit that it was flattering to know somebody wanted her as a partner. She barely knew Gaby at all because they never socialized with bunk 3A. But maybe that silly rivalry had cost her the chance to make a best friend at camp. Gaby was outgoing just like her, and Gaby seemed to want to have fun in drama, just like her. Why not partner up?

"Sure," she said. "It'll be a blast."

▲ ▲ ▲

"I can't believe you did that!" Brynn fumed. They were only ten feet away from their bunk, and Brynn had been yelling at Grace the whole way back from the drama shack.

"Shh!" Grace hissed. "Do you want everyone else to hear you?"

Brynn glanced up at bunk 3C. "Why should I care if they hear?" she asked. "I'm not the one who stabbed my friend in the back!"

Natalie's face appeared in the window, and Candace peered out the door. Grace sighed. Now her disagreement with Brynn would become a bunk-wide discussion. "I didn't mean to stab you in the back," she said for the fifth time. Brynn had been so busy ranting during the walk back that

Grace didn't think she'd heard her the first four times. "I really, really didn't."

"What's going on?" Chelsea demanded, popping out the door of the bunk. Whenever there was any kind of controversy, Chelsea was always the first one to stick her nose into it. "What are you guys fighting about?"

"Yeah, why are you fighting?" Candace asked, sounding much more concerned than Chelsea.

"We're not fighting," Grace said. "We're just . . . disagreeing."

"Oh, please," Chelsea said. "Brynn was totally yelling at you. You are too fighting."

"No we aren't," Brynn said immediately. "Grace and I are friends. We don't fight."

Grace had to smile. Sometimes when Chelsea was rude, it made everyone else band together to oppose her. "That's right," Grace said. "Brynn is just upset because I decided not to be her partner in drama."

"So that's how you stabbed her in the back?" Chelsea asked.

"She didn't mean to stab me in the back," Brynn retorted. "She was just being nice to this girl from 3A who asked her to be partners first. You know Grace—she can never say no to people. She thinks it will hurt their feelings."

Grace blinked in surprise. Apparently Brynn *had* heard her the first four times she'd tried to explain about Gaby and the drama class.

Brynn noticed her expression and laughed. "What?" she said. "I was upset so I wanted to vent. It doesn't mean I wasn't listening."

"Oh. Then do you need me to apologize again?" Grace asked. "Because I will. I never meant to insult you."

"I know," Brynn grumbled, heading inside. "You were just making a new friend. Still, I'm bummed that we won't be partners. What about our pact?"

"We can still audition together," Grace said.

"Okay." Brynn gave her a bright smile. But Grace felt nauseous. What if she couldn't audition? Wouldn't Brynn be even madder at her then?

I won't let that happen, Grace told herself. *Somehow I have to audition for the play.*

▲ ▲ ▲

"Hey, Grace!" Natalie called at free swim the next day. "Are you swimming?"

Grace wandered over to where Natalie had her whole setup on the little beach next to the lake. Nat was an excellent swimmer—she'd been placed in the highest level, blue, immediately, even though it was only her first summer here. But she almost never swam during free swim. She preferred to sun herself and read her fashion magazines. Grace plopped down on the edge of Natalie's super-huge towel.

"I don't know," she said. "My stomach's been

hurting ever since breakfast this morning. I think I finally hit my limit on greasy sausages."

"Shh! Don't say that in front of Marissa," Natalie said. She nodded toward their CIT, who was on her way over to them.

Grace grinned. Marissa had served the less-than-tasty breakfast food, true. But it had been prepared by Pete, Camp Lakeview's official assistant cook. Last year he had been a counselor, but for some reason, this summer he'd decided to torture them by learning to cook. In spite of the bad food, everybody loved Pete. Especially Marissa. She did a bad job of hiding her crush on Pete—all the girls in 3C were sure they were secretly dating. Plus, Pete was a great guy. Grace didn't want to insult either of them.

"It's probably just a stomachache from stress, anyway," Grace said. "The stress of living through Brynn's wrath!"

Natalie giggled. "She was pretty mad at you yesterday. I can't believe you picked that 3A girl to be your drama partner over Brynn!"

"No, I didn't," Grace protested. "Gaby asked me first."

"Are we still talking about the drama in drama?" Marissa quipped as she reached them. She pulled out her own super-huge towel and spread it on the sand next to Natalie's. This had been their free-swim ritual since the second day of camp. It worked pretty well for everyone—you could always leave your stuff with Nat and Marissa while you went swimming.

"I didn't mean to be rude to Brynn," Grace said. "But she's so intense all the time, and I like acting because it's fun. We'd be bad partners. She's too serious and I'm not serious enough!"

"Well, I have to agree with that," Marissa said.

"Besides, why shouldn't I expand my horizons a little?" Grace added. "Who cares if I hang out with Gaby? Aren't we here at camp to make new friends?"

Natalie snorted. "You sound like my mother."

"I have *CosmoGIRL*, *Teen People*, and *Teen Vogue*," Marissa announced, pulling the magazines from her bag. "Who wants what?"

"Ugh, no *Teen People* for me," Natalie said, laughing. "I've had enough of celebrities."

"All right, it's *Teen Vogue* for you and *CosmoGIRL* for Grace," Marissa said, handing over the thick mag. "It's the Back-to-School issue."

"No wonder it weighs five thousand pounds," Grace said, lugging the magazine toward her. "Back to school isn't back to school without three hundred pages of fashion advice."

"Don't forget the dating advice," Natalie said. "And the friendship advice, and the how-to-organize-your-locker advice . . ."

"And the makeup and the hair . . ." Marissa added.

Grace flopped back on the big towel and put the magazine over her face. "I really just wanted a sunshade," she joked. "That much advice will kill me!"

"I can't believe the start of school is so close," Natalie said. "It's only a month away!"

"Summer goes too fast," Marissa agreed.

Grace sat back up. School was the last thing she wanted to be talking about on a perfect summer day. "You guys, we still have half the summer left," she pointed out. "Who cares if the magazines come out early?"

"You're right." Natalie was flipping through hers. "Let's just find a fun quiz and forget about school."

"Now you're talking." Grace turned the pages until she found a quiz in her own magazine. "Here we go. 'How to Know If Your Love Will Last.' Well, Nat? Do you know if your love with Simon will last?"

Natalie swatted her while Marissa laughed. "No one said we are in love. You just wait until you find some cute boy, Grace."

"No thanks," Grace said. "Boys are nothing but trouble."

"You said it!" Gaby appeared next to them, her tall form casting a long shadow over the blankets. "Mind if I sit?"

"Hang on." Grace grabbed her own towel and quickly spread it out. "Have a seat. I've been hogging Natalie's towel this whole time, and it's pretty comfortable."

"Good, then I'll hog yours!" Gaby folded her long legs and sat. "How come you're not swimming?" she asked Grace.

"My stomach feels a little funky. What about you?"

Gaby shrugged. "I just don't feel like it."

"Are you Grace's new drama partner?" Marissa asked.

"Yup! It's gonna be a nonstop party, right, Grace?"

"Absolutely," Grace said. "We should probably choose our audition scenes—we're supposed to tell Bethany tomorrow which ones we're doing."

"What are the choices?" Natalie asked.

"There's a scene from *The Music Man* and one from *The Sound of Music*," Grace said. "I think I'm going to do *The Sound of Music*. Maria has such a good sense of humor. I think I can play her really well."

"Whatever," Gaby said. "I'll do the same one you do. That way we can help each other remember the lines."

"Sounds good."

"Can we get back to the love quiz?" Natalie asked with mock annoyance. "I'm dying to know how I do."

"You're right. Free swim is for goofing around, not for drama talk!" Grace grabbed the magazine. She was just about to read the first question when Julie walked up with Tyler, the swimming counselor. As a rule, Grace didn't like boys. But Tyler was so good-looking that every girl at Lakeview liked him. He and Jenna's older sister, Stephanie, were sort of an item.

"This looks like a party," Julie said with a smile. "What are you guys doing?"

"Magazine quizzes," Marissa told her. "You know how Nat loves the quizzes."

"Yeah, but what about you, Grace?" Tyler asked. "You're usually the first one in the lake."

"I know, but I thought I'd take it easy today," Grace replied. "I'm trying out the lie-in-the-sun-and-read-magazines approach. Natalie and Marissa always look so relaxed and happy after free swim."

"Weren't you reading a book the other day?" Julie asked. "What ever happened to that?"

Grace felt her face heat up, and it wasn't from the sun. "I didn't bring it with me," she said. "I was expecting to swim."

"Tyler!" A voice from the lake interrupted them. It was Stephanie. "Come judge our swimming race! I'm too biased."

Jenna and her twin brother, Adam, waved from the water. Obviously they were the ones preparing to race—both of them were all-around great athletes. But their own sister couldn't call a race for them.

"Be right there!" Tyler yelled back. He turned to Julie. "Wanna help judge?"

"Why not?" she said cheerfully. "See you guys later!" They took off toward the lake.

"Wow, your counselor is big on reading, huh?" Gaby asked when Julie was gone.

"I guess so," Grace told her. She really didn't want to talk about boring books with her new friend—or about why Julie wanted her to read. "What's your counselor like?"

"Lizzie? She's cool." Gaby glanced around the beach. "Although if she catches me talking to all you 3C girls, she'll tease me all night! I'd better go. I just wanted to say hi."

"Okay," Grace told her. "I'll see you in drama tomorrow."

"You got it, partner!" Gaby waved and headed off to find some of her bunkmates.

"Well, well, well," Natalie said, nudging Grace with her shoulder. "Consorting with the enemy, are we?"

Grace smiled. "Yes, we are. That rivalry is just for fun."

"I agree. Gaby seems nice," Natalie said. "But I'm still waiting for the quiz."

"Me too," Marissa chimed in.

"All right, here we go." Grace read the first question for her friends. She was determined not to think about what Julie had said. After all, the sun was shining, she was having fun with her bunkmates, and best of all, she had a brand-new friend!

chapter THREE

"Bunk 5D has Bunk Day on Thursday . . ."

"Psst, Grace!" Valerie whispered from across the table. "Want my hash browns?"

Grace shook her head. All of her bunkmates were holding whispered conversations around her. Nobody ever paid attention to the daily breakfast announcements that Dr. Steve, the head of Camp Lakeview, made. At least not until they heard their own bunk mentioned.

"How about you, Alex?" Valerie asked. "Want my hash browns?"

"No thanks," Alex said quickly. "I'm not hungry."

"You're *never* hungry," Jenna grumbled.

"And the cookout tonight will be for bunk 2B . . . or not to be!"

Dr. Steve got more groans than laughter for his lame joke. Grace glanced over at Brynn, who was now reciting the rest of the "to be or not to be" speech to herself. "I knew it," Grace joked to Alyssa, who sat next to her. "Brynn has gone into total drama mode. Every little thing that happens from now until her audition for the play will be about acting."

"Don't remind me," Jenna said from the other side of Grace. "Remember last year when she tried to lock us all out of the bunk so she could rehearse in private?"

Grace giggled. "She actually dragged one of the counselors' cots over in front of the door to block it."

"But the door opens outward, so it totally didn't work," Jenna finished for her. "We just opened the door and climbed over the bed!"

Natalie laughed, while Alyssa studied Brynn for a moment. "She's really focused," Alyssa finally said. "But from what I hear, you're just as talented as she is, Grace."

". . . a special treat for the third division." Dr. Steve's voice broke into their conversation. Grace spun around to watch him. His balding head looked a little sunburned—he must have forgotten to wear his usual fishing hat yesterday.

"As you all know, the second division and the fourth division have already had their field trips this year," Dr. Steve said.

Jenna grabbed Grace's arm excitedly. "Field trip!" she whispered.

"Now it's the third division's turn," Dr. Steve went on. "Next Thursday you kids will be going to WetWorld, the new water park up in Norwich."

Cheering erupted all around Grace, so she joined right in. In fact, she even climbed onto the bench to celebrate. Two tables over, she saw Gaby do the same thing. They waved to each other over all the clapping and jumping campers.

"Water park! That is so cool," Jenna cried. "I hear they have a three-story-high waterslide!"

"You'll do *that*, but you were afraid to dive off the three-foot-high board?" Chelsea sniffed.

Jenna ignored her, but Grace couldn't keep quiet. Sometimes Chelsea could be really nasty. "Jenna's not afraid of diving anymore," she said. "And I bet you won't go on the giant waterslide."

"Yeah," Candace agreed. "I bet you won't."

Chelsea frowned. "It would ruin my hair. Think of all the chlorine in places like that."

"You're going to have to avoid the whole park if you don't want to get chlorine in your hair," Valerie pointed out.

"Whatever. I'm sure there's a wave pool I can lounge by."

"Not me," Grace said. "I'm going on every single ride in the park. Twice, if I have time!"

Her bunkmates laughed.

"That's okay. Karen will hang out with me and not go in the water. Right, Karen?" Chelsea asked, turning to the shy girl.

Karen didn't look too happy with that prospect,

but she nodded. "Sure," she said quietly. Chelsea smiled, satisfied.

Grace frowned. Why did Karen always go along with anything Chelsea said? She obviously didn't want to spend her time at the water park sitting on a lounge chair. But it was always that way with the two of them—Chelsea called the shots. "You guys are crazy," Grace told them. "One day in the pool water isn't going to do anything to your hair. And besides, it would be worth looking like the Bride of Frankenstein to go on the rides!" She pulled the elastic off her ponytail and quickly teased her hair with her fingers. It never took much to make her mass of red curls stand on end. Within five seconds, she had a mop of hair standing straight up.

Everyone cracked up. Even Chelsea. And, more importantly, even Karen.

Out of the corner of her eye, Grace noticed Kathleen, the head counselor for the third division, leaning over to talk to Julie. Julie always ate with the bunk, sitting at the head of their table. But Kathleen sat with the other division heads, up at the table in the front of the room. What was she doing here? Neither she nor Julie were smiling. It didn't seem as if they were talking about the water park.

"Hey, Grace, have you ever gone on one of those inner-tube rides?" Jenna asked.

"Um, yeah," Grace said, dragging her attention away from Kathleen and Julie. "That's always my favorite ride at water parks. I love when you get to the end and you go down that little tunnel thing. It feels like you're being flushed down the drain!"

Everyone was still laughing, but Grace felt a sinking feeling of dread as she noticed Julie winding through the happy campers toward her.

"Grace, can I talk to you for a sec?" she called over the din.

Grace didn't answer. She just followed Julie toward the door of the mess hall. The sounds of hooting and cheering were all around her, but right now the water park seemed very far away.

"Where have you been?" Alex asked when Grace got back to the bunk. It was chore time, and everyone was busy sweeping, dusting, or cleaning the bathroom.

"Yeah, what did Julie want?" Chelsea added. "Are you in trouble or something?"

"No, but thanks for asking," Grace mumbled. As if she didn't feel bad enough already!

Alex rolled her eyes and gave Grace a smile. "Never mind," she said. "You better get going—it's your turn to take out the garbage."

"Whoo-hoo," Grace joked halfheartedly. But it wasn't the garbage that was bothering her. It was the memory of her meeting with Julie and Kathleen. She'd been expecting the worst, and that's what she'd gotten.

All she wanted to do was hide under her sheets. If her bunkmates found out what was going on, she would be humiliated.

And Chelsea was still watching her like a hawk.

Grace quickly headed over to the cubby where the trash bags were kept and pulled out one for the bathroom garbage and one for the main-bunk garbage. Usually she liked to sing or whistle while doing chores—it got the other girls giggling, and sometimes they joined in. But today she just wasn't in the mood.

"Hang on a second!" Sarah cried as Grace picked up the bathroom garbage can. "I have a handful of hair to throw in there." Sarah wore the bunk's giant, blue rubber gloves, but she still picked hair out of the shower drain with two fingers, holding it away from herself as if it might attack her. "In fact, I think it's your hair," she added, scrunching up her face in disgust.

Grace squinted at the mass of red hair dangling from Sarah's outstretched hand. It could just as easily have been Alyssa's hair, but she decided not to mention that. She just wanted to get her chores over with as soon as possible so that she could go outside and forget about her bad morning.

"After chores, Brynn's going to do a dramatic reading of her *Music Man* scene for the play audition," Sarah told her, dumping the hair in Grace's garbage bag.

Brynn stuck her head out of the toilet area, where she was scrubbing the bowls. "Yeah," she added. "Why don't you join me? We can do it together. Or are you going to do *The Sound of Music* for your audition?"

Grace's stomach felt heavy, as if she had swallowed a handful of rocks. "Um, I don't think I'm gonna audition for the play after all," she said. "I'll just do stage crew again, or whatever Bethany makes us do as part of the drama class."

"What?" Brynn came all the way out into the bathroom. Grace quickly turned and headed into the main bunk, but it was no good. Brynn followed her. "What are you talking about?" Brynn demanded. "You have to audition! You're really good. What about our pact?"

Grace lifted the trash bag and made an exaggerated sour expression. "Sorry, I'm really grossed out by this garbage," she said, trying to sound like she was holding her breath to avoid smelling the junk. "I have to go dump it." She hurried across the bunk and pushed through the door, into the sunshine.

As soon as she was away from bunk 3C, Grace slowed down. She was in no rush to get back. Her bunkmates thought of her as the clown, always bubbly and up for fun. But right now, she couldn't imagine joking around . . . and she certainly couldn't imagine having fun!

She threw the garbage bags into the huge Dumpster near the camp office, then turned to go back. To her surprise, Gaby was trudging up the path toward the Dumpster.

"Hey," Grace said. "You're on garbage duty, too, huh?"

"Yeah, I tried to get out of it, but no one would trade with me," Gaby answered. She held out one of her two full trash bags. Grace grabbed it and hoisted it into the Dumpster while Gaby threw the other one in. They started back down the trail that led to the bunks.

"So what's your problem?" Gaby asked.

Grace was so startled that she almost tripped over a maple root in the path. "Huh?"

"Your problem," Gaby repeated. "You've been moping around all morning. I saw you acting all miserable on your way back from the office earlier, and even now you look like you just ate something sour."

"Well, I did have bug juice at breakfast," Grace joked.

"Funny. Not," Gaby said, completely deadpan.

For the first time in her life, Grace was speechless. She couldn't tell if Gaby was being rude or friendly. Her tone wasn't very nice, that much was certain. But in a way, she was asking if Grace was all right. And that *was* nice. Wasn't it?

"I guess I'm just in a bad mood," Grace finally said.

They had reached the clearing in the woods where all the bunks were. Grace slowed down, automatically taking a step or two away from Gaby. She came from their rival bunk, after all. A few of Grace's friends had already commented on the fact that she was consorting with the enemy. She didn't feel like having to defend herself to 3C right now. She knew they were only teasing, but the situation with her parents had her mega-stressed-out. So stressed that even joking around with her bunkmates seemed hard. "Um, I'll see you in drama," she muttered, speeding up.

"Wait!" Gaby called.

Grace turned back.

"Do you want to hang out during siesta this afternoon?" Gaby asked. "We can practice scenes or something."

Hang out during siesta? Grace could hardly believe her ears. Girls from 3A and 3C did not hang out together. It was an unspoken rule. And Gaby wanted to break it. *How can I say no without offending her?* Grace wondered. Should *I say no?*

"Come on, we'll have fun," Gaby prodded.

Grace glanced over at her bunk. Most of her bunkmates were lounging around on the steps or at the one dilapidated picnic table out front. Natalie was doing Alyssa's nails. Alex was reading lines with Brynn. Candace and Jessie were laughing over a magazine. Valerie and Sarah were practicing some kind of backflip. And Karen was French-braiding Chelsea's hair. They were all paired up, happy in their best-friend twosomes. There was nowhere for Grace to fit in.

How come she had never noticed this before?

"Earth to Grace. Please return to Camp Lakeview,"

Gaby said in a fake deep voice. "Are we hanging later or not?"

"Why not?" Grace said. It wasn't like her bunkmates would care. They already had their camp best friends. Obviously it was time for Grace to get one, too. And Gaby was the only one who seemed interested, even if she was a little hard to figure out sometimes. "I'll meet you here."

"Cool." Gaby started walking backward toward bunk 3A. "Later."

"Later," Grace answered happily.

Grace's happiness didn't last long. As soon as the bunk sat down for lunch in the mess hall, Chelsea turned to her. "You never told us what Julie wanted this morning," she said loudly. "Or was it Kathleen who wanted to talk to you?"

Grace froze with a forkful of bright orange mac and cheese halfway to her mouth. She really didn't want to talk about that, especially not with the whole bunk listening. In fact, all she wanted to do was forget about this morning.

Natalie and Alyssa exchanged a look. "Who cares what they wanted?" Natalie said. "Let's talk about the field trip to WetWorld. I say we go on all the rides together. You know, to show our bunk 3C spirit!"

"Yeah, let's show our spirit," Candace agreed. Grace couldn't help smiling. You could always count on Candace for support. She never had much to say on her own, so she usually just repeated what everyone else said—as long as it was something nice.

"But then what's Grace going to do?" Chelsea asked. "Her new best friend is from 3A. She'll have to be in two places at once!"

A few of the girls laughed, and even Brynn and Alex smiled.

Grace felt her face get hot. She knew her friends weren't really mad at her for hanging out with Gaby. But Chelsea wasn't just teasing—she was being snotty. She was always rude, and everyone in 3C knew it. So why were they laughing along with her as if she was just making a joke?

Grace dropped her fork back down to her plate. She'd had enough of Chelsea's nosiness and her attitude. If her other friends weren't going to defend her, she'd just have to defend herself. "Maybe if my bunkmates acted more like friends are supposed to, I wouldn't have to look for a best friend in 3A," she snapped.

Then she got up and stormed out of the mess hall, ignoring Nat and Brynn calling after her. How dare Chelsea try to tell her who to be friends with!

Once she got outside, though, her stomach did a little flip. Had she really just yelled at all her bunkmates? They hadn't meant to upset her, and she knew it. She'd probably even been too harsh to Chelsea.

Grace sighed. She wasn't mad at them. She was mad at herself, and she'd taken it out on them. How had she gotten herself into this mess?

chapter FOUR

"But I don't understand," Grace said the next day in drama class. She was using a thick British accent and a deep voice. "How could a mouse have unlocked the door?"

"Maybe he had a key," Brynn answered shrilly. She stood on top of one of the black boxes, pretending it was a chair.

"A mouse with a key? Preposterous!" Grace bellowed. "Everybody knows mice never use keys. They prefer to ring the doorbell!" She saw a tiny smile flicker across Brynn's face, but Brynn quickly squelched it. Even though the improvisation exercise they were doing was silly, they both had to take it seriously in order to stay in character. It was hard, though, considering that all their classmates were laughing out loud.

"All I know is that a horrible little mouse came in and stole all the cheese from my kitchen," Brynn cried in her best imitation of a frightened old lady.

Grace's character was supposed to be a gruff police detective. Making him British was a little addition of her own. She loved the improv part of drama because they were allowed to add personal touches like that to spice things up. Picturing a burly English inspector in her mind, she pretended to pull a notebook from her pocket. "Can you describe the mouse?" she asked in her fake voice.

"It was small and gray with a twitchy nose," Brynn said. She added a shudder for effect.

"I see." Grace pretended to write that down. "And can you describe the cheese?"

One of the boys laughed loudly. Grace caught sight of him out of the corner of her eye. He was very tan, with short blond hair and a friendly smile. His green eyes gleamed with amusement as he watched her.

"Ahem!" Brynn said loudly. Grace jumped. Brynn was staring at her, obviously expecting an answer. But Grace hadn't even heard a word Brynn said.

"Oh!" Grace cried. "I'm sorry. I was distracted by . . ." *Think fast,* she told herself. *I can't say I was distracted by a boy.* ". . . by that mouse. I think it's your culprit!" She pointed to a spot on the floor near Brynn's black box.

Brynn gave a little scream and stood up on her tiptoes to get even farther away from the "mouse."

Grace swooped down and pretended to pick it up by its tail. She squinted into thin air and nodded wisely. "This mouse is the thief."

"How can you tell?" Brynn asked.

How can I tell? Grace wondered. She thought fast. "It has cheese breath," she announced.

Everybody laughed again, and most of the other campers applauded. Bethany joined in the applause as she walked toward Grace and Brynn at the front of the room. "Well done," she said. "That was an excellent improvisation."

Grace glanced over at Brynn, who was beaming. She could feel the huge smile on her own face, too. Bethany had assigned each of them a character—the old lady and the detective—and given them the word "mouse." Everything else they made up on the spot.

"If you try out and get a role in the play, this is the kind of applause you'll get," Brynn murmured. "And it will be even more fun than the scene we just did." She'd been trying to convince Grace to audition ever since Grace had said she wasn't going to try out. Grace couldn't tell Brynn the real reason she had to skip auditions, so she'd found herself avoiding her friend outside of drama class. It was awful.

Grace pretended she hadn't heard Brynn's comment. "We're a good team," she said as they took their seats with their classmates.

"Yeah, too bad you decided not to be my partner," Brynn teased her. Grace knew her bunkmate had been annoyed at first, but Brynn seemed to like her new partner just fine. His name was Peter, and Grace had to admit that he was pretty cute.

Her gaze wandered over to the blond boy who'd been laughing so loudly during their scene. To her surprise, he was looking right back at her. He gave her a smile and a thumbs-up. Shocked, Grace sat back so that she was hidden by Brynn. She leaned over to Gaby, who sat on the other side of her.

"Who's that boy with the blond hair?" she asked.

Gaby immediately craned her neck to look over at him. "Devon Something," she said. "He's in 3F. Why?"

"He really liked our improv. He was laughing the whole time."

"Well, it was pretty ridiculous," Gaby said.

Grace didn't answer. She still had a hard time figuring out whether or not Gaby was kidding sometimes.

"That's it for today," Bethany said. "Next time we'll be doing movie scenes." As everybody got up and began heading for the door, Bethany pulled Grace aside.

"Your scene was really funny," she said. "Have you done improv exercises before?"

"Only once. In Drama Club at school," Grace said.

"Well, you're a natural." Bethany smiled. "I hope you're planning to audition for the play."

Grace hesitated. "I don't know. I'm only in the third division."

"I meant what I said, Grace. Anyone from any division can audition." Bethany raised an eyebrow. "Just because a third-level camper has never gotten a lead before doesn't mean it can't happen."

Grace wasn't sure how to answer. Had Julie and Kathleen talked to Bethany? It didn't seem like it. For a brief moment Grace considered trying to lie to the drama teacher. Maybe if Bethany didn't know . . .

But Grace was no liar. She knew she couldn't do that.

"Just think about it," Bethany added. "Someone as talented as you are should really try out."

"Okay," Grace said. She forced a smile onto her face and left. If only people would stop telling her how talented she was! It only made her feel worse that she couldn't audition for the play.

By the time Grace got into her bathing suit and made it to the lake, free swim had already started. Talking to Bethany had made her late, and she'd had to stop at the camp office on the way back to the bunk.

To her surprise, she spotted Natalie in the water with Alyssa. Natalie almost never went in during free swim, but it was unusually hot today. Obviously her latest fashion magazine could wait until after she'd cooled down. Jenna was swimming laps with her brother Adam, and Brynn and Alex were hanging out in a pair of inner tubes, talking. Well, Brynn was talking. Alex just bobbed in the water, listening intently and nodding. She wasn't saying a word. *Brynn must be practicing her audition scene with Alex as the audience,* Grace thought. *I wish Emily was here. She'd let me practice with her like that, too.*

A flicker of guilt stabbed at her. She still hadn't

finished that letter to her best friend. Grace kicked the sand in frustration. She didn't seem able to do anything right this summer!

She tossed her towel onto the ground and stuck her toe in the water. Camp Lakeview rules stated that no one could go in the lake without a swimming buddy, even for free swim. The counselors were pretty flexible about that rule, though. As long as campers didn't swim alone, the counselors didn't care how many buddies they had. Which was good when you were best-friendless. Grace squinted across the sparkling water toward her friends. Maybe she'd ask Nat and Alyssa if she could triple with them.

"Hey, Gracie," Gaby said from behind her. "You're late. I was waiting for you to be my swim buddy."

"Oh." *Gracie?* Grace thought. *Why is she calling me that?* She noticed that Gaby had already dumped her own towel right next to Grace's.

"Let's go," Gaby prodded. "I'm dying from this heat." She waded into the shallow end of the lake without a backward glance. Grace almost yelled after her—Gaby would be in trouble if she swam without a partner. But obviously Gaby was assuming Grace would follow her.

It was kind of weird. Gaby hadn't even asked Grace if she *wanted* to be swim buddies. She'd just decided that they would be, and she expected Grace to go along with that. It was sort of rude. But again, it was also sort of flattering. Maybe Gaby simply figured that they were good enough friends that she didn't have to ask. That's how Grace acted with Emily at home. It was the sort of thing that best friends did.

"Wait up," Grace called, splashing in after Gaby.

▲ ▲ ▲

"Are you kidding?"

It was just before lights-out that night, and Chelsea was looming next to Grace's bed looking extremely demanding. As usual.

Grace marked her page with her finger and looked at Chelsea. Karen hovered behind her, carrying Chelsea's makeup bag. Grace had never figured out why Chelsea had to take the bag to the bathroom every night to wash off her makeup, but maybe there was some kind of magic face-cleaner stuff in there.

"What are you talking about?" Grace asked.

"That book." Chelsea snatched it out of Grace's hands, losing Grace's place. Grace groaned. Now she'd never find the right page again. "Why are you pretending to read *The Call of the Wild*?" Chelsea asked.

"I'm not pretending," Grace said indignantly. "Why would I fake reading?"

"Because there's no way you'd want to read a book at night. You're always the first one to answer every single magazine quiz question that Marissa asks," Chelsea replied.

A few of the other girls giggled. Grace couldn't

argue. The truth was, she would much rather listen to Marissa's nightly reading from some magazine article or quiz. The book she was reading was boring with a capital B. But she had no choice. Marissa was settled on her own cot and ready to start reading aloud, but Grace was going to have to ignore her and read *The Call of the Wild*.

But that didn't mean she wanted to talk about it. Especially not with Chelsea. She held out her hand. "May I have my book back?"

Chelsea shrugged and handed it to her. Grace rolled over on her stomach and flipped through the book, trying to find her place again. She skimmed the paragraphs, but they all blurred together in her mind. It was impossible to remember which parts she had read and which she hadn't. *I guess I haven't been paying much attention to what I've been reading,* she thought. Finally she just gave up, picked a likely place, and began reading again.

"The movie will begin filming in October and is expected to be released next summer," Marissa's voice drifted into Grace's attention.

"That is so amazing!" Sarah cried. "I can't believe your dad is making another 'spy' movie, Nat."

"Yeah, I thought he said he wanted to do more serious roles from now on," Brynn put in.

"He always says that. It's just a way of negotiating with the producers," Natalie explained.

Grace found herself staring down at the page, reading the word "Yukon" over and over while she half listened to her bunkmates' conversation.

"I can't believe we have to wait until next summer to see it, though," Valerie was saying. "That's *forever*."

"Can't you tell us what the plot is?" Brynn asked.

"Yeah, tell us what the plot is," Candace put in.

"I'm not allowed to," Natalie said. "Dad has a confidentiality clause in his contract. He can't even tell *me* everything about the plot."

Everybody groaned.

"Tell you what, though," Natalie went on. "I can ask Dad for a few sneak previews. He's allowed to take pictures on location—he's an amateur photographer, so he takes his camera with him everywhere."

"Wow, he's really multitalented," Alex breathed.

"He's *so* multitalented," Candace agreed.

"As long as the photos don't show the sets or let you figure out what the plot is, I can mail them out to you guys," Natalie said. "It'll be pictures of him having dinner with the director, hanging out with the other actors . . . stuff like that."

"And you'll send them to us?" Valerie cried.

"I promise," Nat said.

That did it. Grace let the book close and sat up in her bed to join in the cheering. What was the point of reading some old, boring book when there was juicy Hollywood gossip to discuss?

"Cool! And we can send pictures from camp to his movie set," she said. "What do you think?" Grace jumped out of bed and struck a pose in the middle of the room, putting her hand on her hip and pursing her lips like a supermodel.

"I think you look like a fish," Chelsea muttered.

But the other girls laughed, and Sarah leapt up to stand next to Grace in the same silly position. "Someone take a picture," she joked.

"Everyone join in!" Grace called. "Then Nat can send the photo to her dad, and the director will see it, and we'll all be discovered."

"The fish-face girls of bunk 3C," Alyssa said, cracking up.

As her friends jumped around, striking other dumb model poses, Grace felt a rush of happiness. This kind of silly stuff was what camp was all about.

She'd read her book tomorrow.

chapter FIVE

"Check it out. There's Natalie and her *boyfriend*," Sarah announced as they all filed into the mess hall for lunch the next day. She spoke loudly, clearly wanting Natalie to hear. Simon's bunk, 3F, ate at a table only a few feet away from bunk 3C's table.

But Natalie just kept talking to Simon as if she hadn't noticed. Grace wondered how she could stay so calm when people were teasing her—especially with Simon sitting right there.

"Yeah, and I think Alyssa's boyfriend is over there, too," Jenna added loudly.

Grace laughed. "You're talking about your own brother," she pointed out. "I don't think you get to make fun of Alyssa for liking *him*."

"Are you kidding? He's the last boy anyone should like." Jenna pretended to bump into her twin brother, Adam, as she walked by bunk 3F's table. But Adam was too fast for her. He grabbed her and gave her a noogie.

"That's one way to handle it," said a voice from behind her.

Grace jumped and turned to see Devon, the blond boy from drama class. "Oh. Um . . ." Grace's heart pounded. She couldn't think of a single word.

"The guys in our bunk are always teasing Simon, and now they tease Adam, too," Devon said. "At least when it's his sister doing the teasing, he can stop her!"

"Yeah." Grace couldn't remember whether she and Devon had ever spoken to each other. "I'm Grace," she said.

Devon looked a little confused, and instantly she felt like an idiot. He hadn't asked her name. He'd been talking about Simon and Adam!

"I know," he said. "We're in drama together."

"Oh." Grace stared into his big eyes and tried to come up with anything to say. But all she could think about was the fact that the back of her neck felt sweaty and hot, and her heart kept slamming against her rib cage. What was going on with her?

"I'm Devon," he said. He stuck out his hand to shake. "I guess we haven't really met officially."

Grace stared at his hand in horror. She hadn't realized it until now, but her palms were totally sweaty, too. How could she shake his hand when hers were all wet?

"Enough with the romance!" Alex cried, pushing in between Grace and Devon so she could get to Natalie.

"Tear yourself away from the boys, and come sit down and eat."

Grace wasn't exactly sure how it happened, but all of a sudden Natalie, Alyssa, Jenna, and Alex were all coming back from 3F's table, talking and laughing. They pulled Grace along with them, yanking her away before she had a chance to shake Devon's hand.

She glanced over her shoulder to see Devon watching. Did he think she'd just snubbed him on purpose? Had she accidentally been really rude?

Devon stuck his hand in his pocket and shrugged. But he was smiling.

▲ ▲ ▲

"I read this book about acting that said an actor's true job is to audition," Brynn said as they ate.

"What is *that* supposed to mean?" Grace asked. She stirred the meat loaf surprise around on her plate. The surprise seemed to be that it barely resembled any meat loaf she'd ever eaten.

"Just that actors spend a lot more time auditioning for roles than actually playing those roles," Brynn explained.

"It's true," Natalie put in. "My dad used to go to hundreds of auditions every year and sometimes he'd only get one part, if that."

"Wow. I bet he's happy he doesn't have to go through that anymore," Grace said.

Natalie shrugged. "He figures someday he won't be such a big star anymore, and then they'll expect him to try out again. For now, he's just enjoying the fact that he gets offered roles without auditioning."

"I can't believe *you're* not an actor, Nat," Karen said quietly. "You know everything about Hollywood."

"Seriously, you know everything," Candace agreed.

"Ugh, no," Natalie cried. "I would never want to live that way. Most actors spend their whole lives being waiters and never making enough money to live on. My father just got lucky."

"I don't care if I have to be a waitress," Brynn said. "As long as I can practice my craft."

Grace shoved a bite of the meat loaf into her mouth to hide her smile. Across the table, she saw Alyssa quickly look down to keep her own smile from showing. Everyone knew how serious Brynn was about becoming an actor. But it was still hard to imagine her carrying trays of food and waiting on other people. Maybe in four or five years she'd be a CIT like Marissa, and she'd get to practice being a waitress all summer long.

"Who wants my pudding?" Alex asked. It was a daily ritual—Alex never ate her dessert.

"Me!" Sarah cried, reaching for the little cup of chocolate pudding. She spooned a bite into her mouth and made a "yum!" face. "Are you ready for your audition, Brynn?" she asked. "You've been rehearsing nonstop."

"I have my lines memorized, but I still have to practice my song more," Brynn said. "How about you, Grace?"

The meat loaf seemed to get stuck halfway down Grace's throat. She'd been hoping no one would ask her about the play, but she should've known that Brynn wasn't going to just drop it. Even though Grace had broken their pact to audition together, Brynn still kept trying to keep up her end. She really wanted Grace to try out. "Um, I'm still not sure I'm going to audition," she mumbled.

Her bunkmates all gasped. "Why not?" Natalie asked. "You're such a good actress."

"Well, that's just the problem," Grace replied fake seriously. She waved them all in closer as if she had a big secret to tell. Once she had everyone's attention, she lowered her voice and said, "I don't want to embarrass all the other campers who can't act at all."

Everyone laughed. "How thoughtful of you," Natalie teased.

"You really aren't going to try out?" Jenna asked. "I mean, I know how competitive it is, but you could probably get a role as a Lost Boy or something."

"Or a pirate," Valerie said.

"Last year Brynn was the only one from our division to get a part at all, remember?" Alex pointed out. "The good roles always go to the older kids."

"But we're a year older now," Brynn said. "And I don't care how it's always been before. This year someone from the third division is definitely getting a part—me! I'm playing Wendy, and that's all there is to it. And Grace can play Tinkerbell!"

Grace couldn't help admiring Brynn's self-confidence. She was so determined to get a part that she might make it happen through sheer force of will. "You know, Brynn, Peter Pan is usually played by a woman," she said. "The character is a boy, but lots of times they get women to play the role."

"Yeah, all the famous Broadway Peter Pans were women," Natalie agreed.

"Maybe you should try out for Peter instead of Wendy," Grace suggested.

Brynn wrinkled her nose. "I don't know if I want to play a boy. Boys are kinda gross."

"But it would be a good acting challenge," Grace said. Everyone giggled.

"Maybe." Brynn didn't sound convinced.

"I could help you practice," Jenna offered. "I know all about being a boy from living with my brother. I can teach you how to belch in public and everything."

Grace watched as her bunkmates laughed and joked around with Brynn. She wanted to get into the spirit of it, but she couldn't stop thinking about the play auditions. She desperately wanted to try out for a role. And she hated the feeling that she was letting Brynn down. But unless her situation changed very, very quickly, she knew she wouldn't be able to audition no matter how much she wanted to.

"Mail call!" Julie yelled, pushing open the screen door with her hip. Her arms were filled with boxes and envelopes.

"Cool! What'd I get?" Jenna demanded, rushing over to grab the biggest box. It had the Bloom family's trademark giant orange stickers on it, which meant it was a care package from Jenna's mom. She always sent enough food for the whole bunk.

"I can't wait to find out—I'm starving," Julie joked. She plopped the rest of the mail down on her cot and began handing it out.

"Nat, a postcard from Tunisia," she called.

"My father's on location there," Natalie explained, taking the oversized card.

"Care package for Karen," Julie went on. "And letters for Valerie, Candace, Alison, and Grace."

Everyone else bounded happily over to get their mail, but Grace was in no rush. She had a feeling the letter was from her mother, and a letter from her mother wasn't a good thing, not this summer. *Maybe it's from Emily,* she thought hopefully. *I would have a great time reading about all the gossip from home.* But she knew her best friend wasn't going to write again so soon. Grace still hadn't answered Emily's first three letters.

She shuffled over to the counselor, hoping against hope that Emily had found out something so juicy that she simply had to write to Grace.

Julie gave her a sympathetic smile as she handed over the envelope.

Uh-oh, that face could only mean one thing, Grace thought. *It's a letter from Mom.*

Grace threw herself down on her bunk and slowly peeled open the envelope. The letter was short, and it said exactly what she had expected it to say. Usually Grace liked to read letters two or three times before she put them away, but not this letter. She stuck it right back into its envelope and slipped it into the box under her bed where she kept her unused stationery and the other letters from her folks and Emily. Then she rolled over on her bed and faced the wall. Even though she'd only read it once, the letter stuck in her mind. Especially the part that said "we're so disappointed in you." Tears pricked at her eyes. She hoped her bunkmates would leave her alone.

No such luck. "Grace? You okay?" Sarah asked from her own bunk.

"I'm fine," Grace replied. She turned back over and plastered a fake smile on her face.

"Are you sure?" Chelsea asked, leaning forward to peer closely at Grace. "Because you look kinda green."

"Thanks," Grace said. "I was going for yellow, but I guess I went a little too far."

A few of the other girls giggled, but Grace could see that Sarah, Alyssa, and Nat weren't convinced that she was kidding. Usually she could joke her way out of any situation, but right now she actually *felt* kinda green, if that was possible. She wasn't really sick, but she was worried and upset. Julie was still over at her own cot, but if she heard the girls talking about Grace's problem, she'd come over to investigate. And then everyone would find out her secret, and they would think she was a loser. *I have to get out of here before Julie gets involved,* Grace decided.

Natalie was opening her mouth to say something—probably something like, "What's really bothering you, Grace?"—but Grace was too fast for her. She leapt up off her bunk and stuck her feet in her flip-flops, all in one motion. "I'm gonna take a walk," she said, cutting Natalie off. "I don't feel like siesta-ing today."

She raced for the door and made it outside before anyone could answer. But what was she supposed to do now? She'd come outside without her book, and almost all of the other campers were in their bunks taking a siesta.

I wish I'd brought my letter to Emily so I could finish it, Grace thought. If only her best friend were here, she'd know how to cheer Grace up. But Emily was far away at home, and Grace was on her own.

Without really planning to, she started down the path toward bunk 3A. Maybe Gaby would want to hang out. That's what best friends did, right? And they were starting to be best friends. Camp best friends, anyway.

Bunk 3A looked exactly like bunk 3C, except that the sign on the door had different names written on it, and the porch had only one step leading up to it instead of two. Grace jumped over the step and landed on the porch. She stared at the door for a second. Was she supposed to knock? All of last summer, and all of this summer so far, she'd never gone to another bunk—unless she was on a raid with her bunkmates. You definitely didn't knock when you were raiding. But how about when you were just visiting? She had no idea what the etiquette was. She'd never needed friends outside her own bunk before.

She took a deep breath and lifted her hand to knock. Before she even touched the door, a short girl with long dark hair pushed it open. She stared at Grace in surprise.

"Uh, hi, Sharon," Grace said.

Sharon raised her eyebrows. "Hi, Grace," she said loudly. Obviously she wanted her bunkmates to hear her. Grace took a step back as a couple of the other 3A girls appeared behind Sharon. They stared at her curiously.

"Is she alone?" one of them whispered. "I bet it's a trick."

Great. They think I'm here to pull a prank or something, Grace thought. "Is Gaby here?" she asked.

Sharon's eyebrows shot up higher. "Gaby?" she asked, sounding even more surprised than she looked. "Yeah. Do you . . . do you want to see her?"

"Yup. Thanks," Grace said. These girls were acting even weirder than usual. Was it really that big a deal for a 3C girl to come to the door? Maybe she should've thought this through a little more.

She heard Gaby's voice from inside, along with a lot of giggling and whispering. Finally Gaby stepped up to the door. She shot Sharon a look. "Thanks. You can go back in," she said.

Sharon nodded, but she didn't move. Clearly she wanted to know why Grace was there.

Gaby rolled her eyes, turning to Grace. She looked her up and down and frowned. "What are *you* doing here?" she demanded.

Grace hesitated. "Um . . . me?" she asked. Immediately she felt stupid. Who else would Gaby be talking to? But the question had taken her by surprise. She'd been expecting a "hello" or a "what's up"—not such a rude welcome from Gaby.

Gaby pushed the door open wider and stepped out onto the porch. A few of the other girls crowded around behind her. "Duh, of course I mean you," Gaby said. "Do you see anyone else who isn't supposed to be here?"

Grace's mouth dropped open. "Am I not supposed to be here?" she asked, confused. Had she missed some kind of no-visiting-during-siesta rule?

"No one from your loser bunk is supposed to contaminate our bunk by touching it," Gaby said. She looked meaningfully at Grace's hand on the porch railing. Her bunkmates laughed.

"Oh. Sorry." Grace picked her hand up and tried to smile. Gaby was just kidding, she was pretty sure. It didn't sound like she was kidding, exactly, but she must be. The bunk rivalry wasn't a serious thing, after all. And besides, Gaby was her friend. Gaby was the one who'd wanted to be partners in drama and again in free swim. So she had to be kidding. She wasn't really being as mean as she sounded. Right?

"Um, I was wondering if you want to hang out," Grace said. "I'm not in the mood to stay in the bunk."

"Who could blame you? I bet it smells in there," Gaby said. Her bunkmates laughed again, and Gaby looked pleased. "But I *am* in the mood to stay in my bunk, and obviously you can't come in here," she went on.

"I . . . I can't?" Grace didn't know what else to say.

"No. How do we know you're not spying on us to help your bunk pull a prank?" Gaby said. "Everybody knows Jenna Bloom wants to prank us."

"Jenna's not planning any more pranks," Grace said honestly. "I think she's retired."

"Whatever. I'm not interested." Gaby stepped back inside and let the door swing shut in Grace's face.

Grace blinked at the dusty screen. Had her new best friend just slammed the door on her? Was this all some sort of joke that she didn't get? Was she supposed to follow Gaby inside?

She didn't think so. But then what *was* she supposed to do? She couldn't keep standing around outside by herself. "Okay. I'll see you later," she called through the screen door. Then she turned and stepped off the porch. She walked off toward the activities shacks as fast as she could. She had no idea what she'd do once she got there. All she knew was that she wanted to get as far away from Gaby as possible. And it looked like Gaby felt the same way about her!

chapter SIX

At free swim, Grace put the tiny nose clip across the bridge of her nose and headed straight for the water. A good swim would relax her—and she needed to relax after the weird day she'd been having. First the letter from her mom, then Gaby's brush-off at 3A! She was totally stressed.

"Gracie, hey!" Gaby called, running up behind her. "Are you going in?"

Grace stopped, surprised. An hour ago, Gaby had been totally mean to her. But now she stood there with a big happy grin on her face, as if nothing had happened. *Maybe she really was playing around before,* Grace thought, confused. It didn't matter, though. Gaby had completely humiliated her in front of all of 3A. Grace wasn't in the mood for any more of Gaby's strange behavior.

"Um, yeah, I really want to swim some laps," Grace said. She tried to step around Gaby without seeming too rude. Sarah and Valerie were already in the water, and if she swam out to them, she knew they'd let her triple with them.

"I was thinking we could just hang out on shore," Gaby said. "You know, put our feet in the water to cool off when we need to. It'll be fun. We can work on your audition scene."

Grace couldn't believe it. Gaby was just assuming they were going to be swim buddies again! Yesterday it had seemed like a good thing that Gaby thought they were close enough friends for that. But after the way she'd acted earlier today, Grace wasn't so sure anymore.

"I don't know," she said. "I was looking forward to swimming. And I don't think I'm going to audition."

Gaby frowned. But before she could say anything, Julie walked up. "Hey, guys," she said. "Grace, I need to borrow you for a minute."

"Okay." Normally Grace would be worried if Julie asked for a private conversation. But right now it was a relief to get away from Gaby. She was just too hard to figure out.

Grace followed Julie over to the canoe stands, where there were no campers. Her feet felt like lead as she tromped through the sand. She knew what was coming, and it wasn't going to be fun.

"Grace, you know I have to ask about your reading," Julie said.

"Yeah."

"How far have you gotten in *Call of the Wild?*"

Grace tried to remember what page she was on. She couldn't. "Far enough to know that I wouldn't want to be that dog," she said, hoping Julie would take that as a joke. The book was about a dog that, as far as she could tell, was in for a really bad life up in Alaska or someplace like that.

Julie didn't smile. "How many chapters have you read?"

"I'm not sure," Grace said. "A few. I think."

"How many is that?"

"Maybe three," Grace told her. "Well, I think I'm almost to chapter three."

Julie's face fell, and Grace looked down at her feet. She loved Julie—Julie was the coolest counselor at Lakeview! The last thing Grace wanted to do was disappoint her, but obviously she already had.

"Oh, Grace, what am I going to do with you?" Julie sighed. "You know I hate acting like a police officer. Why won't you just read the book?"

"It's boring," Grace said. "Every time I start reading it, I practically fall asleep. I'd rather be doing something fun with my friends."

"But you have to read it! You know you won't be able to go to the water park next week unless you finish it," Julie cried.

"I know." Grace kicked at the sand, frustrated. "But I don't even care about the stupid water park. All I care about is auditioning for the play, and I won't be able to do that, either!"

Tears filled her eyes. She'd managed to keep herself from thinking about this for a long time, but now that it was out there, all her emotions came rushing at her.

"Grace . . ." Julie reached out for her arm, but Grace pulled away. It was bad enough that she'd made Julie angry with her—she wasn't going to cry in front of her, too. She turned and ran toward the trees, her vision blurring.

As she passed the last of the canoes, Grace noticed Gaby standing behind it. Her supposed friend looked away quickly, but Grace got the feeling that she'd been hiding there for a while. Which meant that Gaby had heard the whole conversation with Julie.

Gaby knew everything, whether Grace wanted her to or not.

▲ ▲ ▲

"Look at that mop," Natalie teased as Grace shook the water out of her curly hair.

Grace jumped closer to her and shook herself like a dog, spraying water all over Natalie's face. Then she looked up innocently and said, "What? I didn't hear what you said, Natalie."

Natalie laughed and flicked her wet towel lightly at Grace.

"Hey, break it up," Alyssa joked. "No fighting between swim buddies."

Grace pulled her mass of hair back and wrangled it into a ponytail. She knew it wouldn't dry for the rest of the day, but it was worth the messy hair just to get in some swim time. After talking to Julie, she'd managed to calm herself down in the girls' room in time to squeeze in a few laps during free swim, with Nat and Alyssa as her partners. Gaby hadn't come near her since Grace caught her by the canoes, and Grace hoped it stayed that way. She didn't like to think that Gaby was eavesdropping, but there was no other reason for the girl to be hanging out nearby during a private talk.

"Let's get back fast," Natalie said, draping one arm over Grace's shoulders and the other over Alyssa's. "I hate sitting around in a wet suit. I want to be one of the first in the bathroom to change."

They started up the trail that led to the bunks.

"Only a few more days until the water park," Natalie said, bouncing a little as she walked. "I can't wait!"

"Me neither." Alyssa leaned forward so she could see Grace on the other side of Natalie. "We forgot to ask you if you want to sit with us, Grace."

"Oh, yeah," Natalie put in. "Alex says they rent a school bus, so we can all squish into a three-seater."

"Definitely," Grace said. She loved hanging out with Natalie and Alyssa. They were always friendly and never made her feel like a third wheel. "You guys have never been on a camp field trip, huh?" she said.

"Not yet. This will be the first, not to mention the greatest," Alyssa said. "I love water parks."

"Cool, so we're all sitting together," Nat said. She

squealed with excitement. "I can't wait!"

"I can't believe you," said a voice from behind them. Surprised, Grace turned to see Gaby following right on their heels.

"Me?" Grace said. "Why? What do you mean?"

"You're supposed to sit with me on the field-trip bus," Gaby said. "Obviously."

"I am?" Grace asked. "Since when? We never even talked about sitting together. I don't think we ever talked about the field trip at all."

"We're friends, aren't we?" Gaby snapped. "Friends sit together. I didn't know I had to make some elaborate plan about it."

Natalie and Alyssa stepped in closer to Grace, but they didn't say anything. Truthfully, she kind of wished they would—because she had no idea what to say herself. "How am I supposed to know if we're friends or not?" she sputtered. "You wouldn't even let me in your bunk. You were really mean."

Gaby rolled her eyes. "Don't be such a baby," she said. "I was only kidding."

"Oh." Grace felt stupid. Clearly she should've been able to tell that Gaby was joking around at bunk 3A, but it really hadn't seemed that way. "Well, sorry."

"Whatever," Gaby said. "So we'll sit together on the way to the water park?"

Grace bit her lip. She didn't really want to sit with Gaby. In fact, she wasn't sure she wanted to be friends with Gaby at all, let alone *best* friends. It was just too hard to figure out Gaby's behavior, and Grace never felt comfortable around her.

"No, I think I'm still going to sit with Nat and Alyssa on the field trip," she answered slowly. "They asked me first."

Gaby's face turned the same bright-orange shade as Alyssa's hair. Without thinking, Grace took a step back.

"I think she's gonna blow," Alyssa whispered.

"You're a rotten friend!" Gaby exploded, yelling right in Grace's face. "And I don't even care because you probably can't go on the field trip anyway!"

I knew it! Grace thought, horrified. *I knew she was eavesdropping on my talk with Julie!*

"You heard me," Gaby said to Natalie and Alyssa. "She told you she could sit with you, but she's lying. She's not even gonna be there."

"What are you talking about?" Natalie demanded. "Of course she is."

"Grace isn't a liar," Alyssa put in.

"She is, too," Gaby said smugly. "If she doesn't finish reading her lame-o book, she can't go to the water park. And there's no way she can finish it because she's barely even to chapter three!"

Natalie's mouth fell open. Alyssa whirled around to look at Grace. "Is that true?" she asked.

Grace had never been so angry in her entire life! How dare Gaby listen in on a private conversation and then tell everyone Grace's business? How dare she make Grace's friends think she was a liar?

How dare she be such a bully?

"Grace?" Nat said.

Natalie's worried eyes were too much for Grace to take. How could she explain all this to her bunkmates? That she couldn't go to the water park with them, and she couldn't try out for the play . . . and no matter how hard she tried, she couldn't seem to finish that stupid book!

Tears blurred her eyes again, but this time they were tears of anger. She pushed past her friends and Gaby and stomped off toward the office.

chapter SEVEN

Dear Mom and Dad,

I can't believe you're doing this to me! Why are you trying to ruin my life? Now everyone knows that I can't go to the water park. Or at least they will know soon. I'm not sure whether they'll be mad at me or feel sorry for me, but either way they're not going to act normal around me for the rest of the summer. It's humiliating. Why can't you just let me be normal and do the things everyone else gets to do? It isn't fair! I promise I'll finish the books. Just please, please, please let me go to the water park and try out for the play and be normal! I know you're mad at me, but PLEASE don't ruin my whole summer! I love acting so much, and you're taking it away. Please let me audition, and let me go to WetWorld—I'll read as many books as you want!

Grace hit Send and watched the e-mail disappear from the screen. Immediately she wished she could get it back. It wasn't going to help. It would probably just make her parents even angrier at her than they already were, and she couldn't blame them.

She'd barely been able to convince them to let her come to camp this summer—there was no way they were going to let her go on the field trip now that she hadn't held up her end of the bargain.

She stood up and made her way to the door of the camp office. "Thanks, Dr. Steve," she called.

The camp director looked up from his desk and blinked at her. "That didn't take very long, Grace," he said. "Usually you're here for at least fifteen minutes when you send updates to your parents."

"I know. This was a short message," she said. "Anyway, thanks again for letting me use the computer."

"No problem, Grace." He went back to his paperwork, and she pushed open the door and stepped out into the sunshine. It felt weird to thank him for the computer when she didn't want to use it at all. If not for her father's phone call to Kathleen demanding daily e-mail updates on her reading, Grace would have spent the summer happily ignoring her parents. She wouldn't even have known that Dr. Steve had a computer with Internet access that the campers could use. And she would have gone on the field trip and tried out for the play and been totally happy.

She caught up with her bunkmates outside the mess hall, where everyone was milling around as usual before dinner. They all turned to stare the instant she walked up.

"Since I have your attention, I'd like to make an announcement," Grace said. "I no longer have to do chores.

You will all take turns doing my chores for me for the rest of the summer."

Everyone laughed.

"What? I mean it," Grace said, laughing along with them.

"You wish," Alex told her.

"So where were you?" Chelsea asked. "You keep going off by yourself lately."

Natalie and Alyssa wouldn't meet her eyes. Obviously they'd told everyone about the scene between Gaby and Grace, and now they felt guilty. Grace sighed. They shouldn't have to feel bad when she was the one who hadn't been telling the truth.

"I've been keeping a secret from you guys," Grace said, sticking her hands in her shorts pockets. She hated having to be all serious with her friends. Friends were supposed to be the people you had fun with! "You know how I've been reading *Call of the Wild*?"

Everybody nodded.

"It's not for fun."

"Shocker," Jenna said. All the other girls cracked up, but Grace frowned.

"What do you mean?" she asked. "I could be reading for fun. Lots of people do that. Look at Alyssa!"

Alyssa snorted. "Thanks."

"Grace, Alyssa likes to read," Brynn pointed out. "You don't. All last summer, I never once saw you with a book in your hand."

"Me either," Alex agreed.

"All we mean is that obviously you're not reading that book because you want to," Jenna said. "If you actually *wanted* to read it, you'd be done with it by now. So what's the deal?"

This was it. Grace couldn't put off telling them for another second. She bit her lip, hard. Were they going to think she was a total loser? Were they going to laugh at her? "You guys all have reading in school, right?" she blurted. "We have it as a separate class."

"So do we," Natalie agreed. "Every day we go to a different teacher for reading."

"Yeah, well, I failed it." Grace forced herself to say the words. "I got an F."

"In reading?" Chelsea said incredulously. "What kind of idiot fails reading?"

Grace winced. That was exactly the reaction she'd been expecting, and it hurt even more than she'd thought it would.

"Chelsea!" Natalie hissed.

"Chelsea!" Candace cried.

"What?" Chelsea said. "Grace knows how to read—we've all seen her do it. So how could she fail? The only reason people fail reading is because they're dyslexic or something and they need more time for the tests."

Everyone looked at Grace.

"Um, nope, no learning disability," she said. "I just failed."

"What happened?" Alyssa asked gently.

"Nothing really," Grace admitted. "I don't love to read, as you obviously all noticed. And there was always something better to do—talk to my best friend, play video games, act in the school play . . ."

"And?" Jenna prompted.

"And so I was busy goofing off, and I never finished any of the books I was supposed to read," Grace said in a rush. "And they failed me."

"So what now?" Valerie asked.

"You mean after my parents considered locking me in my room with a pile of books until I'm in college? We made a deal. I promised to read the two books I didn't read for class, and they let me come to camp this summer."

"They thought about taking away camp?" Alex sounded faint at the very idea of it.

"Yeah." Grace shuddered just remembering how upset she'd been at the prospect of missing Lakeview this year. "It was the worst. My dad had totally made up his mind that I was going to stay home all summer and read. It took me two solid days of begging before he changed his mind."

"And he came up with that bargain?" Brynn asked.

Grace nodded. "I agreed that during the first session I'd read *Call of the Wild*, and during the second session I'd read *The Jungle Book*. So they let me come." She looked around at all her bunkmates. "You guys, I've never been so upset in my whole life," she whispered. "Can you imagine if they took camp away?"

"But the first session is over," Karen said, horrified. "And you're still not done with *Call of the Wild*."

"That's why on Visiting Day I didn't have as much fun with my folks as any of you had with yours," Grace replied. "My father almost had a cow. He wanted to drag me back home that second."

"Oh, no," Brynn said. "So what happened?"

"They called Kathleen the other day to find out how I was doing with the book. That's when she and Julie called me aside. They made me go call my parents and tell them what page I was on."

"I knew it! I knew you were getting in trouble that day!" Chelsea cried triumphantly.

"Chelsea, don't," Karen said.

Everybody held their breath. Karen *never* corrected Chelsea. How would Chelsea handle it?

"Excuse me? Don't *what*?" Chelsea demanded, turning on Karen.

"It's just . . . you're just . . ." Karen stammered. She looked terrified. "Never mind."

"So what happened when you called your parents, Grace?" Sarah asked, trying to draw attention away from poor Karen.

Grace winced just remembering that awful conversation. "My dad said I couldn't do the field trip or try out for the play until I'd finished *Call of the Wild*. And for this past week, they've been making me go to the office and e-mail them mini book reports so they'll know I'm reading it."

"But you haven't been reading it," Valerie said.

Has everyone been watching me? Grace wondered ruefully. *It's not just Julie. All the girls in the bunk seem to know how much I hate reading!* "I know," she said aloud. "I'm doomed."

"No you're not," Jenna said. "You're just being a flake."

Grace's mouth dropped open. She hadn't been expecting that. All she could think to do was laugh. "Excuse me?" she said.

"It's totally simple," Jenna went on. "Stop fooling around and read the book so you can come to the water park with us."

"Yeah," Alyssa put in. "Just read it. We don't want to leave you here all alone while we're at WetWorld."

"Especially not since you had to have such a fight just to sit with us on the bus," Nat added.

"I know!" Grace cried. "I can't believe Gaby told on me! She listened in on a private conversation between me and Julie."

"Well, you can't trust a girl from 3A," Brynn sniffed. "Anyway, you shouldn't have been keeping this a secret. It's no big deal."

Grace gazed around at the faces of her friends. They all looked concerned. Not one of them seemed about to tease her. Not even Chelsea. "I thought you guys would make fun of me," she said.

"For failing a class?" Alyssa asked. "Why would we make fun of that?"

"Yeah. That's not funny," Candace agreed.

"It's kind of embarrassing," Grace said.

Jenna snorted. "You can't be embarrassed in front of *us*. We're a team."

"You're right," Grace said, feeling better than she had all week. "I should have told you guys."

"That's right," Natalie said. "Believe me, I know how bad it is to keep secrets from your friends. Don't you feel better now?"

"Yeah," Grace said honestly. "I really do. But I don't think it's so simple. I'm not just behind on one book—now I'm behind on *two*! There's no way I'm going to make it to WetWorld."

Dear Grace,

It took a lot of convincing, but I finally managed to get your father to give you one last chance. You know neither of us want you to be unhappy, sweetheart. We know how important it is to feel "normal," and we know how important the camp play is to you. But you made a deal at the start of the summer, and you haven't stuck to it. And reading is very important, honey. You're too smart to sell yourself short by failing a class that you should be able to pass. So Dad and I propose that you take a little quiz. Finish your first book by Sunday, and we'll e-mail you

a list of questions about it. If you answer them ALL correctly, you can try out for the play on Wednesday . . . and go on the field trip on Thursday. We know you can do it, Grace. You're a very smart girl when you put your mind to something. It's up to you.
Love,
Mom
P.S. and Love, Dad too!

Grace's heart beat faster as she read the e-mail from her parents later that night. Kathleen had pulled her away before dessert to tell her that she had a message. Grace had been half expecting them to order her to pack her bags and come home, but instead, her mom was being nice about it. Grace felt a little pang of guilt. She knew her parents weren't trying to be mean by telling her she had to skip WetWorld. She hadn't given them any other choice. She hit Reply and typed in her own message:

Dear Mom (and Dad),

Thank you! Thank you! You're the best parents in the world! I know it's my last chance, and I'm not going to do anything else between now and Monday except read my book.
Love,
Grace

She hit Send, closed out of her e-mail account, and headed out of the office, skipping down the few steps leading to the main trail. Maybe she could go to

WetWorld after all. And best of all, maybe she could try out for the play!

But she still had to finish that whole long book first, and she only had three days to do it. Grace's steps slowed as she thought about *The Call of the Wild*. She knew her parents were being super nice to her and really giving her a second chance. But so far she hadn't even been able to deal with having homework over the summer.

How was she supposed to handle such an important quiz?

chapter EIGHT

Grace was awake and reading before the bugle the next morning. She didn't want to be, but now that there was a chance she could audition for the play, she knew she had to do her absolute best to finish the book.

She read through breakfast. She read on the walk to the mess hall and back, with Natalie and Alyssa holding her arms, steering her down the path. After Candace offered to take over her chores so Grace could finish the book, she read while everyone else was working. But soon enough it was time for their first free choice. Grace reluctantly put down her book. She was almost to chapter five.

"Ready for arts and crafts?" Julie asked, giving Grace's ponytail an affectionate tug.

"Not really," Grace admitted. "I feel like if I put my book down even for an hour, I won't be able to finish it on time."

"Are you liking it any better?" Julie asked.

Grace thought about it. She'd been so busy trying to speed-read the book that she hadn't paid much attention to what she thought about the story. "I guess I am," she said, surprised. "Everyone is being so mean to the poor dog, I want to know how he triumphs at the end."

Julie grinned. "That's what I like to hear. Reading is supposed to be fun, you know."

"It would be more fun if I could act it out," Grace joked. "Although I don't know how I'd play a dog."

"I'll tell you what, my little actress," Julie said. "I'll let you skip arts and crafts today as long as you stay in the bunk and read."

"Really? You rule!" Grace bounced up and down in happiness. "I don't have to skip drama too, though, do I?" she asked.

"No way," Julie said. "I know what your priorities are."

"I just love it," Grace admitted.

"I know. You never take a long time to read scenes that you're doing in class," Julie said. "So obviously you can read fast when you want."

"I'm reading the book fast now, too." Grace jumped back onto her bunk and pulled out *The Call of the Wild*.

"Okay. I'll be back in fifteen minutes," Julie said. "I have a quick meeting with Kathleen and then I'll swing by art and crafts and tell Richie where you are."

"Mm-hmm," Grace said, already back in the world of Buck the dog.

She read straight through lunch and continued in the drama shack right until Bethany called them all to attention. Grace finally put the book away and looked around. Gaby was sitting as far from her as possible. And Devon was standing up in front of the class with Simon, Natalie's sort-of boyfriend.

"Okay, boys," Bethany said. "Show us the scene you've been working on."

For the first time all day, Grace forgot about Buck and the Yukon. The two boys were acting out a scene from an old movie called *The Outsiders*. Simon's character was dying, and Devon's character, his best friend, was there by his side in the hospital.

Most of the kids who took drama at camp liked to goof around and play improv games. But Simon, and especially Devon, obviously took the class seriously. They were really acting. Even Brynn would approve. Grace found herself getting caught up in the lives of the two characters. She could swear she saw tears in Devon's eyes as he spoke to his best friend for the last time.

When the scene ended, she clapped so hard that her hands hurt. Devon shot her a smile and nodded to say thank you.

"Somebody liiikes you," Brynn said in a singsong voice, nudging Grace.

"No way," Grace said quickly. "He was just saying thanks for the applause. You know, from everyone. He was thanking everyone."

"Uh-huh," Brynn said sarcastically.

"He was really good in that scene," Grace added.

"Uh-huh," Brynn said again, wiggling her eyebrows.

"Oh, be quiet," Grace mumbled. "I just think he's a good actor." *And a cute one,* she added silently. She didn't usually like boys, but she wouldn't mind doing a scene with him.

▲ ▲ ▲

When Grace got back to the bunk, she was surprised to hear voices coming from inside. Everyone else was supposed to be at a camp-wide nature meeting. Dr. Steve had gotten an environmental conservationist to come and teach them about endangered species. Grace thought it sounded interesting, but reading was more important right now. She'd gotten permission to go back to the bunk so she could spend her time with Buck in *The Call of the Wild*.

But somebody else was clearly there.

Grace was about to open the door when she heard Chelsea raise her voice. "Because I said so!" she was saying. She sounded angry.

Grace hesitated. Maybe she shouldn't interrupt.

"But, Chelsea, I love water parks," Karen's quiet voice drifted out. "The most fun I ever had was at a water park when I was eight."

"Have you ever seen what people look like when

they go on those rides?" Chelsea argued. "Your hair gets all flat and stringy, and your makeup washes all off."

"I never noticed that," Karen replied.

And why does it matter? Grace wondered. Should she go in there? Part of her wanted to rush in and help Karen deal with Chelsea. But those two were best friends, after all. They seemed to be having an argument, and Grace didn't think she should stick her nose in their business.

"Well, it's true. We'd look horrible if we went on all those rides."

"But it would be fun." Karen sounded wistful. Grace was surprised Karen was disagreeing with Chelsea at all—Karen must really love those water rides if she was willing to fight for them.

Suddenly Chelsea gave a little sob. It sounded fake. "I can't believe you're changing your mind about this," she said. "You promised to hang out with me by the wave pool."

"I know," Karen said. "Don't be mad—"

"You know that swimming makes me sick," Chelsea interrupted. "If we go on those rides, I'll get water in my ears and get an earache. And if water gets in my eyes, it will ruin my contact lenses."

But you go swimming in the lake every day, Grace thought.

"But we go swimming every day," Karen said.

"Yeah, in the lake," Chelsea answered. Her voice wavered as if she were trying to hold back tears. "Where there's no chlorine to sting my eyes. And where I can keep my head out of the water so my hair doesn't get ruined. And I don't get water in my ears."

Grace shook her head. Chelsea was coming up with all kinds of excuses, but Grace suspected that the real reason she didn't want to go on the water rides was that she thought she'd look bad with wet hair and no makeup. Chelsea was so pretty that she'd be gorgeous no matter what. But she took a lot of care with her appearance. Maybe she didn't feel confident without her makeup.

Still, it wasn't fair to keep Karen from doing what she wanted just because Chelsea didn't want to be alone. *Tell her that, Karen,* Grace silently willed. *Tell her you want to go on the rides.*

"Well, if it means that much to you . . ." Karen said.

"Thank you!" Chelsea answered, her voice normal again. "We'll have a great time getting a tan."

"I usually just get sunburns," Karen replied quietly.

Grace took a deep breath and opened the door. "Oh, hi, guys," she said casually. "I didn't know anyone was in here."

Chelsea looked startled. Karen just smiled. "We came back to get Chelsea's sunglasses," she explained. "The light hurts her eyes."

"Plus, who wants to listen to a boring lecture?" Chelsea added, trying to joke. She watched Grace carefully, as if waiting for her to say something. *She wants to know if I overheard them arguing about the water park,* Grace realized.

But she had no intention of saying anything about what she'd heard. She wasn't happy that Karen had given in to Chelsea, but it wasn't really any of her business.

"Julie said I could skip the lecture so I can read," she said, flopping down on her bed.

"We better get back before Julie comes looking for us," Karen told Chelsea.

"Yeah. See you later, Grace."

Grace smiled and waved as they left. It was hard to understand Chelsea sometimes. But right now she had to focus on her book.

▲ ▲ ▲

"Hey, Grace, your *friend* is here." Valerie's tone was sarcastic.

Grace looked up from her book. She'd been reading in the bunk for an hour and a half straight. "Huh?"

Valerie nodded toward the porch. "That girl from 3A. Abby?"

"Gaby," Grace corrected her. "She's here?"

"On the porch. I guess she didn't feel like taking siesta with her own bunkmates," Valerie said.

"I guess I can't avoid her, huh?" Grace murmured. "Did you tell her I was here?"

"Well, I wasn't gonna lie," Valerie said. "Just go out and talk to her. The sooner you get rid of her, the sooner you can get back to reading."

"Yeah," Candace said. "The sooner you can get back to reading so you can come to WetWorld."

"Oh, all right." Grace got up and went out onto the porch. She wasn't in the mood for small talk, but she figured Gaby must have a reason for coming here. She probably wanted to apologize for telling Natalie and Alyssa about Grace's secret. "Hey, what's up?" she said when she reached Gaby.

"Hi, Gracie!" Gaby chirped. "Wanna hang out?"

"I can't," Grace said. "I have to read."

Gaby frowned. "Is this because I wouldn't hang out with you during siesta the other day?"

"No," Grace said honestly. "Although it is a little weird that you feel comfortable coming over to my bunk when you told me to stay away from your bunk."

"I told you I was just kidding about that."

"Yeah, I know," Gracc said. "It still seems a little weird to me, though. And it sure didn't sound like you were kidding. Anyway, I really have to read."

"Look, I'm sorry," Gaby blurted out. "I shouldn't have told your bunkmates that you lied about WetWorld."

It didn't seem like much of an apology, but still Grace felt a little better. At least Gaby realized that what she'd done was rude and wrong. "That's okay," Grace said. "I might get to go to WetWorld after all."

"Cool," Gaby said. "How?"

"I have to finish this book by the end of the

weekend," Grace explained. "And then my parents are going to give me a quiz. That's why I can't hang out right now. I have a lot of reading to do."

"Okay. How about at free swim? Do you want to be swim buddies? It's so hot out, I'm dying to go in the lake."

"Um, I don't think so," Grace said. "I was planning to read during free swim. Julie even let me get out of arts and crafts this morning so I could read."

"Then you don't have to read during free swim," Gaby said. "Give yourself a break. Get some exercise."

"But I can't," Grace insisted. "There's no way I can finish the book unless I spend every single second reading."

"Oh, come on, don't be so boring," Gaby said. "I thought you were supposed to be fun."

"I *am* fun," Grace replied. "Just not right now. Being too much fun is what got me into this mess. If I'd paid more attention to school and spent less time having fun, I wouldn't have to be cooped up in here reading all day."

"It's only one hour," Gaby pointed out. "And we just made up after our fight. Please?"

Grace sighed. How could she say no to that?

"Okay," she said. "I guess I can take one hour off from reading."

Once Gaby had gone back to her own bunk, Grace managed to finish the chapter she was on and start the next one before it was time for free swim. Changing into her bathing suit, she decided Gaby was right. She'd been reading nonstop for hours. She could use a break.

It was hot out, with no wind. The lake barely even had ripples on its surface. Perfect for swimming laps, which Grace couldn't wait to do. When she got in the water, she knew her stress about the quiz on Sunday would start to melt away. She'd cool down, enjoy the feel of the water against her skin, and clear her mind from the adventures of Buck for a little while. She couldn't wait to get into the lake. She put her swimming clip on her nose and looked around for Gaby.

Grace found her sitting on a towel near the shallow part of the lake. "Hey!" Grace called, walking over. "Ready to swim?"

"Oh, I don't want to swim," Gaby said, squinting up at Grace. "I figured we'd sunbathe."

Grace almost laughed. She and Gaby were two of the palest, most freckled kids at camp. Neither one of them was ever going to get a tan—all sunbathing would do was burn them to a crisp or leave them with twice as many freckles. "I'd rather swim," Grace said. "If we were just going to lie in the sun, I would've brought my book."

"I would've brought my book," Gaby repeated in a high-pitched imitation of Grace. "Can't you talk about anything but that dumb book?" she added.

"I have to finish it," Grace cried. "I told you that! You said you wanted to swim."

Gaby heaved a huge sigh. "Oh, all right," she said

as if she were doing Grace a big favor. "Let's go in."

"Cool." Grace turned and started toward the deeper section where they could swim laps.

"Let's just go in over here," Gaby called behind her. "Like we did the other day."

Grace glanced back, surprised to find Gaby standing near the shallow end where all the little kids swam. "Why?" she asked. "We can't really swim there. It only comes up to our waists."

"We don't have to *swim* swim," Gaby said. "We can just splash around and get cooled off."

"But I want to swim laps," Grace said. She tried to remember whether she'd ever seen Gaby swimming in the lake. "Aren't you a green yet?" she asked. Maybe Gaby hadn't learned to dive this summer, in which case she'd still be in the yellow group of swimmers. They weren't allowed to go in the deep part during free swim.

Gaby snorted. "Please. I'm a blue already."

Now Grace was really confused. If Gaby was in the blue group, it meant she was an expert swimmer who'd already passed her swimming safety test. So why didn't she want to go in the deep section? "Well, come on then," Grace said. "Let's go swim."

"But our towels and stuff are over here," Gaby argued. "I don't want to have to walk all the way back from the deep part to get a towel."

"It's a hundred degrees out!" Grace pointed out. "It's not like you'll be cold walking ten feet farther."

"I'm not in the mood to swim," Gaby said. "My contact lenses are bothering me."

"Oh. I didn't know you wore contacts."

"Yeah, and I can't put my face in the water with them in," Gaby said. "So I can't really swim. All I can do is go in over here where I can keep my head out."

Grace frowned. "Then how did you pass your test to be a blue?"

"I wore my glasses that day and took them off to swim. Are we done with the third degree?" Gaby said. "Come on." Without waiting, she walked into the water in the shallow section.

Frustrated, Grace pulled off her nose clip and followed. Wading around in muddy water wasn't exactly her idea of a good time. She was annoyed at Gaby, but she was even madder at herself. No matter how hard she tried, she just didn't seem able to say no to Gaby.

Walking around in the shallow water was boring, so they only stayed in the lake for ten minutes. Then Grace had to sit on shore and listen to Gaby tell gossipy stories about her bunkmates until free swim was over. Grace had never been so happy to hear Tyler blow his whistle.

"Everybody out!" he yelled. "See you tomorrow!"

"Okay, bye," Grace said in a rush, gathering up her towel.

"What's the hurry?" Gaby asked.

"I have to go read."

"Well, hang on, I'll walk with you." Gaby slowly

picked up her towel, shook it out, and folded it neatly. Grace bounced from one foot to the other in impatience. Finally Gaby was ready to go.

"Should we catch up to Marta and Sharon?" Grace asked, spotting two of Gaby's bunkmates on the path ahead of them.

"Nah." Something in Gaby's voice made Grace suspicious. She looked around. None of the other girls from 3A were anywhere near them. In fact, none of Gaby's bunkmates were ever around. It didn't seem as if Gaby hung out with them at all away from the bunk. And based on her nasty stories during free swim, Gaby didn't seem to mind.

"So who's your best friend in the bunk?" Grace asked.

Gaby shrugged. "No one. It's better to have a best friend from outside the bunk."

Grace didn't answer. She'd given up on thinking that Gaby could be her best friend at camp. Gaby was too unpredictable to count on. One minute she was nice, and the next she was mean.

"Oh, hang on," Gaby said suddenly. "I have to fix my shoe." She dropped to her knees and began fiddling with the Velcro on her sandals. But Grace noticed that there was nothing wrong with the shoe to begin with. Gaby had just pulled it open and then started playing around with it. Was she trying to hide from someone? The only people on the path behind them were Julie and

Lizzie, Gaby's counselor. All the other campers were way up ahead.

Julie and Lizzie stepped around them and kept walking. The second they were gone, Gaby popped back up. "Okay, let's go," she said cheerfully.

But Grace didn't buy it. Gaby had been trying to avoid Julie and Lizzie—she was sure of it. "Hey, Julie!" she called without warning Gaby. "Wait up!"

Julie and Lizzie turned around and waited for them.

"What'd you do that for?" Gaby whispered. Grace ignored her and hurried to catch up to the counselors.

"Hey, Grace, I was surprised to see you without your book," Julie said. "Are you finished with it?"

Gaby snorted. "Yeah, right. With how slow she reads?"

Grace felt a wave of anger wash through her body. How would Gaby know how fast or slow she read?

"Don't be nasty, Gaby," Lizzie said seriously. "You finally finished your week in the yellow zone. Do you want to make it another week?"

Gaby shot Grace an angry look. "Sorry," she said, not sounding sorry at all.

Grace waited until they'd reached the bunk area before pulling Gaby aside. "What did Lizzie mean back there?" she demanded. "She said you had a week in the yellow zone."

Gaby rolled her eyes. "Oh, my stupid bunkmate

Christa went whining to Lizzie about me using up her shampoo. So I got in trouble. Christa's such a baby."

A hard knot formed in Grace's stomach. "You were being punished?" she said angrily. "You had to stay in the shallow part of the lake with the yellows?"

"Yeah, can you believe that?" Gaby said. "No swimming in the deep end for a week! Just because I borrowed some shampoo."

Grace had a feeling that Gaby hadn't borrowed anything. Christa was a shy girl in 3A. She'd always reminded Grace of Karen. And knowing their two personalities, Grace thought Gaby had probably just used up Christa's shampoo and expected her not to tell. But that wasn't what bothered Grace most.

"You mean, all week you've tried to keep me from swimming in the deep part just so you would have company while you were being punished?" she asked.

"Well, I didn't want to hang out with the little kids all by myself," Gaby said.

"They're not all little," Grace pointed out. "Some of them just aren't strong swimmers yet."

"Still," Gaby said. "I'm not friends with any yellows."

"Why didn't you just ask me to stay in the shallow part with you?" Grace said, exasperated. "If you'd asked me as a friend, I would've been happy to do it for you."

"What's the difference?" Gaby said.

"You've been lying all week!" Grace cried.

Gaby shook her head. "You should talk. You lied to your bunkmates about the field trip."

"Well, I shouldn't have," Grace retorted. But Gaby was already walking away.

Grace turned toward her bunk with a heavy heart. She clearly wasn't going to be friends with Gaby at all: She hadn't had any fun during free swim, and worst of all, she'd missed an hour's worth of reading time!

chapter NINE

"Hang on a minute, Grace," Julie said as Grace reached for the door of bunk 3C. Julie and Marissa were sitting on the rickety railing around the porch. "We need to talk to you."

Uh-oh, Grace thought. If there was one thing she'd learned in a summer and a half at camp, it was that when both the counselor and the CIT wanted to have a talk with you, it meant you were in trouble. But what could she possibly have done in the five minutes since she last saw Julie on the trail?

She followed them over to the picnic table and sat down.

"Grace, your parents called during free swim," Marissa said. "I had to tell them you couldn't come to the phone because you were busy swimming."

"Oh, no." Grace dropped her head onto the wooden table. "And they were mad that I wasn't reading."

"Yes," Marissa said. "Although I told them that

you'd been reading all day, and that I didn't think there was any harm in taking one hour off to let your eyes rest."

"Thanks," Grace mumbled without lifting her head.

"But that's not what we're worried about," Julie said. "You really buckled down and worked today, Grace. So why did you decide not to read during free swim?"

"Gaby talked me into being her swim buddy," Grace said, looking up at them. "I figured doing a few laps might wake me up a little so that I could read all night tonight. But then we spent all our time in the shallow end, so I didn't even get to do laps." Grace sighed. "Believe it or not, I would rather have been reading."

Julie chuckled. "That's a new Grace, all right."

"Didn't Gaby tell you that she had to stay in the shallow part when she asked you to be her swim buddy?" Marissa asked. "Stephanie told me a week ago that Gaby was being punished." Jenna's sister Stephanie was the CIT for Gaby's bunk.

"Nope." All of Grace's annoyance crept back into her voice as she spoke. "She didn't bother to mention that until *after* free swim."

Julie and Marissa exchanged a glance. "How come you agreed to be swim buddies, Grace?" Julie asked. "I don't mean to sound harsh, but it doesn't sound as if you even like Gaby that much."

"I don't know," Grace said. "She's weird, but it's nice having a friend at camp."

"You have a million friends," Marissa cried.

"Everybody loves you, Grace!"

"Yeah, I know. But I don't have a best friend," Grace said. "Everybody pairs off, but not with me. I guess I thought it would be cool to have one best friend here."

"It's okay to have a lot of friends," Marissa said. "It doesn't mean there's anything wrong with you if you don't have a best friend, you know. It just proves that you're well-rounded!"

"But I miss my best friend from home," Grace said with a sigh. "If she even is my best friend anymore. I owe her a letter, big time."

"You miss your best friend, so you thought you'd feel better if you found a best friend here," Julie said. "And you thought that Gaby was that friend?"

Grace frowned. "At first I thought she was cool, but then she started being mean a lot. Still, every time I try to disagree with her, it's like she turns my words around or something."

"Do you want mc to have a talk with Lizzie about it?" Julie asked.

"No!" Grace cried. "It's totally fine. I can handle her."

"You sure?" Marissa asked. "We're here to help if you need us."

"Thanks, but no. Gaby's fine. I'm just mad at myself because I knew I should be reading during swim." Grace stood up. "In fact, I'm not putting that book down again until I'm finished."

She gave them a little wave and headed for the bunk, her heart beating fast. She hoped she'd convinced them not to talk to Lizzie. The last thing she needed was Gaby to think she'd snitched on her. She knew Julie and Marissa meant well, but she also knew that campers weren't supposed to complain about other campers. It just wasn't cool. From now on, she'd simply stay away from Gaby. If she didn't have a best friend, then she could just take care of herself.

▲ ▲ ▲

"Mind if I join you?" Natalie asked. She held up a romance novel. "Shove over."

Grace grinned at her and moved over on the old park bench. She'd come to the clearing around the flagpole to get in some quiet reading before dinner. Sarah and Valerie had promised to come get her on the way to the mess hall.

"My book is more fun than yours," Natalie said apologetically.

The cover showed two teenagers holding hands and looking all gooey and in love. Grace wrinkled her nose. "I don't think so," she said. "I'd rather read about a noble dog than read some stupid love story."

Natalie shook her head. "I don't know what's wrong with all you guys," she said. "I can't believe I'm stuck in a bunk with so many boy-haters."

"I don't hate boys," Grace said. "I just don't *like* them."

"You're hopeless." Nat opened her book, and Grace went back to reading *The Call of the Wild*. As the minutes passed, the late-afternoon sun; the thick, hot air; and the buzz of cicadas in the trees all drifted away from her mind as she lost herself in the story. She was so focused on it that she didn't even hear anyone approach until Natalie started talking.

Grace looked up and jumped in surprise. Simon and Devon stood two feet away, and she hadn't even known they were there. Simon and Natalie were discussing the WetWorld trip. And Devon was watching Grace. Immediately her cheeks grew hot. Why was he staring at her that way? How long had he been there?

He reached out toward her. Instinctively, Grace pulled away, dropping her book. But before she could grab it, Devon bent and picked it up. "I love this book," he said, handing it back.

"Oh." Grace couldn't think of a single thing to say to that. *I'm only reading it because my parents are forcing me to* didn't seem like the correct response.

"Did you get to the part where he pulls the thousand-pound sled yet?"

"I'm in the middle of that right now," Grace said. "Don't tell me how it ends." She could hardly believe it herself, but she was dying to know whether Buck made it back to his master with the sled. His master had bet a lot of money, and Buck really wanted to win it for him.

"We got a puppy last year, and I made my parents name him Buck after this dog," Devon said.

"Wow. You really *do* love this book," she replied. He blushed a little, which only made him look cuter. Grace couldn't believe she thought he was cute. *He's gross*, she told herself. *All boys are gross.*

"It's cool that you like to read," he said. "It really helps with acting. You know that scene we did the other day? That's from a movie based on a book."

"It is?" Grace asked in surprise.

Simon groaned. "Believe it. Devon made me read the scene from the book *and* memorize the lines from the movie." He glanced at Natalie. "Drama is turning into a tough class, not just your average fun and easy free choice."

"It's all these actors," Natalie joked, her eyes shining as she nudged Grace with her arm. "They take everything so seriously."

"Didn't reading the book help you understand the characters better?" Devon challenged.

"I hate to say it, but yes," Simon replied.

"See?" Devon winked at Grace. "It's good to be a book lover."

"Uh-huh." Once again, she couldn't think of anything to say. Since when was she at a loss for words? The other three were managing to have a perfectly normal conversation, and all she could do was sit there stupidly.

"See you at dinner," Simon told Natalie. She beamed back at him. "Okay."

"Later," Devon added.

"Uh-huh," Grace said again.

Natalie turned in her seat and stared at Grace until the boys left the clearing. Then she burst out laughing.

"What?" Grace said, pretending to ignore the laughter.

"That was priceless!" Natalie crowed.

"I don't know what you're talking about," Grace lied.

"I thought you didn't like boys," Nat giggled. "But maybe you don't like boys because you like just *one* boy."

"No way," Grace teased. "Simon is *your* boyfriend."

Natalie swatted her arm. "I mean Devon, and you know it."

"He's just a kid from my drama class."

"Mm-hmm," Natalie said, her eyebrows raised.

"And he's very talented," Grace added. "I appreciate his acting ability. That's all."

"Riiight," Nat replied sarcastically. "It has nothing to do with how cute he is."

"Is he cute? I hadn't noticed." Grace opened her book and pretended to read, but she could tell Natalie was on to her. She did think Devon was cute. But so what? She acted like a dope around him, and that was no fun.

"Devon and Grace sitting in a tree," Natalie sang under her breath as she went back to her own book.

"Quit it," Grace said. But she knew it was hopeless. When Nat had first met Simon, everyone in the bunk had teased her constantly. It was only fair that she tease back.

"K-i-s-s-i-n-g," Natalie sang on.

"You're such a second-grader," Grace mumbled. Nat cracked up, and after a minute Grace did, too. Even though Natalie was making fun of her, there was nothing mean about it. And when Valerie and Sarah showed up to get them for dinner, Natalie didn't say a word about Devon and Grace. It was their secret.

Grace was half asleep by the time everyone had brushed their teeth and gotten into bed that night. She'd never known that reading could be such hard work—she was exhausted!

Marissa took her place on her cot and started digging around in the milk crate she kept next to it. That was where she stored all her fashion magazines.

"Which magazine are you going to read us tonight?" Grace asked her. "I vote for *Cosmopolitan* horoscopes!"

But Marissa pulled out a spiral notebook, not a magazine. "I'm not reading tonight," she replied. "We have a surprise instead."

All around the bunk, the other girls were pulling out notebooks or pieces of paper. Jenna had a napkin with something scrawled on it in magic marker. "What's going on?" Grace asked, confused.

"We came up with a group assignment during chores this morning," Julie explained. "Everyone had to come up with one question about *Call of the Wild*, and tonight we're going to quiz you to help you study for your parents' quiz on Sunday. And then we'll do the same thing tomorrow night and Sunday morning."

"Are you kidding?" Grace asked. "You guys would do that for me?"

"It's no big deal," Chelsea said. "We all read the book in school."

"Yeah, but still," Grace protested. "You guys didn't mess up your grades. You shouldn't have to do schoolwork over the summer!"

"That's what friends are for," Sarah said.

"We have to make sure you can audition for the play," Brynn added. "How else could we keep our pact from last summer?"

"And besides, it's an excuse for a party," Jenna added. She pulled the box with the orange stickers out from under her bed. "My mom sent brownies!"

"We already brushed our teeth," Alex protested.

"So what? We can brush again later," Jenna said.

"Well, I don't like the taste of toothpaste with chocolate," Alex grumbled.

"Suit yourself," Jenna said. "You never want my mom's sweets, anyway."

"I want a brownie!" Grace put in.

"No way," Marissa said. "You have to earn your brownies, missy. Whenever you get a question right, you get a bite of brownie."

"I want to go first," Alyssa said.

"I'm next!" Valerie cried.

"Why don't we just go around the room," Julie suggested. "Marissa and I will go last."

Grace couldn't believe her luck. After spending half the week with Gaby, she'd forgotten how amazing real friends could be.

"What's the dog's name?" Alyssa asked.

Grace rolled her eyes. "That's too easy. His name is Buck."

Jenna tossed her a little piece of brownie.

"What's his master's name?" Sarah asked.

"Which one?" Grace replied. "He has a lot of masters over the course of the book."

Jenna gave a whistle. "Can't catch her with trick questions," she joked.

"List all of Buck's masters, then," Sarah said.

"Okay. Um, first there's the judge. And then there's François and Perrault. And John Thornton. And Hal and his family."

Jenna threw her another bite-size piece of brownie. "I feel like the dog," Grace joked. "Getting treats when I'm good!"

"Who wrote the book?" Valerie asked. "And when?"

"Jack London," Grace answered. "A long time ago."

Everybody laughed. "I'm going to write down the ones you don't know," Julie said. "That way we'll know what to focus on when we help you study tomorrow."

Grace looked around the room at all of her friends in their pj's, concentrating hard on a discussion about a book they'd all read ages ago. "You guys are the absolute nicest bunkmates in history," she said.

"Aw, you're so sweet," Natalie told her. "But that's not going to make us go easy on you."

Grace grinned. "Okay. Give me the next question. I'm ready."

▲ ▲ ▲

"Just remember: WetWorld," Sarah said on Sunday. "Stay focused on that and you'll ace the test for sure."

Grace took a shaky breath. Her bunkmates had all decided to walk her to Dr. Steve's office to take her parents' quiz. Just having them there made her feel better, but her mouth still felt dry from nervousness. "What if I blank on everything?" she asked.

"You won't blank," Natalie said. "We've been quizzing you so much, you know everything there is to know about this book."

"And besides, I have a giant brownie with your name on it," Jenna added. "You finish the quiz, you get the whole thing!"

Grace smiled. "You saved me a brownie?"

"Yup. And it wasn't easy," Jenna joked.

They'd reached the office. Grace's heart did a flip-flop. Her parents would be so disappointed in her if she failed this quiz. Not to mention all the camp things that were riding on it—WetWorld, and most of all, the play.

"Okay. Wish me luck," Grace said.

"Good luck," bunk 3C yelled.

She stepped inside the office, where Kathleen was waiting for her. Kathleen nodded toward the computer. "It's all yours," she said. "Good luck, Grace."

"Thanks." Grace took a seat at the computer table. Her parents had sent a total of twenty questions about *The Call of the Wild*, which Kathleen had set up for her on the computer. She was supposed to answer all the questions and e-mail them back. Kathleen sat reading the newspaper at Dr. Steve's desk, acting as test monitor.

"WetWorld," Grace whispered. "And brownies." She took a deep breath and began the test.

1. What kind of dog is Buck?

Grace smiled. That one was easy. She typed in the answer: *a mix of Saint Bernard and Scottish shepherd.* Then for good measure, she decided to add a little more detail. *He's a noble dog who leads a pampered life in California until he's kidnapped and brought into the harsh wilderness of the Yukon.* She finished the sentence and sat back with a grin. She wished she could see her father's face when he read that one. He'd be so proud of her.

Grace took a deep breath and moved on to the next question. Remembering all the study questions her bunkmates had asked her over the weekend, she wasn't nervous at all.

2. Who is Buck's favorite master and why?

Grace knew that one. She'd talked about it with her friends, and it had led to a long conversation about everyone's relationships with their own dogs. She typed: *Buck's favorite master is John Thornton, and Buck loves him because Thornton has respect for Buck. Also, he saved Buck's life. And please give Mr. Fluffhead a kiss for me.*

Grace had named her dog Mr. Fluffhead even though he wasn't the least bit fluffy. He had short, coarse fur. But she was only five when she got him, and Mr. Fluffhead was the only name she could think of.

3. Name some of the other dogs on Buck's sled team.

Grace smiled. This was easy! She wrote down the names of all the dogs on the team. And then she just kept going, answering the questions one after another without even pausing to think.

20. How much money does Buck win for John Thornton in the sled-pulling bet?

Immediately Jenna's face sprang into her mind. "I'd pull a heavy sled for that much money, too!" her friend had joked just last night. Grace quickly typed the answer: *$1,600.*

That's Devon's favorite part of the book, she thought. *I'll have to tell him that I finally finished it.* And even though she was sitting in Dr. Steve's office and Devon was nowhere in sight, she felt herself blush. *Stay focused!* she commanded herself.

She finished the whole quiz. Not one single question had stumped her. She read over her answers anyway, just to double-check. Then she crossed her fingers and hit Send.

"Well?" Kathleen asked. "How did you do?"

"I think I aced it," Grace reported. "My whole bunk helped me study all weekend."

"And they're going to help you celebrate if you pass," Kathleen said, gesturing out the office window. "They've been lined up out there for ten minutes."

"Really?" Grace ran over to the window and peered out. Her bunkmates sat in a row in front of the office shack. Nat and Alyssa were playing cat's cradle with some string. Chelsea was sunbathing. Candace, Karen, Jessie, and Sarah were all reading books. Valerie was asleep with her baseball cap over her face. Jenna and Alex tossed a mini soccer ball back and forth. And Brynn was talking to herself. Grace smiled. Obviously Brynn was practicing her lines for the play audition.

"You can head over to dinner now," Kathleen said. "Afterward, come back here to call your folks and see how you did."

"Okay," Grace said.

Kathleen tugged lightly on Grace's ponytail. "I'm proud of you, kiddo," she said. "A week ago, you couldn't have even finished half of those questions."

Grace nodded. "But I have to get them all right or else I can't go on the field trip."

"Try to relax and have fun at dinner," Kathleen said. "There's no point in worrying now."

But it was impossible to relax during dinner. All of Grace's bunkmates kept chattering about the trip to WetWorld. Grace knew they were trying to keep her mind off the quiz, but it wasn't working. The pork chops tasted even more like sawdust than usual. She could hardly wait for dinner to end. Her whole future at camp this summer depended on the results of this quiz. Would she get to go on the field trip? Would she have to start rehearsing an audition piece, too?

As soon as dinner was over, she sprinted back to the office and dialed her home number. "Mom?" she said as soon as she heard someone pick up.

"Hi, honey!" her mother replied. "I'm so proud of you!"

Grace took a huge gulp of air. She hadn't even realized she'd been holding her breath. "You are?" she asked. "Did I do okay?"

"Is that our brilliant daughter?" Her dad's voice came on the line. *He must've picked up the phone in the den,* Grace thought.

"Hi, Daddy!" she said. "How did I do? Did I get them all right?"

"What do you think?" he asked.

Grace considered. All the questions had seemed

pretty straightforward. None of them had given her any reason to doubt her answers. "I think I got them all," she said slowly. "They weren't hard."

"That's because you really read the book," her mother replied. "The questions would have seemed hard if you had just skimmed through the chapters without paying attention to what you were reading."

"You mean the way I usually do," Grace said.

"Well . . . yes. You're always more interested in whatever else is going on around you," her father answered. "But this time you obviously focused on what you were reading and took it in."

"Yeah, I did," Grace said. "I just tuned out everything else and read for hours."

"How did you like that?" her mom asked.

"Not as much as I like hanging out with my friends," Grace admitted. "But I did like the story. By the time I got halfway through, I really wanted to know what happened to Buck."

"That's good enough for now," her father said. "You got every question right, and we're happy."

"Does this mean I can go to WetWorld?" Grace asked. "And audition for the play?"

"Yes and yes," her mother replied. "As long as you start reading *The Jungle Book* right away."

"I will! I totally will this time," Grace promised. "I let you guys down once, and you gave me a second chance. I'm not going to let you down again."

"That's what I like to hear," her father said.

"Good night, honey. We're proud of you," her mother added.

When Grace hung up the phone, she did a little jig all the way to the door of the office. She grinned at Kathleen.

"Looks like you passed," Kathleen said.

"Yup!" Grace ran to the office door and threw it open. Eleven expectant faces gazed back at her. Her bunkmates had all come to wait for the results. *They are the best friends in the entire world,* she thought, touched.

"Well, don't keep us in suspense," Natalie said. "How did you do?"

"WetWorld, here we come!" Grace yelled.

chapter TEN

"What's up, Gracie?" Gaby dropped down on the black box next to Grace at the start of drama class the next day.

Grace couldn't believe her ears. Gaby sounded completely friendly and normal. As if nothing had happened between them. As if they'd never had a disagreement in their lives.

"Did you see Tyler and Stephanie at breakfast this morning?" Gaby asked. "They were actually holding hands."

Grace shook her head. How could Gaby just pretend that things were okay between them? Did she expect Grace to forget her bad behavior? Still, Grace couldn't exactly be rude to her, not when Gaby was acting all nice like this.

"Um . . . I really have to cram," Grace said. "I didn't think my parents would let me audition, so I haven't even bothered to learn the scene." She turned back to her copy of *The Sound of Music*.

"No kidding," Gaby said. "I *am* your partner. I know we haven't been practicing." She sounded annoyed. But what did she have to be annoyed about? Gaby still hadn't apologized for lying about her free-swim punishment, and here she was acting as if *Grace* was the difficult one.

"I'm sorry," Grace said, not entirely meaning it. "We could have been rehearsing an audition scene for you. You never mentioned it, so I just figured you weren't planning to try out for the play."

"It's more fun to have half an hour to play around during drama," Gaby said. "Who wants to spend time practicing?"

"Um, I do," Grace told her. "It's really important to me to get a part in the play this year." Gaby rolled her eyes, but Grace ignored her. "I'm going to do the scene from *The Sound of Music* like we talked about."

Gaby played around with the laces on her sneakers. She didn't seem to want to help, but Grace knew she had no choice. The first half hour of drama was for practicing. Bethany was cool about people sitting and talking quietly with their partners—she knew not everyone wanted to audition. But they weren't allowed to just goof around or wander away from their partners. So if she wanted to rehearse, Gaby was going to have to sit there and listen.

"It's the scene where she's teaching the kids to sing," Grace said, pulling the typed pages out of her notebook. She hadn't even looked at them since the second day of drama. She'd been too bummed about the fact that her folks wouldn't let her try out. But she had the movie *The Sound of Music* on DVD, so she knew the scene pretty well already. "You read the kids' lines. There aren't many." She handed over the pages.

Gaby heaved a huge sigh, as if Grace was asking her to climb a mountain or something.

By the time she'd said two lines, Gaby was yawning. And when it was Gaby's turn to speak, she was busy putting a little braid in her hair and missed her cue.

"You're supposed to be helping me," Grace said, frustrated. "You're the one who wanted to be partners."

"That's because I thought you would be fun," Gaby said. "I didn't know you actually wanted to try out for the stupid play."

Grace noticed Devon and Simon glancing over in her direction. "Shh," she told Gaby. "Other people are trying to rehearse."

"So?" Gaby's voice was as loud as ever.

"Why did you sign up for drama if you think the play is stupid?" Grace asked.

"Who said I signed up for it? I asked for photography, but Lizzie put me in drama."

"Why?" Grace asked.

Gaby shrugged. "My stupid bunkmate Christa is in photography, and Lizzie wanted to separate us."

"Because you stole her shampoo?" Grace said.

"I told you I didn't steal it," Gaby snapped. "Christa's just a crybaby."

Grace didn't answer. She had a feeling there was more to the story than Gaby was telling her. Based on her conversation with Julie and Marissa, Grace thought that Gaby had gotten in a lot of trouble for bullying Christa.

"Bethany, can I go to the restroom?" Gaby called out. When Bethany nodded, Gaby just got up and left without even glancing in Grace's direction. *So much for having a scene partner,* Grace thought, exasperated. *I can't believe I ever thought she could be my best friend.*

"Psst, Grace." Devon leaned toward her. "You can practice with us if you want. We'll read lines for your scene and you can read lines for ours."

"Really?" Grace said.

Devon and Simon both nodded.

"Wow. Thanks." She grabbed her stuff and headed over to them. She tried not to look at Devon's friendly face. If she did, she knew she'd get tongue-tied and not even be able to read her scene. All she could do was hope that it would be easier talking to Devon using words that someone else had thought up!

Dear Emily,

I'm sorry, I'm sorry, I'm sorry. (Repeat at least a hundred times.)

You were right. You said I would be too

busy having fun to write to you this summer. And at first I was. But then I got too busy not having fun. There's this girl Gaby from bunk 3A—that's right, those evil girls I told you about last year. Anyway, most of those girls are actually okay. But this one is mean. Kind of. Sometimes. She started out being all nice to me, and she was funny. So I thought maybe she could be my camp best friend. Not that I'm trying to replace you!! But it stinks that you're not here. So I figured I could be friends with Gaby. And as soon as we were friends, she started being weird. Sometimes she's mean, but then she always says she's only joking. You know me—I have a good sense of humor. So why can't I tell when she's kidding around? I guess I just really missed having one best friend, a partner in crime. But you know what they say—with friends like that! I guess it just goes to show that you really are irreplaceable!

Anyway, I thought I would let you know that I finished The Call of the Wild. Mom and Dad made me take a quiz on it, and I got everything right. Now I just have to read The Jungle Book. I think it will be easy after this one. So, I kept my deal with them to read the book, and now I'm keeping my deal with you. I promised to write and I'm writing!

I wish you were here. You could tell me what to do about the situation with Gaby. I don't think I really want to be friends with her, but I also can't stand the thought of being mean or hurting her feelings. Maybe I'm too soft? Who knows. Cross your fingers that I figure it out soon.

See you in less than a month!

Grace

"Do, a deer, a female deer!" Grace sang as she swept the floor during chores on Wednesday. "Re, a drop of golden sun!"

"Meeee, a name I call myseeelf!" Jenna screeched in a fake falsetto voice.

Everybody cracked up. Grace felt a little bad. They were all probably sick of hearing that song. "Sorry," she said.

"Grace, you've been practicing nonstop for two days," Alyssa said. "Take a break before you make yourself hoarse."

"Yeah, you'll make yourself hoarse," Candace added.

"Besides, you know the whole scene really well," Valerie said. She lowered her voice. "You learned it much faster than Brynn did." Brynn was outside, running lines with Alex as they walked to the Dumpster to throw out the garbage.

"Nah, she's just a perfectionist," Grace said. "Plus, Brynn's had more time to rehearse. Auditions are in an hour and I'm totally not ready."

"Yes, you are ready," Marissa said. "You were singing in your sleep last night."

"Seriously, Grace, you're a natural," Natalie said. "You'll definitely get a part. And then you'll be the huge celebrity at camp, and everyone will forget all about my father!"

Grace smiled nervously. "I'm finished sweeping. Is

it okay if I go over to the drama shack to practice before auditions?"

"Go ahead," Julie said. "Break a leg!"

"Thanks." Grace pushed through the door and bounded down the steps. To her surprise, Karen was sitting on the grass in front of the porch. "Hey. Whatcha doing?" Grace asked.

Karen jumped. "Oh! I'm, um, I'm on dusting duty. I came out here to shake out the duster." She held up their ancient feather duster as evidence.

"You're shaking out the duster while sitting down?" Grace asked, confused.

"No." Karen got up quickly. "I was . . . uh . . ."

"Hiding from Chelsea?" Grace guessed.

Karen's gaze dropped to her sneakers. "No. Of course not."

"Karen, I heard you guys talking the other day," Grace said. "I know you're bummed about having to skip the rides at the water park."

"No, it's okay," Karen said. "Chelsea doesn't like rides."

"But you do," Grace pointed out.

"Yeah, but I don't want to leave Chelsea alone," Karen said. "That wouldn't be very nice. I already told her I'd hang out with her." She gave the duster a little shake. "I better finish my chores." She hurried up the steps but turned back before going in. "Hey, Grace, good luck at your audition," she said quietly. "I think you're the best actress at camp." Then she disappeared into the bunk.

Grace started down the trail. All her nervousness had returned the second Karen mentioned the tryout. It was nice to know that her bunkmates thought so highly of her, but she felt completely unprepared for the audition. She'd had to do all the work on her scene by herself. Gaby hadn't even bothered to check in and see how it was going.

But when she got to the drama shack for tryouts, Gaby was there, sitting in the "audience"—a bunch of the black boxes turned upside down for people to sit on while they watched the auditions. Grace was touched. Maybe Gaby hadn't been the best drama partner in the world, but at least she was there to support Grace when it mattered. It was the first best-friend-like thing Gaby had ever done. Only a real friend would realize how nervous Grace would be about the audition. If Emily had been at Camp Lakeview, she would've been there to show her support. And for once, Gaby was acting the same way. She was being supportive.

"Hey," Grace said, sitting on the box next to Gaby. "Thanks for coming."

"Why wouldn't I come?" Gaby said. "I think I have a pretty good shot at landing a part."

Grace couldn't believe her ears. "You're auditioning?" she asked.

"Of course."

"But you didn't even practice," Grace cried. "You

said you thought the play was stupid!"

"It is," Gaby said. "That's why I didn't bother practicing. How hard can it be to get a role in *Peter Pan*? It's a kiddie story!"

Bethany clapped her hands for attention, so Grace couldn't answer. She wouldn't have known how to respond, anyway. Gaby hadn't come here to support Grace at all. Gaby was only here for herself!

Auditions went in age order, so the younger kids went first. Most of them forgot a line or two, but a few were very good singers. By the time it was the third division's turn, the butterflies in Grace's stomach felt more like a flock of birds. "Third division, who's first?" Bethany called.

"Me!" Brynn leapt up and ran to the front of the room. "I'm doing the scene from *The Music Man*."

"I think I'll volunteer to go next," Grace whispered to Gaby. "I'm so nervous, I just want to get it over with."

Brynn did an amazing job on her tryout. Grace had heard her do the scene a hundred times over the past week, but seeing her perform it today was like watching it for the first time. Brynn disappeared and Marion the librarian stood onstage talking and singing. When she was done, Grace clapped and whistled through her teeth. "Way to go, Brynn!" she yelled.

"Thank you, Brynn," Bethany said. "Who's next?"

"I am!" Gaby called, jumping up and heading to the makeshift stage. Grace almost laughed. Gaby's behavior was so awful all the time that Grace wasn't even surprised anymore when she acted rudely. *It's my own fault for telling her I wanted to go next,* she thought. *I should've known that would make her steal my slot for herself.*

Gaby did the scene from *The Sound of Music*. She forgot half the lines and only sang one verse of the song. But she looked totally proud of herself when she was done. Grace clapped politely, and then raised her hand to go next.

As she passed by on her way up to the front of the room, Devon whispered "good luck," and Simon gave her a thumbs-up. Grace smiled back. They'd been much more helpful to her than her own partner had—they'd gone through the scene with her three times the other day.

Once she got on stage, Grace forgot all about Gaby and her obnoxious behavior. She forgot about *The Call of the Wild* and the quiz. She forgot about the fact that she still had to read *The Jungle Book* before camp ended. She even forgot about the water-park trip the next day. Her entire mind was focused on being Maria, the nun-turned-nanny, teaching the von Trapp kids to sing. She spoke the lines and sang the song as if the words were coming straight from her own brain, not as if she'd memorized them and practiced them over and over. The black room around her became the grassy hills of Austria, and the people watching became the children she was talking to. She loved singing, and she knew the kids would, too. All she wanted in the world was to show these boys and girls how much joy there was in music, so she sang with every bit of happiness she had ever felt in her life.

When her song ended, Grace slowly became aware that people were clapping. She had to shake her head a little to clear away the image of the outdoors and the von Trapp kids. She'd been so wrapped up in her acting that she'd forgotten where she really was.

Breathing hard from singing, she took a bow and headed back out into the audience. Gaby sat with a sour expression on her face, barely clapping. Brynn was practically bouncing up and down on her black box, making whooping sounds as she applauded. Devon and Simon sat nearby, clapping and cheering, too. Grace didn't even hesitate.

She walked right by Gaby and sat with her other friends.

▲ ▲ ▲

"And Devon was amazing, too," Brynn said at dessert that night. "If only we were really doing *The Sound of Music*, he'd be an excellent Captain von Trapp."

"Then you two could act together, Grace," Natalie teased her.

"Don't you want to hear how your boyfriend, Simon, did?" Grace teased back. "I'm surprised you didn't sneak out of arts and crafts to come watch him audition."

"I thought about it," Natalie replied. "But instead I made him a little plate in pottery that says 'Congratulations.'

I can't give it to him until he finds out if he got a part, though!"

Grace shook her head. It was no fun to tease Natalie about Simon these days. She just never got ruffled about it anymore. Not that she'd ever really been bothered by the teasing—if she had, Grace wouldn't have done it.

"I think he'll get a part," Brynn said. "He did a good job. I think we'll all get parts."

"Yeah, we rule," Grace agreed. "Are you still hoping for Wendy, Brynn? A lot of those division four and division five girls were really good." Brynn had done an incredible audition, but Grace didn't want her to get her hopes up too high. Despite what Bethany said, everybody knew that the main roles always went to older kids.

"They were good, but I still think I have a chance," Brynn said confidently. "And so do you."

"Okay, enough drama talk," Julie interrupted from her seat at the end of the bunk's table. "I know you two are dying to go look at the cast list."

"Bethany said she was going to post it after dinner," Brynn replied. "It's not up yet."

"Well . . ." Julie grinned. "I happen to know that she put it up on her way over to the mess hall. She just figured no one would know it was there until after dinner."

Brynn leapt up from her seat. "Can we go now?" she asked excitedly. "Please please please?"

"Go ahead," Julie said. "Good luck!"

Brynn grabbed Grace's hand and pulled her toward

the door. By the time they got to the drama shack, everyone at Lakeview seemed to know that the list had been posted. A crowd of kids stood around the bulletin board on the outside of the shack.

"How are we supposed to see if we're on the list when we can't even see the list?" Grace joked.

"That's a total upset!" one of the division four kids said.

"I can't believe it," another older girl murmured. "I've been coming here for years, and no one that young has ever gotten such a big part."

"Maybe it's one of us!" Brynn cried happily.

Grace stood on her tiptoes, but she still couldn't see the list. "What are you guys talking about?" she asked the older girl.

"A third division girl got the part of Wendy," the girl said. "It's unheard of."

"Oh, it's not such a big deal," Brynn said modestly. "I've been studying acting since I was really little, so it's no surprise."

"Well, you'll probably be surprised to hear it's not you," Gaby said, pushing her way out of the crowd around the list.

Brynn's face fell. "What do you mean? They said it was someone from division three."

"Yeah," Gaby said. "That still doesn't mean it's you!"

"Why do you have to be so mean, Gaby?" Grace

asked, putting her arm around Brynn's shoulders. "Brynn is really upset."

Suddenly Brynn gasped. "I am not upset!" she cried.

Grace glanced at her in surprise. "Why not?"

"Because I may not have gotten the part," she said, "but that can only mean one thing. *You* got it, Grace!"

chapter ELEVEN

Grace woke up with a smile already on her face. It stayed there while she brushed her teeth and packed her backpack for the trip to WetWorld. It stayed there all through breakfast. And it was still in place when she climbed into the field-trip bus and started down the aisle.

She was playing Wendy in *Peter Pan*! And she was allowed to go to the water park! Just a week ago neither of those things had seemed possible.

Natalie and Alyssa had already grabbed one of the back seats, but there were lots of other campers in the little aisle between them and Grace. Ronald from 3E had a backpack as big as his whole body, and he was trying to throw it up onto the overhead luggage rack. Traffic in the aisle stopped as he lifted it again and again, never getting it high enough.

"Do you want some help?" Jenna's brother Adam asked.

Ronald was a twerp, but he had a surprisingly

loud voice. "Not from you," he snapped.

Grace sighed. The rivalry between bunk 3E and Adam's bunk, 3F, was just as strong as the one between her bunk and Gaby's. There was no way Ronald would ever take help from Adam or his friends. She leaned against the back of one of the seats and waited for the path to clear.

"Gracie, back here! I got us a seat," Gaby called. Grace twisted around to see Gaby in the very front seat, right behind the driver. She was waving and grinning as if they were the best of friends. Ever since the announcement that Grace had gotten the part, Gaby had been super friendly and supportive. That was nice enough, but Grace couldn't forget how nasty she'd been so many times before that.

"Um, I'm sitting with Alyssa and Natalie," she called back. "Remember?"

Gaby's face fell. "I thought you changed your mind about that," she said. "I apologized for telling them about your book. Don't you remember?"

Grace did remember. And she also remembered Gaby lying to her about being punished, tricking her into not swimming in the deep end, refusing to help her practice for the audition, and just generally being a bully. She did *not* remember ever changing her mind about sitting with Gaby on the field-trip bus.

But Gaby really did look upset. She was glancing frantically around at the other kids on the bus, and Grace suddenly realized that Gaby had no one else to sit with. Grace thought about it. Gaby didn't seem very popular with her own bunkmates. Whatever had happened between her and Christa must have made them all uncomfortable. And outside of Grace, Gaby didn't seem to have any other friends. Grace sighed. What did she have to lose? She was in such a good mood just being there and knowing about her role in the play. She doubted even Gaby could ruin her happiness today.

She stood on her tiptoes and waved to Nat and Alyssa, pointing back toward Gaby so they'd know where she was going. Alyssa waved back, but Natalie made an "are you crazy" face. Grace just shrugged.

"Excuse me," she said, turning to go back toward the front of the bus.

"You're going the wrong way!" somebody complained.

"You can't get through," another voice whined.

Why did she have to sit all the way in the front? Grace wondered. Gaby was only three seats away from her, but the aisle was stuffed with campers. "Okay, clear the way!" Grace yelled. She jumped up onto the seat next to her and began climbing over the back of the one in front of it.

"Good idea," Devon said.

Grace almost fell on her face. She hadn't realized he was standing so close, only five or six people behind her. And here she was climbing over seats like a . . . well, not like a *girl*. Chelsea would never do something that was so *not* graceful. Natalie probably wouldn't, either. Grace flushed. She was stuck with her left foot on one seat and her right foot on another. There was no choice. She kept climbing, her face on fire. Finally she reached Gaby's seat and plopped down.

"Well, *that* was stupid-looking," Gaby commented.

Grace's mouth fell open. She'd practically done acrobatics in front of Devon and the whole third division just so she could get back here to sit with Gaby, and that was the thanks she got.

"I can do it again," Grace said. "All the way back to Alyssa and Natalie's seat."

"No," Gaby said quickly. "I was only kidding."

Grace didn't answer. Gaby seemed to use that excuse whenever she did or said something mean. By this point, Grace knew that Gaby wasn't really kidding most of the time.

"What ride do you want to go on first?" Gaby asked.

Grace simply shrugged. It was going to be a long day.

▲ ▲ ▲

"This line is too long," Gaby complained at the Flume of Fear.

"You've said that about every single ride so far," Grace pointed out.

"Let's go on Rio Rafting," Gaby said. She stepped out of line and started walking away. Grace didn't follow her.

She was sick of Gaby's attitude—that she got to decide everything and that she assumed Grace would just go along with her. They'd gotten off the lines for the past two rides because Gaby didn't want to wait. In almost three hours at the water park, they'd managed to go on only one actual ride!

This time Grace was going to stay put. If Gaby wanted to leave, fine. Grace would go on the Flume of Fear alone, and then she'd go find her bunkmates. They were probably having a great time. And she'd blown them off in order to hang out with Gaby, whom she didn't even like.

Grace gasped as she realized it. All this time, she'd been annoyed at Gaby, or confused by her behavior, or sometimes even a little afraid of what Gaby would do next. But she'd never stopped to think about her own feelings about their friendship. But all of a sudden it seemed so clear. She didn't want to be friends with Gaby. Gaby was a jerk!

"Come *on*, Gracie," Gaby said loudly, stomping back over to the line. "I don't want to wait for this stupid ride."

"Well, I do," Grace said. "And stop calling me Gracie."

Gaby blinked in surprise. "Why?"

"Because I hate it. In third grade I got caught daydreaming one time and everyone called me Spacey Gracie for the rest of the year."

Gaby laughed.

"You would think that was funny," Grace mumbled.

"It is funny. You need to lighten up." Gaby grabbed her hand. "Come on, let's go on the rafts."

Grace pulled her hand away. "No," she said. "We'll just end up waiting on line there until you get bored, and then you'll leave again, and we'll lose our place in *another* line."

Gaby opened her mouth, then closed it again. She obviously had no idea how to deal with someone saying no to her. Grace wondered if it had ever happened before. Maybe her bunkmates had stood up to her, and that's why she wasn't friends with any of them. "Oh, fine," Gaby finally said. Then she stood there and sulked for the next ten minutes as the line crept forward. She sulked as they got onto the flume ride, and she sulked all the way through its dips and bumps and its one huge drop.

Grace was impressed. She thought it must be hard to sulk when you wanted to scream and wave your arms around like everyone else on the ride. But Gaby stuck to it.

"Okay, now let's go on Rio Rafting," Grace said as they walked out of the flume exit.

"Finally," Gaby exploded. She took off toward the rafts. By the time Grace caught up with her, Gaby was already frowning again. "This line's too long," she said. "If you hadn't made me go on that stupid flume, we could've been at the front already."

"Gaby, it's a water park in the middle of the summer," Grace said. "All the rides are going to have lines. You have to deal with it."

"No I don't," Gaby replied. "Look, there's Christa near the front. Let's go cut her."

"We can't cut her," Grace cried, trying to ignore the dirty looks that the people in line were giving them.

"Sure we can. She'll let us." Gaby strode off toward the front of the line. Mortified, Grace followed her.

"Gaby," she murmured, catching up. "We could get thrown out of the park for cutting in line."

Gaby rolled her eyes. "Whatever. We'll just say Christa was holding our place."

They reached Gaby's bunkmate. Grace couldn't help noticing that Christa did not look happy to see them. Her big brown eyes filled with nervousness at the sight of Gaby.

"We're gonna go on with you," Gaby announced.

"No, I'm . . . um, I'm with Jill," Christa said in a voice so low that it was practically a whisper.

"I don't see her," Gaby said.

"She's in the bathroom."

"Her loss," Gaby said, stepping in front of Christa.

"Gaby, we're going to get in trouble." Christa's voice shook as if she might cry. The people behind her were glaring at all three of them.

"Oh, don't be such a baby," Gaby said. "We'll only get in trouble if you tell. And you won't, right? You already snitched on me once. If you do it again, you'll be worse than a snitch. You'll be a rat."

"Okay, okay." Christa stepped aside to make room for them. She shot Grace a panicked look. *She thinks I'm going to bully her, too,* Grace realized. The thought made her want to laugh. Here was Christa thinking she was a bully when in reality she was just Gaby's latest victim. Obviously Gaby had been pushing Christa around all summer, and for the past two weeks Grace had been letting Gaby push *her* around, too.

She didn't get it. She wasn't a shy, self-conscious person like Christa. Or even like Karen, who got bullied by Chelsea a lot. So why was she allowing Gaby to walk all over her?

"You know what?" she said. "I'm not going to do this."

"Do what?" Gaby asked.

"Cut in line," Grace said. "And I don't care if you call me a baby or make fun of me or whatever you're going to do."

"What are you talking about?" Gaby tried to sound innocent, but it didn't work.

"You know what I'm talking about," Grace said. "You're a bully, Gaby. It's not cool."

"Well, you're a loser who can't even read," Gaby shot back. But she didn't sound mean anymore. In fact,

Grace thought she sounded frightened. She clearly didn't like it when someone stood up to her.

"I am not a loser," Grace told her. "I just didn't pay enough attention to my schoolwork last year because I was busy having fun. With my *real* best friend, who never tries to push me around like you do."

"Why don't you just leave us alone?" Gaby snapped. "I should've known better than to hang out with a girl from 3C." She turned her back on Grace, pulling Christa along with her.

"You shouldn't let her cut you, Christa," Grace said. "She's going to keep bullying you until you say no."

But Christa didn't even have the guts to look back at Grace. *Oh, well,* Grace thought. *Maybe I set a good example for her to follow once she gets up her nerve.*

One of the women in line behind them gave Grace a thumbs-up.

"Thanks," Grace said. She walked away from the Rio Rafting line feeling better than she had since she'd gotten on the bus that morning. She hadn't wanted to be rude to Gaby, but telling her off felt great. Now all she wanted to do was to find her bunkmates and start having fun on this field trip.

She went straight to the wave pool. Chelsea and Karen were lying out on two of the lounge chairs next to the pool. Both of them were completely dry, and Chelsea's hair was perfect, as usual.

"Hey, you guys," Grace greeted them. "You haven't gone on a single water ride all day, have you?"

"No way," Chelsea said.

"It's a water park, you know," Grace teased her.

Chelsea shrugged. "I don't want chlorine in my hair."

"Suit yourself," Grace said. "Do you know where everyone else is?"

"I think they all went to the three-story-high waterslide to cheer Jenna on," Karen said. "No one else was brave enough to go on it."

"I'll do it if you will, Karen," Grace said.

Karen gazed back at her, eyes wide. Chelsea frowned. "Karen's hanging out with me," she said. "I don't want to stay here all alone."

"Then you should come with us," Grace told her. "Come on, Karen. What do you say?"

Karen glanced at Chelsea. Then at Grace. "Well . . ." She took a deep breath. "Okay." She leapt up off her lounge chair and started walking away as fast as she could. *She's afraid Chelsea will stop her,* Grace thought. *And she's probably right.*

"Hey!" Chelsea cried.

Grace shrugged. "Sorry. You can come with us if you want."

For a split second, Chelsea looked as if she might. Then she shook her head. "No, thanks." She sat back in her chair and closed her eyes.

"Come find us if you get lonely," Grace said. Then she took off after Karen.

▲ ▲ ▲

"I can't believe you got us all on that waterslide," Natalie said half an hour later. "That was the most terrifying thing I've ever done in my whole life."

"I can't believe all you guys were willing to go on it just because Grace wanted you to," Jenna said. "You didn't even *think* of going on it to keep me company."

"You didn't need company," Alyssa pointed out. "You were brave enough to do it alone."

"Yeah, Jenna, I think I would have wimped out if you guys weren't with me," Karen said.

Grace grinned. Hanging out with her bunkmates was cool, but getting Karen to come out of her shell a little bit was even cooler. As soon as Grace had announced that Karen wanted to go on the slide, all the other girls had agreed to join in. Everybody knew that Chelsea bullied Karen, but no one had ever had the nerve to say anything about it before. Now that Karen had taken a stand, they all wanted to support her. Grace could tell how much the support meant to Karen.

It's how I felt when they all helped me study for Mom's quiz, she thought. *Like I was surrounded by the best group of friends in the world.*

"Who wants to play Shoot-the-Starfish?" Alex asked.

"Not me," Sarah replied. "But I am a little shaky after that thirty-foot drop. I'll go play one of the other games."

"Yeah, I want to keep my feet on the ground for a few minutes," Valerie agreed. "That slide was fun, but it knocked me out!"

"So let's go over to the arcade, and we'll all play whatever games we want for half an hour," Grace suggested. "Then we can do the Tarzan rope-swing ride."

When they got to the arcade, Brynn took off for the karaoke booth. Alex and Jenna headed to Shoot-the-Starfish. Karen went with Sarah and Valerie to check out the ancient video games like Pac-Man.

"Let's play that Loch Ness game," Natalie said.

Grace glanced over to the game, which was basically Whack-a-Mole with miniature Loch Ness monsters instead of moles. The game looked pretty boring. But playing the game at that moment were Simon, Adam, and Devon.

"Yeah. Let's go," Alyssa said, trying to sound casual.

Grace burst out laughing. "You guys are so obvious!" she said. "You just want to hang out with your boyfriends."

"Adam is not my boyfriend," Alyssa said.

"But you want him to be," Nat replied.

"Not as much as you want Simon to be yours," Alyssa shot back.

"Please," Grace said. "You both like them, and they like you. It's disgusting."

"Well, you like Devon," Nat said.

"I do not."

"Fine," Alyssa put in. "Then let's not go play the Loch Ness game." She exchanged a smile with Natalie, and they both stared at Grace, waiting for her reaction.

Grace thought about it. Devon *was* cute. And he was a good actor. And he seemed to like her. He'd helped her prepare for auditions, and he'd complimented her a few times now. But that didn't mean she *liked* him. Still . . . it couldn't hurt to play the same arcade game he was playing. And her friends really wanted to hang out with his friends. "No, that's okay," she said aloud. "We can play the Loch Ness game. It looks like fun."

She led the way over to the game booth, ignoring the fact that Natalie and Alyssa were totally laughing at her.

By the time they got to the booth, the boys were at the front, each armed with a giant rubber-tipped mallet. A buzzer rang, and the little Nessie heads began popping up from holes in the board along the front of the booth. Immediately the guys went to work, smashing the mallets down on anything they could hit.

Natalie and Alyssa cheered loudly, and Grace couldn't help but join in. When the buzzer rang again to signal the end of the game, Adam had one Nessie hit and Simon had two. Neither one of them qualified to win anything. But Devon had five hits.

"Choose your prize," said the guy in the Scottish hat behind the counter. "A stuffed Nessie or a stuffed lobster."

Devon turned around. "Grace, which one do you want?" he asked.

Grace told herself to ignore the fact that Nat's eyes were bugging out of her head and Alyssa's gasp was so loud that everyone in the park could hear it. It was harder, though, to ignore the heat creeping up her neck, signaling that she was about to turn bright red from embarrassment.

"Um, the Nessie," she said.

The Scottish-hat guy handed over a little stuffed animal that looked like a brontosaurus wearing a plaid scarf. And Devon turned and gave it to Grace.

Don't be a dork this time, she ordered herself. *Come up with something cool to say.*

"Thanks," she said.

Devon just nodded, flashing one of his adorable smiles.

"Now when people say the Loch Ness monster is just a legend, I can show them this to prove it really exists," Grace added. There! That was at least a little bit of her true personality.

Devon laughed. "Yeah, it would be hard to argue with that."

"Let's go play the water-ski game," Adam said. "I'm better at that one." The boys took off toward the interactive games. Devon hesitated for a moment. "Did you know I got a role as one of the Lost Boys?" he asked.

"Yeah, congratulations," Grace said. "I knew you'd

get a part. Your audition was amazing."

"Not as amazing as yours. You have real talent," he said seriously. "But now that we're both in the play, maybe we can run lines together to practice."

Grace felt a strange little tingle move up the back of her neck. "Sure. That would be fun."

"Cool." Devon gave her a little wave as he walked off after his friends. Grace realized that she was still grinning stupidly, but somehow she couldn't make herself stop.

"You were right about that Loch Ness game, Grace," Alyssa said as Natalie collapsed into a fit of giggles. "It *was* fun."

"Fun to watch you flirt with Devon!" Natalie crowed.

"Just because Devon and I are friends doesn't mean I like him," Grace said.

"Yeah, right," Natalie replied.

"It doesn't," Grace insisted. "We're just going to practice for the play together. That's all."

They both smirked at her, and she couldn't blame them. As much as she hated to admit it, she kind of had a crush on Devon. "Okay, we believe you," Alyssa told her, obviously lying.

"Good," Grace said. "Because I don't like boys. It is a cute Nessie, though."

"You guys had Grace for the whole time at the arcade," Valerie said. She grabbed Grace's arm as soon as they all got out into the parking lot where the bus was. "Sarah and I get her for the ride home."

Natalie pouted. "She was supposed to sit with us on the way there and she didn't. I think we should get her now."

"Ladies, ladies, there's enough of me to go around," Grace joked. "Let's just sit right across from one another. That way we all can still talk."

"We'll sit in front of you," Jenna added, following them. "Our whole bunk should sit together."

"Yeah, then Grace and I can practice our scenes for you on the way," Brynn suggested. She was playing a Lost Boy in the play, and Grace was grateful that Brynn didn't seem to be mad at her for getting a bigger part.

With everyone laughing and talking—except Chelsea, who was grumpy because she'd gotten a sunburn—they made their way to the big field-trip bus. Just as Grace was about to climb the tall steps, Gaby walked up next to her and gave her a little shove to push her out of the way.

"Hey!" Grace yelped. "You almost knocked me over!"

"Oh, sorry." Gaby sneered at her. "I guess I'm not supposed to touch you now that you're such a big star."

"You're not supposed to push anyone out of the way whether they're a big star or not," Brynn snapped, stepping up to defend Grace.

"What do you care?" Gaby said. "She stole the part you wanted!"

"She won the part fair and square," Brynn said. "That's part of being an actor, so I have to learn to deal with it. I'm not going to hold a grudge against my friend for doing a better audition than me."

"You wouldn't understand that, though," Alex said, coming to Brynn's side. "You obviously don't know anything about being a true friend."

"Yeah, you don't know anything about it," Candace put in.

"You're just a bully," Chelsea said. "Everybody knows it."

A few of the girls in 3C exchanged smiles. That was the pot calling the kettle black! But it was nice to have everyone in 3C standing together. They really did work well as a team.

"You're all losers, anyway," Gaby said. "I don't know what I was thinking making friends with someone from your lame bunk." She scurried into the bus to get away from them.

"Say what you want, it won't bother us," Jenna called after her. "We know how cool we are."

"So cool that we have the two best actresses in the third division," Alyssa said.

"And Jenna and Alex, the best athletes," Natalie added.

"And we're the scavenger-hunt champs," Sarah said.

"And we're totally going to win color war," Valerie put in.

By now, they were all laughing. "Plus, we're the smartest, prettiest girls in the entire known universe," Grace joked. "And we're extremely modest."

Grace felt a swell of happiness as her bunkmates all high-fived one another. Why had she thought she needed a friend outside of the bunk? They all climbed into the bus and made their way toward the back seats.

Grace noticed Gaby sitting with Christa near the front. Gaby pointedly looked away when Grace passed.

Oh, well, Grace thought. *I guess that's the end of our friendship.* She had lots of problems with Gaby's behavior, but Grace had a hard time staying mad at people. She'd hoped that they could at least be friendly to each other, even if they weren't going to be best friends. But Gaby clearly didn't see it that way.

"Come on, Grace!" Sarah called. "We saved the aisle seat for you."

Grace hurried back to the group of seats her friends had taken over. "It's bunk 3C on wheels," she said. Everyone laughed as she plopped into her seat, letting her stress over Gaby melt away.

Who needed *one* best friend when you had eleven?

Book #4

camp CONFIDENTIAL

Alex's Challenge

chapter ONE

Dear Bridgette,

I'm still here at Camp Lakeview. Just two more weeks left before we can hang out—in person—again! I'm so excited to see you.

Thanks for the letters and manga books you've been sending me. I'm really trying to love anime as much as you do, and I'm getting into some of it. When I read that last one, I thought of you the whole time. I love how the Ninja Supertwins trick their kidnapper into letting them go. You're just like the brainy one (I'm the one who can fly and do flips and stuff—ha ha ha). It's fun to imagine that you're right here with me.

But you're not.

☹

Do you know how much I miss you?

Brynn and I have been keeping busy—we're always swimming or jumping rope or staying up way too late. She can be a handful, though, always wanting me to practice lines with her (you know, she's a literal drama queen) and to help her find the stuff she lost in our big old bunk. I'd like to see her practice soccer with me! She doesn't like sports all that much, and, as you know, I live for anything athletic.

We're so different that sometimes I can't believe we're such good friends.

How's summer practice been without me? If I come back and you're a whole lot better than I am, you're just going to have to teach me your new moves. Deal?

I'm learning some new stuff—from boys, of all people. I get to play with the counselors a lot, which makes me better. But sometimes, I think they let me score points when they shouldn't. I'm not complaining, though. I'm having a blast. Anyway, I can't wait to play with you!

Just know that I miss you and think of you all the time. You don't know how much I wish you were here right now! Ugh. I don't have to pretend around you. You know how it is.

I miss you. Did I say that already? Well, I just said it again!

Best Friends Forever,
Alex

Alex had just gotten into bed and was trying to relax. If only her brain had an off switch! She was deep in thought, wishing she could be one of the Ninja Supertwins. She wished she could just have special powers so her life would be easier. Every time she hit the soccer field, she had to score at least three points for her team. Every time she left the bunk, she had to worry if she'd stay strong for the rest of the day. And every time her camp friends had issues—like when Jenna thought Chelsea had tripped her at lunch—they looked to Alex to keep the peace. Alex couldn't understand why she felt so much pressure and where it was all coming from.

At that moment, Jenna was causing Alex's stress. Jenna was addicted to sugar, and her parents liked to feed that addiction with packages from home. Sometimes, Jenna got cupcakes. Other times, she passed out Swedish fish. That night, she had the largest quantity of Nerds that Alex had ever seen. The round, little balls of candy were pink and purple. As Jenna passed them around—she was totally generous—some Nerds inevitably went flying.

Gnat-sized streaks of unnatural color dashed through the air like Fourth of July sparklers.

Alex couldn't help herself; she peeked up from her letter to watch the scene, her mouth beginning to water. She loved the sharp-sweet flavor of Nerds. Just as she was going back to writing, a handful of the hard sugar pellets nicked her left cheek.

"Agh!" Alex yelled. Those buggers were dangerous.

Some girls started to grumble while others laughed. After six weeks together, everyone knew who'd get cranky (Chelsea) versus who'd get goofy (Jenna, Grace, Natalie). That's what had happened at Camp Lakeview every year Alex had been there, and she'd been going there for a lonnnggg time. The girls grew "thisclose," and sometimes there was this magical warm and fuzzy feeling between them, like you'd met eleven soul mates. Other times, during the War of the Nerds, for example, "thisclose" was a recipe for calorie-infused disaster.

"Hey, did you get any?" Valerie whispered to Alex.

"Yeah, they left bruises on my cheek," Alex said, passing up the sweet treats as usual. This time, Alex went back to writing for real. She started on another letter to her soccer coach. She had to concentrate on seeming busy so the girls would be less likely to pay attention to her. Alex wouldn't disturb a fly—and she liked herself that way. She was the original get-along girl who never instigated feuds or showed up late. She didn't even yell at Jenna's twin brother, Adam, when he pranked the bunk—leaving fake bugs on all the girls' pillows. Though that prank was pretty irritating, not to mention uninspired. Except for Brynn, who was her best camp friend, most people didn't know what made Alex tick. And sometimes even Brynn didn't know.

"Okay, cool," Val said. "More for me then."

"I *know* you didn't just hit me in the eye!" Chelsea yelled into the air. Lights-out was in fifteen minutes, but she was always in bed first. She claimed that her face broke out if she didn't get enough beauty sleep. Chelsea even tried to get the other girls to quiet down early, as if that ever worked.

"Aye aye, Captain Chelsea," Grace mimicked. "You'd better watch out, or you might lose a tongue, too."

"Grace, please stop," Chelsea said.

"Oh, we're just having fun," Jenna added. With so many brothers and a sister, she was pretty good at keeping the peace—as long as she wasn't doing battle with Adam.

"Well, not to be a party pooper," said Natalie, "but I stayed up way too late doing everyone's nails last night." Alex didn't let Natalie put all that colored gunk on her hands or face; makeup just seemed hot and slimy. But Alex did love Natalie nevertheless, who was the daughter of the mega-star Tad Maxwell. *Tad Maxwell!* Alex had taken down her posters of him after she'd found out Natalie's news at the beginning of the summer. It was way too weird to worship her friend's dad. Though Natalie's father *was* the most amazing athlete Alex had ever seen on screen—he even did most of his own stunts in the *Spy* movies. Alex's favorite scene was when Tad jumped off Mount Fuji when the deranged monk was chasing him. Anyway, Alex had to hand it to Natalie; Natalie wasn't stuck-up or glamorous or Hollywood at all. Even if Natalie did love teen magazines, she was down-to-earth.

"Boo!" said Alyssa, Natalie's best friend at camp. Alyssa, a funky, artsy girl, hurled a few more candies at Chelsea teasingly.

"I *said* stop it," Chelsea yelled again. Brynn and Grace talked about the summer play again, and that made the others girls roll their eyes. Natalie put her head under her pillow to avoid all the noise. Jessie and Candace started whining about how hot it was, and Valerie and Sarah started singing "My Dog Has Fleas" for absolutely no good reason. Despite the colorful Nerds that had just been launched around the room, the girls seemed only blue.

Alex just didn't get it. She wondered why it was that every year, people got down in the dumps toward the end of camp. It was that weird time where kids weren't glowing from the newness of Lakeview anymore, and Color War was still a little bit too far away to get excited about. Plus, the kids all knew one another well enough to get touchy about the slightest things. Natalie was worried about Simon, who hadn't looked for her during free period that day. Grace complained about her parents, who were making her read *The Jungle Book*. Chelsea whined that her skin was oily (it so wasn't—no matter how mean she was, she was still super pretty). Brynn didn't know how on Earth she'd memorize all of her lines in time to perfect the voice she needed to deliver them. Alex, of course, had offered to help out as usual.

Alex breathed in deeply, trying not to get teary. She knew it wasn't nice of her to be jealous of them, but she was. She would've traded any one of their problems—she would even take two or three of their issues at once!—to get rid of her own. She wanted to know what it was like to be concerned about stuff you could actually do something about. She would've given her athletic ability—all of it—for just one day where she didn't have to worry, worry, and worry some more. There she was with the girls who knew her best, if anyone knew her at all, and still, Alex felt totally alone.

Chelsea, surprisingly, had risen from bed and walked over to Jenna's bottom bunk in her pink-feathered night slippers that her mom had just sent her. She went back to her bed proudly because she had just scored a new handful of Nerds.

"You want some?" she asked Alyssa, thrusting her hand toward Alyssa's face. Alyssa turned the other way, which was the smart thing to do. If Alyssa had said yes, Chelsea would've yanked her hand away. The girls could handle Chelsea because at least her behavior was predictable.

"You want some?" Chelsea asked, shoving the Nerds in Alex's face next.

Alex didn't appreciate the interruption. She was busy thinking and pretending to write her letter. She tried to ignore Chelsea, but it didn't work.

"I *said*," Chelsea repeated, "would you like some?"

Alex tried to be as casual and distracted as she could when she gave her usual answer, "No, thank you." She started scribbling words onto her sheet of paper energetically. She wanted to look inspired so no one would dare break her train of thought. No one would have, either—no one except Chelsea.

"What? Are you watching your weight?" Chelsea said, heading back to her own bed again and dragging her pink slippers. Under her breath, she added, "Maybe you're like one of those girls in the sappy teen magazine articles with an eating disorder."

The rest of the bunk gasped, especially Brynn. Alex knew it was because Chelsea had been brazen enough to verbalize what everyone else had been thinking all summer long. Everyone wondered why she didn't partake during bunk parties, but Chelsea was the only one rude enough to actually bring it up.

"Maybe you should mind your business," Brynn said to Chelsea in defense of her friend. Alex thought Brynn would sneak over to talk about it, but much to Alex's relief, she didn't. Instead, Brynn whispered something to Sarah. At that moment, Alex felt so weird, so out of touch with everyone.

"Well, okay then," Chelsea said. "Hey, everyone, maybe we should try to be as slim and trim and perfect as Alex," she added as Brynn shot her a dirty look. Alex clasped her pen so tightly that she thought it might snap in half. She poked a hole through her letter by accident. She wanted to scream, to rip Chelsea's slippers to shreds. But mostly, she just hoped that no one could tell how fed up she was getting of everyone wondering what was wrong.

"Just ignore her," Valerie interrupted.

So that's what Alex did, for the moment at least. Staying quiet was easier this time. Infuriated and nervous, she thought about how she had been born with a petite Korean body like her mother's. She thought about eating and how much it terrified her. Since food was definitely an issue for her these days, she had diverted more energy than ever to working out. Alex felt more powerful when she had strong muscles, quick running reflexes, and expert soccer abilities. She was willing to do anything to have those skills. She focused on those thoughts, trying not to think about what Chelsea had just said.

But Alex could barely stand it. She was ready to shout at Chelsea, to tell her what a witch she was for always getting into other people's business and making a big deal about herself. And Chelsea wasn't the only one who would feel Alex's wrath. Alex was ready to tell her whole bunk to just cheer up. She held herself back and got her thoughts organized. Alex never spoke without getting it together first. Her mom and dad had taught her to be smooth and cool and collected, and most of the time, that's exactly what Alex was. But then, with the Nerds fresh on her mind and Chelsea right there in her face, Alex just about exploded—until Julie, their counselor, and Marissa, their counselor in training (CIT)—arrived in the bunk after their staff meeting.

"Lights out!" Julie yelled. Surely, she'd heard the commotion and that's why she had butted in—it seemed like Julie was always coming to the rescue.

Alex was thankful. In her heart, she had wanted to lose it on everyone. But her mind knew better. Starting something with the whole rest of her bunk—girls she loved, well, most of the time—was a disaster waiting to happen. Alex looked up and noticed that all eyes were on her. She hoped they hadn't been able to tell that she was about to lose her temper. Alex's skin turned redder and redder—now because she was angry and embarrassed. Before anyone could say another word, Valerie got out of bed and flicked the lights off fast—it was like she'd been reading Alex's mind. The tension in the room went from thick and gloomy to just plain tired and cranky.

Chelsea threw herself against her pillow, seemingly disappointed that she hadn't been able to get Alex, or anyone else, stirred up. Then, the twelve girls in 3C went back to whispering about whatever they whispered about when the room was dark.

▲ ▲ ▲

"Final electives!" Julie yelled the next morning. Each girl needed to pick her last two free-choice activities for the very last two weeks at Camp Lakeview.

Only two more weeks! Alex thought. Part of her was happy that it was almost over. She couldn't wait to see her parents and her friends from home again. But part of her was so sad, too.

Alex huddled with Brynn to make the big decision. Brynn was such a drama queen, and Alex preferred to have her drama on a theater or television screen. Even though they were so different, their friendship worked—well, most of the time. Brynn created action and excitement, while Alex kept the two of them on time and grounded. Alex admired Brynn's free spirit. Because of her, Alex rarely got bored.

"I have to take drama, of course," Brynn said. "Then I think I'll take nature."

"I have to take sports, of course," Alex answered, laughing. "Then I'll take . . . it's a secret."

"Tell me!" Brynn begged. "Best friends tell each other everything."

"It won't be a secret if I tell you," Alex said, poking and tickling Brynn so she wouldn't get mad at her for not telling.

"Puh-*leeeeeease*!?" Brynn said, this time using the full range of her booming voice. Alex couldn't help it. She caved.

"Okay, okay. Is there any chance I could talk you into taking ceramics with me? Puh-*leeeeeease*!?!" Alex added, making Brynn laugh again. She wished she and Brynn could finally have an activity together. After all, there was no way Alex could take drama—she considered herself allergic to the stage spotlight. She preferred to shine on the soccer field.

"Just take drama with me," Brynn said. "I'll help you! It would be so cool. You never know—you might be a star."

"No," Alex answered, knowing full well that she might as well be in drama since she'd be helping Brynn with her lines like she always did. That's how it had always been between the two friends. "No, no, and no," Alex added. "Come on, do ceramics this once."

"I love you, Alex, but you can't ask me to give up my whole entire life for you," Brynn said, kind of teasing, kind of not.

Alex sighed. "All right," she said. There was no point in trying to change her mind. Brynn was just excited for her big play after all—this year's production of *Peter Pan* was going to be a blast!

The other girls from the bunk flocked to Julie's sign-up clipboard. Julie was always smiling, and everyone loved her. It didn't even bother her to get bum-rushed by a gaggle of excited girls. While Alex waited patiently for the mob to clear, she heard Jenna ask to be in photography with her brother Adam again. Alex was happy to see they were getting along better. Jenna'd had a rough spot a few weeks ago when she pulled a crazy prank, letting all of the animals free to howl and poop and cry during the camp social. Jenna had temporarily lost her brain, but thankfully, it seemed to have found its way back into her head. Grace and Brynn signed up for drama, and they vowed to be partners so Grace wouldn't end up with a bully like Gaby again. Natalie and Alyssa asked to be on the newspaper together, and Val, always the independent one, signed up for woodworking.

"You just want to be with the boys!" Chelsea teased Val. The boys were a divisive issue for some of the girls. Jenna and Alex were on the anti-boy, anti-flirting side, while some of the others were starting to have crushes. Alex couldn't understand why boys were so important. Her friends were talking about them, walking around with them, and worrying about what they did or didn't do. Alex thought it was just easier to be friends with them—just friends—so they didn't take any time away from her already jam-packed life. She had a lot of guy friends—she loved playing soccer with Theodore Cantor and Andre Derstein back home—but that didn't mean she wanted to *hold hands* with either of them. In fact, the idea creeped her out. Alex figured she was lucky she felt that way. Her parents were so conservative that she knew she wouldn't be allowed to date until she was at least thirty.

"Oh, yeah, the boys," Valerie said. "I'm not stupid," she added, flipping her long cornrows into Chelsea's face. Alex knew that Val was just playing along, though. Val was really good at woodworking, whether half the boys happened to be in that class or not. She'd already made a cutting board, a lamp, and a carved plaque with an elephant on it that hung on her bunk. Valerie had the funkiest jewelry and decorations and clothes. Alex was always admiring her stuff in their bunk. She felt like her own choice of decor—plain navy sheets that matched her mostly navy and white outfits—were getting totally boring.

Thinking about trying new, artsy things, Alex got excited again. She had told Grace that arts and crafts were smelly and boring just a few weeks ago, but she didn't feel that way anymore. It was time to try something other than sports. Alex had been inspired by the Ninja Supertwins book she was reading—one of the twins is an awesome sculptor—and by her friend Bridgette from home who had signed up for painting class at the local art museum. Alex had been in a funk lately—she hoped a change of pace would help. So when the other girls had made their picks, Alex made her move.

"Here comes young Mia Hamm," Julie said, making Alex smile, not to mention blush. "So, what'll it be?"

"Ceramics, please," she answered, moving her knapsack—the one she *always* carried—to the opposite shoulder. Alex had seen the necklaces some girls had made in the last session. They were these shiny, round beads that hung from a leather strap. Alex knew her mother, an art teacher, would love to have one. Her mother would be so happy to get a necklace from Alex, too, since Alex was rarely interested in noncompetitive activities. Alex had always known she was a little bit more like her dad, a litigations lawyer who lived for trials that put the bad guys in jail.

"You want ceramics?" Julie asked, totally surprised. She'd known Alex for years, and when she put Alex in arts and crafts three years ago, Alex had cried. (Alex was still embarrassed about that, but she figured she was only eight years old then!)

"Hey, I may be an old dog," Alex started, "but I can still learn a few new tricks."

"I think that's so awesome of you!" Julie said, paying close attention to how Alex felt. Julie always paid close attention to everyone, and that's what made her so special. Julie could have five girls screaming in her ear all at once, and each girl would still know that Julie was listening to her. Alex saw Julie as a role model. She could totally see herself becoming a counselor at Lakeview one day.

"Wait, um, Alex," Julie called a few seconds later. "Could you please do me a favor?"

"Sure, anything," Alex said. Julie's face was wrinkled and unsmiling, and that made Alex worry.

"I can't believe I have to tell you this, but . . .

hmmm . . . ceramics is full, and I would've saved you a spot, but I just didn't have a clue you'd pick an arts activity," Julie said. "I feel so bad about this, Alex."

"Um, well," Alex replied, her hopes sinking into the hungry part of her stomach. "Okay," she added. She mentally kicked herself for not putting ceramics on her free-choice list that Julie kept earlier. *It's my own fault,* she thought. It seemed like she was always missing out on things because she just didn't speak up in time. She could've been the captain of her soccer team back home—she was the best player on her fifth-grade team—if she had just said that she was interested. She hadn't, so one of her teammates got the role.

"But I can put you in woodworking," Julie said.

Alex's faced dropped. She imagined splinters and nails and difficult projects—and way too many boys. Julie patted Alex's back and started to smile.

"Come on," Julie said. "It's so creative. It really is. You can still try new things in there. I absolutely promise that you will have fun."

"Do I have any other choice?" Alex asked.

"Um, well," Julie said carefully, "not really, sweetie."

"Okay, okay," Alex answered, sensing that Julie was about to be disappointed in her.

"Sweetie, you are *the best,*" Julie said, hugging Alex. "I can always count on Camp Lakeview's very own Mia Hamm. Don't you worry, either. There's a really nice instructor in there, and you're always a star at everything you do."

Alex smiled a little bit, even though she was disappointed. When it came down to it, she loved making other people happy, especially Julie. Alex just wished that something would start going her way. She didn't understand why she was feeling so sad.

chapter TWO

When Alex was on the soccer field, there was no Chelsea to antagonize her. There were no free-choice mishaps. There was no Brynn overdramatizing about her drama class. There were no cranky campmates. There was, for once, only Alex. And she was the star.

She had been looking forward to the afternoon because that day, for their usual post-breakfast bunk activity, her mates were taking on their rivals, the girls from 3A. Both bunks had chosen to play soccer.

When the announcement was made, Alex felt like finally she would have a good day, and she was right.

As usual, she had been chosen as the leader of her 3C team, and that made her feel confident. She wasn't the fastest runner—Sarah had that strength. She also wasn't the strongest goalie—Jenna could make that claim. But Alex *was* the most fearless player. The ball was her pet. Alex could skillfully follow it, volley it, chase it, and kick it as if it were attached to her Diadora soccer cleats. The soccer ball met its match every time Alex took to the field.

But the other team, the girls from bunk 3A, were playing a really good game. Alex wanted to win, and the score was six for her team, eight for the enemies, er, opponents. She started to freak out. Alex would rather lick bugs every day for two weeks than lose a game of soccer.

She thought of her favorite childhood book, *The Little Engine That Could*. She knew it was silly, but that story—one her mother had read to her once a week from nursery school through the first grade—always got her spirits up. She'd tell herself *I think I can, I think I can* whenever she got nervous before a test or game or meeting with a teacher. Then during whatever made her nervous, she'd change the words to *I know I can, I know I can*.

Today, with the other team's score creeping up, she added another line to the cheerleader in her head. She thought, *I know I can. I know we can. I know, I know, I know.* She didn't like to brag or anything—bragging was bad manners according to Alex—but she had to get herself psyched to win three more points and take the game. As the next time-out happened, she took charge—something she'd been doing a lot this summer—and gave the only advice she knew that would help them win.

"You all are awesome! You are better than these girls! You can kick their tails—I've seen you do it before.

Now come on!" she yelled. The girls from 3C just watched her.

Candace said, "We can kick their tails!"

Jessie yelled, "You betcha!"

Others stood in the huddle with their mouths open. Some were really passionate about soccer, but most just saw it as a way to have some fun. Those who weren't as competitive were the ones Alex had to get pumped up.

"My shins are getting sore," Alyssa said, bending over to rub them.

"My throat hurts," Chelsea whined, twirling her hair around her pointer finger.

That's when Valerie stepped in, "You all are fine. You have to be! We're gonna win!" Valerie was always like that—she had the sunniest attitude of anybody. Alex was starting to realize that Val was never, ever in a bad mood.

"That's right, we are," Jenna added with pursed lips and furrowed brows. She took soccer as seriously as Alex did.

"Who's the best?!" Alex yelled, relieved that the whiners—there were always two or three on every team—had been shut down. She was even more relieved that Valerie had been the one to do it. She was such a cool girl. No one could argue with Valerie.

"Um, you are," Natalie answered, looking at Alex.

"No!" Alex laughed. "*We* are!"

After the pep talk, Alex started talking strategy. She

told Sarah to run past the other team's best runner—that would distract her from the game at hand. Jenna had three girls to cover. Brynn was supposed to stand near the goal and block anyone who came toward Alex when she went in for the point. Even the whiners came on board for the winning plans.

By the end of the time-out, no one was unmotivated anymore. Instead, their expressions were determined. The girls looked like they took this game seriously, and even better, they looked like they wanted to win.

They huddled up in a circle like a bunch of NFL football stars and yelled their bunk cheer, "We be 3C!" It wasn't poetry, but it was catchy. They high-fived and cheered one another as they ran back to the field.

The other team watched them quietly. Alex could tell her opponents were worried, and she was glad. Her team really did have the edge on the winning mindset, which meant they were halfway there.

Alex was so pumped. She stole the ball from Gaby, wheedled it through the players with ease, and scored. Then she scored again. And again.

Because of Alex's talent and the rest of the crew's enthusiasm, they were able to take the game, and they took it fast. Neither team could even believe what had happened. The girls from 3C, with Alex in the lead, had won. But most surprising was that it hadn't even been very difficult. Alex was proud and happy and confident all at the same time.

Afterward, panting and sweating like happy puppies,

the girls congratulated the other sullen-faced team, and then they hugged one another. They clapped and laughed and basked for just a few extra minutes.

Even if they were getting the end-of-the-summer blues at times, everyone really had bonded over the last few weeks. They'd proven it on the soccer field—whenever someone needed support, another girl ran to her rescue. Together, when 3C needed to rally, they could do it.

Alex couldn't have been more pleased—she forgot all of her problems for that second. Nothing else mattered except that she had done her job, and she had done it well.

Of course, that was typical for Alex. Anytime there were tasks to be completed, Alex was always asked to do them. Teachers knew if they needed help grading papers, Alex was their girl. Moms would let their kids stay out later as long as Alex was with them. Friends could count on Alex to help them with their homework or any other problems that they had. Alex just had this way about her of doing the right thing. But she was really hard on herself—she was a total perfectionist.

Alex wasn't judgmental of others, though. She figured that people had their flaws, and those flaws made them unique, even cute. Meanwhile, she beat up on herself. She couldn't remember the last time she'd received a B in school. Anything but an A-plus was unacceptable to her. Report card day always made Alex's parents so happy—they were big on good grades.

It wasn't just school either. At camp, Alex always got up five minutes earlier than everyone else so she could tidy up her stuff after she got ready in the morning. She'd make her navy and white bed and neatly stack toiletries into her cubbyhole. Even her shoes were lined up alongside the foot of her bed. She never went frantic looking for a lost flip-flop or barrette like Brynn did. Alex never left her room—or her bunk—unless everything was in order. She was always on time (even though she was always sneaking off to take care of a secret personal errand) and during the school year, she always carried around her to-do list.

Alex's mom thought she put too much pressure on herself. She was always giving Alex those relaxing CDs where frogs chirp and water gurgles. Alex knew she should try to take it easy, but it just didn't seem like she was built that way. She hadn't even ripped open the plastic on those calming CDs that were tucked away deep in her summer suitcase.

"It's too bad you're too young to be Color War captain," Jenna said as they headed back to the bunk to get cleaned up for dinner.

"Really? You think I'd be a good captain?" Alex asked, surprised.

"Duh!" Jenna yelled, rolling her eyes.

"But Jenna, you're really good at soccer, too," Alex said.

"I just have to admit that you're better," Jenna

added. "I wish I could be captain—it would be so cool—but I was watching you out there. You've just got *it*."

Alex could feel her heart beating fast, her body getting excited. She tried not to smile too much—she didn't want to be braggy—but she almost couldn't help it. "Got what?" Alex asked.

"It!" Jenna and Brynn yelled at the same time.

That was a big thing for Jenna to say. She had been upset when Alex had turned out to be a better diver a few weeks ago. Alex did everything she could to help Jenna with diving—even spent time with her at the lake—but Jenna just kept getting more and more upset when she couldn't do it right. They worked it out, though, and Jenna even improved her diving.

Alex understood that Jenna could be really competitive. That's why it was especially nice for her to say these things to Alex now. After all, the two of them had been coming to Camp Lakeview together forever. Even though they were close, it always felt like they were rivals, albeit friendly ones.

"Oh stop it, you all," Alex said, hoping that she really would get to be the captain in a few years. She couldn't help but think about how she'd missed being captain of her school soccer team last year.

"You're going to give Alex a big head!" Brynn interrupted, teasing her.

"Nah, we won't," Valerie added, smiling.

"Doesn't that distinction go to Chelsea, anyway?" Grace whispered to Alex.

"Can we stop talking about it, please?" Alex asked, embarrassed by all the attention. She hoped they all meant it—she was thrilled!

Do they think I'm the best at sports? she wondered, smiling.

"Um, okay then," Karen said, and everyone hushed to look at her. Karen rarely spoke out loud. She could only be seen whispering to Chelsea, although lately she'd been standing up for herself more and not letting Chelsea boss her around *quite* so much. "I have a question for Alex. Could you tell me, what's Color War?" Karen said.

Alex liked Karen a lot, even though the girl was a different kind of person. She had about twenty stuffed animals around her bed. Alex understood that some girls still liked their stuffies—but everyone else had only brought one, if that.

"You've got to be kidding me," Chelsea answered, irritation in her voice. She hated when someone else got all the attention.

Alex sidled up to Karen and started telling her all about it—Color War was absolutely Alex's favorite time at camp. "That's when everyone here gets divided up into two groups, Red and Blue. For two whole days, we compete with each other—even with the girls in our own bunk—to see which team will win the Lakeview Champion Title," Alex explained as her heart started beating faster.

"Um, cool," Karen said. Karen wasn't very competitive, so Alex wondered if she really meant it. But at least Karen seemed genuinely interested.

"Most of the competitions are sports," Alex said, "but not all of them. I mean, we do soccer, blob tag, Scrabble, basketball, canoeing, croquet, swimming, and singdown. For the first time all summer, bunkmates could be on separate teams, and best friends could be enemies," she added.

Luckily for Alex, though, she had always managed to be on the same team as Brynn. She couldn't imagine trying to beat out her best friend in anything.

To Alex, Color War was special because, while it tore the camp apart for two days, it also brought everyone closer together at the end. Unlike other camps, at Lakeview, the winners had to do something really nice for the losers—this year, like last, they would have to make chocolate chip cookies. That was always fun because those who make the cookies also get some of the dough, of course. Alex enjoyed the process and the camaraderie and delivering the treats to the other kids at the end of dinner last year. She hoped it would be just as much fun this year—even though she definitely wouldn't be having any treats.

Getting ready for Color War was just as much fun as actually doing it, too. The teams always got together in secret huddles to pick outfits, mascots, and cheers and to make signs and to plan pranks on their opponents. Even though Alex knew the drill by now—she still totally loved Color War at Camp Lakeview.

Last year, Alex, Sarah, and Brynn had been on the

winning team together. Because they understood one another so well, they were able to score the last point for their team during a lay-up competition on the basketball court. After a perfect pass from Sarah, Alex threw the ball into the basket while Brynn cheered them on. They were so happy to win for their division that Alex cried a little while everyone yelled and screamed her name. She was sweaty and hugging her best friends, so she didn't think anyone had noticed how emotional she'd been.

It was a special day and a very lucky shot. She went home savoring her victory. She thought last year was the best time she'd ever had away at camp. She didn't think it could get any better.

"You're going to love it," Alex told Karen, who was a first-year. "I hope we get to be on the same team. I'll show you the secrets to winning all the different events."

Karen was so quiet that Alex hadn't gotten to know her very well. She really did hope that the two of them could hang out some more before it was time to pack up and head home in less than two weeks. But Karen was always with Chelsea, though she had been branching out after the incident at the water park. Alex was so glad that Karen wasn't letting Chelsea be so pushy anymore.

"Alex, you don't have to know everything about *everything*," Chelsea said, taking Karen aside to explain Color War to her all over again.

Alex got tingly because she could sense Karen's suffering, and she *so* wanted Karen to tell Chelsea off.

Alex kind of understood, though. Sometimes, like just now, Alex didn't speak up, either. Alex had the guts, that wasn't the problem, she just didn't like all the drama that came along with speaking up.

"I, um, was just answering Karen's questions," Alex said, moving away from Chelsea and over to Brynn. Brynn would tell the queen bee where to go if it became necessary. That was one thing about Brynn, no one intimidated her, and she was known to mouth off if someone pushed her buttons.

"You were showing off, Alex," Chelsea added, "and you know it. Karen, don't listen to her. I'll explain it all to you."

"I heard her, Chelsea—" Karen started to say.

Chelsea started in, "Well, first of all, it was pretty stupid to not know what Color War is. I mean, come on. Second, I would've told you, honey, if you'd just asked."

Karen hung her head down toward her feet. She was such an abused puppy most of the time, though she was slowly starting to show some teeth. Alex wondered how Karen got to be so mousy.

"I can't believe you," Brynn said to Chelsea.

Karen's face turned red. She put her head back up, and she said, "It's okay, really. I get it now, and there's no reason to—"

"Sweetie, don't you have lines to read or something? I'm sure Alex can help you learn them since she's so good at everything all the time," Chelsea added, pulling Karen ahead of the group so they would be able to jump into the showers first.

"She needs to take a chill pill," Grace said.

"She should really try meditation," Alyssa added, which came out of nowhere. Alyssa often came out of nowhere, but at least she always had something new—and unique—to say.

"Forget about her, you guys," Valerie said.

"Yeah, we just won an awesome soccer game," Alex said, not wanting anyone to argue with each other. "So let's just think about that right now."

Natalie and Alyssa ran past Chelsea and Karen, their way of beating Chelsea to the showers. Everyone was really pulling together, even Karen. It made Alex feel good.

chapter THREE

"Hey, come sit with me," Valerie said as Alex entered the woodworking cabin for their second free-choice period. Valerie had arrived late the day before, so they hadn't been able to share a table. "We girls gotta stick together."

"Thanks," Alex said, sitting down and still wishing she had been able to take ceramics class with her other friends. She liked Valerie fine, she just didn't know her that well. But even worse, Alex just didn't give a flying Frisbee about woodworking. She'd never taken shop class in school for a reason—it sounded really boring. She liked to do stuff that had lots of action, like soccer and swimming and running and volleyball. Wood just sat there and did nothing.

"Hey, Alex," Adam, Jenna's twin brother, called.

"What are you doing here? You're supposed to be in photography with your sister," Alex said, dreading the free-choice period ahead.

"I'm here to make your life miserable," he told Alex, tapping his pencil on the girls' table.

"Yes, you are," Alex said.

He was right—he was going to torment her. Alex tolerated him because she'd known him ever since she started coming to Lakeview. But he had been on her last nerves lately. He had teased her after the soccer game, calling her Lanky Legs and Spider Woman. He had also snapped her training bra the other day. That really ticked Alex off. She knew she was too flat-chested to be wearing one in the first place. Her mother made her wear it because Alex played so many sports. (Alex's mom wanted her to be used to bras for when she really needed them, if that made any sense.) And to have Adam flicking the stupid thing was just embarrassing.

Alex had wanted to ask Jenna to tell him to stop, but that only would only have made matters worse. Jenna *and* Adam would be on Alex's case about her training bra. That would be too embarrassing for Alex to handle. Alex thought he should be spending more time with Alyssa, anyway—ever since the social, they seemed to have a sort-of romance brewing.

"I can tell when I'm not wanted," Adam said as he wandered over to the corner where his friends were hanging out. Alex was relieved. She wasn't in the mood to deal with boys very often.

"Alex, did I just see what I thought I saw?" Valerie asked, tossing her long braids behind her back and out of her way.

"What? Adam Spasm?" Alex started calling him that when they were seven years old. That summer, Adam told everyone he had a magic reaction to peas. Whenever that vegetable was served, he'd eat one and start shaking all over uncontrollably. It had been very difficult to eat whenever peas were served. He'd make everyone laugh so hard, they'd shoot food—including peas—out of their mouths and noses.

"Yeah, I'm pretty sure he's into you," Val said, eyeing the stool she was finishing.

Alex's heart started beating so hard that she thought she'd need to go to the infirmary. "You've got to be kidding me," she said louder than she meant to. "Anyway, I mean, he's Adam *Spasm*!" Her face immediately started going hot, and she looked around to make sure no one else could hear what Valerie had just said. Adam was a friend of hers—just a friend. Of all people to have her first crush on, *if* that were ever to happen, it most definitely would never *ever* be him. Because he was Jenna's twin brother, that kind of made him like Alex's brother, too. *Ewww!* Alex thought.

Besides, she wasn't into boys. She didn't like the way other girls were starting to make such a big deal out of them. Natalie was always planning her day so she could hang around with Simon, Chelsea flirted with some boy in an older division, Grace was flirting with Devon from 3F, and even Brynn was starting to get gooey-eyed when a certain boy from drama was around (though she would *never* have admitted that to Alex). Alex could see it happening all around her, and she didn't like it. She could take or leave boys. She didn't spend that much time thinking about them except with they snapped her bra or smelled bad after playing baseball. She had other important things to think about, like soccer. And something that she just couldn't share with anyone.

"Oh stop it, Val," Alex said matter-of-factly. It had only taken half a minute, and she had gotten control of herself once again. She was absolutely shocked and embarrassed to even think about the possibility of Adam liking her. Then she added, "Adam has a thing for Alyssa, anyway. Didn't you see the way they were hanging out at the social? They're practically each other's prom dates already."

"Where've you been, girl?" Val asked, leaning in to whisper to Alex. At least Valerie wasn't like Brynn when it came to sensitive issues. When Brynn was excited, she yelled out whatever was on her mind, and everyone heard all about it. Sometimes Brynn's enthusiasm was endearing; sometimes it was terrifying. But the dramatic outbursts had really been embarrassing Alex lately. Especially when Brynn had started talking about Alex's training bra in front of Chelsea a few nights ago.

"Why? Where do you think I've been?" Alex said, feeling panicked about something other than Adam. Alex thought Valerie had figured it out—sometimes she'd miss swimming or lunch or evening campfires. That's because she was always running an errand, but Alex couldn't tell anyone what that errand was. Alex believed her problem was really gross and embarrassing. So she would just sneak away a few times a day, take care of it, and sneak back. Alex got away with it by telling everyone she was helping Julie or Marissa. That wasn't a stretch, either, because she *was* always doing stuff with them. She just freaked because she thought Val had figured it out.

"Huh? You really haven't heard, have you?" Valerie said, totally oblivious to the mini panic attack Alex just had. "A couple of days ago, Alyssa started hanging out with Simon's good friend Trevor. She just ignores Adam now. He seemed really hurt about it last weekend. Are you sure no one told you?"

"I had no idea! You're kidding!" Alex said, relieved that Valerie hadn't figured out her real secret. All of a sudden, Alex started feeling bad for someone else: Adam. He really was a cool kid, especially for a boy, despite the pea spasms. Alex certainly didn't want him to be depressed about a girl. Adam was always making Jenna feel better when she was down, and he was a volunteer coach for the little kids, too. He'd show them how to throw Wiffle balls and go dog-paddling. He also played soccer sometimes with Alex, which was fun because he was really good. Alex was surprised that Alyssa would be so rude to Adam. But she liked Alyssa, so Alyssa must've had a good reason to start liking Trevor.

"Maybe I should make sure he's doing okay,"

Alex said, mostly to herself. She thought Adam had been acting weird lately, and that was definitely why. He was heartbroken, and he needed his old friends. She thought she'd ask him to play soccer or something to get his mind off of it.

"I knew you had a thing for him!" Valerie said, getting very excited about this prospect. After all, Alex had never had a crush, and everyone knew it.

"Wait one second," Alex interrupted. "Before you get this all wrong, Adam and I are just friends. He's just feeling bad, and I need to be there for him if he wants to talk or anything. I know he really liked Alyssa. We're like brother and sister, anyway. He knows there is no way on Earth that I'd ever be interested in him. And vice versa!"

"You sure?" Valerie said, completely uninterested in the stepping stool she was making for her dad's garage.

"I'm totally sure. Ewww. I'm just not boy crazy yet, and I don't think I ever will be," Alex added, and she meant it. Other girls said their crushes made their hearts beat faster, distracted their thoughts, and made them want to hold hands and stuff. That just sounded way too complicated for Alex. She didn't understand what they were talking about. She'd never felt that way. Ever. And that was fine with her.

"Me neither, not anymore," Valerie said. "I had a boyfriend in the beginning of the fifth grade, and he transferred out of our school. It broke my heart! Not because we were all lovey-dovey and stuff. But because we were best friends. I missed him! I made close friends with some other girls, though—thank God!"

Alex knew that feeling, her former best friend, Maggie, had moved away in the fourth grade. It wasn't easy getting close to someone else again. It had taken her a year to meet a new best friend at school, a girl named Bridgette. Sometimes Alex really missed her. Bridgette knew Alex better than the girls at camp did. She understood why Alex acted kind of weird sometimes and why Alex had to sneak away. Alex wished she could break down that mystery wall between her bunkmates and herself. She wanted to tell them her secret, but she just couldn't. It was just too awful and embarrassing.

"It's really hard," Alex said. "I'm so sorry you have to go through that."

"It's okay. I'm having a blast this summer," Valerie said, putting down the stool. "Being here makes it easy to forget about how up and down last year was."

"You have a best friend here at least, don't you?" Alex asked. She'd seen Valerie and Sarah together a lot in the beginning of the summer.

"Well, sort of," Valerie said. "But Sarah has been ignoring me lately, actually. She's been hanging out with Brynn. I'm sure you've noticed that."

That was true, though Alex hadn't thought about it that way. Alex had gotten tired of constantly practicing Brynn's lines for the *Peter Pan* play. So she had been so relieved when Sarah started offering to do it. It gave her so much more time to swim and play soccer, the things Alex lived to do. She hadn't even stopped to think about how Valerie felt about the new Brynn and Sarah twosome.

"You're right, she has," Alex said, worrying that maybe Brynn was starting to like Sarah better. "Don't you hang around with them?"

"Nah, only in the rec hall and stuff. I don't feel right. They have so many inside jokes and stuff lately," Valerie said, grabbing a nail. Alex couldn't get a sense of whether she was upset about it or not.

"You okay?" Alex asked, touching her shoulder. She was usually good at sensing how other kids felt. She was starting to believe Valerie, despite her cheeriness, was getting a little bit lonely. That was a feeling Alex could relate to.

"I'm fine," Valerie said. "Now let me show you how to make a cutting board."

"A cutting board?" Alex asked, once again dreading her commitment to woodworking.

"I know it doesn't sound like much fun, but it's the first thing we all have to make in here. It's because a cutting board is simple, and you have to use a lot of the tools to do one. The project is mostly to get you familiar with the tools, honestly. You can give it to your mom, too. I mean, all moms like to chop up vegetables and try to make us eat them, right?" Valerie asked, getting up from their long metal table.

"Oh, yes!" Alex answered. Her mom was always

telling her how important it was to eat broccoli, peppers, carrots, radishes, lettuce, onions, peas, squash, yams, mushrooms, asparagus, artichokes, eggplant, cucumbers, cauliflower, cabbage, zucchini, celery, and Brussels sprouts. Alex's mother was an expert in rabbit food. And, as it turned out, no one ate more rabbit food than Alex.

"My mom will totally love this cutting board," Alex said. She was feeling a little better about missing ceramics. If she couldn't make her mother a necklace, at least she could make her something.

They started drawing on the blank slab of wood that Valerie had brought over to Alex. The slab was the size of a laptop or dinner tray. Alex looked at it, wondering what the heck she'd do with it. It was so drab and dull and, well, *woody*.

Valerie had started on her stool again, but with Alex's wide-eyed look of confusion, Valerie pushed her project aside. Alex thought that was really nice. Valerie picked up a pencil and a ruler and started drawing on the slab; she drew a paddle shape and turned it over.

"Now, you try," Valerie said to Alex.

"Why? You already did a good job on the other side," Alex answered. She didn't see why anyone should do the work twice.

"But my cutting board outline was sloppy. I definitely think you could do a better job," Valerie said, trying to appeal to Alex's competitive streak.

Her approach worked. Alex started making the

shape, using the eraser to fix any wobbly lines. When she was finished, the shape was perfect.

Valerie told Alex that she had a secret gift for drawing, but Alex insisted that if she could draw, it was only because her mother was an art teacher.

Next, Valerie showed Alex how to use the saw to cut the shape into the slab. They thought the spewing sawdust looked like Chelsea's hair in the morning, and they thought the buzzing noise sounded a whole lot better than Julie's alarm clock. Alex didn't realize that more than thirty minutes had gone by. Finally, Valerie got out a wood plane—kind of like a big nail file—to sand the splinters off the freshly cut board. Alex used the tool to rub the rough edges until they became smooth, and it *was* just like filing her nails into the perfect short shape she liked to keep them in. Another twenty minutes later, the girls were almost done with the entire cutting board project. The new boys in the class were barely finished drawing theirs.

"Whoa! What, are you two going to start your own carpentry class?" Adam's friend Jack said to them.

"Maybe we will!" Alex laughed. She never dreamed she'd actually enjoy woodworking. Not only that, she was pretty good at it. She was petite, but also very strong. That meant she could hold the wood against the noisy, gigantic saw that chopped it into usable pieces. Her arms didn't get tired when she was sanding with the wood plane either—back and forth, back and forth, smoothing all the edges. Tomorrow, she was going to stain it a reddish brown color to go with her mother's dishes. It wouldn't look plain or boring at all when she was done with it. She was shocked at how excited she was to start making her next project.

She was also excited because Valerie had been so much fun to partner with. Alex usually spent all of her free time with Brynn, and she realized that she might've been missing out on getting to know other cool girls. Valerie was so helpful, and she didn't complain once. Nor did she ask Alex to do anything for her. She didn't bring up the Adam thing anymore either—Val seemed to have that sixth sense of when to drop things. Alex thought that she and Val just *got* each other. They laughed at the same jokes, they never ran out of things to say, and neither one of them wanted to flirt with all the boys who kept teasing them. Yes, Alex was feeling much, much better about woodworking. The last two weeks of her time at Camp Lakeview might even be a whole lot better than she imagined.

chapter FOUR

The next day, Alex spotted Adam drinking orange juice at the table right behind her at breakfast. He kept poking Jenna, trying to tell her something. Alex couldn't help but notice, now that Valerie had said something, that he did seem to be hanging around all the time. She'd seen him at meals in the rec room, in woodworking, and out on the soccer field. But Jenna had been eating and playing soccer with Alex, so Adam was probably just spending more time with his sister because *part* of what Valerie had said was totally true. Alyssa had been buddy-buddy with Simon's friend Trevor a whole bunch of times. Alex figured Adam was probably upset about it. She imagined that no one, boy or girl, would enjoy getting dumped.

It worked out really well for Alyssa—too well as far as Alex was concerned. She couldn't help but think it: Alyssa got together with Trevor so she could spend a lot more time with Natalie and Simon.

Simon *was* pretty much Natalie's boyfriend. It was really weird how things worked out, and the whole incident just confirmed for Alex how strange her friends started acting once they became interested in boys. Alex thought camp (and school, for that matter) would be a lot more fun if the boys and girls just stayed friends and stopped flirting so much. Alex knew she sure wasn't flirting with anyone. She thought she might even talk to her parents about going to an all-girl high school one day.

"So, I have this idea," Valerie said, hopping onto her stool at their table later that day during woodworking. Valerie was always a few minutes late for class because she was a free spirit. Alex was used to it—no one she knew was as prompt as she was. When Valerie finally arrived, Adam scurried away from the girls' table. Thankfully, Valerie didn't say anything about the situation—surely, she thought Adam was flirting with Alex again. Valerie was so wrong about her theory. Alex and Adam were just good friends!

"You like to play chess, right?" Valerie asked Alex, unpacking her woodworking supplies. Valerie just figured that Alex was super smart. A few weeks ago, when Grace had to read *Call of the Wild* because she had fallen behind in her fifth-grade reading class, Alex was the one who had helped her the most. Alex had read the book two times—for fun. In fact, Valerie guessed that some of the other girls, mainly Chelsea, were even jealous of Alex because she was smart in addition to being athletic and well-liked. This thought made Valerie excited for one reason in particular: because really smart people knew how to play chess.

"Actually, I don't," Alex answered, standing next to the metal table in the woodshop. She had come into class with her soccer ball in her hands, and the instructor—a nice college student named Jeremy (a guy who really needed to take the tape off the bridge of his glasses)—had taken it away from her. He wasn't worried that Alex and Valerie would cause trouble or break things. Instead, he didn't want the boys in the class to start a game of keep-away right there in the cabin. They were kind of wild sometimes, especially Adam Spasm and his friends.

"Oh well," Valerie said, twisting her long black braids and slumping a little on the stool. Valerie was always sitting. Alex always stood.

"Do you play?" Alex asked, putting her hair in a ponytail with the rubber band that was around her wrist. She wished she had a mirror, so it wouldn't look so crooked.

"Yeah, but not here this summer. No one knows how to!" Valerie said. "It's okay." She started getting all the tools together for her next project.

"Wait, I've always wanted to learn to play," Alex said, following Valerie to the supply closet. Alex was telling the truth, too. She'd seen people—all ages and races—playing chess in the park last Christmas when her parents took her to New York City. They were competing on concrete tables outside in the cold—and it was *really* cold in New York in December. Those chess players had the kind of dedication Alex could admire. She asked her parents to teach her, but they didn't know how either. At home, they usually played GoStop, a Korean card game that was totally fun.

"Will you show me how?" Alex asked.

"You can't be serious," Valerie said, staring at her bug-eyed.

"Oh, I'm serious," Alex said, sneaking a peek at Adam across the room. She just didn't get why girls *like*-liked boys so much. He was cute, but he was teaching his friends how to spit really long saliva wads and then suck them back into their mouths. She wondered if Simon did stuff like that when his friends were around and if Natalie would still like him if she saw.

"I'd love to!" Alex added. "I mean it!"

The girls made a plan to get together in the rec room after dinner for serious chess lessons. Valerie told Alex that it might take a few nights for her to pick it up. But then Valerie thought of how fast Alex had learned woodworking. She secretly hoped that they could start playing in two nights because, after all, Alex was really smart.

"So what's your idea?" Alex asked.

"Oh, it's no big deal," Valerie said. "I just noticed that the chess set in the rec room is plastic. And it's all beat-up. My dad always plays with me on this really nice marble set we have at home. I thought it would be really cool if we made one in here to keep at Lakeview."

"That's an amazing idea!" Alex said. She loved doing that kind of stuff. She was always helping the counselors with whatever they needed—and anyone else. Why not help the camp? Maybe they could even carve their initials on the bottom with a dedication. It was the least she could do to give back to Camp Lakeview. And it would be fun to play on "her" board year after year, she thought. The only worry Alex had was that chess would be really difficult to learn. *It will be okay. Val will help.*

"I'm just glad you're into it," Valerie added, walking over to ask Jeremy how the heck they were going to pull off this project. "Because carving out all of those little pieces would take me forever by myself."

The two girls laughed a long time before they got to work. They figured out the dimensions of their board and pieces, and they made a to-do list so they'd be able to get it all done during those last two weeks of camp—or hopefully even earlier. Alex and Valerie were concentrating so intently on this idea that they didn't even notice when everyone else left the room for their swimming period.

"Girls," Jeremy said, "if you don't go now, I'll have to lock you up in here."

"Okay. We'll be fine, Jeremy," Alex said to their instructor while Valerie started gathering their stuff.

"She's not kidding, either," Valerie said, giggling. Alex was still working away.

"I'm glad to see such enthusiasm," he said. "But I was kidding. I missed lunch, and I'm starving!"

"And we have to swim. Come on, Alex, let's go to the lake!"

Alex looked up. "Huh?" she said.

"Class is over. Let's hit the water," Valerie said, now gathering Alex's stuff, too.

They ran to the bunk, threw on swimming suits, and headed out to the diving board. Alex didn't even run her post-free period errand that she usually ran. She was in too big of a hurry. She was having too much of an amazing time with Valerie. Plus, her mind was on the chess set, and she just wasn't being her usual organized, on-time, strictly scheduled self.

"Let's be swim buddies," Valerie said, leading the way toward the blue, or more advanced, section.

That's when Alex's memory kicked back in. She suddenly realized that Brynn was probably standing around the corner waiting for her. But it was too late. Alex and Valerie had already dashed to the end of the dock, and they were all set to hurl themselves into the water. Before her plunge, Alex thought that Brynn would be okay since she had been swimming with Sarah for the past two days. At least Brynn wasn't alone, and she probably didn't even remember that Alex was supposed to meet her since she and Sarah had been so tight lately. Alex thought to herself, *Brynn is really cool—she'll totally understand.* After all, Brynn was always losing her camp projects and scripts and keys and swimsuits and socks, and Alex was always helping her find them. Surely, Brynn would understand this one time when Alex just happened to space out.

"Hey, what's wrong?" Valerie said as she looked from the diving board into the water way down below.

"Oh, nothing," Alex said. She didn't want to worry Valerie with any of it, especially if Sarah had been dissing Valerie for Brynn lately. *What a mess!* Alex thought. *Are Sarah and Brynn becoming best camp friends? I don't understand why everyone can't just have fun together.*

"So, partners?" Valerie asked, getting antsy to just get into the water already.

"Sure," Alex said, knowing deep down that Brynn probably would be upset no matter what excuses Alex came up with. Alex decided to hope for the best, and off the diving board they went, the two of them at one time, even though they were not supposed to do that. Their bodies plunged through the twelve feet between the diving platform and the water. After six more seconds, their heads bobbed back up to the top. Alex and Valerie were laughing and splashing each other so much that they didn't even hear the lifeguard blow the whistle.

"Girls, girls!" the lifeguard called. "We can't have that. One at a time, you know that."

They ran off before they could cause any more mischief. They went to the nearby swimming area where the rest of their friends were sure to be. By the shore, Natalie was lying on a blanket reading her magazines like always. Alyssa was right beside her. Alyssa was so funky and cool, Alex couldn't believe she'd just go and dump Adam like that for Trevor. But Alex would never get involved or say anything to either of them about it—she stayed out of other people's business. Alex decided not to join them and headed toward the lake.

"Hey, Alex," Natalie said. "Hey, Valerie."

Valerie stayed by the blanket to talk for a while. Alex smiled at everyone and said she had to go say hello to Brynn. She and Sarah were floating ten feet off the shore on two separate rafts. Alex swam out to them—assuming she could triple-up with them as a buddy—and gave Brynn a small, playful splash. She acted like nothing had happened, took a gulp, and hoped for the best.

"Ow!" Brynn yelled. "You just got water right in my eye. Geez!"

Alex's stomach dropped. She had been right all along—Brynn was annoyed.

"What were you guys laughing about?" Alex asked, starting to feel sick to her stomach.

"Nothing," Brynn answered, not even looking at her best friend. "You wouldn't get it, anyway."

"Yes, I would!" Alex said back to her. And she did get Brynn's jokes—better than anyone else did, for that matter—and Brynn knew it, too.

"Well, maybe if you had bothered to meet me like you said you would," Brynn added, "I would've told you."

Sarah paddled a discrete few feet away. But Alex

was sure Sarah was in hearing distance. She didn't swim *that* far away.

"You know, that was just so incredibly rude," Brynn said to Alex. She was still on the raft, and she used her toes to flick water in Alex's face. "Sarah wouldn't do anything like that to me."

When Alex looked over to Sarah, Sarah looked away. *She heard the whole thing!* Alex thought.

That really ticked Alex off—she hated for other people to be involved in her and Brynn's business. Besides, she and Sarah weren't close or anything, but they had been friends for the past two years. Sarah was quiet and proper, but still competitive. Alex figured she was from a really wealthy family because her parents had houses in Maine, New York, and Florida. And Alex didn't know anyone else with more than one home. Sarah could sometimes be aloof, but she had the best manners—she always congratulated the losing team and asked politely for Alex's untouched desserts.

Alex had never seen Sarah cry or yell or even get upset. Her even temper was why they played so well together. But now what would she think of Alex? Alex wished she weren't the kind of person who cared what other people thought of her. But she was.

"Brynn, I didn't mean to! I was having such a good time in woodworking, and I stayed in class too long. Then I ran and got my swimming stuff, and everyone was already out here. I just wanted to jump off the diving board so bad before I got here," she said, pleading with Brynn.

"Yeah, with *Valerie*," Brynn said sarcastically.

"What's wrong with Valerie?" Alex asked. "I didn't know her too well, but she's super cool. You would think so, too!"

"I can't think about that right now. Do you know that this kind of stress—you blowing me off—is going to make me forget my lines? I'm rehearsing twice a day now—it's so hard. The play is in just over a week! Do you even care?" Brynn asked, now looking at Alex with teary eyes. Alex couldn't believe being swimming partners—or not—was that big of a deal. She and Brynn had met almost every day for free swim for weeks on end. It couldn't hurt them to hang out with other girls. Surely, Brynn understood that she was still Alex's best friend even if Alex did have a lot of fun with other girls sometimes. Like Alex and Jenna—they often took walks together after dinner at night, something Brynn would never want to do.

"Do you only care about the play?" Alex asked. Brynn was being bratty no matter how wrong Alex had been. Alex started to get a sick feeling in her stomach, and she thought that maybe that moment wasn't the best time to pick a fight with her best friend.

"I can't believe you!" Brynn said. "It's not like *I* was the one who did anything wrong!"

All of a sudden, Alex got so dizzy that her heart started to beat fifty times too fast. She was really scared.

She could just imagine passing out in the water where she might drown or something.

She was so terrified of getting hurt that she forgot all about Brynn for a second. Her head started to fall backward, and she grabbed Brynn's raft to help balance herself. The dizzy feeling went away, but Alex knew it would be back soon, and she pointed her body toward the shore.

"What are you doing?" Brynn asked, pulling her raft out of Alex's reach.

"I, I'm not feeling so good. Just give me a second," Alex said. She moved her body toward the shore, wobbling all over, and tried to get to her knapsack. She reached inside, grabbed the Tums-like tablet and started chewing it. She plopped her bottom down on the ground and put her head between her legs.

▲ ▲ ▲

"You okay?" Valerie said, running over to where Alex had squatted, underneath a tree and away from the rest of the group.

"Oh, I'm fine," Alex answered, her wobbliness going away. She looked up at Valerie's concerned eyes.

"I'm so sorry I let you go out there by yourself," Valerie said. "I guess that's why we're supposed to swim in pairs. You just never know what's going to happen. Did you see a shark or something?"

Valerie was just joking—everyone pretended there

were great whites and barracudas and Loch Ness monsters in the clear, creature-free waters at Camp Lakeview. Alex felt her dizziness going away, and she started laughing. It felt really good to laugh—Alex had been so freaked out just a few seconds before. She really did think she was going to pass out!

Brynn came to the shore and stood next to Alex and Valerie. She saw the two girls talking and then exploded. "I cannot believe you, Alex Kim! You are just so completely overdramatic! Why can't you just face me out there without the act?"

"What act?" Alex answered, wondering which one of them was the drama queen.

"You know what act—you're playing sick to avoid a fight. You know you'll do anything to avoid a fight, Alex," Brynn said, stomping away.

Alex felt too weak to run after her. She really wanted to tell Brynn she was sorry, and she also needed to know why Brynn was making such a big deal out of everything. Maybe something else was bothering Brynn, or else she was just having a really cruddy day.

"What's got her?" Valerie asked, watching Brynn run off.

Alex shrugged her shoulders, worried that Brynn was super mad at her. Alex just hated big old arguments, and she didn't understand why they couldn't just enjoy the last couple weeks of camp together. She and Brynn wouldn't see each other very much during the year, after all. But then again, Alex was starting to feel like she didn't know Brynn as well anymore.

"Probably the same thing that's gotten a hold of Sarah in the last week," Valerie answered.

"What's that?" Alex asked, feeling better and better.

"Well, I think I accidentally made her mad," Valerie said, scooping up the muddy lakeside sand in her hands and squishing it through her fingers. "I told her that I really missed my crew back home, and I couldn't wait to see them when camp was over in two weeks. See, I have these friends Rachel and Shelly from school, and we've been writing a lot of letters this summer, and I just said that I wished they were here. I didn't mean to make Sarah feel bad at all, but she got up from the table and stomped off. Things have been weird between us ever since."

"No way—you could never make anyone mad," Alex said.

"I guess I was a little insensitive, but Sarah . . . you know, it's kind of hard to get her to open up," Valerie explained. "She doesn't share things with me—she keeps secrets, and that's fine. I mean, I love her—she's awesome. I just wish I hadn't said anything."

"Ohhh, that sucks. So that's why she's been buddy-buddy with Brynn?" Alex asked, feeling less alone.

"I guess so. I can't think of any other reason," Val said. Alex noticed how sad she seemed.

"They'll get over it," Alex said. "I hope." *Why don't*

Brynn and I see things the same way anymore? she thought.

"Maybe the mysterious Loch Ness monster ate their brains," Valerie joked.

"Or a shark," Alex answered.

They both laughed, but not for real. They were feeling bad about their friends, or former friends, whatever the case was. They sat together silently for the longest time, just thinking.

chapter FIVE

For the entire rest of the day, Brynn acted like Alex didn't exist. They usually hung out in between their activities and they almost always walked to dinner together.

But Brynn was nowhere to be found at their usual meet-up times. Alex thought that was really strange. If Brynn was mad, she didn't usually have any trouble telling Alex all about it. In fact, Alex dreaded seeing her because Brynn was sure to chew her out.

As it turned out, though, not talking it out actually made Alex feel worse than a confrontation would have. Alex couldn't shake that awkward, uneasy feeling that something was very, very wrong.

She wondered where her best friend had sneaked off to all day, and while she was upset, she also just hoped that Brynn was okay. Alex had not meant to blow her off as swim partners, and she would tell Brynn she was sorry if she ever got the chance. Alex looked for Brynn everywhere—in the rec room, in the woods by the bunk, in the drama hut, but she still couldn't find her.

At dinner, finally, the two girls were together again. Alex didn't know if she should go sit next to Brynn at their table in the mess hall. Brynn was with Sarah, and they were giggling and being loud.

Nervous, Alex plopped down next to them. She decided that would be the right thing to do. Alex took a deep breath and got ready to apologize. Even if Brynn had been a little hard on her, it was just easier for Alex to say she was sorry and end the disagreement. Alex had no problem making the first move, and she wanted the uneasiness to go away.

"Hey," Alex said, smiling.

"Hey," Brynn answered back, not smiling at all.

"Are you still mad about earlier?" Alex asked her while she fiddled around with her napkin.

"I'm over it," Brynn said, rolling her eyes and acting sarcastic. "I mean, really, it's not that big of a deal."

"Oh." Alex was surprised that she didn't get chewed out again. "Because I really didn't mean to—" she started to say.

"It's okay, really. Where's Valerie?" Brynn asked.

"She's coming," Alex answered, feeling awkward about the subject of Valerie.

"Great," Sarah added, rolling her eyes. She was turning out to be a lot more competitive than Alex thought!

"I really think we should all just hang out. It would be fun!" Alex said. It seemed like she was always the one rallying and trying to bring everyone together.

Before they could finish their nonconversation, Valerie arrived, asking if she could sit down with them. Sarah and Brynn shrugged their shoulders in unison, their way of saying "whatever" and started talking super-quietly to each other.

The situation didn't feel any less awkward than it had before Alex tried to be nice. In fact, Alex thought things were getting worse. But since she felt like Brynn was shafting her, she just turned to Valerie, and they talked about their chess set and swimming and the boys who had been teaching one another how to spit in woodworking. They ended up making the best of the situation, and dinner wasn't so bad.

Jenna really helped the situation—she told jokes so goofy that mashed potatoes actually oozed out of Candace's nose. Marissa, who served Pete's poor excuse for food, almost spilled a tray, she was laughing so hard when Jenna told the one about the hippopotamus that rode a bicycle through Weehawken, New Jersey. Marissa was laughing so hard, she had to rush back to the kitchen to calm herself down.

"Hey there."

Julie had been off talking to the camp director, Dr. Steve. Now she sat herself down at the table with all the girls. Relief rushed through Alex's veins. She hoped her counselor had noticed the tension at the table and could help them all to work it out.

"Does anyone have any sparkle lotion I could borrow?" Julie asked, humming a happy little song Alex couldn't make out—it might have been "Somewhere Over the Rainbow." Julie continued, "I can't find Marissa's anywhere, and I don't want her to know that I might have, um, misplaced it."

"I do!" Brynn said, and they started talking about how Julie needed it for her mystery date this weekend. She had the night off on Saturday, and she clearly couldn't wait.

Counselors weren't really supposed to hook up, but it happened, like in the cases of Marissa and Pete, and Stephanie and Tyler. It was cool that Julie trusted the girls enough to tell them about it. They certainly wouldn't spill her secret to anyone. But they did want to know whom Julie liked—and her lips were zipped on that front. A hookup was exciting news even to Alex, who swore she didn't care about boy-girl gossip.

"So, Alex," Julie said, turning toward her, "can you come see me after dinner in the kitchen? I need to ask you something."

"Sure," Alex answered, as usual.

Alex was always helping Julie or Marissa or Pete, one of the chefs, with something. Sometimes they just needed an extra hand to carry something. Other campers were enlisted every so often, too, but it seemed like Alex did the most, which was fine with her. After all, the counselors had their reasons for keeping her busy and keeping an eye on her. She understood. Heck, she appreciated it.

Out of the corner of her eye, Alex could see Brynn and Sarah getting ready to head back to the bunk with the rest of 3C. Was Brynn going to walk off without even saying good-bye?

Without warning, Brynn turned to her abruptly. "See ya later." And then she was off.

Alex tried to calm herself. At least Brynn was speaking to her. She couldn't keep from smiling when she answered, "Cool."

Hopefully, they'd get along well for the night activity a scavenger hunt. Alex loved those things—outsmarting everyone, finding stuff, and digging up clues.

At the last one, Alex led her bunkmates to the winning item that only had the clue: "Something that's shiny and red." She talked Natalie into letting go of her *Teen People* magazine, and her team submitted it. Even though she knew the counselors meant for campers to capture a ladybug, they let Alex's creative idea pass.

Alex walked back into the kitchen. Most campers never went back there. But it was okay for Alex to step right in and start doing something—like cleaning or putting dishes away. She loved helping if it meant she got to hang out with the counselors.

"What are you here for today?" Pete asked.

He was always cooking hamster surprises and spaghetti worm dinners.

Alex told him they were good—even the Soupy Dooby Doo they had last night—because he was funny and sweet. No one wanted to hurt Pete's feelings—especially not Marissa, who had to actually smile when she ate the, well, slop.

"Julie asked me for a quick hand," Alex answered, stacking some cups next to the dishwasher out of habit.

"Julie's not here. But are you sure you don't want to scrub some pots?" Pete asked, snapping his towel at Alex's ankles.

"Um, I will if you need me to!" Alex said, jumping out of the way before the wet towel zapped her. She really wanted to be on time for the scavenger hunt. "But not if you hurt me—then I won't!"

"You are too much, Alex Kim," Pete said, stuffing his surfer ponytail into the hairnet he was required to wear when he cooked. If he wasn't a culinary talent, at least he was into cleanliness; Alex gave him that.

"I'm just kidding," Pete added. "Now go find Julie. I think she's outside."

Around the back of the mess hall, Julie was sitting

at a picnic table filing her nails. She smiled really big when Alex arrived.

"You okay, Mia Hamm?" Julie asked Alex.

Julie reached for Alex's hand so she could file her nails while they talked. Alex was excited—clearly Julie didn't need Alex to help with anything specific, she just wanted to talk. Of course that probably meant she *had* noticed the problems between Alex and Brynn, but Alex didn't care. Spending time alone with Julie made her feel special.

Alex was double thrilled because she was terrible at doing her own nails. She didn't have patience for sitting still to do girlie stuff like that. The only time she'd had her nails painted all summer was when Brynn had done it for her four weeks ago.

"I'm fine," Alex answered evasively.

"You didn't seem fine today at free swim," Julie said, whizzing across the tips of Alex's fingers with the nail file. "You have to take care of yourself."

"I know. I did try to tell Brynn how I felt," Alex answered, trying to sit super still so her hands wouldn't wiggle.

"Oh, that. I didn't know you were having a problem with Brynn," Julie said. Alex was disappointed—Julie had no clue what was going on.

"Oh, no, not really, it's nothing." Alex didn't want to bother her counselor with her silly friend issues. Julie had other things—like twelve campers and zillions of friends and one crush—to think about!

Surely, all of those things are more important than a pair of jousting best camp friends, Alex thought.

"I hope not. You are such a great twosome. You really take good care of Brynn—like when she almost started a bunk pillow fight after everyone had already fallen asleep last week. You don't know how happy I was that you talked her out of it," Julie said, blowing on Alex's nails. "But more importantly, I just want you to take care of yourself."

"Yeah, I know," Alex added, starting to wiggle and squirm. She didn't like where this conversation was heading. She didn't like sitting still. She loved running around.

"So, what I want to ask you is if you'll help in the kitchen for the formal banquet," Julie said, finishing up Alex's ninth finger.

The formal banquet always took place on the very last night at camp, after the drama group's big end-of-summer play, *Peter Pan*. It was 3C's shining night.

Brynn had the part of a Lost Boy, and Grace got to be Wendy. Brynn had actually been really cool when Grace beat her out for that main role. She seemed really happy to be a Lost Boy, surprisingly, and, *un*surprisingly, was putting a ton of effort into rehearsals, fixing the set, and all kinds of other play-related stuff.

"Sure, of course. I thought I already was," Alex said.

"You are the sweetest, I swear," Julie said. "Anyway, thanks. Natalie, Alyssa and Candace are helping out, too.

The four of you need you to come to the planning meeting tomorrow night with the rest of us counselors. It'll be fun. We're going to play Scrabble and stuff after we figure out the menu and plan the desserts. I always like you to have a say on those things, Alex."

She was so happy to be included in any plans that involved the counselors. Alex definitely wanted to be a CIT in a few years, and she thought she'd be really good at it. She loved organizing as many things as possible. With her newly shaped nails—she had to admit they looked pretty good—Alex went back to the bunk in a great mood.

▲ ▲ ▲

Back at 3C, not even Chelsea could ruin Alex's spirits. She and Brynn would work out their differences; Alex was hopeful. Even if Julie hadn't noticed—or given Alex any advice—Alex knew how strong their friendship really was.

"So, what did Julie want, Alex?" Chelsea asked, getting in her face.

"Oh, I'm going to help with the formal banquet," she answered as Chelsea inspected Alex's nails.

"Me too!" Candace yelled enthusiastically. She was too sweet for her own good, but Alex felt kind of sorry for her, too. Candace never had an original thought—ever. At least Candace was good at telling ghost stories. Apparently, she'd learned them all from her older brother.

"Of course you are, Miss Perfect Alex," Chelsea said. "You're always doing whatever you can to kiss the counselors' butts. Just like Natalie and Alyssa and Candace."

"Please, Chelsea," Natalie said, sitting on her bottom bunk on the other side of the room. "What's your problem?"

Alex was glad Nat had chimed in. She didn't know how to react to Chelsea. Today of all days she really wasn't prepared for extra bunk drama.

"You need to mind your own business," Alex said, once she had regained her composure. She looked Chelsea dead in the eye.

The rest of the girls' mouths hung open. But not Brynn. Brynn didn't stand up for Alex. Alex couldn't believe her supposed best friend didn't have her back. Alex really did start feeling sick to her stomach. She didn't even want to be in the scavenger hunt anymore.

"Don't tell me what to do," Chelsea said while Karen ran up to her and tried to distract her. Karen attempted to make Chelsea sit down by offering to French braid her hair. Chelsea finally did sit down, but that didn't mean she would shut up.

"Then don't get in my face," Alex said, wishing she were the kind of person who could give Chelsea's long blond hair a nice short trim in the middle of the night. She hated that this fight was escalating—but Chelsea had managed to push just the wrong button. And right when

Alex had been feeling a little bit better . . .

"Don't be such a drama queen," Chelsea added. "Everyone, just relax. I didn't mean what I said. It was rude."

"You don't say," Alex spat.

"Whatever," Chelsea said, over it and preoccupied with Karen's hairstylings.

Everyone was deadly quiet. After a beat, they tried to go back to hanging out.

Alex looked up to see Brynn walking toward her. Jenna, Jessie, and Candace perked up, watching.

Alex shot them a meaningful look, and they got the hint to mind their own business. They pretended to be busy reading books—except that Jenna's copy of *Are You There God? It's Me, Margaret* was upside down.

"So, Alex," Brynn said, sitting down next to her. "Sorry about that and all. You know how *Chelsea* is," Brynn added loudly so Chelsea would hear.

Chelsea just gave her—and everyone else—an evil eye.

"It's nothing," Alex answered, even though comments like that were everything to her. She was glad that Brynn had at least noticed how hurt Alex had been.

"So, are we on for tomorrow night then?" Brynn asked, sitting down next to Alex on her bed like she always did.

Alex's throat got tight again. *I can't believe what I did!* She had just promised to be at Julie's banquet planning meeting! She wanted to be at that meeting with all the counselors. She wanted to help plan the big dinner and play Scrabble with them afterward! But she had promised to help Brynn paint the *Peter Pan* set for the big show tomorrow night.

Ugh, Alex thought. *How did things ever get so complicated?* She had double-booked, and she couldn't have picked a worse time to do it. Brynn had just started acting like she wasn't mad anymore! Apparently, she hadn't been completely unaffected by Alex's clash with Chelsea. That, at least, was something, Alex thought. Though it didn't exactly solve the current problem.

"So, we are, right?" Brynn said, looking at Alex with her puppy eyes. "I really hoped you could help us."

Alex was no good at painting. She kind of hated it, too. Her mother had made her do way too much of it when she was a little kid. She had only told Brynn she would do it to be nice. She was, however, good at Scrabble. She did like organizing the formal banquet. She would get a say in the menu, and that would be awesome, too.

"Brynn, please don't be mad at me, but I told Julie I'd be at a banquet-planning meeting tomorrow night," Alex said, wishing she had brought her pocket organizer to camp.

"You've got to be kidding me," Brynn said, her voice getting louder and louder. "After today with the swimming and everything?" Brynn stood up, a sure sign that big time theatrics were on the way.

"Please, just try to understand," Alex said, thinking that she'd rather yank off her ponytail at the roots than endure her third fight of the day.

"Understand what?" Brynn yelled, acting like she'd yank out Alex's ponytail for her. "What? That you'd rather hang out with Valerie and Julie and whoever else than with me? I get it just fine."

"I think we need to talk about this. This is not how best friends are supposed to act," Alex said, trying to keep her voice steady.

"Oh yeah, like you're the poster girl for how to be a best friend," Brynn said again, getting all evil-eyed. "Kind of like you were earlier today?"

"You need to get a grip, you are so totally blowing this out of proportion!" Alex yelled. Immediately, she wished she'd just counted to ten first. She knew it was always better to chill out—but Brynn was making that so hard to do!

"Ladies, back to your corners," Grace said, trying to ease the tension with a joke.

"Grace!" Alex and Brynn shouted in unison.

All eyes were back on Alex for the second time in five minutes. She'd had the most up-and-down day of anyone at camp. She had never been in this many fights with Brynn—or anyone else—before. Jenna and Alex clashed sometimes, but they always worked it out. They never yelled, either.

Alex really didn't know what to do. Arguing was

not her style, and she just wasn't used to it. She felt herself mentally checking out of the situation. She just wanted to run out into the woods—and run and run and run. She couldn't make Brynn happy, and she was tired of trying.

"I don't want your help, anyway!" Brynn yelled as the other girls started to whisper about the impending altercation. When Chelsea chewed out Alex, it was easy for everyone to take Alex's side.

But the fight between Alex and Brynn wasn't so clear-cut. Both girls had a point: Alex was standing Brynn up, and Brynn was being self-involved, not to mention bossy. The other girls—Natalie, Alyssa, Karen, and the others—didn't know what to do. They just looked at one another and shrugged.

Only Sarah and Valerie got involved.

"I'll help you, Brynn," Sarah said, moving to stand next to Brynn.

"Come on, Alex," Valerie said. "Cool down for a while, and then try to talk about it again."

Alex wanted to add one more thing before Brynn walked away. "If Sarah helps, then it's okay if I go to the meeting with Julie?" At least she knew Brynn would have an extra hand, which was the important part, anyway.

"I said, I didn't want your help, anyway," Brynn stated, stomping off.

What has Brynn done for me *lately?* Alex wondered. Brynn hadn't even said anything to Chelsea when she harassed Alex just before. Alex honestly didn't think she should be the one to apologize this time.

"It's okay, Alex. Let's just go the scavenger hunt and forget about it," Valerie said. "It will all blow over soon."

"Yeah. Sure." Alex shrugged, trying to shake off the icky feeling the fight had given her. Valerie had to be right. This couldn't go on forever.

Could it?

chapter SIX

When the girls returned after the scavenger hunt—they had lost to their rival bunk 3A—no one was in a giddy mood. Before lights-out, Brynn and Alex used to sit around and talk. They'd often share their dreams and secrets and rehash the day. Nothing of the sort happened that night.

Alex hadn't expected it, but it still stung when Brynn took her script over to Grace's bed and started reading.

▲ ▲ ▲

It was getting more and more awful by the day—not just for Alex, but also for the other girls who felt like they were being forced to take sides. The most worrisome thing for Alex was that Chelsea and Brynn had been talking more. Alex was terrified that the two of them would gang up together against her and make the last days at camp one big pile of steaming Hamster Surprise.

This was not how Alex had imagined the end of camp! She was so disappointed. She'd managed to have a little fun—like at the formal banquet planning meeting—but she just couldn't enjoy the other camp activities with Brynn acting like they weren't even friends anymore. Alex started wishing that she had gone to paint with Brynn that night instead of to the planning meeting. *Maybe then nothing would've gotten this bad*, Alex thought. But then another, less quiet voice perked up inside her head.

Why should Brynn always get her way? Alex asked herself, vowing to stand her ground on this one. *It's like she just expects me to go play with her.*

As the days went on, woodworking was a much-needed break once a day from the girls and their dramas. Valerie didn't care much about it. She mentioned a few times that her friendship with Sarah was totally over.

"If she's that sensitive, and if I can't talk about my girls at home, then so be it," Val explained. "My mom says sometimes friendships fade, and you should let them go gracefully. If Sarah wants to dump me over one little stupid comment I made, I guess we weren't that close in the first place. Hmph."

"It still stinks, though," Alex added, feeling totally dumped herself. "I hate the way Brynn ignores me."

"Likewise," Val said. "Did you see the way they were holding hands at the flagpole this morning? I couldn't even giggle about Dr. Steve's mismatched knee socks—did you see he had one blue and one orange on today?—because I was fuming over the way those two are acting."

"He did?" Alex asked, shocked that she hadn't noticed.

"I am not kidding. He did," she answered. Val never said anything nasty about Sarah or Brynn, and Alex knew she must've been steamed to have an outburst like that. Alex tried so hard not to say mean things about people, either—though sometimes she did drop an opinion of Chelsea. Alex wondered if Brynn was talking badly about her. *Oooh, she better not be,* Alex thought.

"I don't know about me and Sarah," Valerie said, "but you and Brynn will make up soon. Maybe Brynn is just wigging out about the play."

"That's true. She always stresses out before performances," Alex said, rolling her eyes. "It's so stupid. I mean, I don't freak before Color War or soccer games." For Alex, it was just the opposite. She was so excited for the activities she was good at that her mood actually improved when the pressure was on.

"I know," Valerie added.

At least, with Valerie, Alex felt like she had someone to talk to who really understood. Valerie was always cracking jokes to make Alex smile when she felt like kicking trees. Alex's feelings about Brynn were so up and down. One second, she'd hate her for causing such a big fight. The next second, Alex missed her as if she were a long-lost member of her family. Alex would have given anything to have Brynn back the way she had been during the earlier part of the summer.

"Nice."

"What?" Alex looked up to see Adam standing over her. He nodded appreciatively at the wood she was sanding. She had to admit that the chess board was really coming along.

Valerie excused herself and went to the bathroom. Alex knew what Val must've been thinking. Val thought Adam would be a good match for Alex, so she left the two of them alone together whenever she got the chance. Alex wanted her to stay, though! Adam was hanging around too much and making her really nervous. It was weird.

"What are you guys working . . ." Alex trailed off, realizing that by the time she could get her thoughts together into a normal speech pattern, Adam was already gone.

She could see, from where she was sitting, that Adam and his friends were making a wooden table. It was simple, just a round slab of wood with a base and a pole to hold it up, but it was beautiful. Camp would be over soon, and the boys were working hard to get finished. They were sanding down their project and starting to stain the pieces. They hadn't practiced spitting or tried to steal her soccer ball for three whole days. It was nice when boys acted normal. Alex just wondered if they really would finish that table.

She wasn't too worried about Adam anymore—at

least not about his broken heart, anyway. If Alyssa had dumped him, he seemed to be over it. He was laughing and having fun with Jenna and his other friends. He didn't even seem to be bothered when Alyssa/Trevor and Natalie/Simon hung out together in front of him. Alex just thought it was weird that they would parade around considering what had supposedly happened.

▲ ▲ ▲

At lunch, Alex heard Jessie and Jenna gossiping about it.

"Your brother really did get shafted, didn't he?" Jessie said in her usual to-the-point way.

"I wouldn't say *shafted*," Jenna answered. "There's probably more to the story than we realize."

Jenna did not like that Adam was starting to flirt with girls—in fact, she made that gesture with her mouth and her finger where she gagged herself any time the subject came up. But she also didn't like anyone other than herself even remotely putting him down.

"It's just too weird," Jenna said, turning to Alex. "Why does everyone act crazy about boys? And about my brother? Ewww!"

Alex put her granola down; she was done. She didn't think Adam liked her as anything more than a friend. But if he did, as Valerie said, that would completely have freaked her out, and Jenna, too. *Ugh, this is so not me!* Alex thought.

"I definitely do not want to talk about boys," she added.

▲ ▲ ▲

Later, Alex and Val headed to free swim as usual. They had become regular partners by default ever since their respective "friend breakups." Alex kept hoping that Brynn would just come up to her and apologize or at least try to work it out. They couldn't go home for the summer not speaking. That would be awful. But instead of the two of them making up, things just kept getting worse.

Brynn was walking to the shoreline holding hands with Sarah and laughing so loud that people in Los Angeles could probably have heard her. Even though Alex and Val were only a few feet away, Brynn didn't even bother to acknowledge their presence.

At least Sarah and Val were being civil to each other even if they weren't best friends anymore. Brynn was just being impossible. Alex didn't understand what was going on, or what she had done.

"I'm going to talk to her," Alex said to Valerie after they jumped off. The girls were dripping wet, and they were tired from playing Frisbee earlier. Brynn was sitting with Natalie on the blanket, and Alex thought that would be as good a time as ever to work their differences out.

"Are you sure? You want me to go with you?" Valerie said, looking at her waterproof watch. If Alex was going to talk to Brynn, she didn't have much time. Free period was over in five minutes, and then they had to hurry to their Color War meeting to find out which teams they were on.

"I'll be fine, but thanks," Alex said, feeling scared about speaking to Brynn. But she also just wanted to get it over with. This not talking for a few days was just ridiculous. They'd barely gone an hour without speaking before!

Alex headed toward the girls, forcing herself to stop thinking about how mad she was and focus on smoothing it out. Val had been telling her in woodworking not to think any bad thoughts—about herself or about Brynn. Val insisted that not dwelling on drama kind of made it undramatic (and that was a good thing!). Alex thought about how she and Val were kicking tail on the chess set (so what if it was because Jeremy had been helping them?). Things were going slightly better for Alex, so she hoped that Brynn would come around, too.

Natalie and Alyssa watched wide-eyed as Alex walked toward the three of them. They started gathering their notebooks and lotion, taking the hint to go somewhere else.

"Thanks, you two," Alex told them. Then she looked Brynn in the eyes. "Can we talk, Brynn?" she asked. Alex kept standing while Brynn changed positions on her blanket. Alex felt like a tree that was getting ready to topple over.

"I have nothing to say to you, Alex Kim," Brynn

answered, not even looking up from her teen magazine.

"Come on, we've been best friends for so long. We can talk about this," Alex said, thinking about how she kind of missed whispering to Brynn before they fell asleep at night. She missed their inside jokes, and she missed jumping rope together. They had been practicing the double ropes all summer because Brynn complained that she wasn't coordinated enough.

Brynn said jumping rope made her feel more athletic. Alex had a blast teaching it to her. When they had done it, with Jenna and Valerie taking turns twirling the ropes, Alex remembered feeling how great it was to just hang out and get along. It was like they all had a rhythm that went together.

Where has our friendship gone? Alex wondered, lost in her daydream.

"What are you just standing there for?" Brynn asked, annoyed and flipping the pages of the magazine so hard, they almost ripped. "We're not best friends anymore. Can't you just deal with that?"

Ouch, Alex thought. *That was low.* She had meant well, but she didn't know what to say to Brynn anymore.

"Just go hang out with your new best friend, Valerie," Brynn said, not caring that Chelsea and Karen were just a few feet away. Chelsea wasn't even trying to act like she wasn't listening.

Alex was still standing there, and she was still about to topple over. She had to will away her tears. They were going to fall down her face and embarrass her if she didn't run away soon.

But before she took off, she added, "Fine. Then you go have fun with *your* new best friend, Sarah."

Alex stomped away, heading toward the bunk as quickly as her legs would take her.

Back at the bunk, Alex couldn't hold back any longer. She was crying. Really crying. Alex wondered if Adam had felt a little bit like this—totally heartbroken—when Alyssa had dumped him. Alex thought that losing your best friend had to be about a million times worse.

Everyone at free swim had seen the whole thing, even if they hadn't heard what the girls had said. But Valerie was the only girl who followed Alex back to 3C. She hugged Alex and asked her what happened. Alex explained, thankful that she had someone she could count on.

Valerie was turning out to be a much better friend than Brynn had been lately. Maybe they really would be best friends one day—but that couldn't happen overnight. Camp was almost ending, and Alex didn't know for sure if Valerie would be back next summer. Alex would be—she always came back.

"I have an idea that might make you feel better," Valerie said, rubbing Alex's back and handing her tissues. "Do you really miss Brynn?"

"You know, even though she's been impossible lately, I do miss the old Brynn," Alex said, definitely not missing the new Brynn. "We had so much fun together before she started working on *Peter Pan*. I don't know what's gotten into her, really."

"Okay, then," Valerie went on, "I have an idea. . . . But it's kind of weird, and you just have to hear me out."

"Go for it," Alex said, slouching and pulling her knapsack close to her like a security blanket.

"We should do something nice for them," Valerie added, reaching up to mess with her braids as if she were nervous. "Brynn and Sarah, I mean."

"Who? Brynn? Why? She's been nothing but nasty," Alex said. She really did think she had tried as hard as she could. "The ball is in Brynn's court now."

"Don't let her make the decisions for you," Valerie said. "Why don't we make little friendship boxes in woodshop for Brynn and Sarah? Let's just put a note inside them that says, 'Whatever happens, remember the good times when we're all apart next fall. Good luck with everything.' Or something like that."

"Why on Earth would we go to all that trouble for *them*?" Alex asked. She was totally bewildered by Valerie's suggestion. But her tears were drying up at least, and that was a good thing.

"Because it's just the nice thing to do," Valerie added. "My mom gave me this idea. Whenever someone really ticks you off, and you've done all you can do, just give them a nice token of friendship, like a note or gift, and know that you've done the right thing. My mom brings my dad M&M's, his favorite kind—the peanut ones—whenever they've been at each other's throats, no matter who is right or wrong. And you know what? They always stop fighting. No one stays mad when you do something nice for them."

"I don't know about this," Alex said, getting up so she could get dressed for the Color War meeting—she sure wasn't missing *that*.

"Let's just give it a try," Valerie said, getting up, too. "Instead of the chess set. Our friendships are more important than some game, right? We still have a few more days of woodworking. It can't hurt."

"What about the stool for your dad that you were working on?" Alex asked, thinking of ways to get out of going through with this crazy plan. It really did seem like Brynn should be making *her* something nice, but Alex tried to stay open-minded about Valerie's idea.

"I finished it. Jeremy helped me yesterday," Valerie yelled from the shower.

She didn't have anything to lose. Alex decided she'd try it. She did feel kind of good about doing something sweet, even if it was for Brynn. Valerie's suggestion made a little bit of sense, she guessed. Alex was always volunteering to help everyone—especially the counselors—because it made her happy to do so. Good deeds had a way of boosting Alex's self-confidence.

And she could definitely use a boost, she figured.

At the very least, things certainly couldn't get any worse.

▲ ▲ ▲

The Color War meeting was the best. At least Alex thought so. The whole camp—hundreds of kids of all ages—arrived for the meeting after dinner. There was a small campfire burning near the flagpole. Dr. Steve stood behind the fire, creating a stage for himself, as if he were presenting the Oscar nominations or something. Every kid sat with his or her bunk, excited, knowing that the "enemy" could be sitting right beside you. Once they got their assignments, bunkmate would compete against bunkmate for the victory.

But before that happened, everyone sang silly songs like "Green and Yeller" and "Who Stole My Tree?" to get pumped up. Then Dr. Steve made everyone hold hands and meditate (Alex couldn't believe he added meditation to his weirdness this summer) as a show of solidarity before giving his speech.

Dr. Steve went on for twenty whole minutes, just like he did every year, about sportsmanship and no pranks and healthy competition and team pride and camp rivalry and even went on a tangent about how Color War could teach every person about world peace.

"The leaders of our world should come to Camp Lakeview!" he yelled, waving his fishing hat in the air. The kids only clapped a little bit—mostly, just the counselors cheered because he was, after all, their eccentric boss. Alex and Valerie couldn't help but giggle.

"Oh my dog," Valerie said, rolling her eyes and nudging Alex in the side. "He's not even kidding!"

"Oh yes, he means every word," Alex added.

Then, amid hundreds of hushed, anxious campers, the envelopes were handed out. That was something different they were doing this year. Every camper was getting a sealed letter with his or her team assignment on it. For some reason, Dr. Steve thought it would be good for each camper to try to keep his or her team assignment a secret until breakfast the next morning. Then, after breakfast, the competition lists would be posted outside of each cabin.

Color War took place over two days and consisted of a mix of group events and division events. Group events—where kids of all ages competed together in games like singdown and potato-sack race—were worth fifty points for the winners. Division events—where kids competed for their teams against their own age group during games like Scrabble and tug-o-war—were worth twenty-five points for the winners. There were four group events, two per day of Color War, and several division events. The counselors had to do a lot of planning!

Alex couldn't get on board with the secret thing. How was she going to get to bed that night without somehow letting it slip?

"The point is to absolutely torture us, which clearly he considers to be great fun," Valerie said.

But Alex suspected another reason they were doing it this way. Last year, the Blues stayed up all night making confetti that they threw in the mess hall oatmeal. Maybe he was trying to keep night-before pranks to a minimum. Or maybe this was just another "camp challenge."

Julie handed Alex her envelope, and she tore it open. Inside, there was a blank white paper with a small blue dot in the center. Alex was thrilled to be a Blue. It was her favorite color, so it had to be lucky. She just hoped that her closest 3C friends were Blues, too.

"What'd you get?" Valerie whispered.

"What'd you get?" Candace yelled before Jessie could put her hand over Candace's mouth.

"I'm not telling till tomorrow." Alex smiled.

And just then, red and blue balloons fell from a net that was suspended between several trees. Alex was so excited—the next few days would definitely make up for the recent bad ones.

After two more rounds of "Green and Yeller," all the kids headed back to their bunks—some keeping the secret, some surely not—screaming and yelling and acting like wild safari animals.

Camp is awesome, Alex thought. *This is the whole reason I came.*

"Twinkie time!" Jenna yelled as she ripped open a cardboard box from her parents that night. Julie and Marissa were out at a staff meeting, and so it was party time in 3C. Alex dreaded party time. The other girls looked forward to sharing the treats. But sharing time was always a nightmare for Alex.

"I'll give one to anyone who reveals their team!" she yelled.

"I'm a Blue!" Chelsea yelled. Alex hoped she was just lying, but knowing her own luck lately, she probably wasn't.

"I'm a Red!" Jessie chimed in. "No wait, a Blue! No wait, a Red!"

With that, Twinkies started flying through the air.

"Nice pass," Grace yelled as she caught hers.

Chelsea, Karen, Brynn, Sarah, and Valerie tore into theirs. Alex could hear the cellophane wrappers crinkle. She could hear her bunkmates chewing, *mmm-ing*, and *ahhh-ing*.

She knew as soon as Chelsea took the last bite and wiped her mouth, she'd be all over Alex as usual. But worse, Alex couldn't control herself any longer. She wanted to eat one of those Twinkies so bad that she could taste it. It had been seven months—maybe longer—since she'd had such a yummy, sweet, sugary, totally-bad-for-you treat.

"Alex?" Jenna asked, ever polite even though Alex never said yes. She—like everyone else—just assumed Alex was a health nut.

Jenna didn't get it into her head that Alex wished she would stop asking her. To Jenna, not offering a bite to everyone was bad manners. With so many siblings, it was part of her genetic makeup to share. Jenna didn't understand that she was actually torturing Alex.

"I, um," Alex started to say. All eyes were, once again, on her. She hadn't eaten the Nerds or the more recent chocolate peanut butter cookies. And Chelsea had been all over her both times.

In fact, just yesterday, Karen—*Karen of all mousy people!*—had taken Alex aside and asked her if everything was all right. "I, um, like, saw you looking kind of greenish-yellow at free swim the other day," Karen had said one night before bed. "You know, right when you and Brynn started having that fight. You can, um, like, tell me if something's wrong," Karen had added.

Alex appreciated the concern, but she was losing her patience. She told Karen she was fine and offered to look at her sticker collection—just to change the subject. Alex was going to shred the entire camp's pillows. That's how tired she was of everything that had been going on lately. She was sick of Chelsea's nasty words about "Little Miss Perfect" having to stay in shape for soccer.

Alex's walls were coming down.

"You know what? Throw me one," Alex said to Jenna.

"Really? Cool!" Jenna said, glad to oblige. She tossed the Twinkie across the room to her friend.

Alex caught it easily. She didn't squish or harm the Twinkie. *Who knew athletic ability would help keep your snacks safe?* Alex thought. The other girls clapped and whooped. And Alex loved being cheered on, whatever the reason. It just felt good. It felt like belonging. And Alex had been feeling so left out for so long now.

She scarfed that Twinkie down in three seconds flat.

"*Mmm,*" she said loudly. "That was good!"

"You want another one?" Jenna asked.

"I do!" Brynn yelled.

"Me first!" Grace begged.

"Really, I only have one more, girls," Jenna said. "Alex has missed out on all the other snacks. If she wants it, it should be hers."

"I'll take it," Alex said. She opened the other one, wide-eyed. She took one small bite, and then she got up to tuck it into a plastic box in her cubbyhole.

"That *so* won't be there tomorrow," Chelsea said. "I'm going to eat it."

"You will not, or I'll kick your butt," Valerie said.

The girls laughed and enjoyed their short-lived sugar high. They had almost calmed down by the time Julie and Marissa returned from their meeting.

It took at least two more hours before the girls stopped whispering and gossiping in the dark. There was no way anyone was going to get a good night's sleep that night—not with Color War starting tomorrow. Even though Alex had been having a really difficult couple of days, just for that evening, she could forget about it all. She pretended that she was just like everyone else, like she fit in. Sharing in their snacks and pillow fights was freeing. She didn't have to pretend she was writing a letter or reading a book so they would leave her alone. She just jumped right in to join the fun—Twinkies and all. She was determined not to let anything, not even sweet treats—freak her out.

chapter SEVEN

The real roar of wild animals erupted early the next morning.

Bunk 3C was totally not surprised.

It was the first day of Color War, after all.

Instead of Julie's friendly, chirpy morning call of, "Wakey, Wakey!" the girls heard kids outside yelling things like, "Be prepared to get eaten alive!" and "Wake up and get ready to go dowwwwnnn!" and "Red will rule the entire free world!" A whole bunch of kids were up an hour early and running through the bunks in celebration.

No one was supposed to tell a soul which team they were on until the kick-off breakfast that morning, but some kids clearly broke the rule as soon as last night's meeting was adjourned. This year's Reds—at least the ones with hyena giggles and lion roars—obviously weren't concerned about the rules at that moment. They made so much noise—some of them even had lifeguard whistles to blow and pots and pans to clang—that sleeping was no longer an option for anyone.

The crazy Red strategy was obvious. Many of them had gotten themselves to sleep early the night before—those who'd revealed themselves, that is—rose earlier, and then woke up the rest of the camp up. They clearly wanted the Blue team to be tired for the first day of competition. It was a sneaky, sneaky move. Alex admired their ability to work together and strategize, but she also thought the Reds were being silly. Surely, some of their team members would be tired, too. Especially the Reds who were in her bunk still chatting away about boys, life, camp, and one another until the late, late hours of last night.

At least I feel really good this morning, Alex thought. She had been worried that the night before would have her worn out, maybe even sick, for the all-important competitions. But she was fine.

Woohoo! This is great, she couldn't help thinking.

She looked around the bunk, and several girls were missing. The 3C Reds had sneaked out to participate in the morning mayhem. *Now that was really impressive,* Alex thought. She couldn't believe she had been sleeping so soundly that she hadn't heard them earlier. She looked around, seeing who was there and who was not. Her heart sunk. She had wanted certain people to be on her team, and those certain people's beds were empty.

After the initial shock of hearing the noise and seeing who was (and wasn't) on her team, Alex decided there was nothing else to do but make the best of it. She'd have to pump herself up.

There is nothing I love more than Color War, she told herself. She remembered the two whole days of outdoor activities—an all-out Alex fest around Camp Lakeview. Sure, she was surprised that she had liked woodworking as much as she had. But no matter how great it had been to finish a cutting board and to start on the chess set, it was still more fun to punt a soccer ball. Alex's first love was sports, especially soccer. It was time to play ball!

▲ ▲ ▲

Breakfast was mayhem. As usual, on the start of Color War, excitement hung in the air. Kids were yelling, others were telling tall tales about their athletic abilities, others still were hurling muffins and burned toast through the air. She tried to get down some food before kids started spraying silly string—a harmless Color War ritual aimed at ruining the opposite team's morning meal.

A stripe of electric blue shot through the air and landed on her empty plate, narrowly avoiding her cup of water. She wiped her mouth and licked her lips. She smiled. The silly string had missed her watery eggs. She'd already downed everything—somehow—and she was already feeling lucky about the day to follow. Her fingers were crossed.

"Red! Red! Red! We are the best!" someone yelled. Alex heard, and her stomach dropped just like it had earlier that morning in the bunk. It was the voice of someone who'd been absent from the bunk that morning.

It was, unmistakably, Brynn's voice.

When Alex looked up, Brynn was in the front of the long, narrow room doing a cheer with Sarah and a few other girls right in the middle of the mess hall. All eyes were on Brynn, and people were laughing, screaming, or booing—or all three together.

Alex didn't mind the confetti or the cheerleading act. What Alex really minded was that she was a Blue and that Brynn was a Red. In all the years they'd come to camp together, they'd always been on the same team. Sarah was, as fate would have it, a Red, too.

Alex couldn't help but be jealous that Brynn and Sarah would get to spend *more* time together—bonding, laughing, and strategizing. Alex was pitted against her friends—or ex-friends, as the case was—and she was totally uncomfortable with it. She knew she was a strong athlete and Scrabble player, so that wasn't the issue. Alex could compete with anyone at camp. It was just that Alex usually coached Brynn and Sarah and cheered *them* on. The one thing that worried Alex was how skilled Brynn could be at mind games, which was another important element of competition.

Alex knew she could beat Brynn physically, but she wasn't so sure how she'd do against her in the more creative stuff like singdown. Overall, Alex was just sad that they wouldn't be together this year.

"Okay, kids!" Dr. Steve yelled on the mess hall PA system. "We're posting the official team lists outside of the mess hall. You can share your team assignments now!"

"Why the long face, Sport?" a high voice screeched behind her. It was Jenna's, and Grace stood at her side. "We're all Blues! Can you believe it?!"

At least *something* good had happened. Jenna and Alex had never been on the same Color War team. They figured they had been separated on purpose. Really, it was more fair that way, since they were both really good at sports. But this year, who knew what could happen?

The Color War isn't looking so bad after all, Alex told herself.

"We've got to make some signs at the Blue pep rally and put the brakes on those Reds," Jenna said, already wearing a blue T-shirt and shorts, looking ready for a game.

"I'm a better cheerleader than those chicks, anyway," Grace said, joking. That was probably true, too. Grace was always happy and smiling, and she would be a great member of Alex's team. She really would be good at keeping everyone's spirit up. Maybe Alex didn't need Brynn, after all.

"Don't worry, Alex," Grace said, totally reading her friend's mind. "Everything will be okay," she added. It was nice to know that other people could see what was going on, even if Alex couldn't talk about it. Alex refused to think like that for another second. She willed herself to snap out of her funk. Color War was her favorite time—it was a time to shine and show the Red Team what tough stuff she was made of. She just hoped Valerie was on her team.

She thought to herself, *I know I can, I know I can.*

"We're so going to get them," Jenna said. "Even if Chelsea is on our team."

"She is?!!!" Alex said, not even being careful to hide her feelings for the nasty blonde. "I'd hoped she was lying last night."

"I know—ugh," Jenna said. She made a face.

"Come on, let's not think about that right now," Grace added. "I'll work on getting the blond beast in a good mood, and I'll try to get her to play on the Scrabble team." Chelsea was good at word games. The girls hoped that she would turn out to be a useful member of the Blues, and not a total storm cloud.

"Oh, I don't want to think about her. Let's go to our Blue rally. Let's make some killer signs," Jenna said. "I've been stashing art supplies all summer for this very occasion. I just need you all to come up with ideas."

"So, is Valerie on our team, too?" Jenna asked.

"Yeah, that's what she told me," Grace said. "You, me, Chelsea, Natalie, Alyssa, Alex, and Valerie."

That left Karen, Candace, Brynn, Sarah, and Jessie on Red. *It was weird for the teams to be uneven*, Alex thought. There must have been an uneven number somewhere else in the division that they were compensating for.

Jenna and Alex shared a knowing glance, and Jenna said, "Grace, go grab Valerie some toast and bagels. The Reds will steal all the food soon. People don't compete as well when they're hungry. Alex, do you need some snacks, too?"

"No, I'm good," Alex answered.

"What about you, Grace?" Jenna asked.

"I'm all filled up and ready to *par-tay*," she said, putting some treats in her pockets for Valerie and whoever else didn't get a chance to eat. She was fighting kids from the Red Team who were up there hoarding stuff, too.

Why does food always have to be such a big deal? Alex wondered as she ran over to the arts and crafts shack for the Blue rally.

The crackle of the PA system indicated a new announcement from Dr. Steve.

"Apparently," he said, clearing his throat, "from the outburst this morning, we saw that one team in particular—some members of the Reds, specifically—didn't keep their team affiliation secret. As a result, all Reds will get a twenty-five point deduction!"

Some Reds hissed and booed and threw bagels at the Reds who had set up the abrupt morning wake-up.

"So, Blues, you have an advantage. Use it wisely. Now good luck to you all!"

The Blues—Alex, Jenna, Grace, Val, Alyssa, Natalie, and even Chelsea—whooped and screamed in celebration.

▲ ▲ ▲

Day One started with a rally. Marissa had made everyone blue wristbands, and Jenna and Alex made some kick-tail signs. They sung songs like "We Are the Champions" as they got ready for the big competition. Both days would start with a camp-wide competition—today's was the singdown. Then the divisions broke up and, instead of their regular free-choice activities, there were division competitions.

The first one each day would be sports, like basketball or soccer, and the second one after lunch would be a less athletic, like blob tag (*so funny*, Alex thought) and Scrabble. This went on for two days, and full schedules were posted on each bunk. In the evenings, kids could work on their missed activities (*like woodworking*, Alex realized) if they wanted to during free time.

Since much of Color War dealt with athletic ability, endurance, and prowess, Jenna and Alex went back to the bunk with the others to put their heads together to strategize for their division soccer game. As long as they let Julie know where they'd be, they were allowed a little more independence during "Color War–designated hours." When the competition ended for the day—or during meals, of course—everyone traveled as a bunk again.

As they scribbled "We're seeing BLUE!" and "BLUE

will rock your world" on pieces of poster board, they plotted out ways to win.

Since Scrabble would be soon, Alex knew the time had come for her heart-to-heart with Chelsea. Chelsea was really good at the game, so she could help the Blues earn their twenty-five points. And the only goal for Alex was to win, win, win.

Alex tracked her down in the bunk and willed herself to be patient with her grumpy teammate.

Needless to say, Chelsea did not exactly appreciate the pep talk. "Whatever. I know what this is about. You just won't be able to stand it if I'm better than you, right?" she said, wrinkling her nose.

Alex, for the first time, actually felt sorry for Chelsea. When she stopped and thought about it, Chelsea rarely smiled. Even when she got to do something she liked—like Scrabble—she didn't seem to enjoy it.

She just seems like she doesn't know how to be happy, Alex thought. Again, for the first time, Alex didn't get mad at Chelsea. Instead, she pitied her. She thought Chelsea's entire existence was just sad.

"I need you to be the best, Chelsea, even if that's better than me," Alex said. "I don't care which one of us wins, as long as *we* win together. It's all about the Blues. It's not about me. And it's not about you, either."

Chelsea just stuck out her tongue and answered,

"Always Little Miss Perfect . . . *always*." With that, she pranced away to talk to Karen.

Meanwhile, on the other side of the bunk, right in Alex's line of vision, she could see Brynn hugging Sarah—overdramatically. Brynn glanced at Alex just to make sure that, yes, Alex had seen the two of them bonding—*without* Alex. Alex smiled at Brynn. Alex didn't want Brynn to think she was getting to her, even if Brynn kind of was. To Alex, Color War was healthy competition; maybe it was a healthier way to work through their differences.

Heck, she'd tried everything else, hadn't she?

▲ ▲ ▲

Alex, Jenna, and Val headed out to the porch to work on a Blue Team cheer. Jenna was frantically racking her brain for a word that rhymed with "stupendous" when Alex heard a familiar voice.

"Too bad we're on different teams, Alex."

Alex looked up. Adam was making his way toward the bunk. She thought he was actually on his way somewhere else, but then he stopped and stood there like he wanted to talk. Alex was happy to see him, but she was also nervous. Something was up, definitely. She noticed the way he was sweating, too. Then he added, "So are you and Valerie both Blue?"

Something in Alex's brain clicked. Maybe Adam Spasm had been hanging around all of the time because of Valerie. *He likes her!* Alex thought. That made sense to

Alex—Valerie was confident, cool, outgoing, cute.

Adam and Val? Alex thought as she noticed an ant crawling across her sneaker.

"And Jenna, too," Alex said, her heart beating a little too hard. "We're going to *kill* the Reds."

Her *words* were confident. So why was her body shaking like the laundry spin cycle?

I do not want to think about crushes and stuff, she thought. *Especially not now. I need to focus.*

"*Maybe* you girls will survive without me," Adam joked, "but don't be so sure."

"Yeah, *maybe*!" Valerie called after him, shaking a fist menacingly.

"He's *so* weird," she said, once he had gone.

"Yeah, what was that!?" Jenna asked, being nosy.

"Right?" Alex asked. Her heart rate had returned to normal and the flush she'd felt in her cheeks had cooled. And Jenna seemed clueless that Alex had even been thinking . . .

Nothing! You were thinking nothing!

"Let's get back to that cheer," Val said, nudging them both. The small smile on her face suggested that *she* might have an idea what Alex was thinking.

Nothing, Alex reminded herself firmly. *Nothing at all.*

"And fifty points goes to the Blues for the singdown!"

Pete yelled. He smiled. His face was painted red, and he wore a headband with devil horns to show his spirit. Even though his team hadn't won the first competition, he was just as enthusiastic and happy for the Blues. He was a great sport.

Marissa, a Blue, turned to her team. "You guys rock."

"When you came up with song that had the word 'burger' in it, I was so impressed!" Marissa said to Alyssa.

"Cheeseburger in Paradise? A classic," Nat quipped, clapping her friend on the back good-naturedly. Alyssa only grinned, semi-embarrassed at her retro-music knowledge.

Alex, Jenna, Grace, Valerie, Natalie, Alyssa, and Chelsea had another competition together that day. They were on the same tug-o-war team. Alex knew that she'd be against Brynn and Sarah there. Brynn loved that game, and she had a will as strong as chain links.

"Don't worry about them," Valerie said as the teams lined up on either side of the thick, white rope. Val reminded Alex that they had to finish their wooden boxes—their gifts to their ex-friends—later that night during their evening free time. Working on a gift for Brynn was just about the last thing Alex wanted to do. "Whether you two are close friends again or not," Valerie explained, "with these gifts, at least you two won't be enemies."

"We'll be frenemies, instead," Alex said, wondering how she'd let Valerie talk her into this crazy gift idea.

"Are you talking about Brynn?" Chelsea said, interrupting.

Alex and Valerie immediately clammed up. They definitely didn't want Chelsea to get involved. Chelsea would surely think of a backhanded putdown or something—anything—wicked to say.

"Please. Like I don't know what's going on," Chelsea snorted.

"Nothing's going on," Alex insisted, looking across the thick competition rope for Brynn. Brynn was laughing—make that cackling—about something with Sarah.

Instead of getting sad, Alex got determined. The girls lined up for tug-o-war, bracing their legs and feet into the ground as if they could grow roots.

"On your mark, get set, go!" Julie yelled. She was the counselor-in-charge once again. She had on an all-red outfit, and had painted cat whiskers on her face. Alex didn't know what that had to do with anything, but it was funny.

"One, two, three!" Jenna yelled, telling them to all yank together. She was the anchor of the team, meaning she stood at the end of the rope, her feet and body leaning toward the earth. Jenna was the strongest of the group, so she was the unofficial team leader for that game.

The immediate strain on the rope knocked the wind out of Alex and dragged her off her feet, taking her completely by surprise. Her strength was draining away, as if the rope was actually sucking it out of her body.

Shake it off, she thought, determined to keep trying. Her grip was so tight that it burned. She looked up and saw Brynn's eyes shut, her face scrunched up into a wrinkled ball. Brynn loved tug-o-war, and it looked like she was about to win at it. Unbelievably, Alex's confidence sagged.

Slowly, the Red Team inched their way backward. The Blues' bottoms hit the ground as their last bit of sheer willpower washed away. They slid forward, defeated.

"Go, Red!" Julie yelled. "We rule!"

Brynn and Sarah and Candace and Jessie and Karen hugged one another. Tears nearly sprung from Alex's eyes. She couldn't believe the Blues had lost. She blamed herself because she hadn't tried hard enough. She couldn't believe that she was an outsider to her ex-best friend.

"It's okay," Jenna said. "None of them are good at basketball. They might as well take this win while they can get one."

"Except for Sarah, she's, like, good at everything," Chelsea said in a voice that was much more quiet than usual.

Chelsea was right—Sarah was a great athlete. But Alex team-hugged Jenna. Together, they wouldn't let the Reds win again.

I think I can, I think I can, Alex thought to herself.

I have to.

Alex started strategizing. She wondered and

calculated and figured what she'd have to do to get back in the right mindset to win. She thought of the Ninja Supertwins. In tug-o-war, she had her former best friend's determination and spirit. It was what she loved best about Brynn, and seeing it had made her wistful. That sad, longing feeling took away Alex's competitive edge. Alex was uncomfortable playing against Brynn; it was like an allergic reaction. It made her throat get thick and her head ache. Alex turned her thoughts to soccer that afternoon. It would be easier.

⛺ ⛺ ⛺

After lunch, the bunk headed off to the soccer field. Alex rubbed her temples. Her head thumped with a dull thud. As her mind wandered, Alex realized that she'd left her knapsack in the bunk. She figured she was just tired from the night before. *I'm fine,* she told herself. Then her head started to spin. She paused, glancing back toward the bunk.

"I, um, just have to grab one thing. I'll be back in five minutes," Alex said.

"Oh, no you don't," Natalie said, smiling and teasing Alex. "I know you don't really want to compete against Brynn again. I could see it during tug-o-war. But you're not bailing on us for soccer. We *need* you for soccer."

"I'll be right back, I just have to go—" Alex started to say.

"Let's go, girls! We're running late!" Julie

yelled. "Everyone on the soccer field! It's time for midfield shots."

"Midfield shots!" Candace yelled, crazy enthusiastic even though she wasn't so good at them.

Jenna cheered. Nat shrugged and winked at Alyssa. Grace and Valerie clapped like crazy because they were awesome cheerleaders.

Alex watched as Brynn and Sarah started frowning. Clearly, those two knew that the next round would be tougher for them than tug-o-war had been. Alex told herself to get excited and to do it fast. Soccer was her *thing*.

"Alex, you okay?" Julie asked, breaking into Alex's thoughts.

"I'm fine," Alex answered, even though her brain was throbbing as if a jackhammer was right next to her head.

"You sure? You seem tired," Julie added.

Before Julie could make a big deal out of anything, Alex turned toward her teammates.

"Okay, girls. I've got an idea. Here's how we're going to win," Alex said, drawing the Blue team into a huddle.

After, the girls, Blue and Red, lined up on opposite sides of the goal net. They would take turns kicking three-point shots, kind of like a game of H-O-R-S-E, but using a soccer ball and with points. Everyone had three turns. If you hit either edge of the net, you got one point. Hitting the edge of the goal got your team two points. Scoring a goal was three full points. At the end of the game, the points were dropped, but the winning team added a full twenty-five to their team's overall total.

Alex forgot that she needed her knapsack and willed her headache to calm down so she could concentrate. It didn't matter if Brynn was prancing around with Sarah. It didn't matter if they were on opposite teams. It didn't matter if she was still getting over Brynn's decision to be mad at her. Alex still loved being the athlete. She figured she deserved to shine in her element.

She deserved to win.

"You can do it, Brynn," Sarah yelled as her friend stood poised to kick.

Alex didn't get down this time like she had during tug-o-war. She stood there, watching what Brynn would do with the ball, and she thought of the day as a competition, not as anything to do with the breakup of their years of friendship.

Brynn tried to look focused, but she kept glancing over at Alex. Alex was glassy-eyed, staring at Brynn's kicks instead of looking directly at Brynn. Brynn missed all of them.

Alex was up next. Valerie and Jenna patted her back and told Alex how awesome she was before she made her way to the line. Alex dribbled the ball nine times before going for her first kick.

Sure!

Her team cheered because she'd made a goal, scoring three whole points. Alex's heart pounded. She was so intent on scoring nine points that she didn't pay attention to anything else. Her energy had drained. Her breath was short. Her heart fluttered.

She thought she was just pumped to win.

She dribbled ten more times, slowly, her eyes never leaving the net. She lifted her right foot to launch the ball into the perfect position in the air. On one side, her team members stood in anxious silence—giving Alex the moral support she needed to concentrate. On the other side, the girls screamed and yelled, trying to break her thoughts and her lucky streak.

Alex felt like she was in a movie. She could see both teams of girls moving in slow motion, the outlines of their faces and bodies going grainy, like a blurry photograph.

Alex didn't think anything of how fuzzy she was getting. She thought it was just the buzz of adrenaline. She didn't realize what was happening.

She didn't realize she was going down.

Hard.

chapter EIGHT

"Oh my God!" Brynn yelled.

Alex could barely make out her former friend's voice through her haze. Through tiny slits in her mostly closed eyes, she saw Brynn's face hovering anxiously overhead.

The rest of the girls were stiff with worry. Valerie looked on the verge of tears. Jenna ran off, yelling to the others that she was going to the infirmary to get the nurse. Sarah stood back, uncertain. In a surprise move, Chelsea hovered nervously at Alex's side.

"Where's your knapsack?!" Julie asked, about to hyperventilate herself. "We need your knapsack."

"She left it in the bunk," Valerie yelled, pulling herself together.

"I know where it is, I'll get it," Chelsea said, running off before anyone else could do it.

Julie patted Alex's face gently, trying to keep her awake.

"Alex, honey, come on. Don't pass out. Stay awake. We're here, and we're going to take care of you. Help us out by staying awake, honey," Julie said.

Julie was trying to stay calm, but it was clear that she was worried. Her hands were shaking uncontrollably. "Come on. You can do it.

"Jenna went to the infirmary, right?" Julie asked, turning to the rest of the group.

"Yeah, what can we do? Just tell us what to do!" Valerie asked, pacing around Alex.

"What's wrong with her, Julie?" Brynn asked, desperation in her voice. "What's wrong?"

Brynn's face was turning blotchy red. Brynn was much more upset than anyone else—and she wasn't even being overdramatic for once.

Sweaty and breathless, Chelsea appeared back on the scene, Alex's navy blue backpack in her hands. Julie grabbed it, and she fished around frantically inside. She pulled out the little tablets that Valerie had seen earlier and also a small bottle of water.

"Alex," Julie said, breathing fast and quick. "Keep your eyes open, just keep them open for me. I'll take care of you. We'll take care of you."

"What? What happened?" Alex murmured softly as she kinda-sorta began to wake up.

"Oh thank God," Julie said, her voice quivering. Sweat drops lined the sides of Julie's face. "Open your mouth."

"Look under my bed," Alex mumbled to Brynn, who was sitting on the ground just to Alex's left side. Alex's eyelids fluttered as if she were having a super difficult time keeping them open. "My kit's there."

Brynn wiped the tears from her eyes. Her shoulders were slumped—so unlike her usual confident stance—as she ran off toward the bunk in a blur.

Julie pried open Alex's mouth and placed an unwrapped candy between Alex's lips. Then Julie poured water, also from Alex's knapsack, over the candy and into Alex's mouth. A whole lot of the liquid ran down the sides of Alex's face. But her eyes began to stay open, and her eyelids stopped fluttering so much.

Just seconds later, the nurse arrived with an oxygen tank and a couple of counselors. Brynn was not back yet.

"Good job, Julie, good job," the nurse said. "I'm really impressed. Now, girls, please step back." The nurse whispered something gently to Alex. The counselors whisked Alex away to the infirmary. She was mumbling to them, "Did we win? Did we win?"

The rest of the girls rushed to Julie, and Julie struggled to catch her breath. Her forehead was sweating, and she leaned over her knees, trying to get herself together. Brynn arrived on the scene with a little white medicine box, totally out of breath.

"I don't think I've ever been so scared in my life," Julie said, more to herself than to the girls. "That was close."

"What's wrong with her?! What's wrong with Alex?!" Brynn yelled, upset.

"The nurse has her, Brynn," Julie said, patting her back. "And now she has her kit, too. She's going to be okay now."

"Are you sure?" Valerie asked. She paced around the group of girls, rubbing the palms of her hands together.

"She has juvenile diabetes," Chelsea said, interrupting. She sat down on the ground and rubbed her temples.

"How did *you* know?" Julie asked surprised. "She didn't tell anyone."

"My cousin has it," Chelsea said. "It's awful. Really awful."

"So you knew about Alex this whole time, and you still always give her a hard time about eating snacks?" Valerie asked, clearly annoyed.

"I didn't know!" Chelsea said, still not making eye contact with anyone. "I just figured it out when I saw the tablets Julie put in Alex's mouth. I swear! I didn't know until a second ago!" With that, she stood up and ran back to the bunk.

▲ ▲ ▲

"An insulin kit, thank you, dear," Nurse Helen said, taking Alex's box from Brynn and placing it on an empty cot.

Brynn had raced Alex's kit to the infirmary. Now she stood awkwardly next to Alex's bed.

"Luckily, I also have this stuff on hand here. So do me a favor, and make sure you put this back exactly where you found it. And Alex, no more Twinkies for you, okay?"

"Okay," Alex muttered softly. Her voice was tired. She hadn't regained her normal strength yet, but at least she wasn't dizzy anymore.

"Hi," she said weakly, turning to Brynn.

"Hey, girl," Brynn said, reaching for Alex's hand.

Alex let her take it—she was in no position to do anything else. Alex's heart beat hard. She really didn't know what to say to Brynn. She did know that somehow, she was relieved to see Brynn there at the infirmary. Deep down, Alex knew that Brynn would get over whatever was eating her brain lately. Alex knew that Brynn would come through for her if she really needed her to. And Alex needed her to right then.

"Is it too late to say I'm sorry?" Brynn asked, rubbing Alex's thumb the way Alex's mother might have done if she were there.

"For what?" Alex asked, winking at Brynn.

"I've been so awful," Brynn said, her eyes tearing up for about the fifth time in the last thirty minutes. "I love you. You really had me worried just now! I couldn't bear to think that I had been so mean to you—while you were so sick!"

"I'm not that sick," Alex said. Slowly, the energy was flowing back into her veins. Her body was acting like she'd been at a slumber party all night—and hadn't slept a wink. But other than that, Alex felt okay. It definitely helped that Brynn was there—and ready to reconcile.

"You have diabetes, though!"

"I do?" Alex asked, feigning shock.

"I'm so serious! I'm not making a joke. You looked like you could've died," Brynn said, moving her head around as if she were on stage.

"Oh, I just shouldn't have eaten all that junk last night," Alex said, waving her hand as if to say *pppshaw*! "And I didn't get a shot this morning like I usually do."

"So that's where you go every day before we clean the cabin!" Brynn said, her hands in the air.

"Yes, and you thought I was staying after breakfast to help Pete," Alex answered, smirking. "That's what everyone thought, or so I hoped. Even if it meant getting teased by Chelsea."

"It all makes so much sense now," Brynn said, rubbing her forehead. "But why didn't you just tell me? When did this happen? Last year you ate all kinds of junk!"

"I got diagnosed last fall. I was tired and thirsty all the time," Alex said, a serious expression on her face. "The doctor said I'd have to totally change my diet and get shots once a day, so that's what I've been doing."

"I'm so embarrassed that you didn't think you could tell me. When you stopped eating snacks even I thought—"

"Eating disorder," Alex said, lying in the cot and turning her gaze to look out the window. "Or some weird soccer diet. I know."

"I can't believe you! Why didn't you just tell us?" Brynn asked, her voice louder. "The bunk, I mean. We would've understood. I definitely would've understood."

"First of all, everyone at school back home knows about it, and it's like I get all this attention that I don't want," Alex said, sitting up on the cot as her energy returned more and more.

She continued, "I don't want anyone to feel sorry for me, and I don't want to be known as the girl with diabetes like I am at home.

"It's so much better here. I mean, I'm just known for being good at soccer. What could be better than that?"

"Oh my God, Alex!" Brynn said, turning her voice down as the nurse looked her way. "You don't have to be perfect all the time. We would've understood—and we would've still thought you were our resident Mia Hamm. I don't get it."

"But I really don't want to cause any trouble or extra fuss. I just want things to go smoothly—and if everyone knew, I thought it would be a big deal or something," Alex explained, surprised at how relieved she was that she didn't have to hide it anymore. She was just sorry her bunkmates found out the way they did. Especially sorry since she passed out—she had a bruise on her butt where she smacked down onto the soccer field.

"I know I haven't been the best example of this lately," Brynn said, "but your friends accept you for who you are. If you have an issue—*hello,* I have about a hundred—that just makes you more interesting. I'm so sorry I was so jealous and awful to you the past few days. I thought you were choosing Valerie and Julie and your woodshop friends over me. I was just worried that you were about to dump me, and I shouldn't have acted the way I did."

"Brynn, I would never do that to you!" Alex said. "I just wanted to do my own thing—like hang out with Julie sometimes and play more soccer. But all my free time was supposed to be with you."

"I know, I know. I wasn't very nice at all. Are you going to hate me forever? Because I'm pretty sure that I would hate me forever if I were in your shoes. I mean, when I saw you passed out just now—like you were going to die or something—I have never felt so guilty and evil and awful in my whole life. I'll never act like that again. Not to anyone. Ever."

"Stop it, I'm so serious," Alex said, blushing.

Her heart was beating a lot now, but because she was happy. She could tell by the concern in Brynn's eyes that she had gotten her old best friend back. Alex couldn't have been more thrilled. At least something good had come out of her diabetic breakdown.

Alex wouldn't let herself get that bad again—she just had to be better at watching what she ate! She would definitely stay away from the sugary treats. Julie and the others always had Alex in the kitchen to make sure there were enough diabetes-friendly goodies for her. Alex would stick to those foods—special puddings and cookies and candies made with artificial sweeteners—from now on.

Valerie and Sarah burst through the door, not even giving Helen a chance to stop them.

"Are you okay?" they asked in unison. They were panting, so it was difficult to understand what else they were trying to say.

"She's fine," Brynn said, explaining the insulin kit and Alex's drop in blood sugar that caused her to pass out and everything else she had just learned at the infirmary.

"She'll be fine, as long as you girls don't encourage her to eat sweets—*no more Twinkies*," Nurse Helen interrupted. "She can even leave now if she wants to."

"Really?!!!" Alex sprang out of her cot, and she tied her sneakers. She was ready to go canoeing.

"Take it easy today—no more sports in Color War, Alex," the nurse said. "And I want you to stop in before bed tonight."

"You've got to be kidding me!" Alex felt her heart sink. What was the point of Color War if she couldn't play sports?

"I have a feeling you'd make a great coach tomorrow," Nurse Helen said. "You have to do it. You have to give you body time to recover. You just went into diabetic shock, Alex Kim. You're lucky you're not in the hospital."

"Ahh man, that's not good," Brynn whispered into Alex's ear.

"Ugh, I know, I know," she answered, knowing she'd just have to deal. The soccer episode had scared her to death. And she didn't want to go through that again. She'd do what she could to help the Blues from the sidelines. At least she could still play Scrabble.

One good thing: Alex had always been stopping by the infirmary to get her blood sugar levels checked—and to get her daily shot. She was tired of sneaking around and super relieved that she wouldn't have to do it ever again. The four girls joined hands and headed back to 3C.

Together.

chapter NINE

Alex passing out on the soccer field had made everyone want to get along. All the girls were so scared—a few of them worried that Alex was really and truly dead for a moment—that everyone wanted to reaffirm their friendships. It became clear that things could change for the worse in an instant. And in the midst of that change, the girls realized that they wanted to be nicer. After all, there were only three more days left of camp.

Sarah and Valerie had a long talk that night. Sarah wanted to work things out with Valerie once and for all. It turned out that Sarah was upset when Valerie hadn't signed up for ceramics with her, and Valerie had honestly forgotten that she had said she'd spend the last free-choice period with Sarah. Sarah had started hanging out with Brynn just to get her back, and Brynn was trying to get back at Alex. It had turned into a complicated, nasty, nonfriendly mess for everyone.

"When we're mad at each other in the future, let's promise to talk it out instead of all of this dissing," Valerie said, attaching another carved wooden elephant to her bunk.

"Let's call ourselves the Twinkies," Alex joked.

The other girls shifted uncomfortably. Since they all had found out that Alex had juvenile diabetes, they learned that her body couldn't process sugar. They also figured out that Jenna's Twinkies the night before had probably set off Alex's diabetic attack. But no one blamed Jenna. They didn't blame Alex, either. Chelsea hadn't even piped in to offer her "advice" on what had happened. In fact, she'd been sitting on her bed by herself. Karen was starting to hang around with Natalie and Alyssa more, and Chelsea didn't seem one bit happy. Her lips were pursed and her eyes creased as she brushed her hair and pulled it into ponytails using a small hand mirror.

"It's just a joke," Alex said, laughing at their wide-eyed, afraid-to-laugh expressions. "It was meant to be funny!"

"I thought it was funny!" Candace said, laughing.

"I don't care what you all call us," Natalie said. She'd seen many friendship feuds in her private school in Manhattan. Though she would never have gotten in the other girls' business, she was more relieved than anyone to see the bunk work out their differences. "As long as you take care of yourself."

"Alex, that just can't happen again," Jenna said,

changing into a pair of pajamas. Jenna had been trying to share her goodies with Alex all summer (and the summer before that). She had almost a nauseous gurgle in her stomach about it. She could've killed Alex—and she almost did yesterday. "It just can't happen again."

"It won't, I promise," Alex said, coming over to hug her friend.

They went to bed, all getting along. Tomorrow was the last day of Color War, and even though it wouldn't be the same without playing sports, Alex looked forward to much more friendly competitions.

▲ ▲ ▲

The second day of Color War was amazing. Chelsea and Alex kicked some tail at Scrabble, and Jenna kicked some butt of her own in basketball.

In the Scrabble competition that morning, Alex knew it was something they could do. Last year, she and Chelsea had picked off campers—like Gaby from 3A and Trevor from 3F—left and right. Obviously Alex and Chelsea weren't exactly friends, but when they had to, the two girls could work together. They had team spirit.

And Nurse Helen was right, the Blues in Alex's division needed a good coach—and the counselors were willing to let Alex take over. So that day, Alex stood on the sidelines strategizing, and her team always ran back to her for advice. She was so happy because she had still gotten her sports fix. And her Blues had done a terrific job that day. According to Alex's point calculations, she had an idea of which team had won. But sometimes there were surprises—like the deduction Dr. Steve had taken for the overzealous Reds who had woken up the camp—so Alex had to wait until the banquet later that day to see the final tally.

But first, there was a play to see!

Brynn and Grace's play! Alex thought, excited. She couldn't wait to see her friends on stage.

"Okay, makeover time!" Natalie called. Natalie had a makeup kit the size of a tackle box. She'd gotten it from her famous dad's super-famous model girlfriend. It was so fancy—Alex figured the products had come straight from Rodeo Drive in Beverly Hills.

"Me!" Jenna yelled, surprising everyone. She was such a huge jock—and she didn't usually care about those things.

"Are you kidding?" Natalie said, laughing.

"Well, just a little bit of blush," Jenna answered, blushing naturally. "I thought it might be fun to try for a change."

"I'm doing my own," Alyssa said. She liked to wear black mascara really, really thick on special occasions. Candace, Jessie, and Sarah got in line next. Grace had gone first. She had the lead female part of Wendy—a *huge gigantic deal* because usually the leads went to the older kids. Grace had been so excited the past few days that she'd been waking up extra early. Brynn was excited, too—she was a Lost Boy—but she didn't have trouble sleeping in. Brynn had busily done her own eyes, cheeks, and even hair. She loved doing that stuff before her plays.

Both Grace and Brynn were already backstage, preparing for their debut. All day long, their mouths had been moving silently as they went over their lines. They were so worried that they would forget something or say the wrong line when it really mattered. The two drama divas had huddled together and seemed nervous at breakfast, especially Grace who hadn't done as much acting as Brynn had in the past. Brynn taught Grace her deep yoga breaths, and everyone laughed at them as they chanted, "*Ooooommmm. Ooooommmm. Ooooommmm.*"

Chelsea had a pink dress with tiny little flowers that was way fancier than what anyone else had brought. Natalie let a few of the girls, including Alex, borrow her extra skirts. Alex hadn't even brought a skirt to camp—she never did. She paired Natalie's jean skirt with one of her navy blue polo-style shirts, and checked herself in the mirror. While the other girls were cuted up with makeup and lip gloss, Alex went plain-faced. She loved being *au naturel*. Her only concession was to let Nat take out her ponytail and fluff her hair up with some gel. She dabbed on some moisturizer and was ready to go. She grabbed Valerie, and the two of them—the first ones ready in the bunk—were good to go.

"Sarah, hurry up!" Valerie said as Alex pulled her by the arm to wait for everyone outside by the door. She was impatient—like everyone else in the bunk—and ready to party!

Sarah was still standing in front of the wall-sized mirror in the hot, humid bathroom that really did need a good cleaning.

"I'm almost done!" Sarah yelled, seeing her friends heading off without her.

"It's okay. Take your time," Alex said, sitting down to wait for her friend. Sarah was soft-spoken, but very cool. She made these quiet, dry remarks that cracked Alex up.

Alex had forgotten how well she and Sarah had gotten along earlier in the summer—before Brynn went wacky on her. Alex didn't like to think about how hurt she'd been just a few days before. It was all over, and she was trying to forget. There was no sense in dwelling on the bad.

Just twenty more minutes, and Alex would see Brynn and Grace up there on stage.

"So, how do I look?" Julie asked, twirling around. Her shoulders sparkled because of all the glitter lotion she had on.

"You don't look like you're going to a play! You look like you belong in a music video," Alex said, rushing over to Julie with the rest of the girls.

"I think she's going on a date," Val said as Sarah looked at her, winking.

Julie's face turned bright red. Alex was standing next

to her counselor—the one who'd secretly counseled Alex about her diabetes all summer long—and Alex noticed that Julie's skin was hot.

"You're awfully excited to see *Peter Pan* tonight. Don't you think?" Alex asked, teasing Julie.

Julie had been such a fantastic friend to Alex. She was always reminding Alex to get her insulin shots from Nurse Helen and making sure that none of the other girls heard her. Julie had tried to get Alex to tell her friends about her problem, but when Alex didn't want to, Julie respected Alex's decision.

Instead, Julie had Alex hang out in the kitchen a lot because the other counselors knew about her condition and accepted her for it. Julie figured that Alex needed a few friends who understood. She also wanted to make sure that Alex got enough to eat. Julie was always slipping Alex celery sticks and carrots and other snacks that Alex was allowed to have.

"I'm seeing my 'date' at the show!" Julie exclaimed, her blue eyes sparkling more than her shoulders.

"Who? Who?" Alex yelled.

"You have to tell us!" Valerie said, chiming in.

"Come on—just tell us!" Sarah begged.

"Oh, please," Chelsea added sarcastically, rolling her eyes. No one paid any attention to her.

"You'll find out soon enough," Julie said, spraying on just a tiny bit of perfume—too much, and the mosquitoes would eat her alive. Then she headed out the door.

The rest of the girls followed, going straight to the rec hall where *Peter Pan* was about to debut.

▲ ▲ ▲

The music came out of a CD player, but it was still amazing. The instrumentals were light and airy, as if Tinker Bell herself had been playing them. Grace did a fantastic job in her role of Wendy. Alex loved how Grace made Wendy a lot more punk and hip than she was in the original. Grace wore leg warmers and had a pink ponytail extension in her hair. But that was just like Grace; she had a way of livening everything up. Whenever she spoke on stage that night, the rest of Camp Lakeview—nearly four hundred kids—literally went silent to hear her.

Not to be left out of the spotlight, Brynn did a great job as Peter Pan's right-hand man, as well. She played Nibs, the Lost Boy who was the main character's smart and debonair best friend. Alex laughed when Tinker Bell, played by a tiny eight-year-old girl, sometimes acted like she had a crush on Nibs. Brynn's Nibs never noticed anything but his best friend—Peter Pan—and followed Peter's every order. Alex figured all those yoga breaths that Brynn did were helpful—she didn't miss one line. She even delivered her words in a brisk, deep boyish tone. Alex was astonished at how Brynn could transform herself on stage. She was so girlie in real life but such a boy when she needed to play one.

Grace's real-life crush Devon played the minor part

of another Lost Boy. Sparks flew when Grace was on the stage with him (though Grace did a good job of acting like she had a thing for the boy who played Peter Pan, too). But Grace and Devon were so flirtatious and sweet that Valerie kept nudging Alex. They'd had a thing for each other for a while—that much was clear just by the way they interacted on stage.

What does it feel like to have a crush? Alex asked herself. *I don't think I get it.*

"Oh my God, did you see those two?" Val whispered in a hushed, high voice of pure disbelief. "They are so into each other!"

Alex couldn't help herself: She thought of Adam and wondered if she would ever have a crush. She just knew he liked Valerie, and she had to admit she was a little disappointed by that, which made no sense, not even to her.

Just then, the kid playing Michael, Wendy Darling's youngest, most rambunctious brother, knocked down a ten-foot cardboard ship. It was an accident, but a big one. Once the ship came down, the other set pieces—a tree, a fake crocodile, a few hooks lying around—also came down.

Alex gasped. Her heart started to sink. All of the hard work that Grace and Brynn and the rest of the cast had done was brought down into shambles.

For a moment, everyone on stage froze. It was as though no one knew what to do.

Then Grace stepped forward.

"It is now time for our intermission," she said, pulling the curtain closed. She shoved another kid, a seven-year-old girl who played Nana the dog, in front of the closed curtain. The kid stared, wide-eyed, looking as if she were about to cry. But just when everyone was least expecting it, Grace peeked her head out of the curtain and whispered something to the pint-sized dog. Then the dog started singing the song, "You Are My Sunshine." The audience—especially Alex, Valerie, and Sarah—laughed so hard that their heads almost exploded.

"Grace is awesome," Alex said, her face getting sore from so much giggling.

A few minutes later, the show went on, as the ship and other set pieces had been set back up (though they weren't as straight as they had been before). Even with a minor catastrophe, Camp Lakeview's *Peter Pan* had turned out great. It was definitely the best thing Alex had seen there.

She was so impressed with the actors—they had put so much emotion into their lines. And the set was cool, too; Sarah and Brynn had a done a fantastic job painting everything and setting it up. Alex couldn't help but think that Brynn would be a great set designer one day if she ever wanted to go that route. Brynn would be great at anything she set her mind to.

When Grace came out to take a bow after the show was over, the audience roared. Brynn bowed right after her, and Alex stood up and started a standing ovation. Since Alex was the first out of her seat, she could see clear to the back of the room. She nudged Valerie and couldn't help but point.

"Do you see that?" Alex said, jumping up and down, for the show and for what she was witnessing.

"Oh my goodness!" Valerie said, turning bright red.

"They are so cute together," Alex said, tugging on Valerie and Sarah's arms.

Julie was sitting in the back of the room holding hands with their woodworking instructor, Jeremy. They two of them were nuzzling like love-struck puppies. Julie had never looked sparklier—and it wasn't from the lotion she had borrowed from the girls in 3C.

The applause continued throughout the drama shack. All the kids—four hundred of them—were standing and cheering for the young actors. Still smiling, Alex turned to watch Brynn and Grace take their final bows as Nibs and Wendy from *Peter Pan*.

Alex was so proud of them.

chapter TEN

After the play, Alex rushed to the stage to hug Brynn and Grace. Then she rushed to the mess hall with Natalie and Alyssa because she was helping with the banquet dinner. She helped pull several pans of vegetable lasagna and several more pans of meat lasagna out of the oven.

Pasta was especially good for kids with diabetes—the sugar released more slowly into their bodies—and so were vegetables. So she picked her favorites to help everyone make with the meal: green beans cooked with bacon, salad with cheese, and honey cookies for dessert. (She could have those because honey was better for her than other kinds of sugar.)

Alex was more careful about what she ate than most kids with diabetes were. She figured out when she was first diagnosed that if she watched her food carefully—saying no to all the yummy stuff she really wanted to eat—she didn't have to get as many insulin shots during the day. She was down to one per day, and she didn't have to sneak off to see Nurse Helen anymore. Now that everyone knew, she could walk there without making excuses. She realized how much more relaxed she was with the counselors' support, and without having to hide or sneak off and make excuses. And most of all, without someone like Chelsea tormenting her every other day.

When Alex worked in the kitchen, she was happier than ever. She and Brynn were better. Valerie and Sarah had patched things up. The play had been awesome. And even she had to admit it: Color War was still fun, even from the sidelines.

She was suddenly surprised by a towel that snapped in her direction. The whip of it just barely missed her right knee. Pete was at the other end of the weapon, laughing his face off.

"I *know* you're not really going to get me with that thing," Alex said, grabbing a goofy-looking hairnet. She was required to wear it whenever she helped out. Pete and the others had them on, too.

"So I hear you whipped some tail at Scrabble this morning," he said, turning around to stir a huge bubbly pot of bright red tomato sauce that was making a mess all over his stove. Alex thought she had better taste it. Pete wasn't the best cook—someone might have to sneak in and fix that sauce so it didn't wind up tasting like

Play-Doh. He was busy fixing extra spaghetti in case the campers ate up all the lasagna.

"I did pretty well!" Alex answered, grabbing a towel to snap him. If she got his attention away from the pot, she'd be able to sneak in and taste the sauce.

"More than *well*," Pete said, snapping her back as she washed her hands, preparing to dunk her finger.

What Pete said was true. Alex had taken the entire Scrabble tournament that morning. She had beaten the older kids, the counselors, even Chelsea. And she was beaming about it.

She didn't want to brag or anything, so she tried really hard to beam inwardly. The thing with Chelsea had been pretty easy. They wound up playing against each other in their division—after they'd already won for the Blues. So they played it out to see who could be the ultimate winner.

Alex, Natalie, Candace, and Alyssa helped Pete and the other cooks in the kitchen for fifteen more minutes before dinner was finally ready. Alex chopped while Marissa scrambled in and out to finish setting the tables. Alex couldn't wait to sit with her friends and have fun at the formal banquet that night.

"Alex, do you want me to save you a seat?" Brynn yelled into the kitchen.

"Yes, please!" Alex yelled, taking off her hairnet and rushing out to hang with her friends.

"Where do you think you're going?" Pete asked,

pretending that he was about to flip sauce onto her navy blue shirt.

"I gotta eat," she yelled, knowing that she was done for the night. She had helped plan and prepare, and now she just wanted to have some fun.

In honor of the banquet, the mess hall had been completely transformed. All of the banners that different campers had made for Color War were plastered across the wall, and red and blue streamers hung from the rafters. A centerpiece of red and blue balloons had been placed on top of every table. The entire room was abuzz with excitement—the fun and glamour of being dressed up for a special occasion, as well as the imminent announcement of the winners of Color War had everyone hopped-up like three-year-olds on a sugar rush.

"I'm sure everyone wants to know which team won the Color War," Dr. Steve said, stepping up to the front of the room with a devilish glint in his eye. Everyone clapped and cheered in anticipation. "It should be no surprise to anyone that the victors were. . . the Blues!"

The campers went crazy, stamping their feet and pounding on their tables. Dr. Steve laughed. "The point totals were . . ."—he paused, dragging the moment out for all it was worth—"Red, three-seventy-five. And Blue . . . four hundred!"

The room shook with noise and energy. The Blues—what sounded like six thousand of them—whooped and hollered. The Reds booed in good nature. They were pretty upset, because if they hadn't broken Color War rules by raiding the camp the first morning—and losing twenty-five points for their team—then there would have been a tie.

"Ha! In your faces, Red!" Chelsea shouted, pumping her fist in the air.

"No one lost, Chelsea," Brynn said. "Not really."

Green beans and dinner rolls were thrown through the air until the Julie and Marissa convinced everyone to stop before the mayhem got out of hand. Alex was glad there wasn't a food fight that particular night: She had her good clothes on for once in her life!

As the Most Valuable Players were announced—in their division, Jenna was named for the Blues—everyone cheered some more. Alex was glad that Jenna had won. Jenna had played a great game of basketball earlier that day and she had two more overall points than Alex did. When Jenna got her award—an MVP necklace made out of clay—Alex clapped the hardest.

"And we can't forget Alex Kim," Julie announced, still all rosy-cheeked. She stood up at the front of 3C's table. "She is our top-winning Scrabble player *ever*." With that announcement, Alex turned the color of a lobster and picked up a ceramic necklace Julie had made just for the occasion. The gift was so thoughtful that Alex almost cried. Even if she hadn't been able to be in ceramics for her last free choice, she still got the necklace she had wanted to make.

The winners—the Blue team—got up to serve the chocolate chip cookies to all of the losers. Alex only ate one—others had three, four, or five—and no one gave Alex any trouble about it. Not even Chelsea, who had seemingly made up with Karen. They were sitting together at the end of the table, laughing and talking. Karen was doing *a lot* of talking!

Chelsea didn't seem to mind too much. She turned to Alex. "I'm glad you're feeling better, even if I do think you cheat at Scrabble."

Alex smiled despite herself. Chelsea could always be counted on to be . . . well, Chelsea. It was almost endearing.

The mood was happy but quiet as the girls, totally exhausted but running on adrenaline, made their way back to the bunk for the last night at camp. Alex was satisfied that she had learned a lot that summer—about bullies and sports and Twinkies and friendships.

Did I learn anything about crushes? she wondered as she saw Adam walking with Jenna, whispering to her about something. They saw her looking at them, and they started coming her way. Her heart sped up by about a hundred beats.

"So, um, Adam," Alex said, her voice quivering from way too many nerves, "I heard you won blob tag for the Blues. Congrats!"

"Thanks. Can I talk to you?" he asked, his eyes serious and wide.

"Um, I guess. What do you want?"

"Uh, excuse me," Jenna said, a tad overly loud. "I have to talk to . . . Natalie!" She turned her whole body away to "subtly" give Alex and Adam some privacy.

But why? Alex wondered.

"I just, um, wanted to see if you'd be here next summer?" Adam asked her, while he bent down to tie his shoelaces. Alex could see that his hands were trembling. *Why are his hands trembling?*

"I'm here every summer. They're good about catering to kids with diabetes here, kids like me," she answered, proud to be talking about her condition in the open. She wished she had just blurted the truth out before—her summer could've been a lot easier. "I can't wait to come back here."

"Me neither," he said, looking at her.

"Cool, see you later!" Alex said, smiling as she took off toward her friends in 3C. *Next summer will be even better!* she thought.

chapter ELEVEN

"You what?" Natalie was screaming when Alex got back into the bunk.

"I broke up with Trevor," Alyssa said. "It's the end of the summer. Why not?"

"You're such a heartbreaker!" Natalie teased Alyssa, throwing her pillow at her best-camp-friend.

"It's about time it's that way around," Alyssa answered, flipping her Day-Glo hair up into a high, messy ponytail. "I was so bummed when Adam told me said he just wanted to be friends."

Alyssa looked directly at Alex, meeting her eyes. Alex froze, but luckily, Alyssa just smiled and looked away.

Adam dumped Alyssa? Why? Alex asked herself. This certainly put a new and confusing spin on things. Alex figured she wouldn't think about it anymore. This stuff just wasn't her business.

Before Alyssa could get another word in,

Natalie dove into her bed headfirst. "I can't believe the summer is over!" she whined.

"Oh, Simon, how I love thee!" Grace teased. *"I can't go back to Manhattan without you! My dahhhlling!"*

"My dahhhhhhling!" Candace yelled, getting a laugh from the rest of the bunk.

Another pillow flew into Alyssa's face, knocking her off balance and into her sheets.

"Oh, stop it," Alyssa said to everyone. "Natalie will see Simon in the fall."

"Really?" Grace asked, still beaming from her performance as Wendy. She looked happier than she had all summer.

Grace had something else to be proud of, too: She'd caught up on all of the summer homework her parents had given her. She'd be heading back to school well-prepared in the fall. Her bunkmates had enjoyed helping her when she couldn't get through a book like *Call of the Wild*. Alex had really liked getting to know Grace better. Alex was going to miss her!

"I hope we get to hang out," Natalie said. "He lives in Westport, Connecticut. That's close to New York City. We think we'll hang out in September."

Her facial expression got all dreamy. Alex was pretty sure she wasn't ready to get *that* into a boy.

"Brynn, will you be auditioning for all the school plays?" Natalie asked, clearly trying to get the attention off her romantic possibilities.

"Um, yeah, and Grace is going to audition for parts at her school, too," Brynn added while doing a post-drama-production sun salutation, a yoga move.

Brynn told Alex that it helped her calm down. Alex was used to Brynn's moves.

In the other corner of the room, Valerie was talking to Chelsea, and Karen was standing there, too. Alex definitely wanted to get the full story later.

When the excitement died down, and that took at least twenty minutes after all those honey cookies everyone had eaten, Valerie ran over to Alex and hugged her. She added, "You didn't forget, did you?"

"Of course not!" Alex reached around under her bed and dug into the large suitcase to find a few sacks she had hidden there. Inside the sacks were two wooden boxes. "Now is the perfect time."

Valerie grabbed Brynn and Sarah. The three of them came over to Alex and walked just outside the bunk.

"Don't go too far, girls," Julie yelled.

"We have to give out the bunk awards next! Alex, I think you might be getting one . . ." Marissa teased from the bathroom mirror where she was fixing her hair.

"Okay," Alex said, trembling. "This is for you." She handed one sack to Brynn.

"And this is for you," Valerie said, handing the other one to Sarah.

Both girls looked puzzled. The girls tore into them. Once they realized what the gifts were, they shrieked with excitement. "This is amazing!" Brynn said as she opened and closed the box. Hers had flowers carved on it. The wood was cedar, and Brynn stuck her nose in to take a whiff and went, "Ahhh."

"It is. But why did you do this?" Sarah said, admiring the stars and moons that were carved on her wooden box.

"There's one more, actually," Alex said, feeling suddenly shy. She dashed back into the bunk, pulled another bag out, and rushed back outside to hand it to a very surprised Valerie.

"One for me, too?" Valerie asked, bewildered. Her box had a simple, round elephant carved on it.

"Valerie, you are awesome. Yours is a huge thank-you," Alex said, hugging her friend. She looked at the other girls.

"Brynn and Sarah, Valerie and I made these thinking that they would help us all make up and be nice to one another again—it was a gift we wanted to give you." Alex blushed, feeling like she was in an after-school television special. "Valerie thought of doing it. She's the generous one, not me," Alex said, admiring Valerie's cornrows that were piled festively on top of her head. "She's also the talented one, I mean, she taught me *how*."

Brynn wiped tears from her eyes—she really could cry on cue—and ran over to hug Alex. "This means so much to me. I'm so sorry for everything the past few weeks."

"Stop it. That's so yesterday!" Alex yelled. "I'm just glad you like it!"

Brynn reached over and hugged Valerie, too. But she had to wait her turn. Sarah was saying something to Valerie that got Valerie all teary-eyed.

"Enough of this sappy stuff," Alex said, wanting to party and not get sad. She would miss her camp friends *sooo* much.

"Wait, Alex," Brynn answered. "You're the only one without one of these!"

"No, she's not," Valerie said, smiling from cornrow to cornrow. "Here you go, girl." Valerie handed Alex a wooden jewelry box with soccer balls carved on it.

"You are too much!" Alex said, hugging Valerie.

She did feel like these girls knew her well. She didn't have anything to hide. She was sure that this summer she had belonged at Camp Lakeview. She really wanted to cry because she was so happy. But she held back—she wanted to celebrate, not get sappy.

After the gift exchange, Alex, Valerie, Brynn, and Sarah went back inside the bunk with the rest of 3C.

"Snack time!" Jenna yelled, pulling out a small cardboard box—the last of her snack stash.

Alex's throat tightened because that was her conditioned response. Every time Jenna had snacks, Alex would have to dodge them.

But then her muscles relaxed all over. This time was different because everyone finally knew the whole truth.

"Alex, you first," Jenna said.

Alex's throat tightened again—this time because she was surprised. Jenna knew she couldn't have any.

Alex's face scrunched up. She had hoped that awkward moments like this one were in the past. She thought it was all over!

"Just look in the box! Go on," Jenna chided, smiling and giggling. The other girls stood back like they were all in on a joke.

Alex looked in and she saw packs of sugar-free pudding. Her face broke out into an enormous grin. She reached in and took one, along with a spoon. The other girls waited their turn.

"We want you to know we love you," Brynn said, passing out the sugar-free treats to everyone.

Even Chelsea took one, looked up, and smiled at Alex. "We're with you this time."

Alex just beamed, and finally, she couldn't hold back the waterworks that gushed out of her eyes. She wiped her cheeks with the insides of her arms and then she tore open the pudding. It was the very best thing she could've eaten. And that's because she was eating it with her very best friends.

She held up her plastic tub filled with smooth chocolate yumminess and yelled, "Cheers to 3C!"